Critical Acclaim for SURVIVOR

"A real page-burner . . . delivers passion in fifteen shades of purple . . . Tabitha King's best book to date . . . I couldn't put it down."
—Thom Jones, author of *The Pugilist at Rest* and *Cold Snap*

"A monumental novel . . . on par with the works of Joyce Carol Oates."
—*Rocky Mountain News*

"Chilling . . . suspenseful and enjoyable."—*Booklist*

"A novel of great insight and empathy, filled with believable, troubled, complex characters."—*Kirkus Reviews*

"A big book in the way that books used to be big—a large cast of characters drawn in bold, often ingenious strokes, all engaged in vigorous, exciting drama. Like life, but better. An immensely likable book, and one that is, once begun, impossible to resist."
—Pinckney Benedict, author of *Dogs of God* and *The Wrecking Yard*

"Grips readers by their throats and drags them along a roller coaster ride."
—*Springfield Sunday Republican*

"Tough and gritty . . . compelling, captivates the reader just as a speeding car captivates the driver who desperately wants to get it under control."—*Publishers Weekly*

SURVIVOR

TABITHA KING

A SIGNET BOOK

SIGNET
Published by the Penguin Group
Penguin Putnam Inc., 375 Hudson Street, New York, New York 10014, U.S.A.
Penguin Books Ltd, 27 Wrights Lane, London W8 5TZ, England
Penguin Books Australia Ltd, Ringwood, Victoria, Australia
Penguin Books Canada Ltd, 10 Alcorn Avenue, Toronto, Ontario, Canada M4V 3B2
Penguin Books (N.Z.) Ltd, 182–190 Wairau Road, Auckland 10, New Zealand

Penguin Books Ltd, Registered Offices:
Harmondsworth, Middlesex, England

Published by Signet, an imprint of Dutton Signet,
a member of Penguin Putnam Inc. Previously appeared in a Dutton edition.

First Signet Printing, April, 1998
10 9 8 7 6 5 4 3 2 1

Grateful acknowledgment is made for permission to use the following song lyrics:

*"Zombie Jamboree (Back to Back)," words and music by Conrad Eugene Mauge, Jr.
Copyright © 1957 (renewed) Hollis Music, Inc. New York, NY. Used by permission.*

*"Word Up," written by Larry Blackmon and Tomi Jenkins. Copyright © 1986 All
Seeing Eye Music and Better Days Music. Used by permission. All rights reserved.*

 REGISTERED TRADEMARK—MARCA REGISTRADA

Printed in the United States of America

For Anne, who loved it best

As always, this work could not have been completed without the assistance of others. Julie Eugley, Marsha DeFillippo, and Shirley Sonderegger and Nancy Gilbert, our office staff, provided the necessary secretarial support. Nancy was invaluable in researching hockey. Susan Kominksy very kindly read the manuscript to check my legal fictions against mundane practice. Dr. Philip Mossman provided me with access to some details of head injuries and their treatment. Lynn and Dave Higgins and Andy England resuscitated my MacIntosh computers when I attempted to croggle the framjets. Some folks are always there—my agent Chuck Verrill, my spouse and children, my siblings and parents, who are my first and most patient readers and often read more than one draft. Billy Abrahams, my editor, was wonderful, and I thank my publisher, Elaine Koster, for bringing us together.

TAKE YOUR HEAD, COLLECT YOUR BONES, GATHER YOUR LIMBS, SHAKE THE EARTH FROM YOUR FLESH! . . . THE GATEKEEPER COMES OUT TO YOU, HE GRASPS YOUR HAND, TAKES YOU INTO HEAVEN.

—Old Kingdom Pyramid Text

1

The girls came from nowhere, emerging from darkness suddenly, into the street directly in front of her. She was above them behind the wheel of her Blazer, and as the girls lurched in her lights, the hilarity distorting their faces turned to terror, their arms upthrust as if against the glare. She was by then standing on her brakes. The Blazer shuddered and bucked, tires shrieking. Only inches from her bumper, the two girls seemed to reel as if in a strong wind.

And as suddenly as the girls had appeared in front of her, the small, low car that had been behind her was loudly beside her, swinging around her on the right. The two girls were still looking at her as she hit her horn and they stepped in front of the little car. They rose into the air as the little car hit them and then they fell down again, their limbs flopping disconnectedly. One of them was thrown against the Blazer, rocking it slightly on its tires. If there were any sounds of impact, she did not hear them over the music.

The impact did not slow the little car, which she saw now was a yellow T-bird. But the driver must have braked, because it swerved and leaped and finally jerked to a stop yards past the Blazer. The driver lowered his head to his arms, embracing the wheel. Then he sat up straight again and opened the door without haste. He looked all of seventeen. He moved with the mincing gait of a drunk trying to walk a line.

She snapped on her four-way flashers and set the hand brake before she jumped out of the Blazer. Once out, she stood in the street, uncertain what to do next. There was a wobble of panic, a tightness in her lungs, as if she would discover when she tried to take a breath that there was no atmosphere to breathe. She knew this street well—the trees that were monuments in their old age, the outlined ramparts of the nineteenth-century dorms and the old gymnasium glimpsed beyond them, the banality of the line of shops on the opposite side of the street—and yet the very familiarity felt false.

One of the girls was lying on the side of the road. She looked like one of those Halloween effigies of no one, sets of clothing sewn together and stuffed with leaves and left slumped on porches or stoops or lawns. This girl looked like them—like something cast off.

The kid who had hit the girls began with a sudden barking noise to vomit into the gutter.

She took an involuntary step back, putting her hand out to the hood of the Blazer for support: it was hot from the engine running and it was dirty, too. She had been meaning to get it washed but hadn't gotten around to it. Now her right hand was dirty and she wiped it on the side of her thigh, on her Levi's.

She did not want to turn around and look at the other girl. When she did, she saw first only a heel, emerging nakedly from underneath the Blazer. Somehow the girl had come to rest almost completely under her truck. The heel was just a young girl's, tapering toward the ankle, and flawless, no bruise or scratch or trauma—just a bare heel as innocent as if it were peeking out of the bedclothes in the heat of the night. How could that happen? For an instant, she had a nightmare vision of the girl, crawling, twitching, groping spasmodically, into the hot darkness underneath the truck in the few seconds that it had taken for her to dismount from it.

The air had turned foul with the products of human bodies and the smells coming off the vehicles, the burnt tires and brakes, the stressed metals of the engines. She felt ill.

The kid wailed, "I couldn't stop!" He was trembling and filthy, and he raked his hair with both hands and reeled in the middle of the street.

There were sirens, closing. The onlookers drawn to the scene of the accident milled about, and a campus security cop, with a flashlight in his hand, began to gesture them out of the way. There were many more lights and the glare was strong in her eyes. Abruptly weak and dizzy, she sat down on the curb and started to cry.

The campus cop bent over her and asked if she was all right. She knew him—had exchanged smiles and civilities many times with him at the checkpoint by the main entrance as she went on and off the campus. But her mind was a blank; she could not think of his name.

"I was driving the Blazer," she told him.

Of course he knew it, knew her vehicle and her as its driver well.

His name came to her suddenly: Chick.

"Sit tight, honey." Chick patted her shoulder. "There's an ambulance on the way."

He moved off to the kid who had hit the girls. The kid was still standing in the middle of the street, arguing intently with fate.

"I couldn't stop," he insisted.

Chick spoke sharply to him and the stuffing went out of the kid and he began to sob.

The ambulance arrived, the regular police right behind it. Chick gestured with his flashlight—the victims, the kid, her. They all looked at her, the ambulance guys and the city cops and the campus cop and the dozens of gawkers who had materialized out of the night onto the sidewalks.

One of the cops reached into the Blazer and all at once the music stopped. It was the first she realized the Clash had still been rocking the Casbah from the Blazer's speakers. In her shock, she had left the vehicle running. And once the music was gone, she heard its absence and was glad of it: it had become babel, something to fall through.

She stood up, wanting to tell the cops she had almost killed the two girls herself. Once on her feet, though, she was woozy again. Then a cop was at her elbow, steadying her. She closed her eyes to make the world stop spinning, and leaned against his shoulder.

"Take your time," the cop said. "Take it easy."

He was young, only a few years older than she. Lately she had been noticing more people her age, all dressed up and acting like grown-ups, while she was still a raggedy student.

"I almost hit them," she told him.

"Don't say anything," the cop said. "Don't talk. Just be quiet and take it easy."

He supported her across the street. Once she had to stop again, to keep from falling down. Leaning against the cop, she looked down and saw the other girl, the leaf-dummy girl.

The girl was dead. Anybody could see she was dead. There was something intensely mysterious about her dead face staring up at them. One of her eyes was open, reflecting all the lights that now made the street bright. The socket of the other was a cup of blood. The jaw was noticeably displaced, and in the excess of light, the face was mottled and patched and quilted into something like a primitive mask.

The cop tucked her into the backseat of the blue-and-white unit for safekeeping. His name was Michael Burke. His father had never gotten out of blue, never gotten past sergeant, but not for lack of ambition. Michael Burke had ambitions too, and one of them was that what had happened to the old man was not going to happen to the old man's only son.

"What's your name?" he asked casually.

She told him. It was unlikely enough to be for real.

"Got some ID?"

"In the truck," she said.

"I get it for you?"

She nodded.

He smiled as he straightened and closed the door on her. As far as he was concerned, she had just given him permission to search. Not that he expected to find anything in particular, but sometimes people in shock forgot what they had tucked away in their vehicles and you never knew what might prove useful.

Burke's partner, Pearce, was checking the license and registration taken from the driver of the T-bird. Head down and hands cuffed behind him, the kid was in the backseat of the second blue-and-white. Drunk and in shock, the idiot still knew what he had done. Killed somebody, probably two somebodies. Fucked up his own life royally. He was weeping. Somebody should.

The impacts with the bodies of the girls had marked the T-bird, dented it, and left tissue and blood, of course. Autopsy would establish where their bodies had been broken by the T-bird, and where by impact with the road, and there would be paint from the T-bird on them. On the Blazer, the young cop saw no dent or other sign of collision with a human body. The T-bird had left rubber in a juddering pattern that could be read by any eye: too fast, too close, brake too late. The track marks of the Blazer showed an immediate stop from a lesser speed.

Inside the Blazer, he found no bottles, no cans, open or empty. No smell of cigarette smoke or pot, but the windows were open. Ashtray closed. Opened, it was pristine. Not an ash for Holmes to analyze. A faint odor of bleach prickled his nose. On the backseat, a damp towel hung out of an open gym bag. The keys were still in the ignition, a Sowerwine University key fob in the shape of its caricature mascot Spectre dangling from them. He didn't see anything that looked like a handbag. There was a camera bag on the floor, along with a collapsed tripod. The cop snagged the strap of the bag and pulled it over. Tucked among the camera gear inside, he found a wallet. Driver's license, student ID. The name was different from what she had given him, but probably she had blurted out her nickname. He extracted the registration from the glove box and noted yet another first name.

Papers in one hand, camera bag in the other, he returned to the unit and called in the numbers. He handed the bag to the girl over the back of the seat. "Howyadoin'?"

She shrugged.

"Are you Kristin or Caitlin Mellors?"

"Kristin," she replied. "Caitlin's my mother."

"You told me earlier you were Kissy Mellors."

"I am, it's my nickname."

He asked her if she was high and she said no. He did not see any sign that she was, nothing that could not be explained as shock. Then he identified himself to her and asked if she understood she had been involved in a fatality. She cleared her throat and managed a yes, and they went through the routine about the blood alcohol test and how she could refuse to have it and she said she understood. The registration, he pointed out, was not in her name, and she explained that though it was her vehicle, her mother held the title and paid the insurance to minimize the insurance costs. It was a common arrangement for drivers under twenty-five. He explained that the vehicle would be impounded to allow a forensics examination. She didn't look happy about it and asked if she could have her things out of it and seemed to be comforted when he said sure.

"You know, if you got some weed or something else in it you think will get you in trouble, you better tell me now," he said. "Be honest with me now or I'll be tough on you later."

She seemed to be paying attention to him. A faint disbelieving smile softened her mouth and she shook her head wearily. "I'm not into that shit." She closed her eyes and rested her head against the seat back.

He looked at the license again and her picture.

Kristin Elizabeth Mellors, three weeks past her twenty-first birthday, a year left on her current license. A year ago her hair had been black and buzz cut except for a long rattail. She was wearing her hair a little longer, but unevenly shorn as if somebody had held her down and clipped it off while she wriggled around and tried to escape. As he thought of it, the idea made him smile.

Her hair was not black anymore. It was bleached white in a ragged feathery cut, in contrast with her taut young skin. The short, light hair made her dark eyes stand out. No bra harnessing her exceptional knockers, which was fine by him, the forearm feel he had gotten assisting her across the street a pleasurable recollection. He looked at her in the backseat and then at the picture: same girl, with the left ear pierced three times with studs and the other with a safety pin in it.

Again he looked at her picture, then at her. The unit's map light threw little light into the back; she was intermittently lit by bubble lights of an emergency vehicle in the street outside. The weirdly strobing light brought out her bone structure, the slight crookedness of her nose, sexy with the possibility it had been broken at some time. Given the weird hair and the studs, never mind the size of her knockers, he would expect to remember her if he had ever seen her around. The campus was an enclave with its own security that kept a modicum of order and controlled traffic on campus but did little more than take reports of more serious crime and pass them on to the municipal police department. The Peltry police did not have the kind of sense of the campus that came of constant presence on the beat. Burke retained some understanding of the campus from his own undergraduate years, but no longer knew the student population, changing with every year, the way he once had. As a graduate student in the law school, he was only on campus for his night classes.

He left the unit to talk to his partner. "She's a student. Sober and insured. Blazer's in her name. I'm waiting on the computer to tell me if she's got a jacket. How 'bout you?"

"James A. Houston. Premed at Sowerwine. Master James has himself a sheet, all right. Three priors. First bust at twelve—public intoxication, possession by a minor. Lost his license when he was sixteen on an OUI and then again last year, surprise, another OUI. Just got his license back again a couple months ago. The T-bird's in his name. Valid registration. And, happy days, we have a witness who was getting ready to cross the corner down there says when he passed her he had a bottle to his mouth. She could read the Bud label like it was a halftime ad on TV."

Burke laughed. "No shit. Victims?"

"One's Dead Right There. Both students, Chick says. Smell of beer on both of them. My guess is they had been to a party and were headed to another one, or maybe a bar."

"It's early yet," the young cop said.

Pearce glanced at the kid in the back of the unit. "Never too early to be shitfaced, right?"

The cop handed her the duffel. The degree of relief she felt surprised her. Kissy did not think of herself as a person who cared about things, but it was hugely comforting to have her stuff back. She signed a receipt for the Blazer and he gave her a number to call to find out when she could get it back.

Then he asked her if she would make a statement. He explained how it would work: he would tape it, right then and there. She was just a witness, she was not being charged with anything.

"They stepped out in front of me," she said. "I almost hit them and then the kid in the T-bird did—did she die? The girl who was still alive? Is she dead?" She did not wait for an answer. She wiped at her wet face with the back of one hand, then with her fingers. "What's going to happen to him? The driver."

"There's nothing you can do for him," the cop said. "It's

better you don't think about him. Think about the two
girls. One of them's dead, the other may be soon. He did
that. He was driving drunk and too fast and he passed on
the right to get around you and that's what happened."

"But it could have been me! I could have hit them!"

"But you didn't. You were sober and you were proceed-
ing at a safe, legal speed and you were able to react in
time."

"They practically jumped in front of him trying not to
get hit by me!"

The cop fixed his eyes on her intently as if to force her
to believe what he said and do what he told her. "My advice to you is to keep that thought to yourself. It wasn't
your fault and you shouldn't invite anybody to try to make
it your fault. Now, is there somebody we can call to come
and meet you at the hospital to take you home?"

She shook her head no. "I'll call my roommate."

Giving her another of his reassuring smiles, with an appropriate little tinge of solemnity and sadness, the occasion not forgotten, the cop nodded.

Her roommate was waiting for her when she came out of
the blood lab. Mary Frances was a few years older and
tended to mother her. "You okay?"

"No," she said, "I saw somebody get killed, Mary."

Mary Frances drew her close, an arm around her waist.
"Poor baby. Tell me about it."

But she could not. All at once she was ready to fall apart
again. Mary Frances hurried her outside to her Subaru. Eager for the air, Kissy rolled down the window on her side.
She was wrung out. She had submitted to a test that would
satisfy the authorities that there was nothing in her veins
but her own healthy blood and maybe a few molecules of
chlorine. For her trouble, she had a bruise forming in the
hollow of her elbow under a cheap hospital Band-Aid.

She settled back and closed her eyes. A few minutes
later, when their forward motion was arrested and they
came to a halt, she opened her eyes again. They were at an
intersection, stopped by a red light on Riverside Drive
where it crossed College Avenue. If she looked right, she
would be able to see the place on College where the accident happened. She turned her head slowly. The emergency vehicles were gone and there was no sign of any

accident. It was as if it had never happened. The light went green. She kept her eyes fixed on the place where the accident had happened until they were through the intersection and she could not see it anymore. Then she stared straight ahead, no longer able to close her eyes.

The Dance River divided Peltry on a northwest-to-southeast diagonal. The ground-floor apartment she shared with her roommate was on the northern outskirts, on the east side of the river. Crossing the river, Mary Frances took the Mid-Dance Bridge. It arched high over the black gleaming water. Suicides homed to it, and so there were barriers, ten-foot-high storm fencing that curved inward at the top. The fencing cut the view of the river into diamonds, making Kissy feel as if she were looking at it with insect eyes.

The water rushed below, its surface roiled and braided in its relentless passage. She remembered the first time she had entered it, more than a little gingerly, a kid of eleven, breaking the unbreakable rule: *Thou shalt not swim in the river.* The cold of it, even on the hottest day of summer. And its strength, pulling at her with its chilly grip like the irresistible tug of the ocean.

It was only a flow of water, made up of the same indifferent substance as a drip from the faucet, a rainsplat on the window, but it was once the way into the wilderness and the reason Peltry existed. Since her first sight of it, she had been drawn to it, and understood the mind of those would-be and still, even now, sometimes successful suicides: it would be all right to die in it, borne away by it into nothingness, the way it was as she slipped into sleep at night. That was how dying would be, like the river, a cold irresistible embrace, taking her swiftly and powerfully where it willed. The road rose up on the other side to meet them. She pressed her face against the cool glass and her breath fogged it in flowing shapes.

The Clash blared from the component system mounted at the head of her mattress. She sat up straight, her heart in her mouth. In her exhaustion the previous night, she had forgotten about the dub she had been running in her tape player as her wake-up call for the last few weeks. Punching it off, she sprawled for a moment on her bed, the accident and the night before coming back to her.

She slept in a small back bedroom. On arriving home, it had seemed like a good idea to finish off a bottle of cheap, metallic-tasting white wine, but it had set Kissy's gut aroil and there had been no rest in her sleep, only a long drowning struggle. Her stomach turned over violently and she stumbled to the bathroom. To clear the sour taste of vomit from her mouth, she chugged some mouthwash and spat it out. Her armpits were acrid, as if she had been sick abed with fever.

The smell of coffee brewing and a cigarette on fire seeped into the bathroom as she dressed. Ryne had let himself in by the kitchen door and was helping himself to breakfast, dripping a butt over a frying pan of egg he was scrambling. Last night's gig had probably kept him at Skinner's until past three. Four nights a week he worked a shift as a butcher at the House Of Meat, getting done early in the afternoon and getting sleep between two or three and nine. At the abattoir, he wore a head rag over his recently shorn hair. His rimless glasses and a discreet earring made him look just like another one of the hordes of students, though he had dropped out of Sowerwine in his first semester.

She poured herself coffee in a mug he had stolen from Denny's. It was a private game of his, walking out of Denny's late at night, early in the morning, with a mug or a plate or salt and pepper shakers or a set of utensils. What had once seemed eccentric to her had long since become an irritating affectation.

Mary Frances shuffled through on her way to the bathroom without speaking. Waking up was hard to do for Mary Frances, and she especially did not like to do it for Ryne.

"You had a night," Ryne said. "Heard it on the radio on the way home. You okay?"

She yawned. "I'm okay." Actually she felt as if she had spent the night moving furniture. Pianos and sofas and major appliances.

There was a newspaper on the table. They did not have it delivered. Ryne must have picked one up on the way, an unheard-of event unless there was some chance of publicity about his band. She snatched it up and scanned the front page.

"I knew her," she said slowly. "Diane Greenan. I can't believe it. I actually knew her."

The picture on the front page stared up at her: a high school graduation portrait—studio lighting glinting off hair spray, pearls, and pastels. It did not look any more like the Diane Greenan she had known than had the woman last night. She had looked right into the woman's face in the instant before Diane had stumbled into the path of the T-bird. She had looked right into Diane's dead face afterward and not recognized her either time.

"I didn't really know her," she amended. "She was in my dorm, freshman year. Lived on the second floor."

Diane had been a preppy blonde with money on her back and her pick of dates and sororities. The university did not allow freshmen to live off campus, and there were no actual sorority houses at Sowerwine, either, so the pledges stayed in their dorms, only moving into off-campus apartments with their sorority sisters in the sophomore year.

Abruptly, Kissy recalled something else. She had been looking out the window of her third-story room. It was night and she had wanted to look at the moon. And as she gazed at the low-riding moon, its pale bloated face smirking back, a movement flickered at the corner of her eye. She had glanced down into a glassed-in porch that formed an ell with the dorm. Alone inside the porch, a couple was fighting. At first it was apparent in their tense postures, stiff gestures, and in their angry faces. And then she had actually heard their raised voices, muffled by the distance and the enclosure, as they shouted at each other. One of the quarreling lovers she had recognized as Diane Greenan. And then, the boy in his rage had spun suddenly about and kicked out one of the glass panes.

Her memory was patchy. The violence, emotional and physical, had arrested her at the time, but she had felt far away from it, as if she were seeing it from the face of the moon. It had seemed like a play, a play about something private and shocking. Remembering it, it seemed like something witnessed as a child that only made sense once she had grown up.

But all at once she recalled a single detail, the shape of the boy's ear, and realized instantly who he was. Someone she knew better than she had ever known Diane Greenan. She had forgotten the incident so thoroughly, she had not connected him since with Diane.

"I saw her break up with a guy once," she said.

"Small fucking world," Ryne grunted. He divided the eggs between two plates, handing one to her.

Sitting down, she read through the story.

The second victim was a junior, Ruth Prashker, a sorority sister of Diane's. There was a blurry snapshot of her at a party, with other people incompletely cropped out. Her condition was critical, the paper reported.

It was disorienting to look at pictures of the accident scene. In the foreground of one shot, Diane Greenan's body was made anonymous and more lifeless by an obscuring sheet of plastic—and by the newsprint itself, Kissy thought. In the background was her own Blazer, looking shabby, and the T-bird, smaller and with dents in it she had not noticed at the time. Another picture framed melodramatic dark stains on the pavement.

But she was not there—she herself, Kissy Mellors, was absent from the scene the film documented. Her name was there: "driver of the other vehicle." But the camera had omitted to record her—indeed, she hadn't noticed the presence of the photographer—and now she was no longer sure she had really been there.

There was one of the kid who had hit Diane and the Prashker girl, as he was being taken into the police station. Unshaven and cuffed, he looked as if he had already spent a couple of years in solitary confinement somewhere. His name was James Houston. He was twenty, a student like Diane Greenan and Ruth Prashker and herself, at Sowerwine University. In premed, the paper reported.

Kissy covered her face with her hands.

"Big fucking mess, huh?" said Ryne.

"Yeah."

"You need a booster?"

She ignored the offer.

As he helped himself to what was left in the coffeemaker, he eyed her appraisingly. "Maybe you should ditch class." Angling to take her to her room. Scraping and shoveling, he ate standing up, one eye on her. When he saw she wasn't eating hers, he picked up her plate.

"Where are we, Ryne? Are we going anywhere?" she asked him, more curious than anything else.

"Little heavy for this early in the morning, baby." He laughed. It was almost the very first thing he had said to her after she had allowed her curiosity to take her to bed with him. *Let's not let this get heavy, okay?* She had laughed rudely at him, at the idea sex with him was so overwhelming as to enthrall her instantaneously. He had been insulted. They had been making up and breaking up ever since.

His band took up most of his time. She had her own life too, and was not about to give any of it up to hang around waiting for Ryne to notice she was waiting for him. But eventually, against her best intentions, she had become one of the band's girlfriends. The bitchy selfish one, who wouldn't let them use her Blazer when the van was broken down, or lend them rent money, or money to get instruments and amps out of pawn, or money for beer or drugs. The witch who ran them mercilessly out, if they asked for a patch on the floor, just till they could get a new place. She was twenty-one now, not seventeen, and it was all too easy to see the drift of his life and her own, and to wonder if that was all there would ever be.

"Don't call me baby," she said. "I mean it."

His smile faded. He crossed his arms and leaned back against the countertop. "What is this? You want to play games with me, Kissy? Put me through some hoops?"

She could walk in front of a car today and lose everything. The panic and terror of that instant when the two girls came from nowhere and stepped in front of her washed over her.

"You want me to say we're going to get married."

She shook her head. "No, I just asked if we were going anywhere."

"But that's what you want me to say.

"You said you wanted to call it quits. I thought you just needed your space," he went on. "I need space too. I thought by now we would be back together. Now you're on some white-gown-and-veil trip." He paused for a reaction and when he got none, became angrier. "It's goddamn confusing, Kissy. You want a ring, you want to be engaged? You know as well as I do, it doesn't mean fuck-all. We could get married tomorrow, file for divorce the day after."

"Yes, I know all that," she said finally. "I don't want a ring, Ryne. Three years and everything is just exactly the way it was when we started. Nothing, absolutely nothing, has changed. Doesn't that bother you at all?"

"It's a hard go," he said, "you know that. It can take years to make it in this business. This is really mind-blowing, hearing you sling this shit."

"It's about I'm twenty-one now, and you're twenty-six, and I don't feel like a grown-up. When do we get to be grown-ups, Ryne?"

"I can't fucking believe you're saying this. You know better. Being a grown-up is suicide to an artist." Behind her, he put his hands on her shoulders. "Come on, Kissy, let's get close again."

She shrugged her shoulders, shaking off his touch. "No, Ryne. Fucking won't do it. It isn't enough."

"Which means you're fucking somebody else, doesn't it?" Fury incised his face in straight pale lines, nose to chin.

"I wish," she said. "If only to meet your expectations."

He stared at her a moment. "You fucking bitch." He turned on his heel and slammed out.

"Right," she muttered. "I guess that answers the question."

She sloshed the carton to gauge the level of milk, closed the box on the remaining couple of eggs, and returned them and the dish of butter to the nearly empty refrigerator. The kitchen, such as it was, was depressingly dingy and dirty even after her efforts to clean up. She ought not to give a shit—most of the time she didn't—but it wore on her sometimes. Sometimes she just wanted some money. Enough money.

Her schooling was covered by a scholarship. She had bought the Blazer with her own earnings, accumulated summer after summer since junior high working every kind of available job, double shifts, overtime, holding down two jobs when she could. Her mother had helped her with the insurance coverage on the Blazer but was struggling herself, a single mother with a young child. After her parents' breakup, Kissy had watched her mother shed her old identity and start all over, as a textile artist in an arty tourist trap town on the coast. They had become more like sisters distanced by several years, and not close ones either, than like mother and daughter.

Mary Frances rushed into the kitchen, knapsack in hand.

"You need a ride, I'll drop you off. Can you get that ass-hole's key away from him or do we have to have the locks changed?"

"Sorry, 'fraid so—" She hurried to gather up her gear.

2

Work was the best thing for her; it would drive the accident out of her thoughts. She had film to develop and printing to do. As always, the alchemical odors of the darkroom made her heart leap. But the darkroom itself, the sense of enclosure, absence of light, and the heat and stale air, often seemed suffocating—at least until she lost herself in work. This time, it was the worst ever; with no one else working in the student darkroom at Sowerwine, it was like being buried alive. The mistakes she made rattled her into more. Everyone had difficult sessions, but rarely had it ever been so complete a bust for her. She gave it up for a bad job.

On impulse, she hiked over to the hospital. The weather was pleasantly brisk and the walk cleared her head. She found her way to the Intensive Care Unit, which seemed to be organized into islands of machines. At the nurses' station, she asked where Ruth Prashker was.

"No visitors except immediate family," said the woman curtly.

"I'm her twin sister, Rachel," Kissy told her.

That worked nicely. Muttering "Oh, my," the woman summoned an elderly woman in a smock with a pin that identified her as a volunteer, who led Kissy to the right place.

The patient was suspended like a paralyzed insect in a mechanical web. Her head was heavily cocooned in bandage, her face so distorted by edema that she hardly resembled the girl in the paper. But the chart read "Prashker."

A sliver of lifeless white showed between her swollen eyelids. Her sheeted chest pushed up and fell down in a robotic rhythm. Her fists were clenched on her chest. She wore a collar like some techno-jewel that accessed and maintained the hole in her trachea. Her flesh, a patchwork of bruise and abrasion and doughy white, hung shapelessly upon her bones. Shockingly, there was dried blood flaking on her brow, crusted in her eyelashes, smears of dirt on her bruised face, and her hands were dirty too.

"Who are you?" a woman's voice asked.

Kissy spun to face the voice. It belonged to an older woman, her French-braided white hair coming down around her shoulders. This was an elegant woman, falling to pieces. The white of her hair was soft and pure, not the deliberately harsh, bleached white of Kissy's. There was a striking resemblance in this woman to the photographs of Ruth—nose, slant of eye, mouth, chin. In her pallor, in the dark wells of her eyes, the woman seemed also to reflect the traumatized condition of her granddaughter.

"I'm Kissy Mellors."

The older woman blinked. "Mellors was the name of the other driver."

Kissy nodded. "Me."

"I'm Ruth's grandmother, Sylvia Cronin."

"I'm so sorry," Kissy said formally.

"Of course you are," Mrs. Cronin agreed. "It's brave of you to visit Ruth. It must be very difficult. I understand from what I've been told that you were not at fault in any way." She indicated the chairs by the bed. "Perhaps you'd like to sit down a moment."

Kissy took a step backward. "I don't want to intrude."

"You're welcome to visit."

Kissy hesitated.

"I understand." Mrs. Cronin smiled reassuringly. "It's very difficult."

"I'll come back," Kissy said quickly. "If nobody minds."

"The doctors say Ruth may be aware of us," the older woman told her. "Please do come, if you can bear it."

"I will," said Kissy. "I will."

The commitment brought an unexpected peace. It was something she could do.

Head bent into the wind, Kissy was turning over ideas for the Oriental Seagull paper in her backpack that she had just picked up at the photosupplier. She had stepped off the sidewalk before she realized that she was crossing College Avenue at the place where the accident happened. Pulse vaulting, she stopped in her tracks and looked both ways again. There was no danger, nothing coming, but she broke into a lope. She reached the other side of the street in a cold sweat.

Under the trees was the break in the yew hedge that walled the campus from the street. This was the way the girls had come. The path was unpaved, beaten out of the grass by the passage of feet. She had taken this route herself many times, particularly when she had lived on campus. It was shabbily familiar, even to the bits of trash stuck in the branches of the hedge. The nearest structure was the old Victorian-era gymnasium, superseded by the new Athletic Complex with its high-tech weight rooms, lap pool, and the arena that showcased the glamour sports of ice hockey and men's basketball. The old gym, called the Field House, now provided a home floor for the women's basketball team, hoop courts for the student intramural leagues, and space for gymnastics, wrestling, dance, and aerobics.

On the other side of the hedgerow was a copse of old white pine like huge columns. The ground was gold with pine straw that the wind lifted occasionally in little puffs. A pale flutter on one of the pines caught her eye. At the foot of the tree were asters and the red-leafed branches of some shrub in a plastic milk container cut off to make a vase. Drawing closer, she saw the flutter was a photograph in a plastic sleeve, nailed to the tree only at the top, allowing the wind to slip under its bottom edge and lift it. She held a bottom corner down: it was a picture of Diane Greenan.

In her pack she carried a box of pushpins. She had to blink against the wind at her eyes. She pinned the corners of the photograph flat to the tree so the wind could not tear it free.

He was watching for her. Sooner or later he knew they would cross paths at the gym when she was there to swim or work out. The varsity weight room was on the second level, the hall outside it an open gallery overlooking the civilian weight room below. The setup allowed the jocks to check out the action. It was from there he sighted Melons. He would have stopped to watch her settle into the tri-fly machine anyway; it was the sort of thing he could take home and put to use. Her buddy was with her, the one who was supposed to be an ex-nun.

Sensing his eyes on her, she looked up with more than recognition. She was braced too, knowing they would stumble across each other, and likely where.

The first time he had ever seen her was lost to his memory. On campus, between classes. In the library. He remembered the rattail and the pin in her ear and the tits. How could he not? Then somebody told him what her name was. He had to look it up in the Student Directory before he believed the name.

She had turned up in the civilian weight room, with her bunny-faced buddy spotting her. He believed the rumor the buddy was an ex-nun; she had an eagerness in her face, as if she were ready to take her ups in a softball game with the fifth graders. There was something monastic in the ex-nun's gray sweats, even more so in the inch of carroty hair covering her scalp that made her look like she had just taken the veil instead of having jumped the wall.

Once, on an impulse, he had stopped by Melons as she did presses. "I like that place right there," he had told her, gazing down at her on the bench. Not with any expectations, just buying a lottery ticket. He had heard she was living with some musician.

The ex-nun had begun to blink rapidly, like an out-of-order traffic light.

Melons had looked down where he had focused, at the sweaty dip in the loose, low-cut neck of the cut-off T-shirt she had been wearing that had allowed him to look at her cleavage in the first place. It was damp there, which he liked, and the hair in her armpits was also wet and sticking to her skin.

"I'm Junior Clootie," he had told her, though he expected she already knew it.

"Lucky you," she had said on the exhale, heaving the bar into the cradle.

Not a good start, but in for a pint, in for a pound. "You want to have a cup of coffee or a beer with me when you're finished?"

"No," she had said, "and I don't want to fuck you either. Go stare down someone else's tits, will you?"

The ex-nun had smiled at Junior with an infinitude of Christian compassion.

Palms raised in a gesture halfway between surrender and self-defense, he had backed away, smiling.

"Sorry 'bout the language, Mary Frances," she had said to her friend.

"She can spin her head around and projectile vomit pea soup, too," the ex-nun had said to him, and the two women had had themselves a good snigger.

Dykes, he had shrugged it off to the guys who had seen him flame out.

As he had skimmed through the student paper sometime later, a picture and then her name—*photo by kissy mellors*—under it had caught his eye. It was a shot of a couple making out under a tree on the quad, from an angle that made them unidentifiable. Hotter than it looked at first glance. Not only was the girl's shirt strained over her nipples, the guy had a rise in his Levi's. But it was not like some soft-focus aftershave ad. The bodies of the lovers not perfect, nor their skin either, and barely in the frame, a passing maintenance worker, a bearded long-haired tub of guts, glancing at them in amusement.

He could remember Diane Greenan sneering—*pretentious art school crap*—when he pointed it out. He had not disagreed, mostly because it was not worth discussing, but also because Fine Arts *was* full of bullshit artists. He had taken the art survey courses—guts, all of them—to fill requirements, and arrived at the conclusion that the ability to sling paint at a canvas or carve a stone weenie was overrated as a source of moral authority. Diane, though, had probably just been putting down someone else to build herself up. For all her easy charm and beauty, Diane had been a snob whose vanity made her an easy mark for anyone willing to suck up to her. She had surrounded herself with women who would suffer by comparison with her.

Melons had published a lot of pictures in the paper, and he had seen her work hung in the galleries and corridors of the School of Fine Arts. It was not that they had gotten to know each other but that each of them knew who the other one was. Then this thing had happened. And, weirdly, she had been involved in it.

He went down and spoke to her. "How close are you to finished?"

"Twenty minutes."

"I'll wait outside. I want to talk to you."

She nodded.

He waited patiently, sitting cross-legged on the floor, bouncing the tennis balls he carried with him against it, working his reflexes, his wrists. He could outwait an ice age. It was his one virtue, his mother liked to say, which he thought was a little harsh. His own mother could surely find at least one or two other virtues in him. Self-discipline, say, considering how hard he worked at his game. A good sense of humor. Clean ears, clean underwear. Not smoking butts. And lots more, if he wanted to think about it.

Crouching down next to him, Melons sighted on one of his ears.

"I can't believe she's dead," he said. "You know? Must have been a shock. You okay?"

"Getting by."

"It's so weird. You being there. Somebody else I knew. You saw it happen." He shook his head.

"I'm sorry."

"It's the shock, that's all. You don't expect somebody you know to die."

"I didn't even know it was her until the next day." As soon as it was out of her mouth, her face changed and she bit her lip.

He stared at her for a moment and then cleared his throat. "Do you know about the memorial service?" He didn't wait for an answer. "I feel funny about it. I want to go, I feel like I should, but I don't know her family or anything."

She almost grinned. "Me too. Exactly."

"I'll go with you," he said. "If you want. Or you can go with me. Whatever suits you."

The grin got out. "Clootie, is this a date?"

It was the kind of irreverence he might need to get him through it. "Why not? I've never made a date for a funeral before."

"Memorial service," she corrected him. "The real funeral's back in Trust Fund, Connecticut, isn't it?"

He nodded. His smile vanished. "What if I get there and

it's the wrong Diane Greenan? She isn't really dead, is she?"

Melons just looked at him pityingly.

"Shit," Junior muttered, gathering himself for the push to his hind feet, "I was afraid you'd say that."

Diane had died on a Thursday night, eight days ago, a week and a day, and he was waiting for Melons again, on the stoop of the building where he lived. She had said she would meet him there. She had laughed when he told her he lived in the Barnyard.

Once it had been the Bagnaide, a few crowded river-bank blocks of shanties whose permanent population was largely female—originally French and in the guise of laundresses offering services to woodsmen and seamen. In the rude bathhouses and flophouses, the lads had gotten de-loused and barbered and their linen cleaned. They had also roistered and roostered and contracted social diseases, hangovers, and busted heads. In no particular order. Though doubtless the laundress-whores much preferred the fellows who bathed first.

A succession of fires had destroyed the Barnyard but always it had been rebuilt, achieving a degree of semi-respectability as the port of Peltry itself declined. Keeping only its anglicized name, it had become a working-class tenement neighborhood, and then, in the 1960s, it had been invaded by students in search of cheap accommodation.

In a jacket and tie and real shoes instead of sneakers for the occasion, he occupied himself wondering what she would wear. Black, he figured. As a Fine Arts major, she should have plenty of choices. Fine Arts majors were the major market for black clothing in the universe; the Gap wouldn't exist without them. The denizens of the School of Fine Arts drank black coffee, smoked black hash, and bathed with black soap. He had seen some black soap once; it came from Spain. *The world is so full of a number of things. I'm sure we should all be as happy as kings.* Once he'd written a paper about the philosophy expressed in that rhyme. A+. He thought it about covered the major issues.

He was in fact a philosophy major—not only were the reactions to that revelation a continuing entertainment, it was equally amusing to collect credits for sitting around bullshitting. The obdurate simplemindedness that had served him so well in the face of authority since junior high was tailor-made for the Socratic dialogue. He made the philosophy faculty all feel like fucking geniuses, plus they got a charge out of having a jock sitting at their collective of pallid bony feet. They loved his ass—in some instances, he suspected, *fantasized* about his ass—and he aced their courses effortlessly, raising his grade point average to the highest on the hockey team. It was a great scam. There was no danger of his ever going pro as a philosopher; he expected to run out his eligibility without taking a degree. He had been drafted as a senior in high school and had a pro career waiting for him.

When she came walking up the street, he was disconcerted. He hadn't expected her to be on foot. He could have picked her up easily enough. At least he had gotten the shirt right. Over the black tee and a man's weskit, her usual ragbag Levi's and scuffed cowboy boots, she'd hung a man's thrift shop tweed jacket. The layers of clothing minimized her superb chest a little too effectively for his taste. She wore red plastic-framed shades. He wished he had thought of shades. A nice sort of Joan Crawford touch, covering his tear-swollen eyes.

Removing them, she tossed her silly hair. With the shades off, she looked haggard, her eyes dark shadowed, her skin wan.

He ruffled her duck's down hair playfully. "You okay? You look beat."

She shrugged. "Cramps."

Just his day to leave the Midol in the medicine cabinet. He dug the keys to his truck out of his jacket pocket. "Oh. Well, we'd better get going."

Light filtered through a stained-glass window behind the altar of the Sowerwine Chapel. Its central figure was a rearing white horse, from which a skeleton tumbled loosely. Underneath it, a banner bore the legend SO FALL-ETH MAN FROM LIFE INTO DEATH. The window, and the chapel itself, memorialized a student killed in a fall from a horse a few years after the founding of the school. Vaulted and ship-carved, the dark paneling of the walls and pulpit and stalls of pews was polished to a coffin sheen, and streaks of colored light from the windows spilled over the mourners like stains. Motes hung in the gloomy light, and the air was dusty in the lungs.

Eulogies by a sorority sister, her major adviser, and a minister educated them in the details of Diane Greenan's life. She had had a younger brother with cerebral palsy—the kid in the wheelchair at her mother's side. Diane had spent her summers since she was fifteen as a music counselor at a camp for CP kids. Her older brother was an aspiring actor; her father, a psychologist. Her mother played third violin in a symphony orchestra. Diane had played cello and planned a career like her mother's.

Junior tugged at his tie and rolled his shoulders in his corduroy sports jacket and picked at the knees of his Levi's. "This is worse than the Annual Athletic Achievements banquet," he whispered to Kissy.

The corner of her mouth twitched. He put his arm around her shoulders. She hiccuped and her hand went to cover her mouth and she squeezed her eyes shut. Wet gleamed at the corners of her eyes, but he thought it was a reflex thing, from the hiccup. Her breathing hitched and her bosom heaved wonderfully, making him glad he was at a funeral where he could keep his eyes cast down with perfect propriety.

The minister launched into a Shakespearean finale:

> *Rough winds do shake the darling buds of May,*
> *And summer's lease hath all too short a date . . .*
> *But thy eternal summer shall not fade.*

He invited them to come forward and offer their condolences to the family. Kissy rose and moved toward the line. Junior seized her by the hand.

Low-voiced, he asked, "Is this a good idea?"

She went forward anyway, amid some whispering. He followed, regretting he had brought her to this thing. And that he had come to it himself.

Mrs. Greenan stood between her son in his wheelchair and her husband. She blinked at Kissy. Her gloved hand groped toward her and Kissy took it.

"I'm Kissy Mellors," she said. "I'm so sorry."

Next to his wife, Mr. Greenan's body jerked as if from a blow. He stared at Kissy.

"Oh," Mrs. Greenan whispered.

Junior gripped Kissy's elbow and nudged her along. Kissy craned to look back. The Greenans stared after her.

"Fun, fun, fun till the Peltry PD took my T-bird away," Junior muttered, tearing off his tie and stuffing it into his pocket as he drove.

Distracted by the memory of the way devastation had marked the faces of Diane's family, Kissy made no response.

A moment later, at a red light, he drummed the wheel restlessly. "I feel like getting shitfaced. Wanna get shit-faced with me?"

She took a moment to consider it, in itself not a great sign. "I don't drink much," she finally said. "Not to get drunk, I mean. I don't see the charm of throwing up."

Junior made a face. "You don't have to get drunk till you puke. I'll do that for both of us. You know, it might help those cramps."

Again she paused to think about it.

"All right. I'll have a drink with you. Where do you want to go?"

"Got beer at my place. Drinking out is a little expensive for me this week."

"Your place."

He raised his palms in mock horror. "All you women ever think about is sex. I want to get drunk. I'd like some company to get started." He winked at her. "Of course, if I get drunk enough, I can be had."

She laughed. The right kind of laugh, from the belly, no sarcasm in it. Sex in it, though. Their eyes met. She was coolly amused with him; he was challenging her, teasing her.

"I don't like beer all that much," she said.

"How 'bout vino? I got that too."

"Screw top?"

"My favorite label. Life's too short to wait for a wine that's not ready to be drunk when it comes out of the vat."

"Barbarian," she said, but smiling.

He had an efficiency, a single room with a mattress on the floor, a stereo component system and TV, a tiny galley kitchen in one corner and in another, a bathroom. It was cluttered—hockey sticks and pads and spare gear of one kind or another. All worn, and she thought it must be his own stuff, too well loved and too much part of him to ever discard. The hockey gear emitted a distinct smell of its own, rather like old wet dirty mutt, but the place itself wasn't dirty. The mattress made up and no fossilized pizza wedges apparent. The walls were papered with posters and snapshots and newspaper clippings. She cruised them swiftly and intently.

She nodded toward a glossy of him, taken with some suits in front of a microphone when he was drafted by the Islanders. "That still on?"

"All it means is I go to camp with them—they've got first dibs to sign, trade, or sell me, or they could just waive me for a stiff," he explained, giving her a glass of red jug wine. "They don't call'm owners for nothing. If they want to deal and I don't, they could trade me to Tierra del Fuego, where I'd have to make the best deal I could or not play. I'm a Spectre this season. If I do my job well enough, I might improve my position with them, but right now, it's pie in the sky."

"I wonder what pie in the sky tastes like," she said, thinking aloud, and then, quickly, "Don't answer that."

He grinned at her. "It was right on the tip of my tongue."

The choice of a place to sit was limited—the mattress, the toilet, the bathtub, the floor, or one of three chairs. Two of them were stools at the kitchen counter. The third was a rocking chair with the arms gone that looked as if it had been salvaged from curbside on a garbage pickup day. She chose the rocking chair.

Junior put on *Sergeant Pepper.* If she didn't like the Beatles, fuck her. And fuck her if she did, a sentiment fueled by the immediate elevation produced by alcohol fumes from the wine and the little parry over the word *pie.* She had started it, another good sign. He picked up the reading lamp from the floor next to the mattress and turned it over to pop the bottom, extracting the half ounce of weed he kept in the base for special occasions. He showed it to her. She shook her head no, which surprised him a little.

"Sure? A little rope's as good for cramps as a glass of vino."

"You have a lot of trouble with cramps?"

"Not your kind, no."

She tapped a family snapshot. Ma, Dad, himself, his younger brother and sister and the dog, taken on the porch at camp during the summer, with the self-timer on the old man's camera.

"Your brother's going to play here?"

"Next year. He's got a lot to learn. That's my dog, Ed."

He hung up his jacket, kicked off his shoes, and took his glass of wine and the jug to the mattress. He fixed up the pillows for a backrest and got comfortable because he might as well be and she would not be unless he was. His comfortable did not last long.

"I saw you break up with Diane," she said.

He almost strangled on the mouthful of red he had going down. He could not cough it out either; it would stain his good shirt. She sat there looking at him as if it were a perfectly normal reaction.

When he had gotten himself under control again, he shook his head in disbelief.

"I lived in Melville then," she explained. "My freshman year. I moved out of the dorm then. It was cheaper to share a place off campus."

He rolled his shoulders, trying to relax again. "I met Diane at some mixer and we started going out. We were just kids using each other not to feel out of place. Probably if she hadn't fucked me over, I would have done the same to her." His mouth twisted in disgust. "All the same, fucking her English professor—how stupid can you get?"

"Putnam?"

"Right. It's his hobby, knocking over numb little freshmen. You could run a pool every year on which one he's gonna nail." He emptied his glass, without incident this time.

"I guess what shocked me," she went on, "was when you broke up with Diane, you kicked out a pane of glass."

"I was immature," he said, and laughed at himself. He got up to top her glass for her. "I could not believe she fell for that asshole. A bottle of Amaretto, some hash, and some poetry, and she believed he was gonna leave his wife for her." He shook his head. "Diane was a blip in my life. She's dead and I don't feel all that much. A little bit amazed that someone I used to fuck is dead." He studied his glass of wine, didn't see any bugs or body parts in it, and had a good knock of it. "I know you've been through a shock, seeing her get killed, but you didn't really know Diane, did you?"

Kissy rocked back gently. "No."

"Did you know the other one? Ruth Prashker?"

She shook her head no.

"That asshole—the drunk driver?"

"No."

"It must have been a horror show. You must think I'm a real shit, trashing Diane."

"I knew you were a class act."

"How'd you get named Kissy?"

"My older brother Kevin couldn't say Krissy, let alone Kristin." Her full lips pursed with mild contempt. "Guys have been calling me Kissy Melons since I first had bumps on my chest."

Heat in his face as always reinforced his embarrassment by revealing it. "You could insist on Kristin—"

"I'm not changing anything about me because some ass-holes haven't got past tit jokes. They're the ones who have the problem, they should do the changing."

Thinking of the times he had referred to her as Melons, Junior swished the wine around his glass. She could have changed her first name. She could have had an operation, gotten herself a B-cup. She didn't wear a bra half the time. Bouncing around like that, it was her own fault. But these days, women thought they could have it both ways. Maybe they could. They had that persuader between their legs.

"I heard the news today oh boy," filled the momentary silence, returning them abruptly to the occasion.

A little wine for her belly's sake, her mother used to say, giving her a glass for her cramps. The tanker burgundy was only moderately watered down, and it was warm in her mouth and, indeed, in the pit of her belly. The cramp did ease. She licked moisture from her upper lip.

" 'The darling buds of May,' " Junior said. "That tore me up. Some powerful stuff, you know."

Kissy watched him. Pushing out of the rocker, she sank to her knees next to him. He watched her progress to-ward him with a sudden glitter in his eyes. Her fingers sought his jaw, pushing gently, and he let her turn his ear toward her.

She leaned toward him, the tip of her tongue flickering around his ear. He shivered, his hand on her forearm tight-ening. Then her teeth grazed the lobe and he jerked away from her. She put her hands down flat to catch herself and came down on all fours.

His face was flushed, his throat too. He cupped the back of her neck to push her head down to his as he rose toward her. His tongue was in her mouth immediately, his fingers groping up the back of her neck to hold her head where he wanted it. The other hand found the base of her spine and pressed her toward him so she couldn't maintain her balance and collapsed onto him. He caught one of her hands as she sought purchase on the mattress or him and brought it to his penis. She did not resist him, and he let go of her hand and she kept it there. His hands went to her breasts and his touch was agreeably light. His cock rose harder against her hand. His tongue felt huge in her mouth. She couldn't breathe past it and was a little dazed. He withdrew it and lowered her onto her back, rocking his hard-on against her thigh as he tried to kiss her again. She got both hands on his chest and pushed and he rolled off her onto his side.

Clearing his throat, he reached for his glass. "What is it? We were doing good. It's no big deal if you started already. I don't mind." He handed her glass to her.

She sat up to drink from it. "No, I haven't. It's not that. I don't know what I want to do."

"That's all right," he teased, "I'll make the choice if you can't make up your mind. I hear there's nothing better for cramps."

The music had ended so he got up and changed it to *Abbey Road*.

She put the toe of one boot to the heel of the other. He knelt to help her pull it off, and then the other. As she relaxed against the pillows, he pulled off her socks and waggled her big toe and she snickered. He crawled up and over her body and settled gently over her.

"Come together," Lennon's voice insisted over his shoulder.

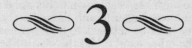

3

It was like waking, cramped and aching, from a wet dream about someone she had not known she ever wanted. When she hauled her shirt, already tugged loose of her waistband, over her head, he inhaled sharply and caught her elbow still up and his tongue flickered in her armpit, tasting it. She plucked at his shirt and he shucked it hastily and pressed her to the mattress again. He scrunched up suddenly to rub his face in her crotch. His head there, his face, so unexpectedly, made her catch her breath. When he came up for air, his fingers were on his flybuttons.

"No," she said, "I'm not safe."

He sat back on his heels. "I thought if you were getting your period, you couldn't be fertile."

"You're wrong."

"I'll pull out," he said quickly, seeing his chance slipping.

She shook her head. "I got pregnant that way once."

He looked at her. Licked his lips. Made his own confession. "I've got skins."

So he knew she had had an abortion and she knew he had been willing to try to hustle her into a risk so he would not have to diminish his own sensation. It was, she guessed, a species of intimacy.

"All right," she said.

He flashed a smile that was a rush in itself, that made her feel powerful and generous and amused and sweaty, all at once.

Undoing her buttons, he pulled her Levi's off her hips and right off her. Standing over her, he shuffled his pants off hastily. He put his hand on his chest as if he were about to salute the flag and glanced down at himself, seeming mildly abashed at the flush there and below, the sheer improbability of his own erection. As if he were searching for something, he groped between her legs. Finding it, he bestowed a kiss so enthusiastic, so hugely pleased, she laughed through it. Her laughter turned to gasps when he kissed his way down her body and gave her head. It took her a while to come, but he didn't seem to find it burdensome. On the contrary, he applied himself as if he had no other desire. At times she grasped him by the hair of his head and bucked into his face and he made noises like he was laughing.

As she was panting in the lee of orgasm, he took her by the jaw and kissed her again. His mouth, his face, was flavored and scented with her. It really had taken her some time, she realized: the record had reached the lullaby of "Golden Slumbers." His cock was hard against her leg, and he drew her hand to it and sighed at her touch. Then he produced a skin.

She had never much enjoyed the awkwardness at the beginning, the man's body on top of hers. The knob of his cock pressed her vulva and he sank it into her with a shudder.

Wet from his mouth, still upon the plateau of her previous orgasm, the feel of him inside her made her frantic. She struggled beneath him and he responded. It was rough and wild, both of them gasping and noisy but not talking. *Abbey Road* spun out irrelevantly in music hall jingle and the noises they were making were suddenly loud in the room. He brought his mouth down upon hers bruisingly and they kissed frantically as they fucked each other. She sucked his tongue into her mouth as he came. He kept on fucking her and she came again herself.

Their breathing was harsh in the modest space, and in her heaving chest, her heart racketed. She put her hand on his chest and it was the same, his heart pounding like a fist upon a door. Propping herself on her elbow, she reached for her glass to sip it. She was aware of him watching her but said nothing to him.

He reached down to his cock for the skin. "This is bloody. You're bleeding." He grinned. "Got you going, huh?"

She got up to take care of it, retrieving from the breast pocket of her jacket the tampon she'd been carrying around in anticipation. Just a trace, really. She felt used, as if some internal machinery had been oiled. She splashed water on her face. Already, she could hardly believe she had let Junior Clootie fuck her. But she had. In the mirror, she wore a secretive smile.

He was half asleep on the mattress, lazing like a cat after a big meal. She started to dress.

He opened one eye. "Are you okay?"

As she shoved her feet into her boots, she shot him a quick smile. "Sure. Thank you, Junior."

"My pleasure. You're welcome."

They both laughed, and she hunkered down to kiss him lightly, with more mocking politeness, before she left.

He wallowed, stirring up the olfactory ghosts of their bodies fucking that clung to the sheets. Warm with the feeling of damn-I'm-good. Recollecting in tranquillity the poetry of her white hair damp against her neck from exertion. Looking down at her, watching her face contort as she came, he had had a revelation. She was O—the woman in *The Story of O*—who had worn the mask of an owl in her sadomasochistic games. That was what her hair, white and feathery and shaped to her head, was like. Even if it was not deliberate, it had had—and still had—a powerful effect on him. Whatever he had imagined O's face to be, it was now hers and always would be.

Weird that it was Diane dying that had put them together. He hoped Diane somehow knew. He didn't know why he should feel guilty just to be alive and savoring the lingering warmth of a woman's body, the afterglow of getting laid.

There was a boyfriend, he thought drowsily, some musician. So there was a risk, she might tell the guy, the guy might turn out to be an asshole. Not exactly red alert time, but any time you dicked some other guy's piece, anything could happen. Might be fun, tying some junkie musician into knots.

"I made my own soy sauce," Mary Frances explained. She was making tangerine chicken, which she had never done before, and had been at it for over two hours. "Really it was skinning all the little tangerine sections that took so long."

"Don't they come all skinned in little cans?" Kissy asked.

"I thought they'd taste better if I did them myself. I'm an idiot, aren't I?"

The laughter the two women shared was low and warm, a pleasure in itself.

Kissy watched Mary Frances finish slicing chicken into paper-thin slivers. A series of small, precisely aligned bowls containing already prepared ingredients were arranged in order of cooking next to the range top. Another, segregated, bowl contained a mix of vegetable pieces that Mary Frances judged imperfectly sliced for this dish but that she would puree into soup.

Mary Frances cooked for invited friends every Sunday night. It took her most of the day to prepare the meal. She had confided to Kissy that occupying herself helped her to ignore the sense of panic she always felt that day because she had not gone to Mass. Sometimes it made her angry that she still felt it, and then she was likely to burn something or leave out a vital ingredient.

"My dad called," Mary Frances said.

Since the sudden death of her mother the previous spring, Mary Frances had become the focus of her father's life. To her brothers and sisters, Mary Frances's single status meant their father should be her charge. Their father, for the same reason, saw her as his charge. The struggle over who was going to take care of whom was an endless frustration to them both.

"He's had a brilliant idea. He wants us to do a Grand Tour of Europe next summer, after I graduate."

"What do *you* want to do?"

Mary Frances grinned. "I'd love to spend the summer touring Europe. Especially the dyke bars. All I need to do is fix him up with a girlfriend so he'll be busy enough nights not to ask what I'm doing with mine."

Kissy paced around the kitchen. "You're not going to believe what I did after Diane's memorial service."

Mary Frances glanced up from her knife. "Don't tease, baby, spit it out."

"You know I went to the service with Junior Clootie—"

Mary Frances went wide-eyed, her transparent skin mottling. She stamped her feet. "Tell me about it!"

"It was"—Kissy burst out in throaty laughter—"pretty

wild, actually." Fishing a slice of water chestnut from the dish of rejected vegetables, she popped it into her mouth. Her face was warm and she wasn't sure, now that it was out, how much more she wanted to tell her friend. She still did not know how she herself felt, but she was thinking about it more than she had expected she would.

Mary Frances cast her eyes heavenward in mock piety, but her pink cheeks were a more accurate measure of her shock. She swept the chicken slivers into a bowl and put them in the refrigerator, then carried the knife to the sink to wash it meticulously, dry it, and replace it on the knife rack. "Aren't you the Kissy Mellors who told me you'd decided you needed a man like a fish needs a bicycle? How did you get from there to Junior Clootie? I mean, what would any sane straight woman want with Junior Clootie?"

"To fuck him," Kissy said, as she masticated deliberately. Putting it as crudely as she could not just for Mary Frances but for herself. She swallowed. "I'm not moving in with him."

"I should hope not." Mary Frances shuddered theatrically.

Mary Frances might long to tour the dyke bars of Europe, but if she ever did, it would be all looking and no touching. She had confessed to exactly one sexual experience with another person in her entire twenty-seven years. Kissy couldn't imagine how that had happened, or rather, she could, but she couldn't imagine anyone out there with patience enough to wait for Mary Frances to redecorate the bedroom first. Despite endless clinical discussions of how to induce an orgasm by masturbating, Mary Frances had never managed one, probably because she was too numb after two hours of whatever the masturbatory equivalent of skinning tangerine sections was.

"Come on," Mary Frances said, "let's have the juicy details while we finish the table."

Kissy pretended nonchalance as she circled the table, putting down place settings of Mary Frances's fine china and real silver, which she only brought out for her Sunday dinners. "Just the usual. We were animals, tearing each other's clothes off."

"Of course, but how much of the Kama Sutra did you get through?"

Kissy giggled. "Get a life, woman."

"You were putting paid to Ryne," Mary Frances speculated, as she carefully straightened the place settings that Kissy put down.

"Maybe," Kissy said.

"You okay?" her friend asked.

The quiet concern in Mary Frances's voice affected Kissy. She nodded. "I'm getting by."

The Monday after the memorial service, the Blazer was released. Mary Frances dropped Kissy at the Peltry PD impoundment yard. Her vehicle sat in lonely less-than-splendor with the yellow T-bird, off by themselves as if they had BO and the other vehicles wanted nothing to do with them. Her Blazer suffering guilt by association. It was dirty, much dirtier than she remembered it having been when she last saw it.

She had not driven since the accident, just bummed rides from Mary Frances. Her palms were damp, her stomach churning as she keyed the ignition. The wheel slipped jerkily through her fingers and she bit her lip. She drove too slowly, with ridiculous caution. Fuck you, she raged inside at the impatient drivers behind her, blatting their horns, wait'll somebody bounces off your bumper and dies. Or worse. She swung into the nearest car wash. The Blazer inside the tunnel of the car wash became a cave on wheels, dark as a confessional.

She thought of things she had done in automobiles. She put her palm down on the seat of the Blazer. Front seats, back seats. Explorations and experiments. What had seemed bad and wild then now seemed merely mawkish. Then there was Ryne, for three years that weren't, in retrospect, all that different from the fuck-and-runs with the others. She was better at getting herself off than any of them had ever been. Until Junior. She had not expected anything but the same-old-same-old, but it had been different. Just exactly how and why, she was still sorting out.

A few months ago, while looking for something else, she had spilled a manila envelope of pictures she had taken of the boys she had dated in high school. It had struck her how they were all just boys. Pictures did that. Time was one of their dimensions. And in those pictures, she was younger than she had ever felt then. It was the first time she had had an inkling how quickly time passed, how life flew by.

The reality of high school had had all the substance of a fading photograph too—four flat, grainy, overexposed years of faking it, serving her time in limbo, waiting to get on with her life. She had known since she first put her eye to the viewfinder of her father's Nikon what she wanted to do with her life. He had abandoned her within reach of one of the best schools in the Northeast for fine arts. To qualify for a scholarship, she had made Honor Roll every semester.

Other than photography, her only interest had been swimming. She had taken a place on the swim team no one else wanted. Never placed, and also had never lost the twenty pounds the coach kept demanding she take off. But she was still there at the end, to receive her letter and her fourth varsity medal from a still-grudging coach.

Inside the Blazer, the world shut out by the noise, the rush of spray, the whirring of brushes, the slap of sodden felt strips, she thought of her second statement, recorded a few days after the accident by a guy with a little machine on a little stand in a little room at the District Attorney's office. She had answered questions over and over about many small details. She wondered how many more times she would have to tell it. Till she got it right, she thought suddenly, and chuckled wearily to herself. Expelled with a jolt into the natural light, she immediately felt freed. The Blazer was clean again. She opened the windows to breathe.

Down a crowded corridor, she saw James Houston. She was bolting from a class, on her way to make five o'clock laps. He was out on bail, she supposed, and there was nothing else to do but go on with his classes while the legal process worked itself out. Avoiding eye contact, he carried books and moved with purpose in the surge of students. He was unshaven, his skin pallid; he looked as if he lived under a rock.

Twenty minutes later she was crouched at the edge of the pool in the Athletic Complex. As she straightened into the dive, the instant of being airborne became an exhilarating fraction of a second of free fall. Then she sliced cleanly into the water and it flowed around and over and under her.

At the other end, turning, spinning, she reversed directions. Swimming was an automatic process, unthinking, habitual to the point of ritual, but it was also overwhelmingly sensual. The water flowed over her. She moved the water, nudged it and stroked it and slithered through it, forcing it to part for her and receive her and bear her onward.

In the shower later, she remembered James Houston, the way he had looked, how he had not made eye contact with anyone. She could not help remembering, guiltily, that she had promised Ruth Prashker's grandmother that she would return to visit Ruth. She would and soon; it was only that she had been busy.

Sleep, when it came, brought vivid disturbing dreams of the accident, happening again and again, except that she was unable to avoid hitting the two women. If she managed to sleep through the impact in the dream, her dreaming self would leave the Blazer to examine the bodies. She had come to dread that part of it as much as the moment of impact, for the faces the bodies wore were unpredictable. Sometimes it was Diane or Ruth who stared up at her, sometimes it was someone else. James Houston. Her brother Kevin. Her mother or even her father. Mary Frances once. Another time, herself. The dreams not violent were sexual. She was jolted awake often, with a sense of congestion in her belly mingled with the anxiety that seemed to coalesce inside her, under her breastbone, in her guts.

Very early one morning she woke as if from a blow. Her body ached with tension and she was shaking and overcome by tears. It had been Junior's face this time, but she was wracked with weeping for them all. It was stupid, she told herself, this ridiculous grief. People died; it was the bottom line.

It was four-thirty. She pulled on sweats in the dark and slipped from the house. With the first inhalation of clean, cool air, her head cleared of the last dregs of nightmare. She took the Blazer across the Dance to the other side of Peltry, to the Valley. Taking Drumhill, she drove past the house where her brother Kevin had lived for a while after he had dropped out of Sowerwine in his first semester. They had not been close since Kevin decided to introduce his younger sister to better living through chemistry by giving her an acid-spiked beer without mentioning to her

what was in it. It had been a very bum trip indeed, shatter-
ing her trust in Kevin and her confidence in her own sani-
ty. If she was well rid of the prevailing bullshit about the
joy of drug use, she sometimes felt it as a loss of naïveté
that kept her from indulging with her peers. Her brother
had skulked out of Peltry without saying good-bye; her
mother had received a postcard from him a few months
later but no one had heard from him since. The postcard
had been from Sturgis, South Dakota, where a big annual
Harley meet was going on.

A heavily wooded gorge cutting through the west side of
the town, the Valley channeled a turbulent tributary of the
Dance called the Hornpipe. The Valley had remained wild
while Peltry grew up around it. Periodically the desperate
poor had thrown up shacks along the Hornpipe, but sooner
or later a fiercer-than-usual spring flood would sweep
them away. The only residents of late were bums, inca-
pable of constructing more than cardboard hooches. Peltry
had designated the Valley as a public park, and it was indeed a place where runners ran and joggers jogged and
bikers biked and dogwalkers walked dogs. In good weather
there was picnicking, and in the spring, when the water
was at its height, a gleeful white-water race.

But the Valley was a place of shadows. In the obscurity
of its woods and the overhang of its rock faces and beneath the interstate overpass and the several roads that
bridged the Hornpipe and in the solitude of the cemetery that bordered it—the cemetery itself divided by the
highway—the winos found refuge and fornicators and
adulterers trysted and drugs and sex were bought and sold.
Occasionally a rape was perpetrated, and once or twice a
year, a murder or a suicide. Amid the stones of the cemetery, on the lush grass of one of the oldest of graves, she
had herself laid down for the first time with a boy.

She had her night vision, there were arc lamps at strate-
gic points and she was able to jog at a reasonable pace. As
the dark began to thin, she was intensely aware of the
emergence of detail, of edges and depth that had only been
implied. She heard the passage of isolated traffic on nearby streets. As she slowed to turn onto the uphill path that
would take her out of the Valley, there was the whisper of
gravel underfoot, the loud breath of exertion, of another
runner.

Farther uphill, she looked back and through a break in the trees saw the path she had just left, and the other runner on it. She jogged in place, watching him. His sweats, his hair, clung to him damply, and his breathing was exhausted. Yet he was running hard, too hard, with no sign of letup. As if he sensed her observation, he glanced up and saw her. It was James Houston.

She bolted as if she thought he had been in pursuit of her.

Street lamps still glowed uselessly along the empty streets. She found herself sitting in the Blazer outside the hospital. She thought she might have been asleep for a few minutes. It was six by the clock visible through the glass walls.

Sylvia Cronin was sitting next to her granddaughter's bed as if she had never left. The warmth of Mrs. Cronin's smile at the sight of her made Kissy feel even more negligent. The older woman had recovered some poise since their first meeting. She wore an expensive suit of royal blue. Her hair was bound, by itself, in a deliberately old-fashioned and elaborate arrangement of braids. Her ears were adorned by antique filigreed silver drops, and around her neck, a silver sphere of a locket, chased with some antique pattern. The silver was so burnished it had the warmth of gold.

Ruth seemed diminished. Her visible bruises were discolored with healing, but the flesh that had gone undamaged was bloodless. The color of her hands was the same as the sheet on which they rested. The fingers, nails still tipped with red polish except for one that had been torn from its roots, cupped nothing. Her hands were neither beautiful nor ugly; they seemed rather childish and unfinished.

The photographs of Ruth in the paper and on TV had not given Kissy any strong sense of her looks before the accident. Like Diane Greenan, Ruth, in the pictures reprinted in the *Peltry Daily News,* had had health and youth and grooming to make the most of her looks. Perhaps in that first widely disseminated one, the cropped one, there had been a certain visible eagerness to please, something in her eye that made Kissy think of a spooked horse. Coltish, skittish, was the way Ruth had looked.

But the woman on the machines was expressionless.

Nerveless. Inanimate. Unreachable. This Ruth Prashker was a blurry vision of her photographs. And the face of Ruth Prashker in the moon-colored lights of the oncoming Blazer had been a mask, unreal as the face of the body in the machine limbo, and as desperate and terrified and frantically laughing as the girl in the snapshot. Kissy could not have sworn it was the same person. Could not believe it. It. The intermediate and accidental face of Ruth Prashker did not, in Kissy's memory, even have a gender.

To Ruth she murmured, "I'm Kissy Mellors. I was here before. I was driving the first car, the one that didn't hurt you. I'm sorry this happened to you." She stepped back and sagged into the nearest chair and put her face in her hands.

"You're just exhausted, aren't you?" Mrs. Cronin said.

Kissy nodded.

"Come on," Mrs. Cronin said. "Let's go get some cocoa."

In the canteen, she handed Kissy a cup of instant cocoa from the dispenser and nodded toward a table. "I'm worried about you."

In her strung-out weariness, Kissy blurted a confession. "I'm having nightmares."

"I'm not surprised. I've had a few myself lately. In fact, I think I'm living one." Mrs. Cronin stirred her cocoa distractedly.

The cocoa tasted much better than it should have. Suddenly Kissy was hungry. She bought some cereal and milk and ate it under Mrs. Cronin's approving yet ironic eye.

"How is Ruth? I mean, how's she doing?" Kissy asked.

The older woman flapped an age-spotted hand disconsolately and made a disgusted clucking noise in her throat. "The first week, every minute I wasn't actually at Ruth's side, I was in the library here, or buttonholing doctors and forcing them to talk to me as if I weren't an idiot. Once I sorted out the jargon, there's nothing much left. She has suffered a diffuse axonal injury to her brain, a kind of injury that has the worst prognosis for recovery. Even if she woke up tomorrow and all the tests were suddenly hopeful, the odds are that she would be facing at best a future of severe disability. It would take a miracle to bring her back to the point of hope, never mind settling for total dependence just to have her conscious some of the time and maybe flickering her eyelids to communicate." Mrs. Cronin's voice wavered at the end.

Kissy swallowed a suddenly awkward lump of sodden cereal. "Is she in pain?"

"Oh, no. Can't feel a thing without awareness." Snatching a paper napkin from the dispenser on the table, Mrs. Cronin wiped at the corners of her eyes shakily. "That's supposed to be a blessing," she snorted.

"I'm so sorry," Kissy said.

Mrs. Cronin smiled sadly at her. "Sartre said other people are hell. Nasty little narcissist, I always think whenever I'm reminded he said that. By that definition, Ruth's in heaven, since she's in a condition where she doesn't have to deal with other people."

"She's in limbo," Kissy said, "if there is such a thing."

"Yes." Mrs. Cronin nodded. "And we are too."

Kissy clutched the napkin in her hand, stained with the cocoa she had wiped from her mouth. "I wish I could do something."

Mrs. Cronin cocked her head. She looked like an old cockatoo, a magical one that not only talked but dispensed magical conundrums. "Get some rest, dear."

"I'll come visit again," Kissy volunteered.

"Do that." Mrs. Cronin patted her hand. Her touch was light and dry as a dead leaf. And then her hand went to the locket. She caressed it gently and then looked up at Kissy in wordless supplication.

Kissy nodded. With shaking fingers, Mrs. Cronin unhooked the locket and its chain and passed them to her. The locket was body-warm as a living heart and chased with the most delicate arabesques. Kissy opened it. Inside was a picture of a young girl of about ten. Ruth. Her dark eyes merry, her smile gleeful, teeth white against sundarkened skin.

"She was such a happy child," Mrs. Cronin said.

Kissy studied the image. She felt a little ill, to know this delightful child was the broken woman in the Intensive Care Unit. It was hardly thinkable, or bearable, and her chest hurt and she wanted to flee.

When she looked up, Mrs. Cronin was still as a statue, her hands in her lap, but her face was wet with silent tears.

The dashboard clock had just gone seven as she started the Blazer in the hospital parking lot. The traffic in the streets was steady. She was calm and fully awake. Climbing the stairway at her next stop, though, she was suddenly nervous again. She knocked at a door. When there was no response, she knocked again, more loudly.

From inside came a mumbled "Shit, all right." And the sound of bedclothes flung aside, bare feet on the floor, a snap of cloth, snap of elastic, more bare feet, approaching. Junior cracked the door and stood there blinking. He yawned and squeezed his penis, which distended the front of the boxer shorts she had heard him pulling on.

"Jesus," he said.

She slipped past him and he closed the door behind her.

"I could have had somebody here," he said.

"You don't."

He grinned and scratched his chest. "So what are you here for? Coffee and a heart-to-heart?"

Primly she took a seat in the rocking chair and looked up at him, and then her gaze dropped.

"Oh," he said. He yawned again. "You think just because I let you take advantage of me once, I'm a slut you can have anytime?"

She managed not to giggle.

Twice was still an experiment, she told herself. A little craziness was good for her.

Ryne was the first man she had wanted, knowing what she wanted from him. With Junior, she wanted the experience of fucking him, being fucked by him, far more intensely than she had with anyone, even Ryne. It had been ignited, she thought, with the return of her memory of him kicking out the pane of glass. The light of that night, as she recalled it, had been a dreamlike zombie one, falling from that moon over her, too. She remembered having read—with a vagueness that suggested it must have been in childhood in some kid's story, maybe—that moths were drawn to flame because they mistook it for the moon. And she could see in her mind a vast flight of moths drawn upward like a contrail to the moon.

All she could read as she straddled him was the glaze in his eyes that begged her not to stop. She had been making a joke of it with Mary Frances, but there was truth to it, too; they were animals together, doing an animal thing, and she found the crudeness of their coupling was just what she wanted. A momentary obliteration.

She was not sure what she was doing with him had

much, or even anything at all, to do with Junior. Maybe it was all her. A suddenly realized capacity, like the first time looking through the viewfinder. The moment of Amazing Grace: I was blind and now I see. Or when she really swam for the first time, finding all at once the rhythm of turning her head to take in a breath at precisely the right point in the cycle of stroking. Later, turning the wall without a hitch in her stroke or her breathing. Or the night her major adviser, Latham, poured her first glass of vintage wine and she held it in her mouth as he had instructed, realizing it was all true, all the seemingly silly blather about wine. It was in her mouth, the texture, the complexity of flavors, the whole vivid sensual and ancient and undeniable experience.

Distractedly, she wondered how much else she had been missing. And then she laughed, with amazement and wonder and pleasure. And Junior heard her and, seeming to understand exactly the source of her merriment, laughed with her.

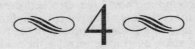

4

Toad's wild ride, Junior thought, when he could think again. *Froggy went a'courtin'*. He went courtin' Miss Molly. Must have been the same Miss Molly in the Little Richard song: *Good Golly Miss Molly she sure like to ball.*

Her skin was damp and flushed. Eyes open, blank and wide. He lifted himself on one elbow to look at all of her. Legs open, the pelt between her legs wet, notch visible and engorged, her stomach hitching now and again, one arm up, the other slack at her side, so one breast was lifted, the other flattened on her chest. He had not considered himself a tit man, but hers would get anyone's attention. And then they had that amazing quality all tits, big or small, did: there were two of them. A fact that might indeed be proof that God had a dick.

He flopped back and closed his eyes a moment, catching his breath before he peeked at her again. Dead asleep. Mouth a little open, a bubble of spit in the corner. Eyes shadowed deeply in the slackness of sleep, she looked as if someone had coldcocked her.

Later, as he cradled her in the bathtub and they played a meaningless game with their feet, rubbing and scratching and flexing on each other, he asked her, "Who would ever think the two of us could get something going?"

She only laughed in response, way down, so he felt the vibration of her body against his. A reminder of what it felt like, her laughing, when he was inside her. He squeezed a sponge and watched the dribble of hot water studded with clear soapy bubbles over her breasts, around and between them, slicking the cleavage, making it gleam like polished stone. The muscle from swimming and lifting underneath made it smooth and sculptural, supporting her full breasts. Though she had the triangular, wide-shouldered, slim-hipped build of the swimmer, her thighs were heavy with muscle and so was her bottom.

He had never been able to hold on to a woman for more than a few months at a time. Women were like plants—however easily acquired, you had to water them and keep track of whether they liked sun, shade, or partial shade. To satisfy science requirements he had taken Botany and Horticulture. The geek who taught the latter class had quoted Dorothy Parker gleefully at every opportunity: *You could bring a whore to culture but you couldn't make her think.* It was Junior's one lasting lesson from that class. Once the season started, dating was a pain in the ass. Between classes and conditioning and practice, he would not have much time and energy for horticulture.

One-night stands were even more unpredictable than dating—even one scene with a wasted, hysterical slut who would not go away was more than enough for him. For all there was some truth to the idea the worst was still wonderful, fact was, it was not all the same. There was career highlight, and then there was the good, the bad, and the indifferent. That last time with Diane—bumping into her at a kegger in somebody's apartment, both of them drunk, not saying a word to each other, just going into the bathroom to toot a little of Diane's cokey-dokey, and then he had fucked her, up against the wall. Hard work for such an anorexic little rush, he remembered—the blow was famous for that. Diane had buttoned up her Calvin's and with a glancing check in the mirror at her hair, walked out and gone off to die that night.

Whereas with Kissy it had all been highlight film. Like they had just invented fucking, the two of them. Nothing so intense could stay that way. Though as long as it was, he was not going to turn it down. He still did not have her phone number. She had made all the first moves so far, and he was inclined to let her offer it. Sometimes it was better to wait for something. Except sometimes you knew you should step out and meet it. What he was really waiting for was the moment he knew whether to step out. It did not matter; it was just a game to play with himself.

"We're soup," she said drowsily. Moisture beaded her

upper lip and the roots of her hair were damp. "Cannibal soup."

He laughed and licked her ear. "Who's the missionary this time?"

Fishing for a sock among the tangle of clothing in his duffel, Junior realized he was going to have to settle for a damp one. On the bench nearby, Zoo examined the edges of the tape on one of his sticks. They were nearly alone in the locker room after practice, with a few other stragglers, guys consulting the trainer, sorting or mending equipment.

Zoo picked at the tape and realigned it. "You nailing her?"

"Who?"

"Melons. Saw her Blazer outside your place this morning. And you got that, I dunno"—Zoo looked up and grinned— "special glow about you."

The sock snagged on his toenail. Junior yanked it off and examined the nail, which had a ragged edge. Frowning, he peeled off a strip of the nail.

"You are," said Zoo.

"Hard." Junior grinned. "You got a nail clipper?"

He tossed him one. *"You gotta cut your nails or you gotta stop havin' that kinda dream,"* Zoo quoted a line from the first *Nightmare on Elm Street* movie. He laughed. "Hoot, you are one twisted pup. She goddamn near killed Diane."

"Life goes on. I should give up a perfectly good fuck because Diane got waxed?"

Junior flipped the clipper back.

Dionne's lumpy face appeared in the door of the trainer's room. He had an ice bag taped to his right shoulder. His pupils were pinpoints from some painkiller. "Diane? Diane Greenan?"

"Hoot used to go out with her," Zoo explained.

It had been before Dionne's time. He was a class behind Junior and Zoo.

"No shit." Dionne blinked. "Wow."

"He's ramming Melons. How's that for sick?"

"Melons?" Dionne's eyes bulged. "I heard she was the one really hit Diane and the other girl. They bounced off her truck and onto the other car—"

"You're a fucking moron," Junior interrupted. "Guy that

hit those girls was two point shitfaced. They tested her too and she had nil blood alcohol. It was right in the fucking paper."

"Cover up," Dionne said. "They do it all the fucking time."

"And you got proof, just as soon as you bend over and yank it out of your ass," said Junior.

Dionne looked injured and then, through the sludge of painkiller in his head, he remembered something relevant. "Hey, you always said Melons was a dyke."

Junior cupped his balls and hefted them. "Not anymore."

"You moron," Zoo said to Dionne. "Just because the sign says it's a one-way street, you think you can't drive down it anyway?" It was always a good time, messing with Dionne's head.

The black and white colors of the Spectres would make for powerful graphics against the white ice, Kissy thought, watching the players skate out to warm up. Glove still off, Junior showed her a thumbs-up. The preseason opener she had been assigned to shoot put the black travel uniforms on the ice against the white-trimmed-with-black the Spectres wore at home, as they split into two teams for the Black-White scrimmage.

She had wangled a special assignment from Clarissa, the assistant editor of the student paper.

Roger Day, who regularly shot sports, had gone into a snit. "She doesn't know shit about the game!" he had repeated several times, while Clarissa blew smoke at him. "What is this, Dykes Giving Dykes a Hand Week?"

"I'd ask you not to be an asshole," Clarissa had retorted, "but I can see it's too late—"

By way of a compromise, Roger was at the game too, supposedly backing her up, showing her the ropes, but expending most of his energy treating her like an idiot. They both wore laminates that allowed them access between the plexi and the seats. There were strategically placed holes, big enough to allow a lens, in the plexi. The locations were widely spaced, so during actual play Roger would be occupied, working his hole in the plexi while she worked another one, at the other end of the ice, near the runway to the Spectres' locker room and the goal the Spectres defended for two out of three periods of every home game.

The cold of the ice crept up through the extra pair of thick socks in her boots and she was glad of her long johns under her Levi's.

"Explain it to me," she had asked Junior.

"Nope." He had grinned at her. "You're a girl. The mysteries may only be known by the men of the tribe——" Her hand drifted between his legs. "Oh, all right, yes, yes, it's simple, clear the puck out of your zone, get it into the other team's net, yes, let me teach you everything I've ever learned——"

With Junior's distracted and rudimentary instruction as a base, she had done a little reading and looked at a lot of photographs of hockey action from periodicals. The goalie's mask had evolved from the eerie inhuman featurelessness of the first ones, revived by the murderous Jason in a series of horror movies, to the current generation of masks, sophisticated articulated helmets protecting the whole head while simultaneously functioning to provide a totemic identity. A goalie for a team named the Bears, for instance, could don the fearsome snarling face of a grizzly or a black bear, like some primitive shaman or warrior. Junior had a new mask that harked back to the anonymous white nullity of the Jason look at the same time the skull it so graphically depicted achieved a startling gruesome realism. A human skull, of course, was perfectly proportioned to the face it masked, as no Lion or Tiger or Bear face could be. Catching the liveliness of Junior's eyes peering out from the bony cage of the mask, she foresaw making some extraordinary and eerie shots.

She was taken with the sheer intensity of his waiting, as he shifted in his gorilla crouch, for the action to reverse in his direction. Bulky as the gear was, his swiftness and fluidity were that much the more striking. He was as forlornly alone as a forest ranger in a tower watching for smoke over vast tracts. The puck could come hurtling the length of the ice in a single stroke at times, and he had always to be there, to be ready. Yet even in his solitary stints while the puck was in the opposition's zone, Junior was vocal, chattering to his teammates across the ice. He used a voice pitched higher than his normal range to get their attention above their own calls to each other and the chalkboard screech of blade, the chattering of sticks and the booming of bodies into the boards, a voice that had gotten him nicknamed "Hooter."

"Loose puck!" he would cry out, scuttling to defend the corner as the forward and defensemen dug it out of the boards.

Or he would singsong an alarm to someone being caught from behind. He would call out the offense as he read it, urge on his own offense, his voice at their backs. With a peacock cry of triumph, he would shoot out to stroke the puck out of the zone and fall back like a yo-yo on a string to the crease.

At game's end, as she packed her gear, he paused on the runway, headed for the locker room. "Kissy," he said. He tipped his elbow. "Bird's."

Roger, trudging up to join her, caught it. A nasty grin spread on his face. "Comes the dawn," he said. "You're trying out for the team. It's too fucking perfect."

Bird's was a jock hangout on the waterfront near the town marina. It had never been Kissy's kind of place. Bright lights, lots of noise, and hordes of jock sniffers—the owner was one and didn't look too closely at IDs from Sowerwine athletes. The others, most of them middle-aged and male, were eager to buy drinks for the golden boys and recount tales of their own days as young gods.

When she arrived, Junior was holding down a corner table with Zoo and Zoo's girlfriend, Brenda, and Dionne, with a thin girl Kissy did not know by name but had seen around the weight room. The table next to them was all hockey players too—and some girls. Some girls. There were always some girls around the jocks. And some beers. And somebody to buy another round for the boys.

Junior jumped up to meet her, his breath warm and beery, and she thought of how she liked the taste of beer in a man's mouth so much more than she actually liked to drink it. He crammed a chair for her in next to his own. As she sat down, he took her hand and drew it out of sight beneath the table, onto his crotch. Under the flybuttons, his penis jumped at her touch.

He whispered in her ear, "See what you do to me?" And laughed. To his friends, he said, "You know Kissy?"

Even the girl Kissy did not know nodded. Knowingly. She was with Junior; all that was necessary was known.

They were in the middle of something. Nobody troubled themselves to explain what they were talking about but just left her to sort it out on her own. Some political thing on the team, somebody not pulling his weight. It had the sound of a chronic bitch. It gave her a chance to look around and check out the place. In a bar, with a little booze short-circuiting their inhibitions, people were a carnival that made her itch for the camera she had left in the Blazer.

Junior bought her a glass of house red. He glanced at her often but did not say anything, focusing on his friends. The hand not cupping his beer relaxed on her thigh, her hip, her waist, her hand, reassuring himself of her presence, or her of his.

A girl approached them unsteadily. She leaned over the table, her bosom shifting heavily forward, her eyes a little glassy. Though the conversation continued, everyone at the table picked her up on their radar.

"Hooter?" Her voice was both rushed and husky. Between her long, red-tipped talons trembled a drink mat with a name and a sequence of numbers written on it. She extended it to him as if offering a business card. "Call me?"

Kissy pushed the mat away.

"Fuck off," she said.

Everyone except Junior laughed.

The girl looked her up and down sneeringly. "Who is this bitch?"

"My wife," Junior said, "and you're offending the shit out of both of us."

Zoo and Dionne writhed in their chairs, tears squirting from their eyes. Brenda and Dionne's date sniggered into their fists.

The girl blinked uncertainly. "Oh." She sniffed and pushed the mat toward Junior. "Lemme give you my number."

"He's got your number, and so do I," said Kissy, and flicked the mat to the floor, where it landed in a puddle of spilled beer.

For a second, the girl hovered, working out her best strategy. She tipped her chin and twitched away.

Junior's friends burst out laughing again.

Brenda leaned close to Kissy. "Get used to it."

"Wife?" Zoo choked, eyebrow hooked at Junior.

"Sorry," muttered Junior, squeezing Kissy's hand.

Dionne and his girl saw somebody they should say hello to and Brenda announced she had to go to the ladies' and Zoo said he thought he had better go tap a kidney too.

"Don't worry about my friends," Junior told her, when they were alone. "They're all right. They just don't know you. They're as freaked by you as you are by them." After draining his beer mug, he glanced at her glass. "You want something else?"

She shook her head. "To drink? I was just being polite. I should have told you a tonic would do."

He gave her a speculative look. "I'd like to see you drunk someday."

She raised her eyebrows.

He played with a drink mat, a circle printed with the name of the place and its logo, a cartoon gooneybird with bugged-out spinning eyeballs. It was the same as the one the girl had tried to give him, lacking only a phone number. "Let's clear out of here."

"I'm driving. You can pick up your truck tomorrow."

For a fraction of a second, she thought he was going to be angry.

"I'm all right," he protested mildly, but when she held his gaze, he shrugged.

He put a couple of dollars on the table by way of a tip and they cleared out on the crest of an exchange of jeers with his teammates, by which she gathered the winners of the scrimmage had been sucking up beer at the expense of the losers.

Friday brought another exhibition game, this one against some Red Bloc Comrades. Though they were alleged to be students, nearly all of the visiting team looked to be at least thirty. Except for one, who appeared to be about fifteen. Not only was he shockingly pretty, unlike his teammates, he had all his own teeth, on constant display in a high-wattage, thigh-dampening smile.

As the Spectres took the ice for warm-up, Kissy was at the near shooter's hole.

On his last circuit of the ice, Junior slowed and put his face to the shooter's hole in the plexi. "Gonna make me look good?"

"Got my stud lens on. Women will get pregnant just looking at your picture."

He laughed. It was an enormous lens she had attached, one that required a monopod to help support it.

With the camera at her eye, she didn't close the other eye, which looked at him unblinkingly. The camera split her face as if she were some kind of android, half her face a black box with a black mirror of an eye in it, and half that of a real woman, the real eye fixed and amused. Her beak looked like sculpture with that camera next to it.

He let himself slip backward, receding from her as if drawn on invisible wire.

The Comrades shelled him. Not just him—Zoo and his line, Dionne and his—they all looked like Pee-Wee Leaguers. The most descriptive shot of this game would show Junior out of focus, blurred, an immeasurable fraction of a second behind where he needed to be. And a second choice: he tipped his mask and drank thirstily, his throat working as if the water were rock, his hair plastered to his damp skull and the sweat running down his drained face like rain.

And later, facing the media, he smiled, he made the right noises, parroting how the game showed they needed to do some tuning up. The struggle to be cool and amused and in charge made his face more interesting—the false face tense, the true one wounded and childish and tremulous underneath. She wanted to follow him around, try to get him at an unguarded moment, but Clarissa had asked her to look around for off-ice postgame action too—the coaches, the visiting team, the fat cat donors and university bigwigs. And the mascot.

The seven-foot-tall Spectre, with his skull face like a shell of scoured bone, loomed over everyone, causing a stir among the Comrades. The teen idol Comrade was as entranced as a kid at Disney World. Inside the costume was a mild-mannered communications major who loved climbing into the ring and scaring hell out of everyone. In recent years the mascot had become mildly controversial. Objections had been raised that because he wore a horned helmet on his skull, he was altogether too demonic. He did not so much walk as lurch, and little children had been known to burst into tears at the sight of him.

As she was starting to pack up, Junior emerged from the crowd.

"You used the wrong lens," he said, "the dud lens."

"Rough night." It wasn't offered as commiseration, only as observation.

"I sucked." Meant to be observation too, but it came out flat. He lunged from it. "We're hosting the Comrades—taking them out for a few beers. You want to go, don't you?"

"You have a beer. I'll drive."

He looked at her. "This is turning into an obsession. You'd almost think you'd been in a drunk-driving accident."

She shrugged.

He put his arm around her waist. "Follow me to my place, I'll drop off the truck."

At his place, though, he asked if he could drive the Blazer. "Just going. You can drive back here."

He was humoring her. So she gave him the keys. But he didn't drive to Bird's. He cut downtown.

"Where are we going?" she asked.

"Skinner's. We're all meeting there. So the Comrades can check out the local color."

"Whose bright idea was it? The band sucks. So does Skinner's." She tried to be flippant. Since the morning after the accident, she had managed to avoid seeing Ryne even in passing. He had left a note in the mailbox the previous weekend, asking her to meet him at Skinner's, but she had not. Most nights she had spent with Junior, only returning to the apartment for a few hours at a time to change clothes or work at her Mac.

"My idea." He glanced at her. "You're just worried about the drummer. Your boyfriend."

"He's not—don't call him that."

Junior seemed pleased. "Well, he can't expect you to become a nun. He'll be busy playing anyway."

"Let's go to your place."

His face set. "A couple of beers. Then we'll cut out."

Shrug it off, she told herself. More than likely she would discover Ryne would be more interested in showing her how easily he could get another girl than in butting heads with Junior, if that was what Junior was looking for.

* * *

Skinner's was housed in the subbasement of an abandoned department store. It served as the primary venue for local bands and brought together the university punks and the townie skinheads, greasers and longhaired metalheads, often with violent results. The brick exterior was painted black and covered with graffiti, mostly bumper sticker wit that ran the gamut from moronic to smutty. It was entered through what had been the rear of the building, and by way of a short stairway that turned around a landing where a bouncer could collect a cover charge or sell a ticket if the band warranted anything so exotic, or maybe challenge the possibly underaged, if he felt like it. The bouncer recognized Kissy and then did a double take on Junior, became effusive and wanted to shake his hand and waive the cover charge.

Inside the place was darker, the air a noxious brew of smoke, sweat, piss, vomit, and sour beer. The music matched the assaultive stench in its decibels, harshness, and breakneck beat. Amy, the singer, was writhing around the mike stand and shrieking. Jose and the bassist, Leo, were sweating nearly forehead to forehead over their guitars. Ryne's forearm muscle was pumped as a weightlifter's with the exertion of drumming, and his T-shirt hung on him like a damp second skin.

The Comrades and Junior's teammates were already on the dance floor, whooping and throwing themselves about spastically. Dragging her with him, Junior plunged into the sea of bodies. He began to pogo ecstatically. Some of the regulars, recognizing Junior and his teammates and identifying the Comrades as yet more invaders, began to bump and push them with malice that was, at least initially, mistaken for all-in-good-fun.

Junior threw his arms around her enthusiastically. "What a blast!" He had to say it directly into her ear.

Of course it was. Or had been once. Abandoned dance, the music blocking out the outside world and driving the pulse. At times it had seemed like the closest thing to sex and sometimes better, since conversation was impossible. Only bodies were possible in the scrum.

"Yeah," she agreed, having to hang on him in turn to speak into his ear.

"You come here often?"

Not as much as she used to. "Once in a while. It gets old."

He did not seem to hear her. Maybe he could not. She could hardly hear him, even with his tongue practically in her ear. But maybe he was telepathic. All at once he took her by the jaw and did tongue her ear and then kissed her enthusiastically. Somebody near them bellowed "Fuck her, man! I did!" and other people broke into laughter.

Though she knew it was not Ryne's voice, she could not help but glance his way. And when she looked at Junior, he was smiling ironically at her; he had seen where she had looked.

His arm tightened around her waist, and he pointed toward their right, where the thin girl, her denim skirt up around her hips, was riding Dionne's shoulders. She had taken off her shirt. Her small breasts bounced in the spot the light board man immediately put on them. The thin girl swayed on Dionne's shoulders and then he lost her and she fell backward, shrieking a long terrified scream, into eager hands. She disappeared amid the writhing bodies. Dionne scrabbled after her and began to throw people to one side or another and one of them turned on him and punched him in the ear. Hardly anyone paid any attention. The band kept on bashing; most of the other dancers kept on dancing.

"Thanks," Junior said into her ear. "It's a trip."

As people got more beered up, the music became steadily louder and the dancing wilder. The beautiful young Comrade climbed to the stage and began to dance there. He did not look old enough to be in the club; he looked like someone's little brother who had snuck into the big kids' party, gotten pissed on a stolen beer, and was now playing the idiot. The band ignored him. He grabbed at Amy and she punched him in the gut. He vomited over the stage and into the crowd and was dragged down into it by skinheads eager to pound on him. His teammates came to his rescue, beating back the skinheads while Junior and the other Spectres cheered them on.

The skinheads began to collude in their assaults with the headbangers. Zoo and Junior conferred, agreeing that as much fun as it would be to tear some heads off, it would be much better to let the Comrades do it for them. Without informing their ostensible guests, they tapped shoulders quietly, and by twos and threes and fours, the Spectres slipped out of the club.

5

Springsteen moaning on the stereo—*down to the river down to the river I go*—Kissy gasping with him, Junior urging her on—and then an inarticulate scream of rage like the howl of an animal burst over them as someone hit the door hard enough to make it jump in its frame. They separated with a jolt, Junior pulling out and into a defensive crouch, Kissy rolling up onto her knees, clutching at the sheet. Springsteen's voice continued in his dirge from Junior's speakers. Kissy jumped up and hit the power button, silencing the singer's voice. Turning back to Junior, she caught a glimpse of his face in the streetlight from the window above them—the gleeful passion of the previous instant twisted into fury, as if he were the screamer at the door. She was stunned with terror. He moved naked away from her, away from the door, and then turned back, a hockey stick suddenly in his hand.

"Fucker!" Ryne screamed, his voice recognizable this time, and he hit the door again.

Junior reached for the door.

She understood instantly he meant to open it. Ryne would not be expecting the stick. Shocked almost numb by the violence of Ryne's anger, she couldn't let murder happen. She scrabbled to her feet and went for Junior's hand on the door, clawing at his wrist.

He yelped.

"No!" she hissed.

It was enough to make him hesitate, and she put her back to the door, just as Ryne threw himself against it again, with another howl.

"I'm gonna kill you both!" he raged.

A long crack jagged like lightning in the door panel.

The light glinted off Junior's bared teeth.

"Get out of the way," Junior told her softly. "That door's coming apart."

"Ryne, goddamn it!" she shouted, "I'm calling the cops!" She dove for the phone.

The threat only produced another cursing, thunderous assault on the door.

"Come and get it, asshole," Junior bellowed, and yanked open the door.

Kissy threw aside the phone to try to get between the two men, but was too late. Junior's stick was up and arcing, aimed between Ryne's eyes, and Ryne was lunging toward it. Kissy tackled Junior, throwing off his aim. The stick hit high, glancing off Ryne's forehead. The blow slowed but did not stop him as he went for Junior's throat with both hands. Junior, unbalanced and with Kissy hanging on his waist, staggered. At close quarters, the stick was harder to use, and he dropped it, trying to get his arms up and between Ryne's. He succeeded. He thrust his arms wide and both men's left fists, driven outward, caught the side of Kissy's face as she struggled to her feet.

She dropped like a stone, too stunned to even cry out.

Junior went under Ryne, threw him casually over his back and knocked the wind out of him.

Sirens were shrieking. There were neighbors peering out of their apartments outside the open door.

Junior stooped over Kissy. "Baby, you okay?"

Ryne crabbed to his knees and hurtled himself at Junior, who got him in a headlock and began to pound his head on the floor.

The open door filled up with large men in blue, wielding nightsticks and shouting.

Kissy flattened to the floor, her arms over her head. The place was full of shouting men and the sound of sticks hitting meat and suddenly the lights came on, bright and fierce. And then the shouting stopped and someone crouched over her and she felt cloth.

"Here, cover up, honey," someone said, and she took the sheet blindly, recognizing its texture, and covered herself.

She raised her head and looked into the sympathetic eyes of Officer Burke. He smiled, and she felt a rush of gratitude.

"Why, it's Kissy. You remember me—Mike Burke?"

She nodded.

"You're bruised up," he said, studying her face critically. "We'll get an EMT."

"No," she whispered, but he ignored her.

Still naked, Junior was face down on the floor and Ryne a few feet away, both of them with cops manacling their wrists behind them. Ryne was bleeding from the head and nose, some of it Junior's doing, some of it the cops. Ryne hardly seemed to know where he was. His eyes were red and unfocused.

"Shit," she muttered.

Burke's hand on her arm tightened, and when she glanced at him, he nodded toward Ryne. "What?"

She turned her face away. "He's baked."

"On what?"

"I don't know. Blow, probably."

"He a user?"

"Sometimes."

He left her side, spoke to another cop, whom Kissy recognized as his partner, Sergeant Pearce, from the night of the accident.

Burke and Pearce prodded Junior onto his knees and then to his feet.

"I'm at a disadvantage here," Junior said. "Any chance of letting me have my shorts?"

"Oh, I don't know." Pearce grinned. "It don't look like much of a disadvantage to me."

The other cops laughed.

"What's going on?" asked Pearce.

"Old boyfriend being an asshole," Junior said.

Pearce sighed theatrically. "Figured as much."

"Howyadoin'?" Burke asked Kissy. He had seen it before, other women with an ice pack to the face, trying to be invisible. The bruises were purpling up despite the ice.

Kowanek was in a unit on the street, almost ready to transport. Clootie had gotten into some shorts and was giving his statement to Pearce.

Burke drew water for her and brought her the Excedrin sitting out on the counter by the sink.

She swallowed hard, her throat as tight with tension as

her face. Burke watched the effort of her swallowing with interest.

"I'm sorry," he said.

He caught a flash of fury as she lowered her eyes.

He prodded her. "Kowanek's your boyfriend, he caught you with Clootie—"

"He's not; we broke up a while ago—"

"Tell me what happened."

She told him tersely, hurriedly, wanting this to be over, wanting to flee his presence.

The place smelled like a fuck factory. He doubted he was the only man there aroused by it.

"And the bruises on your face are from accidental blows from both men as they fought and you tried to stop them."

"Yes."

"Where's Ryne get his shit?" he asked.

She closed up on him fast, like a pupil contracting in the beam of a flashlight. She shrugged. "Anywhere. Everywhere."

He held her gaze, so she would understand he knew she was bullshitting. "Whatta you think, should we legalize'm?"

She snorted. "I thought they were."

That made him laugh, and then he grew serious again. "What are you going to do? We're holding Kowanek overnight, but he'll be on the street tomorrow. You could offer not to press charges against him if he'll stay away from you. He's in enough trouble with other charges, he might listen."

"All right," she said. "I'll go along with that."

Burke sighed. "You got a right to go where you want, but you could save yourself grief by staying out of his face. If you know he's at Skinner's, don't go there, especially with some other guy. He has to deal with you being with another man, you're liable to stir him up again."

"Oh, the hell with him," she said, all the anger rising up again. "I will press charges and you can leave his ass in jail—"

He let her rage. Whatever she did, Kowanek would be in jail on other charges at least overnight, postponing Round Two, if there was going to be one, until tomorrow night.

Burke had never hit a woman except in the line of duty, in self-defense, usually fending off some bitch gone berserk on booze or drugs. But he had moments when he had wanted to hit a woman. Women knew what buttons to push; many of them could play a man like a pinball machine. Some women made a hobby of driving men crazy. It added something to those weekend nights, getting wasted, working each other up, trading some slaps or outright punches, getting the guy aroused enough to throw a fuck into her that would make it all worth it. In Burke's view, it was natural selection at work—females testing males for survival traits, males battling each other for possession or just slipping one past the other guy when he's busy poking an anthill with a stick, looking for a snack to buy himself some of that same honeypot. All of it unthinking, instinctual, the itch demanding to be scratched, but all wrapped up in the romance, the bullshit of the same old story, the fight for love and glory. Play it again, Sam.

"Oh baby," Junior said, his touch caressing on the side of her face. "I hate it you got hurt."

The cops were going out the door, the young cop, Burke, watching them quizzically. Then the door closed. It was badly cracked, so the heat went straight out and they breathed night air, cold and sharp, and felt exposed.

"The asshole had nose candy on him, as well as in him," Junior told her. "It'll be on the blotter, nothing they could do for me about that." He grimaced and fidgeted at his crotch. "My balls hurt. Christ, what a night." He glanced at her. "I'm not liable to forget this one. You're gonna think I'm nuts, but I'm really hungry. Want to go get some breakfast?"

She was still shaky inside. Food might sop up some of the excess adrenaline.

The only thing open intown was Denny's.

At the restaurant, Junior ordered a huge breakfast for himself and dug into it enthusiastically. Halfway through, he looked up at her and grinned. "It was a blast."

"I'm glad somebody enjoyed it. I was terrified," she said. She had managed to eat a piece of toast. "And it was so much fun having half the cops in this town checking me out stark naked."

"You forget I was standing there myself balls-and-bare-ass," Junior said.

Her mouth twisted as she fought a smile. "Not likely I'd forget."

"No," he agreed with a grin. "I guess you wouldn't. They won't either." He shrugged. "Sometimes somebody gets past you. It happens. Nobody ever stops everything. You have to live with it sometimes. Never mind. It's over, baby. New game tomorrow."

"Don't call me baby."

"Will if I want to. Baby, baby, baby," he taunted. And then his grin faded. "You don't care about that asshole anymore, do you?"

"No. If you thought you were fighting over me, you were mistaken. You were just butting heads."

He wiped egg off his plate with a corner of toast and chewed it and swallowed before he spoke again. "I wasn't fighting over you, I was protecting you. And myself. That asshole wanted to hurt you. If you'd been there by yourself, you'd be in the hospital. Or dead."

Recalling Ryne's violence, she was hard put to deny she had been in some danger. It had all happened so quickly, all she had been able to do was be frightened. But now, in the ordinary light of Denny's, she didn't want to believe it had been that scary. She didn't want to believe Ryne would ever have really hurt her, any more than Seth, her grave-yard first-time lover, meant to, when she was fifteen and knocked up.

The ache in her face throbbed.

Seeing her confusion, Junior reached across the table for her hand. "We'll take a bath, get relaxed, get some sleep."

Later, with his mouth to her ear, holding her from behind with both of them on their knees in a way that made her feel entirely in his physical power, aware he felt it too, he asked her, "Am I better?" Her answer was a sobbing cry with an odd note of triumph in it. It satisfied him.

In the years they had been roommates, Mary Frances had never asked Kissy to account for herself. Kissy had always come and gone as she pleased. Ryne had never lived there with them—Kissy would not allow him to stay the night—and, in fact, he had acquired a key in a brazen con. Claiming Kissy had lost hers, he had borrowed Mary Frances's from her and had it copied. Kissy had broken up

with him over it and eventually made up with him, while
he had retained the key. Mary Frances had put a lock on
her bedroom door, and so, for that matter, had Kissy, to
make sure Ryne could not get at her Mac or her stereo
components or camera gear. Mary Frances was never
happy about Ryne but she coped. In the face of Kissy's involvement with Junior Clootie, Mary Frances wilted.

It was from the start a greater involvement—Kissy
spent many more hours with Junior than she ever had with
Ryne. When she came home with her face swollen, her
friend could hardly bear to look at her. Everyone would
know now; it was on the police blotter and Junior was
somebody in Peltry, and it had been on the radio the cops
had been to his place over a domestic disturbance, and in
the morning it would be in the police beat column.

"I'm all right," Kissy told her.

Stricken and white-faced, Mary Frances daubed at her
eyes and blew her nose. "Latham says you pick them—"

"He should talk. Look, it's over. Ryne's in too much
trouble to give me any more shit. Let it go. I'm all right."

And Mary Frances nodded, agreeing with Kissy because she wanted it to be true.

The autumn sunlight fell on Ruth Prashker like a cruel
knife, rendering her face mineral and translucent. The
edema had gone, and now the flesh was closer to the bone,
as if her fabric had been taken in by a skillful seamstress.
The discoloration of bruising had disappeared except for
the splotches over accessible veins, where test blood was
drawn and various lines tapped into her bloodstream. She
was pale as moonstone. She was breathing now without a
ventilator. The rigidity of her posture had been treated with
a drug, and her limbs could now be moved through exer-
cises that were intended to prevent contracture of her ligaments, as well as stimulate her blood circulation.

She had been moved to her grandmother's house on
James Street in Peltry, where a front parlor had been converted to her needs. It remained a pleasant room, despite
the addition of the sickroom accouterments. The windows
had sheers in them as well as blinds. A spider plant hung in
one of them; in another, a gift from Kissy, a kalanchoe as-
terisked with clusters of waxen orange blossoms. Comfortable chairs were arranged around the bed for visitors,

and the beribboned plants and cards on the windowsills
and fireplace mantel testified that Ruth's friends and sorority sisters had called upon her.

Displayed prominently on a side table was a collage
of snapshots of Ruth and her friends and relations. As
Kissy examined the photographs, her uneasiness and distress welled up again. This girl had had a life. She had
made faces with her girlfriends at the camera at someone's
birthday party, had stood with her parents, her graduation
cap tipped precariously over one eye, at her high school
graduation; she had stroked this dappled pony lovingly,
and shot a shy glance at the camera; she had straddled the
shoulders of this grinning boy standing in a swimming
pool in teenage exuberance.

The bedside table, however, arrayed medicines and tissues and other necessities of care. An indwelling catheter
served Ruth's bladder, but the processes of her bowel were
a major preoccupation for her caretakers, and it was necessary to reposition her frequently to prevent bedsores. This
was Ruth's life now.

Mrs. Cronin had welcomed Kissy with an eagerness that
made Kissy suspect the burden of care was already wearing her down. Ruth's mother was in attendance every day,
but her father never visited. There had been a terrible argument in the hospital, her father shouting that Ruth was
dead, that the young woman in the bed was no more than a
corpse being maintained in order to enrich the quacks, that
his wife, her mother, and Ruth's brother, Daniel, were all
being victimized in their grief.

It had seemed best, once her condition stabilized, that
Ruth be transferred to Mrs. Cronin's home—Dan had
small children at home taking up all his wife's energy. A
retired grade school teacher and the widow of a lawyer,
Sylvia Cronin was in sturdy good health, lived alone, and
was more than willing to center her life and household on
Ruth. She had acquired a specially equipped van to transport Ruth, who would occasionally need a trip to the hospital for testing or therapy, and who might, at some point,
benefit from an outing, though she had not been in any
way responsive. The house had been modified with ramps
to allow passage of a wheelchair so Ruth could be moved
from room to room. Mrs. Cronin had had special bathroom
facilities, including a whirlpool for various water thera-

pies, installed. She had organized all the necessary care for Ruth, performed by herself and Ruth's mother, supplemented by Ruth's brother and his wife and by the occasional visits of a public health nurse.

Mrs. Cronin read to Ruth from a novel about a man who had recovered from a coma and discovered himself to be clairvoyant. Kissy, watching Ruth closely, saw no reaction from her. When Mrs. Cronin paused to sip a little water, Kissy asked if she could take some pictures.

For a moment Mrs. Cronin studied her with a sharp, inquisitive eye, and then said, "Yes, I think perhaps you should."

Kissy worked quietly, spending long moments watching Ruth, or Ruth and her grandmother, then composing and shooting as unobtrusively as possible. When she put the camera down, she sat and held Ruth's hand for a time. Following Mrs. Cronin's example, every time she touched Ruth, she spoke to her directly, telling her she had been taking her picture.

Later, in the trays in the darkroom, the images of Ruth formed upon the paper first as ghosts and then developed depth and dimension. It was good work, with a dignity that would gratify Sylvia Cronin, Kissy thought. If there was anyone who should see them, it was her.

The weekend brought the first away games, back-to-back, at Arkham in Rhode Island.

Junior went into the first game sweating and, for the first few minutes, experienced a definite wobble. His defensemen were there for him, blocking a wraparound and then a wily attempt at a rebound. He sucked the water bottle, wiped the sweat from his face, and squinted down the long, glowing white plain.

Zoo's line glided off ice as Dionne swung a leg over the boards with his line behind him. Dionne misplayed the puck and Arkham broke away with it. Stepping out, Junior met it like a door catching the cat's tail, stopped it, and flipped it with a stroke to Dionne's left wing, Golem.

Later, he gave up two goals. But he stayed cool. It happened. Overdone-with-tout-finis. Dwelling on goals would take him right out of the game. The time to examine failures was after the game and before the next one. So the internalized coach in his head reassured him. He stepped out

to shoot the puck that was skidding straight in ahead of the
pack, back into the neutral zone. The Spectres scored three
goals to win and he got out with his goals-against per-
game average unchanged.

Without discussing it with anyone, even Zoo, he ate a
postgame meal, knocked back a beer or three, and hit the
rack, instead of going out with some of the other guys. His
roommates, Zoo and Onsrud, for instance. There was another game the following evening, and he needed to have a
great year, to position himself. Coach Stannick would
know he had stayed in, just as he would know who had
gone out and partied. The whole club would get the message, without anything needing to be said, that Junior
Clootie was not fucking around with the season.

Early to bed did not necessarily make it easy to sleep.
He was still dieseling from the game. Experience had
taught him partying did nothing for his game, but he had
yet to find another way to unwind.

In the second game against the Warlocks, he gave up a
single goal and the Spectres won again, 2–1.

While changing, they heard the last fatal play of the sixth
game between the Sox and the Mets on the trainer's ghetto
blaster. Cries of outrage, of disbelief, a rain of curses—their
own game was momentarily forgotten. They kept going
back and forth, on the bus, as they played cards or snuck
beers, chewing over their own sweep, then bemoaning the
ball lost between Billy Buckner's legs.

After a while, Junior stared out the window. It was rain-
ing hard. Miles and miles to go. He dozed. A sudden jud-
der as the gears shifted jolted him, and he wiped drool
from the corner of his mouth. He had been dreaming.
Dreaming about Kissy. He sighed and shifted in his seat,
pressing down on the erection that the dream had raised, or
that had raised the dream. Next to him, Zoo snored softly,
sure of having a bed warmed by Brenda at the end of the
ride. Junior closed his eyes again, hoping the dream would
return.

The stands at the Sowerwine Arena filled early on Halloween Eve, with nearly everyone costumed and in a carnival mood. The most popular among the disguises were
variants of the mascot Spectre. Seemingly every other

spectator was suited up as one of a ragtag militia of skeletal grim reapers. They made a notably rowdy crowd.

With Coach in mind, Junior pretended not to notice Kissy at her spot in the plexi. Just as well, as a single sighting of her had already burned her image on his retinas. She was wearing a skeleton costume, white bones painted with anatomy chart accuracy on a skintight black bodysuit. Only the ribs were incomplete: they stopped beneath her breasts, making a grisly bustier. Her face wasn't painted yet because she had to use the camera, but it would be.

The game was a knockover, 3–0, for the Spectres, against a team they had expected to be a lot stiffer. The crowd seemed to rattle the visitors, on its feet most of the game, shaking the building with an earthquake roar.

"They were into it," Junior told Zoo as he unlaced, after the game was wrapped. "It was the costumes, wasn't it? Like they were all somebody else and could do anything they wanted."

"Tell me about it. Hey, buddy, it's party time."

On the other side of Zoo, Dionne and Golembiewski howled.

6

The dead walked everywhere on the Sowerwine campus. The conjunction of a weekend Halloween with a mild night and a full moon had had a powerful effect, like the rip of a spring tide, when the earth and moon come closest at the same time the sun, earth, and moon are in a straight line. It was as if it had triggered a weird rupture of dimensions. Abe Lincoln and Marie Antoinette and Michelangelo's David and the Tasmanian Devil and Minnie Mouse and the Marlboro Man and Madonna and Michael Jackson and the President and Mrs. Reagan and Queen Elizabeth and Adolf Hitler and Traci Lords and Freddy Kreuger and Kareem Abdul Jabbar walked the campus. Ichabod Crane held hands with the Headless Horseman, not only unhorsed for the night but with his head obscenely attached to a lifelike dildo sticking out of the front of Ichabod Crane's pantaloons. There were tribes of punks with multicolored mohawks and pins through their ears, several Alice Coopers with painted faces, and legions of spooks and demons and vampires, flitting to and from parties. The association of the school's Spectre mascot and the holiday of the dead had inspired skeletons, zombies, and the undead far out of proportion to the not-inconsiderable variety in other costumes.

The carnival surged in and out of dormitories and fraternity houses across the quads and through the Commonses and on and off campus and in huge eddies at the three costume balls. Representing the largest number of students, the Student Senate sponsored one at the Campus Convention Center. The Greeks were throwing theirs in the men's gymnasium. And the Guild of Fine Arts Students, known informally as the Freakers, had possession of the women's gym in the Field House. The Freakers' annual ball had in recent years been nicknamed the Homo Hop because of the high proportion of openly gay and lesbian students in Fine Arts.

The smallest available venue, the women's gym, was nicknamed "the Pit" for good reason. Taking the name as a theme, the Freakers had decorated the dark, narrow, high-ceilinged gym as the Circles of Hell. Before the upper-story stands were locked as a matter of safety and security, the Theatre majors doing the decorating had filled the house with otherworldly spectators. In some sections of the stands, shrieking and moaning sinners suffered demonic torture and flame that did not consume. In others, the seats were occupied by dusty, cobwebbed bones and mummies. A deejay costumed as a red devil spun music from one of the corner sections, and a lighting tech in a troll mask beside him worked a lightboard. At the farther end of the gym, a dais bore a crude, European-style wooden coffin. Deposed upon its upholstery was a real human skeleton named Mr. Bones, the official host of the ball. Rumor had it Mr. Bones had been unearthed from an Indian burial ground.

The floor was packed with dancers. Gelled lights washed the floor in violent flares of red and green and purple, lighting faces and masks weirdly from underneath. Black light, rigged to strobe to the beat of the music, fluoresced the white of bones painted on black body stockings, a costume so popular that much of the crowd appeared to be lurching, writhing skeletons. Oingo Boingo was the music of the moment:

Going to a party where no one's still alive.

It was nearly midnight when the mascot Spectre loomed, brandishing tickets, at the door. An entourage, including several Jasons in hockey masks, the Monster of Frankenstein and the Monster's Bride, and a female skeleton, crowded in behind. At the Spectre's appearance the revelers cheered and applauded. They parted for him, some of them bowing and kneeling in obeisance, receiving him as their lord and ruler, as he lurched to the dais. He leapt to it effortlessly.

The horned wraith commanded seven feet, his seemingly

long-weathered skeleton a tromp l'oeil illusion, the bones standing out in strong relief from a black ground that blended with the ragged-edged black cloak swirling about him. His fingerbones were metal-tipped talons, and he carried an enormous scythe. By black light, the ivory carapace of his skull face gleamed and the whole costume came to life. Back to life.

The Spectre pranced and swung his scythe to Rockapella.

> *Back to back, belly to belly,*
> *I don't give a damn*
> *'cause I'm stone dead already.*

He brought the scythe in a huge parabola to his crotch and rode it obscenely. Then he cast it aside and threw himself to the floor to dry-hump the air. The crowd loved it and urged him on. Leaping up, he strode to the edge of the dais, where he pumped his hips lewdly and mimed masturbation. Then he aimed a talon at the crowd, describing circles and waves with the point of his finger until finally he fixed upon the Bride of Frankenstein. With a roar, the crowd pushed the Bride forward and the Monster himself participated. She entered into the spirit of the thing with shrieking and swooning and was handed up to the Spectre.

He swung her to her feet. His jaws moved in some instruction to her, to which she replied with a grin before he threw her down and faked copulation with her, with air visible between her rolling hips and his thrusting body. After a moment, he rolled to his feet and helped her up, but once she stood, he swept her off her feet again and threatened to throw her to the crowd. It clamored for her, she shrieked obligingly, until he pitched her off into waiting arms.

Unsatisfied, he resumed his capering and crotch clutching. A missile arced above the crowd below him. The Spectre spread his body open, stretched up one arm, and caught it neatly: it was the Headless Horseman's head. He held it up to the pleasure of the mob and then lowered it to his crotch and pumped into its face. After a few thrusts, he raised it again and shook it in disgust. Taking up his scythe, he tossed the head upward and batted it with the curve of the blade, back into the crowd, where hands reached for it as eagerly as fans at a ball game for a foul, or bridesmaids for a bridal bouquet.

While the Spectre brandished his scythe triumphantly, another missile rose and he snatched it one-handed from the air. It was Ichabod Crane's dildo. The Spectre displayed the dildo at his crotch and masturbated it and humped the air with it and then jacked it into the pelvic bones of the skeleton in the coffin.

Returning to the edge of the dais, he pointed his talon again, in search of another mate. Dancers abandoned their partners to rush to the stage to offer themselves. The wraith played to them for a little while, surveying his choices. Then the moving finger steadied and fixed upon the female skeleton. The crowd seized her and passed her overhead to the dais.

Of all the skeletons at the ball, she was a triumph of the makeup artist equal to the Spectre's own costume. But while he wore an articulated skull mask, the flesh of her face had been transformed, as if stripped to bone. The sockets of her eyes had been blackened into holes in which the orbs of her eyes seemed to float. Her nose also had been blackened into an absence at the center of her face. Heavily whitened, her lips blended into the bony plates of her face. White hair stood in wiry twists and horns from a bone-colored skullcap that covered her ears and erased them. The strobing black light picked out the bones of her skeleton. The outline of her body in the black body stocking was as visible as the flesh in an X ray.

She tried to roll away from the Spectre, but he seized her and yanked her onto the dais. Landing lightly on her toes, she leapt away from him. He pursued her, Harpo-ishly, around the stage, to the delight and encouragement of the crowd. Eventually she allowed him to catch her and the two fell into a slow exaggerated erotic bump and grind.

The skeleton slithered up and down the Spectre, and the spectators bayed and bellowed.

The beat surged with Cameo:

if it's music we can use it
if we can dance
we don't have no time for psychological romance

The skeleton and the Spectre became fevered in their dancing courtship. The wraith surrounded her, pressing her closer, spreading his fingerbones over her hipbone. She tilted it toward him receptively. She stroked his thighbone and his tongue flickered snakelike from between the teeth of his skull face, into the air near her teeth, as if he were searching for her mouth.

An ominous hesitant chord announced another change of music: the Honeymoon Killers' cover of a legendary Beatles anthem. A voice growled, *"Why can't, why can't, why can't . . ."*

It had a dramatic effect on the Spectre, sending him into a rutting frenzy. He ground hips with his partner. His bony fingers with their razor nails plucked where her jaw and skullcap met and suddenly tore downward, rending the black to reveal pale living flesh, somehow more obscene, more corrupt, than the illusion of skeletal bone. In a single savage rip, the Spectre exposed the skeleton's breasts, to the eruption of a full-throated roar from the spectators.

The skeleton became more lewd herself, grasping the Spectre's skull as he knelt on one knee before her, thrusting her chest to allow him to tongue her bared rigid nipple. The voice of the crowd was thunderously lascivious, and in some corners, so was its behavior.

The Spectre rose, gathering the skeleton into the folds of his cloak and lifting her off her feet. She buried her face in his shoulder as he jumped from the dais. Amid the wild enthusiasm of the crowd that parted for him, he strode across the gym. In a moment he was out the doors and gone into the night, bearing his consort with him.

Outside, the figure of the Spectre staggered with his booty into the night and into a copse of old trees. There upon the pine duff, he and the skeleton writhed in a horizontal *danse macabre.* On the trunk of a tree nearby, the moonlight illuminated the photograph of a dead girl.

The Spectre removed his head behind the wheel of a truck parked in a nearby lot. He inhaled deeply and raked skeletal fingers through sweaty hair.

"So how was it for you?" Junior asked.

Still shaking with adrenaline, Kissy leaned back against the window on the passenger side.

He grinned at her. "I'd better get this rig back into the locker or it's my ass. Oh, shit!" He gave himself a knock between the eyes with the knuckle of his fist. "I forgot the fucking scythe!"

Kissy burst into nearly hysterical laughter.

They encountered each other's eyes with a degree of mutual embarrassment. It had been bareback; he had come inside her.

"It's going to be all right, isn't it?" he asked.

"How would I know?" She sat back, anxiously tugging her torn costume over her nakedness.

He reached out with his deadman's hand to pat her thighbone.

Pulling into shadow near a side door, he struggled out of the costume. While he changed into sweats and high-tops, Kissy peered down the legs of the rig and discovered everything below midcalf was false—as it would have to be to turn its wearer into a seven-footer. When the wearer placed his foot inside it, he was forced onto tiptoe. The Spectre's typically lurching gait must be unavoidable.

He grabbed the costume, glanced over it, and cursed. Then he bundled it all up and slunk to the side door, reappearing in only a few moments.

"Slow down," she cautioned him as he peeled out. "You'll draw attention to yourself, speeding."

He slowed immediately and then patted his knee. "Head down, baby, you're still all made up."

His thigh made an agreeable pillow. He touched her gelled and spiked hair sticking out of her skullcap.

She looked up at him. "Hey, there's an all-night pharmacy on Seventh Street. Stop there, I need a douche kit."

"Oh. You think so?"

With her costume in tatters, she could hardly go into the store herself, so he did. When he couldn't find what she needed he had to ask the clerk, and somehow it was more embarrassing than buying skins, which was something he'd only been doing with any regularity since he started up with Kissy. Most girls took the Pill. He could hardly wait until hers kicked in. About douches he knew nothing. He accepted what the clerk handed him.

The first thing she did at his place was bolt for the bathroom.

After a little while, he gave the door a quick rap. It wasn't locked, so he peeked in. Starkers at the basin, she was creaming off her makeup. The douche kit was in the trash and the remains of her costume were on the floor.

"You want to shower?" he asked.

"I'm whipped."

He was close to it himself.

"Hungry? I could eat the mattress. Want some scrambled eggs and toast?" he offered.

She gave him a grateful nod.

He had the toast ready and the eggs starting to curd when she emerged from the bathroom. She fell on the toast and eggs like a junkyard dog. Since she was so hungry, he handed over the toast he had made for himself and went back to make more.

And when he glanced up at her again, she was sprawled on the mattress, a piece of toast clutched in one crumby hand, and she was dead to the world. Her hair was still all corkscrews and twists like little horns. Like a butch Medusa. Her mouth gleamed with butter from the toast, and there were crumbs in the corners. She'd missed some of her makeup, left a smear of white under her ear. The darkness of exhaustion pitted her eyes.

He took the toast from her fingers and licked the crumbs from the corners of her mouth with great delicacy. He covered her up. He looked at the toast, shrugged, and shoved it into his mouth. Slowly and carefully he lowered himself beside her. His fingertips drifted to her breast. This must be love, he thought. Snorting hysterical laughter, he had to hide his face in the pillow.

The rush of the shower wakened him. Eyes still clenched shut, he sniffed at the pillow that bore the impression of her head and at the sheets, still warm from her body. He stretched and yawned luxuriously and remembered the previous night. As the stew of sensation recalled coalesced into historical fact, the cat-in-the-cream smile faded from his face. Junior opened his eyes and flat bright light smote his retinas.

Kissy emerged, glowing, from the bathroom. It occurred to him that seeing her emerging from the bathroom was a pleasant thing in itself.

"Hey," he said, throwing off the sheet, "look at this."

She was more amused than impressed, but before they

finished, he reckoned he had her complete attention: she came like a freight train and took him with her.

The munchies followed as the night the day. He heated some soup and made tuna sandwiches and they picnicked on the mattress.

"I've been thinking," he said, "we should live together?"

She hooted softly in disbelief.

A little stung, he asked, "You got a better offer?"

"Junior, thanks." She swallowed a bit of sandwich. "I don't know. We don't know each other all that well—"

"We'll get to know each other fast, living together. Do you know how good we are together, Kissy? It's not that way with just anybody."

She finished her sandwich and studied the scatter of crumbs on the sheets.

"If it doesn't work," he offered, "we'll just say so, okay? We'll still be friends."

She was still warm and relaxed from making love, and she had a full belly too. It was tough to argue with the way she felt, the possibility of feeling this good all the time. Most of the time anyway. She had to admit she had had more sheer fun with Junior than with any other guy. When they went places together, he didn't ignore her; he had never asked to borrow the Blazer or tried to con money out of her. His place was really small but that was not totally negative. And it was not forever. Just for as long as it lasted. On the other hand, there was Mary Frances, who would be hurt if she left, and then there was a little matter of having just paid November's rent.

"I just paid the month's rent—"

"Mine's paid too—"

"We go halfsies—"

"Sure," he agreed. "Absolutely. I can give you November, though, as a gift, can't I? It isn't going to cost me anything more—"

"You can't give me November; it's a month."

He lifted the edge of the T-shirt she was wearing and smooched noisily on her navel and made her laugh.

Working quietly so as not to disturb Mary Frances, she muscled her amps and stereo components into the Blazer. They were the heaviest things she owned aside from her mattress, inherited from a previous tenant, which she decided to abandon. She finished packing up her clothes, her books, her Mac, her camera gear. She looked around the suddenly stripped room that had been hers for two years and was not sad to leave it. She had started to feel more than a little claustrophobic in it. If it did not work out with Junior, she did not want to come back anyway. She slipped the house keys from her fob and left them on the table, holding down a slip of paper with the address of Junior's place and the phone number.

She made herself coffee and sat down to wait.

Soon Mary Frances stumbled into the kitchen, in her pajamas and robe. She squinted at Kissy. "Night you had, I'm surprised you're up to moving furniture."

"I'm moving in with Junior—"

Silently, Mary Frances slopped coffee into a mug and slumped into a chair. "I knew it was coming—I just want you to be happy, Kissy—"

"Mary Frances Donohoe," Kissy said, "tell the truth and shame the devil."

Mary Frances stared at her, eyes bright with challenge. "All right. I hope you're at least as miserable as I'm going to be. I'm expecting some great pictures out of you, Kisser. Just don't let some hard-on distract you."

Kissy laughed. "Never." She jumped up and bent over Mary Frances, to whisper in her ear. "It's okay, Mary Frances. I love you even if you aren't a saint."

Mary Frances caught her hand and kissed it.

A Friday-night win and no game on Saturday meant Coach Stannick would cut a little slack for the guys who had performed. None for the guys who hadn't, but that was their lookout. Video at three—so Junior hit the ground running, taking a circuitous five-mile route to campus. The air had a tonicky bite in it that amplified the headiness with which he began.

Zoo stopped him on the way into the weight room.

"Something up?" asked Junior.

"Rumors all over campus. Somebody used the Spectre costume last night at the Homo Hop, bopped some chick, or chicks, right there, in public." Zoo covered his mouth as he laughed. "A drug-crazed orgy or a black mass, take your pick."

"Who thinks this shit up?" Junior grinned.

"Barry the custodian told me the costume locker was definitely jimmied. The costume was there but it's been used." Zoo poked Junior in the ribs. "The scythe was found this morning, planted in front of the women's gym with a fake decapitated head at the foot of it. Barry says the A.D. came into the office right after they found the locker open and campus security's been here too."

"Shocking," Junior said. "Unauthorized use of the mascot costume at a black mass."

Zoo lowered his voice. "Just remember we were all at my place, okay?"

"Eleven to one," Junior said.

Zoo shook his head. "Maybe you should cool it with Melons for a while. There were people who knew who she was, even if nobody but us knew you were playing mascot. Those gazongas are memorable, you know. Though if the administration decides to have a lineup to identify them, I want to be there."

Junior hung an arm around Zoo's neck and whispered, "She's moving in with me."

Zoo moaned.

"I've been looking for a regular thing," Junior said. "She makes me hard, man. We get along."

"Junior, you're thinking with your dick—"

"Fuck you," Junior said genially.

Zoo just shook his head.

With a slight tremor in her hands, Sylvia Cronin replaced the photographs of Ruth carefully in their folder. "You'll take more, won't you? Make a record?"

"Of course."

The public health nurse was there, checking on Ruth's tubes and bottles and needles and readouts. Ruth was on an antibiotic feed for bronchitis. Her breath whispered in the tubes like a cold wind outside the frosted window. One eye was closed, the other partially opened. Instead of hospital issue, she wore plaid flannel pajamas and flannel booties. With her hair cut short to make it easier to keep neat and clean, she looked younger. She wore no earrings, and the holes in her lobes had closed to dimples.

Sometimes Ruth's mouth worked as if she wanted to speak. Sometimes she moaned. She cried, too—sometimes a silent slick of tears, sometimes audible sobbing. The doctors said it was probably nothing more than random electrical activity in her brain, of no more significance than an occasional twitching of her limbs and eyelids, the rolling of her head from side to side.

Kissy had not heard Ruth laugh, though, or seen her smile. Surely to laugh or smile was as likely a random event as weeping and moaning. Or perhaps it wasn't. The longer Ruth remained so, the more mysterious her condition seemed to Kissy. This was limbo, neither heaven nor hell, neither dead nor alive. Kissy merely watched, expecting nothing, but interested in witnessing this transition of Ruth's, in whatever direction it moved and at whatever rate.

Junior had never lived with a woman before, a woman of his own. Aside from the sense of maturity, of having come into another aspect of manhood, it was a kick, having a woman to come home to, a woman waiting for him. If she was not there, her return was something to anticipate. She left signs of her presence. Spoor. Her stuff in the bathroom, the odd piece of clothing and the bedding that bore her scent. Her books and her music and her computer set up on the counter. Her pictures were everywhere, mounted by slipping them between parallel rows of pushpins. They were Polaroids and work prints with a raw unfinished quality he found seductive.

He talked to her about shit he had never talked to anyone about. He could not get enough of her. His own feelings surprised and unnerved and excited him. If this was being in love, he never had been before, and no wonder people sang its praises. They were not going out much, partly because time and money were short for both of them, but also because they were finding each other more interesting than anyone else. Their friends were mutually aghast at their pairing. There was an element of lying low, too. Nothing had happened, officially, at the Homo Hop, of course—nothing could be proved—but the thing was already the stuff of myth.

She had taken him to dinner one Sunday at her old place, and while they ate Pad Thai that her buddy Mary Frances had prepared, he got a look at the people Kissy called her friends. Art School denizens like her, and all of them the kind of people who took social handicaps and ran with them like wheelchair marathoners. Bemused, he had to wonder if she had some Diane Arbus in her, some attraction to freaks, which naturally raised the question of what freakishness in him attracted her.

He had trouble sorting out who was with whom and realized it was part of the subcultural ethos; they were all lover-chummy with each other. Apparently to be clearly with someone was exclusionary and impolite. Or some shit like that. There was only one other straight couple, and one seemingly single straight guy, and the rest were happy faggots and hearty dykes, including Latham, the department head, who was more accurately described as a hearty faggot. Bearded and bull-chested, Latham had worked through a repertoire of fag jokes that would be the envy of any straight locker room. The lot of them had looked at Junior like he was the gorilla in the zoo and they were expecting him to throw his shit at them. He resisted the instinct to do just that. And then there was Mary Frances, the bunny nun. She didn't like him, he could tell.

"Interesting bunch," he told Kissy in the Blazer on the way home. He had the window rolled down to breathe the crisp air and be himself.

She gave him a skeptical glance.

"Really," he said. "I couldn't tell who was balling whom—"

"A for grammar," she said.

"Let alone who might have been your lover."

"Why would you want to know?"

He shrugged. "Raging jealousy, of course. Set off by your little fuck-buddy Kowanek. That guy, Gordon"—naming the straight guy on his own—"he acted like he'd had something with you."

"Fuck-buddy?" She hooted softly. "Once when I'd broken up with Ryne for a while, I went to a retrospective with Gordon. American International stuff, low-budget horror films. We got into a drive-in mood and did some necking, but we decided to stop there. He thought about it some more and decided he was in love with me but by then I was back with Ryne." She squeezed his hand. "Now we're even. I know about Diane and you know about Ryne and Gordon doesn't count—don't be jealous of my friends—you're my fuck-buddy now."

He chanted, "Fuck-buddies forever."

"I'm not the only romantic in this duo," Kissy jeered.

At home again, Junior slipped his hands under her sweater. "I wish I'd known you in high school."

"Why?"

"We'd have had so much fun together."

She closed her eyes, amused for the moment by the very ludicrousness of the idea. He would have been one of those guys who never looked above her collarbone and never said anything to her that didn't have to do with the size of her tits. She tried to imagine them, six years younger, in the cemetery. Junior instead of Seth, the boy who had been there with her. She had wished, on occasion, that she re-membered more of it. Not just the first time for both of them but the anticipation of love that had been the draw be-tween them. Is this it? Is this all there is to it? she did re-member asking him. Another thing spoiled because of being wasted. Once they had done it, everything changed. Her sweet, funny Seth had turned humorless, possessive, domineering, demanding. She might have put up with the constant fumbling and grinding at her but the possessive-ness drove her wild. As little as she could remember of that first time, she had perfect recall of every instant of the last time she ever spoke to Seth. Dry mouth, pounding heart. I'm pregnant, Seth. Sixty seconds of terror as he lashed out, verbally and physically, breaking her nose, and then she was on her ass on the cemetery access road that was their makeout spot, as Seth, swearing and sobbing simultane-ously, yanked the car door shut. The tires of his father's Cadillac spitting bits of gravel at her and her too numb to even raise her hands to protect her face.

Junior's fingers moved in patterns on her skin, like someone weaving a cat's cradle that would, in a magic in-stant, simply dissolve.

7

It was his turn to cook, and he knocked himself out with the recipe on the macaroni package. She was late. Out shooting. He grew ravenous and could not wait any longer. Then he poured another glass of supermarket red and hit the books. When she finally blew in, he had a crick in his neck and he was hungry again.

He had left a place setting on the counter, a supermarket rose in a vase next to it. She stopped to sniff it.

"Want to look at some pictures?" she asked, handing him a box. "Handle them by their edges, okay?"

"Sure." He had noticed how she did it when she was putting up pictures.

"It's me," he said with a grin of pleasure at the one on the top. With the next picture, his grin faded. "This is the other girl, isn't it?"

She nodded.

When he had shuffled through the rest, he closed the box. "You want some supper, a glass of red with it?"

"Yes."

He took out the pie to reheat, the salad. "Been to visit that girl?"

"Uhuh."

"Little morbid, isn't it?"

"No," she replied blandly. "I was there tonight. Shot some more."

Finding out where she had been without having to go through the humiliation of phrasing it that way made him feel better. Not that he couldn't tell, he assured himself. He would know in a minute. He filled a glass for her and one for himself and leaned against the counter to watch her continue to eat, which she did heartily, her appetite undiminished by visiting the near dead.

"Ghoul," he said.

She laughed low in her throat, her eyes devilishly alight.

Another road trip took Junior away. She could have gone with him. The student paper couldn't afford to send her to away games, but the *News* had asked her to act as a stringer, offering to cover gas, a cheap motel room, a per diem. On this particular weekend, however, she had class work to complete and work she wanted to do on her independent study project in photography. And she told herself she was not about to become a camp follower, arranging her life around Junior's, with the likelihood she would be abused by some bitch trying to get at him. It was his problem, not hers.

She visited Ruth. Mrs. Cronin left her alone sometimes, or used her visiting as a respite. The quietude of Mrs. Cronin's front parlor offered no distractions from the wretchedness of Ruth's condition. But there was another, unexpected benefit, that of the confessional. Sitting at Ruth's side, Kissy told her the things that had happened to her, the things she had done. It seemed a lot, once articulated, and much of it made little sense to her.

Ruth had no reaction. Ruth offered no advice. She merely took in breath and pushed it out. A sticker on the calendar on the wall marked her birthday, at the end of the month. Ruth's mother and brother and his family would have a party here, cake and ice cream and birthday cards, in the hope that Ruth, in her nether world, would hear their panpipe of love for her.

Gently, Kissy squeezed Ruth's flaccid hand. Then she rose from the bedside chair to pick up her camera.

At New Year's there was a break in the schedule long enough to allow a trip to Junior's hometown, Kingston, five hours away on the Canadian border. They traveled in separate vehicles because Junior was going to leave his truck at home. He had made a deal to let his brother, Mark, who was good with electronics, use his truck for a month in exchange for repairing his damaged amp.

He had grown up in this small town that huddled bleakly on a branch of the St. John River. Meanders of streets lined with peeling wood-frame houses led to a granite-and-red-brick downtown that was still modestly alive because it was so far to anywhere else. The little town seemed a redoubt, less against marauders than the isolation, the loneliness, underlined by the flatness of the glacier-dozered land about it.

"Welcome to East-End-of-the-World," Junior told her, helping her from the Blazer in his parents' driveway.

Making a joke of it as he cast his hand wide in a theatrical gesture of display, he had the look of a man just realizing what he had escaped. Her doing, Kissy thought. He was seeing it through her eyes for the first time. The house was an old ark, high ceilings and big unheatable rooms and chimneys that predated central heating. It had been an Episcopalian parsonage, Junior had told her, until the congregation had grown too small and elderly to support both it and the church next door. His maternal grandfather, who had been a builder, swapped the 'piscobles, as he called them, a modest frame house a block away for their obsolete parsonage. Then he had turned around and presented the parsonage to his daughter as a wedding gift. He had not had much hope of his son-in-law amounting to anything.

The brother from the snapshot, a junior version of Junior, flung open the door and the Saint Bernard erupted from the house and landed on Junior. Watching the two of them tussle, the dog on its hind legs, was like watching bears dancing.

Brother legged over the porch rail and introduced himself. "I'm Mark." His eyebrows jumped. "You must be Kissy."

The parents emerged next, with welcoming smiles. Kissy was introduced to Dunny and Esther, who in turn urged her into the house, out of the cold. Inside, the first thing she noticed was that the floors, linoleum or wood, were heavily scarred, as if a pack of huge dogs had been allowed to furrow them with their untrimmed nails. Then the kid sister clomped into the kitchen on skates and Kissy realized that the damage had been done by a single huge dog and children allowed to wear their skates indoors.

"I'm Bernie," the girl said, "and if you call me Bernadette, I'll punch you out."

Kissy laughed and agreed.

Like many a fourteen-year-old, Bernie Clootie had

achieved her full height and mature figure and could easily pass, with the right makeup, hairstyling, and clothing, for eighteen or twenty. Without makeup, her long hair in a sloppy French braid, she was still a kid sister.

The whole place smelled like a locker room. It was apparent the Clootie family's highest standard in furnishings was sturdiness, with stain-resistance and comfort second and third, and plaid trailing fourth. The only pictures on the walls were family photographs. The Christmas tree was still up, listing to one side and mangy from needle loss, the lower limbs denuded of ornaments by a pair of slant-eyed overweight cats, one of whom appeared to have a piece of tinsel hanging out of its asshole.

They did not stay in Kingston but went on to camp, on a frozen pond yet another two hours into wilderness. Once there, the male Clooties and Bernie immediately rushed to prepare the surface of the ice, while the dog, named for Mr. Ed the talking horse, frolicked among them. Junior had acquired the dog in high school, Esther Clootie told Kissy, after seeing the Paul Newman hockey movie, *Slapshot,* which featured a Saint Bernard. Kissy had become familiar with the movie. It was extremely popular with all of Junior's teammates, who commonly recited lines from it at each other.

Junior came stomping into the camp to announce he had a late Christmas present for her. Unwrapping it, she found she was the owner of a new pair of skates. Hockey, not figure skates. It appeared she was going to have to take to the ice with the rest of them, a suspicion confirmed when Esther plumped down to lace on a pair of blades. No wonder Junior had insisted Kissy pack long johns and snow pants.

Junior tended goal, with Esther and Kissy as his defense against his father and Mark and Bernie. Though all in good humor, the bruises were real enough, for none of them, not even Esther, pulled any punches. They wanted the puck and they wanted to shoot it. Bernie hit as hard as her brother Mark. Being a rank amateur only made Kissy fresh meat.

She came inside wanting nothing more than a long hot soak for her aches and bruises, to discover that the Clootie camp facilities had only a small water heater auxiliary to the woodstove. There was hot water for washing dishes and hands but not for bathing. The family used a sauna

they called the steambath, followed by a starkers plunge
through a hole cut in the ice into the heart-stopping cold
water of the pond. The sauna was only large enough for
two at a time, a relief to Kissy since Mark had been eye-
balling her relentlessly since her arrival.

"Don't mind him," Esther advised. "You're the only girl
Junior's ever brought home. Dunny," she addressed her
husband, "you keep Mark out of the bushes so Kissy and
Junior can take their steambath."

"I don't know about this skinny dipping in a frozen
pond," Kissy told Junior.

He grinned evilly. When she was just about melted to a
puddle in the sauna, he carried her out and dropped her
into the hole in the ice and dove in after her. Once she hit
the water, shrieking was the only reasonable reaction. The
hole was on the shoreline, over water shallow enough to
stand in, with chunks of ice floating in it. It came to her
this must be what it felt like to be the olive in the martini,
chilled and shaken.

They had blanket robes and moccasins waiting on shore.
Half frozen, Kissy could hardly move. Junior bundled her
up and carried her into the camp. Mark was lurking by the
stove, anticipating inadvertently exposed flesh. Bernie
crept up behind him and put her hands over his eyes. He
jumped up and turned on her, but she was already scam-
pering away with a peal of laughter, behind her father.

"G'wan," Dunny Clootie growled at Mark, thrusting
chunks of wood into his hands, "haul in your eyeballs and
go take your bath." By then, Junior was rolling Kissy into
the bed they were to share in the camp's small second bedroom. The room was no more than a cubicle, curtained off
from the main room, with a pine-paneled wall dividing it
from Esther and Duncan's room. Mark and Bernie shared a
loft partitioned with a bookcase. The old and sagging mattress smelled of woodsmoke and damp, but it felt heav-
enly after a forced introduction to pond hockey, steambaths,
and ice water baptism. Junior climbed in to warm her up—
sex was inevitable.

"Can they hear us?" she whispered.

"We can always hear Mom and Dad," Junior murmured
into her ear.

After dinner, they huddled around the fireplace, exchanging late Christmas presents.

"Mother and I got something to announce," Dunny said suddenly.

"Shit," Junior muttered.

Esther's eyes were downcast; Mark's mouth, down-turned. Bernie hugged herself, as if to hold what she knew tighter.

Dunny cleared his throat. "Mark's goin' to college next fall. Mother and I, we decided we'd go with 'm."

Junior immediately relaxed.

"Nothin' to stay here for," Dunny continued. "We stay, we'd never see Mark play. The way we hardly ever saw Junior play the past few years. So we're renting out the house, letting George Labree run the shop here, and we're going to take a place near the college. Bernie likes the idea of going to a bigger high school. I figure I'll rent a little hole-in-the-wall, run a one-man shop. Mother wants to get her cap. She should be able to get on at the hospital part-time as a PN while she does it."

"You got it all planned out," said Junior. "I thought you were going to tell me you were getting a divorce."

"Junior!" Esther was horrified.

"I was just afraid neither one of you would want Mark and Bernie and I'd get stuck with 'm." Junior grinned.

"There's an idea," Dunny said. "I'll keep it in mind."

"It'll be much easier to see Junior play occasionally too," Esther put in, "with the Peltry airport to hand. And I want my cap. I've got this practical nursing thing knocked and I know I can do more. So we're doing it."

Junior applauded. He got up and kissed his mother. "The day you get it, I'll be there."

As Kissy and Junior were packing to return to Peltry, he announced he wanted to bring Ed with them, now he had someone to look after Ed when he was on the road. Bernie flew into a rage and was not mollified when Junior pointed out that it was only a matter of months before she would have the dog back again. Kissy argued against it, telling him not to count on her staying home to look after his dog, and pointing out how small the efficiency was. Junior had made up his mind. Ed was in the Blazer with them on the ride back. Five hours confined with the dog in the cab of the Blazer convinced Kissy she was right.

But the first weekend Junior was away again, she discovered she was no longer afraid to be alone. She had Ed there, a very large warm breathing farting friend, always happy to see her, always delighted with whatever she fed him, always deliriously eager for a scratch, a little horse-play, a pat on the head. He made a huge dog hummock on the mattress next to her at night. The nightmares that had plagued her since the accident finally stopped entirely. All she had ever needed, she thought, was a damn dog. It made her laugh. Someday she would tell Junior how easily she could replace him.

The gloom of the library stacks was darker for the fluorescents spilling queasy light against the strata of books. It gave Kissy the spooks to be there, particularly late at night, but she had a paper due and the references were proving elusive. With a printout in hand of the books she was seeking, she drifted down the gulches of the stacks. Someone coughed, destroying the illusion she was alone. Peering around the end of the stack, she saw a student in a study carrel. And with a stumble in her heartbeat, recognized him. James Houston. Laboring like some Dickensian clerk with pen and papers and huge splayed tomes like gutted turkeys. He had cut his hair to a stubble and was so thin he looked like a penitent monk at the end of a particularly flagellant Lent.

She must have made some noise, squeaked bootleather or inhaled sharply, she didn't know, but he glanced up. His dark eyes passed over her hastily and returned guiltily to the papers. Then he raised them again, his pupils widened, his lips parted slightly, and what little color he had draining from his face.

Kissy cleared her throat. "How are you?"

He stared at her without reply for a long moment and then he laughed, a high loony sound with a dusty, hysterical edge. It made her want to flee, but she steeled herself and held her ground. The weird laugh collapsed upon itself and he looked down at his papers again and then at her yet again.

"Beg pardon," he muttered. "It's kind of you to ask. I'm not used to people speaking to me anymore."

"I'm Kissy—"

"I know who you are. Would you go away now?" He stared down at his papers, waiting for her to go.

She didn't know what else to do, so she did what he asked.

The third week of February brought a long sweet thaw. The light was thin and delicate. The warmer air gave her a chance to shoot out of doors without having to keep the camera warm inside her jacket between shots. She took Ed with her on a tramp around the campus. He was delighted to be unleashed to romp at will while she made pictures.

Eventually they worked their way around to the copse where Diane Greenan's photograph was pinned to the tree. Someone had decorated it with demonic horns and a mustache. The defacement was in marker on the plastic sleeve, so the picture inside was unharmed. It would be a simple task to peel the sleeve and laminate the photo to protect it. The homemade vase had been knocked over, the dead and ruined flowers scattered amid the debris of leaf and needle on the ground. Kissy pried the photo off the trunk of the tree and slipped it into her backpack.

She returned to the copse to pin the laminated picture to the tree trunk. The thaw had passed and it was frigid again, with a cold that was harder for the false spring preceding it. At the base of the picture tree, someone had left another chopped-off plastic container, a liter soda bottle, with a bundle of clumsily arranged roses in it. The roses had gone black from freezing. Kissy took black-and-whites of the scene, thinking how it would look if she handcolored the roses.

As soon as she had prints in hand, she wanted them seen at once, as they were, and published them immediately in the campus paper, over a paragraph about the impromptu memorial. Unexpectedly, the *News* picked it up and then the local television newscasts.

The school and Diane Greenan's family subsequently announced that in addition to a scholarship endowment in her name, a more formal monument would be located in the copse. It would be a modest granite plinth in which a photograph of Diane would be embedded behind glass. A brass vase would be attached to it for floral remembrances and a park bench installed among the trees to encourage visitors. A dedication was scheduled for Graduation Day in June.

*   *   *

After an exhausting semifinal struggle—four overtimes, a sudden death goal eleven seconds into the fourth OT—the Spectres lost the final for the national championship. And then it was all over. Junior felt like a Slinky, end over end down a flight of stairs, at first deliberately and then faster and faster until he was all ashiver at the bottom. There was a certain amount of the usual bullshit afterward—media, receptions, banquets, which were flat for him, flat as he felt, as if the Zamboni had rolled right over him. He shook it off as best he could, but the sense of disorientation kept recurring.

With courses to complete, he applied himself, though it was irrelevant whether he passed or failed as he was short three credits of a degree and had no immediate intention of acquiring them. It filled the time; it killed some of the obsessive replaying of what had gone wrong in his head. In April, Kissy began a six-weeks' internship at the *News*. Her classes were over, her honors project submitted and prints from it chosen to be hung at the Student Art Show. All of a sudden he had more free time than she did.

Since he was six years old and his dad finished tying on his first pair of skates and put a stick in his hand, he had wanted to be a pro. Now it was only months away. He thought about it obsessively, making it difficult to concentrate on anything else. But there was Kissy. Realistically, he didn't have, and couldn't be sure he would have, money enough to support a wife. The professional hockey season was long, with a lot of time on the road.

"We've got most of the summer," he told her one Sunday afternoon when they were in the bathtub. "What happens then?"

"You'll go to camp and go someplace to play hockey. I'll keep on working."

The light irony with which she spoke flustered him and made him forget the careful formulations he had imagined. The negotiation that would keep her his, yet not commit him to the unimaginable reaches of forever.

"I don't want to break up," he blurted. "I want us to stay together. We could get married."

His words fell into her silence like the slow drip of the faucet. He hadn't actually asked her, just put it out on the table as a possibility.

She slithered around to face him. "Let's see how the next year goes."

Sensible girl. More sensible than he was. And he hid his relief by making love to her aggressively.

The sound of the fire amazed her. It was so noisy, like a windstorm, some monstrous thing on the rampage. She had never seen a building of this size burn. The abandoned textile mill on the bank of the Dance was heavily involved before the first report. The main road ran by the mill, and traffic was a problem as the big trucks and pumpers maneuvered into position and passersby slowed down to gawk or parked at the sides of the roads to get out and rubberneck.

Kissy worked a couple of likely vantages of the fire itself, using a wide angle to capture the sense of chaos at the scene. The smoke was great, though it made her cough and she worried about soot on the lens. A sudden flurry of activity at one of the mill's windows caught her eye. The weathered plywood boarding up a tall, narrow ground-floor window splintered outward under a fireman's ax. Smoke and flame belched from the breach like a dragon's breath, and in their midst, the dark outline of a fireman appeared. Kissy fired the camera even as she registered the fact that the fireman was carrying a body.

A few yards from the burning building, the fireman fell to his knees and was surrounded by other firemen and emergency personnel. The body slid from his shoulders to the high grass that was pale and dead and beaten down by the scurrying of the firemen. She framed the corn silk shock of the victim's hair in the firelight and the pallidness of the fireman's face, strained with effort and smeared with soot, as he removed his mask. EMTs moved in with oxygen for both fireman and victim. Immediately there were angry shouts and curses. Someone had fucked up— the oxygen tanks were empty. The rescuing fireman's face was a conflagration of emotion, his fury and despair as consuming as the fire wracking the structure. Then he swayed and collapsed next to the victim. His head lolled. An EMT anxiously sought a throat pulse. The others bellowed and cursed one another over the oxygen.

A man emerged from the mob of firemen and EMTs and dropped to his knees next to the apparently forgotten victim. The man seemed to fall on the victim, and Kissy realized he was administering mouth-to-mouth. An explosive burst of light from the fire revealed he was not a fireman, not an EMT, but a uniformed policeman. His action galvanized the others and an EMT went down on his knees beside him to help.

Kissy kept shooting as the rescue workers moved the victim to an ambulance, while continuing the attempt at resuscitation. The man who had begun it stepped back from the ambulance as the EMTs took over. Kissy closed in on him. As she framed his face, weary with defeat, she recognized him. Mike Burke. Looking up at the flash from her camera, he flinched as it temporarily blinded him.

"Sorry!" she shouted over the roar of the fire.

He shook his head and then, as if he had a bug or something equally nasty in his mouth, he spat several times onto the ground. He turned away and headed toward the road.

She caught up with him quickly.

"Fancy meeting you here," he said with a grin.

She flicked the plastic tag clipped to her vest. "I'm interning with the paper."

"I see." He indicated the road. "I gotta get back to work. I'm supposed to be keeping rubberneckers out of the way. My partner's out there trying to keep traffic moving."

She fell back.

Julius Horgan, the reporter with her, loped up. Short and barrel-shaped, he wheezed with any physical effort. "Did you get a shot of the cop?"

"Yes."

"Gotta get a quote." Horgan huffed after Burke.

Behind the wheel on the way back to the paper, Horgan was still twitchy with excitement. "Somebody's gonna get their ass fried over those oxygen tanks. The town could get sued, you know. Not by the fag they dragged out there, he's nobody. The fireman, Kimball. The union'll have somebody's head on a pike."

"You know the victim?"

Horgan grinned at the opportunity to impress her with how well he knew the town. "Donnie Hebert. Hasn't breathed a sober breath since he was maybe thirteen. Keeps himself in booze and drugs working the Valley on his knees. That's why the EMTs weren't in any hurry to give him mouth-to-mouth. Afraid of AIDS. They all got a bug up their asses about it. To my knowledge, there's only half a dozen cases in town, all of 'm guys who caught it somewhere else. It's like herpes, you know. Scourge of God. A good scare sells a lot of newsmagazines. Fact is, you gotta work at catching it. Shoot smack or take it up the ass. I can't get worked up about something that kills junkies and fudgepackers, you know, honey?"

Kissy peeled his wandering hand off her knee. Horgan was in his early forties, married, losing his hair. One of those guys who, once stricken with the gut-wrenching fear that this was all there was, grabbed every tit and ass going by. It must be male instinct, something built in, because so many of them were afflicted with it—the sudden over-whelming conviction that all they needed to make up for the receding hairline, the advancing belly, the tired wife and surly teenage children, the realization they were just ordinary joes and afflicted with mortality, was a (surely) hot fuck with a young woman. Or sometimes a young man, according to Latham. She wanted to have some compassion for the guy, but basically he was pathetic.

8

"**G**et any tongue?" Pearce asked Burke, showing him the front page of the paper where the photograph of the younger cop trying to resuscitate Donnie Hebert was prominent above the fold. Pearce had pulled the paper out of the vending machine on the sidewalk outside the cop shop as they went off shift early on the day after the night of the fire.

It was just the beginning of the shit Burke was going to take from the guys. He grinned anyway. He had not succeeded in kissing Donnie back to life, but he wasn't a fairy-tale prince and Donnie sure hadn't been any kind of princess. Queen maybe. Fairy tail, all right. The only real good Burke had done was for himself. With top grades in his sergeant's exam and a commendation in his file, he was sure to get his stripes when Don Harkness retired in July.

And his folks would love it. His mother would call as soon as she saw it. She would get a print from the paper to frame and hang next to the old man's commendations and pictures. His dad had made sergeant at twenty-five. Of course, the old man had not been going to law school at the same time. Instead he had had a wife and kid. And had not yet crawled inside the bottle. The old man would come to the phone to congratulate him too. It meant everything to make the old man proud of him.

After the night he had been in on the call to Clootie's place, he had not seen anything of Kissy. Months later, she puts him on the front page, and that very afternoon, he goes into Denny's on a french-fry-and-burger mission and there she is at the counter.

"Hey," he said to her, "I owe you one. My mom loves that picture."

Kissy laughed. "You're welcome. My editor loved it, too, so we've both got gold stars on our charts."

"So you're working for the paper now?"

"Just interning."

"I think you might be good at it."

She shrugged. "Thanks."

"When's your case, the Houston case, come up?"

"This summer, last I heard. It takes a long time, I guess."

"Yeah." The places on either side of her were taken and no one volunteered to move. "I'll see you around. Good luck with the job."

She gave him an agreeable smile.

He found an empty booth and opened his paper. He could ask her to join him, but sharing a booth might look like they were together. Side by side at the counter—that could just happen. Better to be mere acquaintances. He did not need anybody speculating the picture might have been a put-up job.

He happened to glance toward her just as the last bit of burger went into her mouth. Tip of her finger pushing it too. She licked her lips. She didn't look up from the book she was reading. Her lips shone damply. Burke took a deep breath. But he found himself sneaking another peek. Clootie's name came up once in a while. Of course, the least reliable source on the face of the planet was a fucking doper, who would invariably claim to have sold the Pope a little shit. But it was always reefer Clootie was supposed to score, which in Burke's experience meant Clootie burnt a little ganja occasionally. Like most of the rest of the student body.

The onslaught of a powerful memory overwhelmed rational consideration, and not for the first time: the call to Clootie's, her body momentarily on view for them all. The contrast of her white hair with the lustrous black pelt of her pubic hair. All of them looking at her. Nothing to breathe in that room but the smell of sweaty fucking, as intoxicating as reefer. They had all had a good look at Clootie bare-ass too. There was a story going around about the mascot costume that had gone missing Halloween Eve—a black mass at the art school ball, the one they called the Homo Hop, that put Kissy on the altar, Clootie in the mascot costume playing the demon. He could be-

lieve it. Conscious of the flush on his face and chest, he was
more than a little aroused at the thought not just of Kissy
but of Kissy with Clootie. Jesus, he thought, get a grip on
it. Mrs. Burke's baby boy was obviously suffering from delayed ejaculation. That redheaded legal secretary—Penny—
who had flirted with him last Friday at Happy Hour at
Bird's—she looked like she could take some dictation.
Surreptitiously, he checked out Kissy again.

The sound of running water placed Kissy in the shower.
Eight-by-ten black-and-white prints were spread like a
hand of solitaire on the kitchen counter. Her honors project, her submission to the Student Art Show, which she
had said she would bring home to show him. Junior
propped his bat against the counter and slung his catcher's
mitt and mask into the rocking chair. He had had the kind
of game that made him think he had missed his calling, but
it was just a city rec league he was playing in, for fun. He
drew a glass of water and looked at the prints.

They were finished, ready to matte. It was weird, seeing
himself, sometimes pieces of himself, this way. If all anyone ever saw were the close-ups, they wouldn't know it
was him, but he was recognizable in other ones that she
evidently meant to show with them.

The water stopped and she stuck her head out, toweling
her hair as she spoke. "What do you think?"

"I'll never live it down," Junior said.

She was naked herself, pink and moist from the shower,
but she hardly seemed aware of it. Her gaze left him, went
to the prints. "They're good, Junior. They're really good."

"You got permission to hang them."

"Yes."

"You showed them to somebody to do that. Jesus. I can't
believe you did that."

She tossed the towel aside like a fighter getting ready to
go to the center of the ring. "You knew I was taking pictures of you."

"I didn't think you'd ever print them, let alone some
fool would give you permission to hang them."

She stalked past him to the counter. Layering the prints
in tissue, she swept them into a carrier box. "You've spent
half your life in locker rooms bare-ass-naked or in nothing

but a jock; there's easily three dozen hockey players, half a dozen coaches, assistant coaches, trainers, and dozens of fat-cat alumni donors who've seen you in your birthday suit—"

"Not with a hard-on," Junior said. "Fight fair, Kissy. You wouldn't want me whipping out my wallet to show beaver shots of you—"

"They're not beaver shots," she said. "Latham called them classical life studies."

Latham. Oh, sure.

"Latham's a fag, he probably had a boner, for Christ's sake, you let Latham see them?"

"He's my major adviser, he had to approve them for the show—"

"You show those goddamn pictures and we're through."

She stiffened. "Draw a line in the dirt, Junior, dare me."

"You told me an ethical photographer would never use anyone's photograph without permission."

Her angry eyes clouded, her gaze drifting away from him. After a little silence, she admitted, "Yes. That's right."

"You don't have my permission."

"You won't do this for me?"

He shook his head. "No. It's not fair to ask it."

She turned her back and went rummaging for her clothes. "They're mine," she cried suddenly. "My work. It's not fair!"

"They wouldn't exist without me—Kissy, you don't have the right to do this to me."

She bit her lip. And hung her head, surrendering.

He felt like a turd.

If Zoo and Brenda hadn't been getting married in New Haven the weekend the art show opened, he would have had to look around for something else to get him out of town. Kissy couldn't go with him, she said, because of the show, but he thought she just didn't want to go. She never had gotten comfortable with his friends. Or he with hers. At the last minute, he almost begged her to go anyway, call in sick or something and come with him. But he didn't. He kissed her warmly and told her how much he would miss her and threw his garment bag with his rented tux in it behind the seat in Dionne's truck and hopped in, belted up, and left her standing on the sidewalk, watching them leave.

Since he had refused her permission to use two of the pictures of him, they had both been knocking themselves out being good to each other. Her being generous so as not to look like a spoilsport in defeat, him acting like it never happened. But there was a scar there. A cold place. All he had done was exercise his right to say no. He should not have to feel he had been selfish. She should not have asked for something he could not give her.

Sitting there sucking on the roach Dionne had fired up and passed him the minute they were out of sight of Kissy, the road rumbling suddenly with the bridge under them, right up through his bones, he glanced sidelong at the river, and all at once, he jerked against the sensation of falling, the familiar clutch that everyone suffers, from time to time, drifting off to sleep. But he was not drowsy. And everything was the most real it had ever been. Like a 3-D movie. So vivid it was lurid. He could smell the water, he could feel it rolling, like some enormous animal gathering itself to explode into an attack. He was sweating. Along his hairline, under his arms, down the crack of his ass. Sick to his stomach with it. Trying to gather his thoughts was like trying to put together a jigsaw puzzle of all-black pieces. Black as the river, flowing through his fingers. His nausea suddenly the lurch of a raging lust to be face-first between Kissy's legs, flossing his teeth with black hair. He giggled weakly, appalled at the realization he was headed in the wrong direction, and helpless to turn back.

There was nobody to go home to after the opening except Ed, but that was really a relief. Kissy was wrung out. She took Ed running. Five miles through the Valley and then a long hot shower, a plate of pasta, a glass of wine, and she began to think she would live. In any case, she would sleep.

On Sunday night, Junior came clambering up the stairs two at a time. He threw off his clothes and burrowed, shivering, between the sheets with her. His skin was all goose bumps as he wrapped himself around her. It was as if he'd been chased home by a headless horseman. He didn't say hello or glad to see you or anything. Neither did she. It was wordless. It was a collision.

At the end she was resting her head in the palm of one hand, arm crooked up. His hands were underneath, lifting her up against him. As their hips rolled almost imperceptibly, he bent his neck to tongue her open armpit. He lifted his face to hers. Sweat dewed his eyelids, his upper lip, his throat. He licked his lips and sought her mouth. His dazed tongue moved like a charmed snake in her mouth. With a cry he lifted her body off the mattress and drove it back down as he collapsed onto her. She went with him with as little resistance as a shingle being lifted by the wind.

His hand groped for hers. "Oh Christ baby I love you," he mumbled into her damp hair.

"Ssssh," she whispered, stroking the back of his neck.

"I suspect you won't be with us long," the managing editor, Earl Fish, told her. "But we can give you good solid experience."

Which meant entry-level pay. Kissy thanked him. The paper had been good to her, using her occasionally as a photographic stringer on campus, giving her the internship. Its art reviewer had admired her prints in the art show. She would make something resembling a living. She left Earl's office in a state of barely suppressed excitement, full of the anticipation of telling Junior her good news.

He had been following her around all week like some aimless retiree. Telling her all about Zoo and Brenda's wedding, the ice sculpture, the eight bridesmaids. Zoo's nine-year-old nephew who had gobbled hors d'ouevres at the reception until he puked. She got the idea he was trying to convince her he had had a good time.

The only time he shut up was on the mattress. The wordless intensity of Sunday night repeated itself every day or night that week. She didn't think much about it. She knew he felt guilty about refusing her the two prints. And he was worried about what the summer would bring, whether he would do well enough in camp to get a pro slot, and what would happen to them when he went away. She gave him what he wanted, what he seemed to need.

Her good news, though, seemed to go right by him. Like he had more important things on his mind. It was an undeniable letdown, and it angered her too. She had always been happy for his successes.

Friday she got up sore. It stung to pee. Too much of a

good thing, she assumed. Later in the day she started being
hot and then cold, in waves, and her throat hurt. She had
picked up a chill, she guessed, maybe shooting that high
school baseball game in the damp cold of spring the day
before. She skipped her workout and her swim and canceled out on Dionne's big party, the last big blowout.

Surprisingly, Junior made no attempt to dozer her into it.
He went off to Dionne's by himself and came home early
and sober. Settling in beside her on the mattress, he opened
a book but never turned a page. He kept sneaking looks at
her. Finally clicked off the light and turned onto his side
without so much as a good night.

She woke up and his side of the mattress was empty. It
was two-thirty and there was a sweet seepage of reefer under the bathroom door. She was almost too groggy to believe it was real. And she slipped off again and in the
morning, when she woke, he was heading out the door.

He and his buddies were filling up the weekend with a
volleyball tournament. After work on Saturday, she went
by the field to shoot some pictures. Junior ignored her.
When she got home, he had gone out again. She was just
dropping off when he came in and she couldn't rouse herself to ask where he'd been. She rolled over and fell off the
edge into deep sleep.

Glass breaking, cursing, woke her early in the morning.
Even though she was startled awake, her ears were
nonetheless able to pinpoint the disturbance as in the bathroom. Ed scrambled to his feet and followed her. In the
bathroom, Junior had wrapped a towel around his left fist.
The mirrored door to the medicine cabinet hung from a
single hinge. He seized it with his right hand and tore it
away completely. She grabbed Ed's collar to keep him
from going into the bathroom and picking up splinters of
glass in his paws.

"I'm okay," Junior said. "Just some cuts on my knuckles."

"What happened?"

He stared at the exposed shelves of the cabinet. "Catch
stuck and I couldn't get it to move. I wanted some aspirin.
I just meant to knock the catch loose, that's all. It was an
accident . . ." His voice trailed off as his gaze dropped to
the towel around his fist.

She held out her hands, expecting him to let her peel off

the towel and examine his wounds but he jerked the fist away from her.

"Go back to bed," he said. "I'm okay. I'll take care of it."

She did, and to the best of her knowledge, he did.

Whatever bug she had contracted, she was still fighting. It wasn't a cold—at least she wasn't congested. Just the glands in her throat swollen up, and the fevers and chills that meant her body was fighting something. It had definitely gotten into her bladder. She wondered if she had picked up something swimming. She stayed away from the pool, for fear of infecting others.

By Monday her throat was almost normal and she wasn't feverish anymore. Passing water was still an adventure. She noticed a slight discharge and decided maybe she had two things going on, maybe a virus and a yeast infection. She had never had any problem with yeast but she knew swimmers who did. No one had ever mentioned they hurt.

At the student clinic, a physician who did not appear to be any older than she listened closely to her recital of symptoms and then said he wanted to do an examination. He seemed a little distant, as if something about her made him uncomfortable, and for a moment she wondered if he was gay and then decided he was just a cold fish or maybe it was nothing more than he had problems of his own.

To her surprise, the internal exam actually hurt. When she winced, the nurse took her hand and squeezed it to reassure her.

When she was dressed again, the doctor returned, carrying an ampoule of some medication and a needle. He placed them on the counter and clasped his hands as if he didn't know what to do with them. He cleared his throat. "Have you had any sexual contacts since the onset of these symptoms?"

Kissy was too stunned for a moment to answer. Then she blurted, "You think I have some kind of VD?"

The doctor had to clear his throat again. "STD. We call them STDs now. It's a possibility."

"I'm living with someone," Kissy said, "I haven't been with anyone else. There's no way—"

"I think you have gonorrhea, Miss Mellors."

For an instant she was dizzy.

The doctor took the pen from his breast pocket and stared at his clipboard. "We'll know for sure in forty-eight hours, but I'm going to treat you for it now. The law requires I report it. I'll hold the report for the test results, but I have to ask you for the names of your recent sexual partners."

"Junior," she said, her mouth almost too dry to get it out. "Clootie."

The doctor wrote the name swiftly.

"Spell that D-E-A-D," she told him.

He didn't laugh. "I'm going to give you a shot now. Would you expose your hip, please?"

The needle bit like air in a cut and she flinched.

"Beg your pardon," the doctor murmured.

"If it's not one prick, it's another," she said.

He smiled but she could see he was disconcerted. Unpleasant job, telling people they have the clap. "You should refrain from sexual activity until you have a negative test or else use a condom—"

She laughed rudely.

"These things happen to the nicest people, Miss Mellors. In one sense, you're lucky. Many women don't have symptoms with gonorrhea. They go untreated, it scars their tubes and makes them infertile. You came in early. I can't guarantee there's been no damage but at least you've minimized it."

She buttoned her Levi's with trembling fingers. "It's a real consolation, Doc."

He gave her pills, an information pamphlet, a number to call about the test results, and asked her to make a return appointment.

"Junior's been here, hasn't he?" she said. "You knew when I came in what was wrong with me because he's been here and been tested and given you my name. You know my test will come back positive."

The doctor reddened. "Miss Mellors—"

"The fucker was supposed to tell me and he didn't. What were you going to do, let me go on in blissful ignorance and become sterile?"

"Discussing another patient with you would be a breach of ethics." The doctor blinked rapidly. "In STD cases, a positive test requires a follow-up of the patient's partners. If we had your name, we would have contacted you shortly—"

"Thanks." She snatched up her camera bag. "That's another big consolation."

The chickenshit bastard wasn't home, which was lucky for him, because if he had been, he would be bleeding out from where his dick used to be. If she had to guess, he was probably cowering somewhere, smoking something to calm his nerves.

It took her an hour to load the Blazer with her things. Everything except her music and her stereo components. Her music was all mixed up with his. She was not going to sort it out now. She couldn't stand being there one more minute. Ed kept getting underfoot, whining at her, as if he understood she was leaving.

Her guts were in a knot. She had to keep wiping her eyes. Breaking up is hard to do. Oh yeah.

Her whole childhood had been one long move, from one base to the next so often they never ever finished unpacking. Goose Bay or Huntsville or Fargo, whatever the climate, the housing had been the same ticky-tacky boxes, the schools, the hospital—everything built to one linoleum-dull plan. They had been living in Peltry seven or eight months when the Famous Family Row had broken out. At dinner one night, her father started talking about applying for a new assignment that would mean another move. She had been getting her period, and all she could think about was how much harder it got with every move to make friends. The weeps had overwhelmed her. When her father had mocked her and chivvied her for being a whiner, Kevin had jumped into it. They had nearly come to blows before her mother got between them. Her brother had been seventeen and at odds with his father anyway. Then later her parents had had a huge row in their bedroom and her father slammed out of the house. Off to the Officers' Club to drink. In retrospect, it all had a numbing inevitability. Her mother, she figured, had been as tired of moving as her children were. And her father had been tired of them. He had left for good within weeks. If it ever had, dumping a wife and kids did not hurt a military career anymore.

Mary Frances had already broken up housekeeping and was roosting at Latham's until graduation. But he had a big house and enjoyed the trials of being a host. Kissy could think of nowhere else to go.

* * *

Latham was in his garden, cutting asparagus. He squinted up at her, sliding from the Blazer. "Kissy."

He took in the state of her eyes, her wilted posture. Just when she thought she was all done, she started flowing again, sheets of tears. Her T-shirt was wet from it.

"The prick," he said, holding out his arms. "What's he done?"

She let him hug her. "I need a place to stay for a little while. Just till I find another place."

"Of course," he said. "Happy to have you here, dear. Mary Frances will be ecstatic. Perhaps you can get her out of my kitchen——"

"It shouldn't take me long to find someplace else——"

"Don't even think about it—oh, Christ, you're not——?" He was theatrically alarmed.

"No."

He blew a great loud sigh of relief. She herself breathed deeply, feeling somehow safer for a roof over her head. The garden air was heady with the scent of lilac.

Mary Frances jittered like the lid of a pot on the boil, steaming at the chance to offer Kissy comfort.

"I don't want to talk about it," Kissy said, and then, to soften it, "not now."

"Of course not," Mary Frances agreed eagerly.

Latham pressed a glass of wine upon her. "Nature's own sedative——"

Then he showed her a bedroom as if he were a landlord, renting it, bustling in to fling open the window. "Don't you touch a bag, I shall buttle for you——" But it was necessary for her to pick through what she had thrown into the back end of the Blazer, sorting what she would need from what could be left there.

Once her duffel and camera gear were in the guest room, she flung herself onto the bed. Latham clucked.

A while later his step was in the passage, his knock at the door, and he stuck his head in. "Are you all right?"

"Fine."

"Really?" He bore a tray. More wine, bouillon and sourdough bread, and a vase full of lilac and orange tulips with blossoms as big as the bowl on a brandy snifter. Shaking a napkin over her lap as she sat up, he settled the tray on her knees. "Sustenance, darling. Must not fade away." He settled gently into a lotus posture next to her. "If you want to talk about it—"

"Thanks, Mom. Don't worry about me."

Latham chuckled, kissed her forehead, and went away again.

Kissy shut herself up in the bathroom, showered for fifteen minutes, and still felt unclean. In the guest room again, she retrieved the pamphlet from her backpack and read it again, then returned it to her pack, to discard somewhere on campus where no one would know it was hers. Flat on the mattress, she spread her fingers over her stomach, as if to feel the germ working inside her. She was full of a disease that Junior had put inside her. In her throat, in her female organs. It had traveled into her bladder, her kidneys, her brain—it was all through her, borne by her blood. It might already have scarred her tubes. She might be sterile now, never be able to have a baby. All the thought she had ever given to babies was avoiding one. Though she was not sure she would ever want one, she resented like hell the possibility that Junior might have carelessly taken that particular future away from her. Robbed her of it. All at once she was crying again. It hurt too, and she got up and soaked a washcloth in cold water to put over her eyes. She had to stop this shit. Next weekend was graduation. If she spent the week bawling, she was going to look like Yoda after a binge.

She filled her lungs with the lilac-honeyed air coming in the open window and set about visualizing, in detail, the individual small flowers bunched like weightless grapes, swaying on their twigs. As she concentrated, she could feel the jerk and thud of her heartbeat, the rigidity in her chest, the knot in her stomach that made her gut quiver.

9

He should have known once he made up his mind to tell her, it was already too late. Ed heard him at the door and woofed anxiously. Which meant Kissy wasn't there. Simultaneous relief and panic knotted his gut. It only took a glance to see her gear was gone, except for her stereo components and music—she had left in that much of a hurry. Ed's expression was one of mournful reproach.

He checked the bathroom just to be sure. Toothbrush, shampoo, makeup, the shit she used in her hair, and the raggedy towels—she hadn't left so much as a stray tampon. He wanted to kick something, but there was nothing in the place except the few sticks of furniture and Ed, and Ed didn't deserve to be kicked. He supposed he could find a window to kick out, but what he wanted was to kick the moon out of the sky.

Dionne, with his fucking blow they had to do, fucking Dionne and his fucking hookers at Zoo's bachelor party. They're fun, Dionne had said, hookers are fun. Life is short, kid, one day you wake up and you're fifty, you don't wanna miss nothin'.

He had been high and it all had made sense—he and Kissy weren't married, she didn't own his dick. He was pussywhipped. He was in a rut. He needed some contrast to remind her she didn't own the only one. And what she didn't know, didn't hurt her.

Dionne, fucking Dionne.

The prick was home, unshaven and mildly hung over, as he opened the door to Junior.

"Hey," said Dionne.

Junior punched him in the nose.

Blood gushing, Dionne staggered back.

Junior strode past him, headed for the refrigerator in Dionne's kitchen, where there would surely be something that passed for beer, which was all beer had to do, philosophically speaking.

"The fuck!" Dionne cried, lurching after him.

"How's your dick, asshole?" Junior snarled. "Or are you too fucking numb to notice?"

Dionne smeared blood across his face with his forearm and groped his crotch with the other. "You got some kind of bug up your ass?"

"Up my dick," Junior said, "the fucking clap I got off that hooker. You fucked her too, you must have it."

"Clap?" Dionne frowned. "You sure?"

"Got a positive test at the clinic."

Squeezing himself thoughtfully, Dionne wandered to the sink and stared at the faucet until he remembered his mission. He turned it on, wet a rag, and wiped at his nose.

"The fuck," he said. "How do you know you might have it?"

"Feels like you're pissing razor blades."

Dionne dropped the rag into the sink, unzipped, and aimed at the sink. He produced a brief squirt. With a sage nod, he tucked himself away again.

"Yeah, I guess it does sting some." He brightened. "So I get some penicillin, right? Big deal." Problem solved, he turned his attention to Junior. "Hey, I seen dead people look better than you. You got it worse or something?"

"You got any weed left?"

Dionne took out a beer and popped it. "Had a party, remember? Up in smoke, darlin'. What's happening?"

Junior hunched his way to a chair as if he had an abdominal wound. "Kissy bailed on me." It was a lot harder to say than he expected.

Dionne stood over him a moment, processing the information. He belched loudly. "Well, fuck her."

Water welled in Junior's eyes.

Dionne slumped into the nearest chair. "Well rid of her, ol' buddy. Things wear out, man. They all wear you out, you give 'm a chance." He shrugged in world-weary resignation and then was moved to consolation. "The world's full of pussy. Too bad every one of 'm's attached to some bitch."

Junior was in no mood for philosophic speculation. "I need to get paralytic."

"Sounds like a plan." Dionne scratched behind his ear, then moved on to his crotch. "How much you got to spend?"

Junior turned out his wallet and his pockets and started counting. Dionne did the same.

"Whatcha wanna do? Drink it or smoke it?" asked Dionne.

"Drink it. It'll last longer."

"Let's don't stop till we're in jail." Dionne grinned.

The door was a little unsteady as Junior groped for it. On the other side, Ed barked furiously. The dog had been cooped up since Kissy left. Three days. Three nights. Junior suspected the way he himself was feeling must be what it feels like to rise from the dead. Moldy. Shaky. Disoriented. He was none too fragrant either. Smelled like a long-buried bone Ed might have unearthed.

"Yeah, yeah," Junior muttered, but the dog's strident bark did not let up.

Once he got the knob by the neck, he aimed the key. It took a few tries before he was able to work it into the keyhole. The next thing he knew he was on his ass in the hallway and Ed was going over him on the way to the stairs. Dionne, squatting by the door to be closer to the floor in case he fell down, laughed crazily.

The two of them crawled into the apartment. Then it seemed like a good idea to stand up. The floor was mined with Ed's turds and puddled with dog piss.

"Jesus," Dionne complained, "this is rank, man. Ed's colon must be the size of the Eisenhower Tunnel."

Junior got a garbage bag and some newspapers and started trying to clean up. He found the mop and pail and slopped a load of Mr. Clean into some water and pushed the mop around. Ed bounded back up the stairs and stood outside the open door in the hallway, barking and growling in a kind of doggy lecture. Scolding him.

Junior's feet went suddenly out from under him. The side of his foot struck the bucket of water and flipped it. The mop flew from his hands as he went down on his ass, slipping in the shit. Trying to give him a hand up, Dionne lost his footing too and wound up flat on his back. Junior gained his feet on his own and threw himself into a skate-board slide through the soup of shit and piss and soapy water on the floor. Dionne joined the game and they did it until they were red-faced with effort.

"Fuck this." Dionne bent over and grasped his knees as he panted. "Let's sell the stereo and go buy some shit."

He started yanking wires out of the backs of the speakers. It took ten minutes to boost the components down the stairs to the back of Dionne's truck. Junior slipped on the last few steps and they dropped the last speaker. It rattled ominously when they picked it up again.

"It's fucked," Junior observed.

"Maybe Mack won't notice."

"Hey, Ed," Junior called.

The dog raced around the corner of the building and nearly knocked Junior down again. Then he loped off.

"He's crazy from being cooped up."

"Jesus." Dionne was moved to reverence. "He's doing it again. Look at that. It's bigger than your head. He shits bigger than you do, Clootie."

Junior called Ed again and this time succeeded in getting him into the back of the truck with the stereo equipment.

"He's wiping his ass on that amp," Dionne said. "Maybe Mack won't notice."

With the money, they paid a visit to a guy they knew, then made a stop at a 7-Eleven and bought more beer. They were closest to Junior's, so they returned there. They filled the dog's dish with beer and the smell made them thirsty so they got down on their knees and slurped it up with Ed. The dog seemed to get the idea it was a game and he barked once in a while in a way that sounded like he was having a pretty good time. So they barked some too. Then they washed down a couple of hits of blotter.

The beer was all gone sometime next day. They smoked another bomber and had a contest to see who could get his tongue deepest into an empty longneck. Junior won, as usual, but this time it merely seemed to make him morose, and he pitched his bottle against the wall. The smash sounded good, so Dionne pitched one too. It was clearly time to get more beer. They collected the rest of the returnables. Junior bundled up what remained of the buy in case someone tried to break into the place and steal it. He stuffed it into his buttonflies and they flipped a coin to see who was going to drive and Junior lost, which meant he had to do it.

Neither of them noticed the door failed to latch. Nor did they notice the dog following them. Dionne slung the garbage bag of empty beer bottles into the bed of his truck, and Junior got behind the wheel and threw it into reverse. As the truck began to move backward, Ed barked somewhere behind them and then there was a thump. A big heavy one like they had dropped a load of garbage bags off the tailgate and backed into it. Junior couldn't get the door open at first, and the truck was still in gear, still moving backward. Dionne fumbled for the gear stick and knocked it into park as Junior fell out the door. The truck shuddered to a stop and Junior crawled on the ground, screaming for Ed.

Junior held the dog in his arms. Ed's tongue lolled, his usual slobber gone pink, his eyes dead as flat beer.

"Oh, Jesus," Dionne moaned.

Junior tried to get up. He tried to lift the dog, but it weighed as much as he did.

"We gotta get him to a vet," he sobbed.

Dionne helped Junior hoist Ed into the truck. It was like trying to move a broke-back couch up a crooked flight of stairs. He took the wheel while Junior stayed with Ed. Dionne stomped the gas and the truck shot into the street. It was a blast, pedal to the metal, taking corners on two wheels and ripping through red lights. Dionne blew four of them before he realized he didn't have the faintest idea where there was a vet or an animal hospital. He skidded to a halt and got out and went back to talk to Junior, stretched out on the truck bed holding the dog. Ed's body was slack, and as Junior shifted, lifting himself to peer at Dionne, the dog's head rocked against his chest. It was obvious to Dionne that Ed was lapping up beer in Pooch Heaven.

"Junior, he's dead. The fucking dog is fucking dead."

"No," Junior protested. "Hurry the fuck up, the vet can save him."

Dionne just stood there. Junior was crying. Junior had cried several times in the last few days and Dionne was more than a little sick of it.

"You shoulda been more careful!" Dionne was suddenly possessed by a righteous fury. "Fuck you, you asshole, you killed Ed! You killed your fucking dog!"

Junior sobbed harder, his face buried in Ed's blood-stained ruff.

Dionne got back into the truck. He didn't know where he was supposed to go, but he was sure of one thing; he was sick of Junior fucking Clootie and Junior's goddamned dead dog and the bitch had had the right idea, leaving the sorry-ass clapped-up dink. He drove slowly along the street, trying to get his bearings. He needed a plan. He yanked at the rearview mirror and got sight of Junior in the back, sitting up now, cradling the dead dog and talking to it. Begging it to come back from the dead or forgive him or some insane fucking shit like that.

Dionne was almost through the next intersection when he registered the sign that said PELTRY DAILY NEWS on the pink stucco building on the corner. On the right was the Civic Center, a notably ugly construction that looked like it was built of garish playing cards, behind a thirty-foot statue of a mythical logger named Peter Gallouse. The statue bore a striking resemblance to Charles Manson and figured in the nightmares of many of the children of Peltry. It was rumored at the local high schools that it turned into a killer clown on Halloween, but the ones who had seen this transformation admitted it helped to do a stamp first.

The important thing about the *News* building, Dionne recalled, was Junior's snotty bitch Melons worked there. He spun the truck into a U-turn and sped back down the block. The employee parking lot was next to the building. He cruised up and down the ranked vehicles until he saw her Blazer. He pulled up behind it and got out.

"Come on, you crazy fucker," he told Junior. "Take your goddamn dead dog you fucking killed yourself and get it the fuck out of my truck. The bitch's truck is right here, asshole."

Junior didn't argue. It was true he was the murderer of his own dog. He saw Dionne's logic at once. Ed had traveled many happy hours in the Blazer; even Kissy would understand how fitting it was that the Blazer be his final mode of transport. And the sight of Ed's remains was sure to move her to take pity on him. They would be united, tragically, in their grief over Ed. He dragged Ed to the tailgate of Dionne's truck and jumped down.

"Still got a set of keys to this fucker?" Dionne asked.

Junior patted his pockets. Not on him.

Dionne rolled his eyes heavenward in long-tried exasperation. He fetched a tire iron from under the seat of the truck and smashed the rear and then the driver's side window of the Blazer. That was so enjoyable he was inspired to go around and knock the lights out of the motherfucker and whack on the body a few times for the hell of it.

An advertising copywriter sneaking out of work a few minutes early shouted at them in surprised outrage. Then he seemed to realize he was challenging two burly young thugs, and he dove hastily into his Toyota.

Junior and Dionne hardly noticed. Dionne lent a hand moving Ed to the back of the Blazer. Then Junior climbed in and tore the ignition assembly loose. He needed to strip the wires and he didn't have anything on him, but he remembered all the shit Kissy kept in the glove box. He punched the button, the door dropped open, and the shit spilled everywhere. Among the maps and crap there was, as he knew there would be, a little Swiss Army knife.

Dionne leaned in at the broken window. "You're doing that wrong. That won't fucking work."

The ignition fired like a Bronx cheer. Junior displayed a rigid middle digit to Dionne.

"Hey, Melons," Julius Horgan called down the darkroom baffle. "Your boyfriend's beating the shit out of your heap."

The nasty edge of his laugh convinced Kissy he was not having her on. She dropped the developing reel she was threading with film into a drum, slapped on a lid, and hurried through the baffle to the nearest window with a view of the parking lot. Other people had had the same idea, and she had to shoulder her way to get a look.

Dionne was leaning in at the Blazer's broken window and she could see Junior's head bent over the wheel. They were two floors below her and the angle left something to be desired, but the broken glass from the Blazer's lights was scattered like seed on sterile ground at the four corners of the vehicle.

"Hot-wiring it," someone said helpfully. "Somebody dial 911."

The rear window was gone. She could see Ed's bulk in the back, huddling as if he knew something screwy was happening.

She had seen enough. Erupting from among the gawkers like a flushed quail, she tore down the stairs and out into the parking lot. The wail of approaching sirens electrified the air like ozone before a lightning strike.

She stood on her tiptoes to scream, "Junior, you shithead, what are you doing?"

But he was driving away.

Dionne turned toward the sound of her voice.

She ran up to him. "What is he doing?"

He shrugged.

"Why did Junior take my car?"

"I didn't want him in my truck anymore," Dionne said, enunciating with great care. "He's a fucking crybaby."

The sirens drowned the sound of traffic in the street. Suddenly the two exits of the parking lot were blocked by incoming units.

In her weeks at the paper, Kissy had gotten to know the local cops by face if not name, and they all knew her. Several of them, she reflected bitterly, had seen her naked. The two most familiar, though, were Pearce and Burke. Spotting them immediately, she abandoned Dionne to his own devices.

Mike Burke rolled down the window and craned out at her.

"Junior took my Blazer," she told him breathlessly, and recited the license number as he wrote it down.

He handed off the notepad to Pearce, who was already on the air with the dispatcher.

"He must be loaded," she said.

"Which direction did he take?"

"North on Main."

Pearce threw the unit into reverse and they roared away in hot pursuit.

It was a roller coaster for a while, sirens and lights and going too fast, the other traffic frantically trying to get out of the way, but then the immediate charge of adrenaline began to slacken. It came to Junior that this might be a mistake. The sirens coming down on the parking lot at the *News* had thrown him into a panic. All he could think to do was drive faster and harder.

Then he saw the sign ahead and everything fell into place. All at once he knew where he was going. He accelerated the Blazer as if he were going to go straight ahead through the intersection, but at the last instant made a hard left. And he was on the Mid-Dance Bridge with the lights and sirens shooting past the turn behind him.

Not until he was on the bridge did he register the suicide fencing along the sides of the middle span. He stomped on the gas pedal and yanked the wheel to the left crossing the opposite lane. As tires and brakes of oncoming traffic were put to the panicked test, the Blazer rammed the guardrail and the fencing above it. The fencing buckled and dented outward but did not break. Junior bounced headfirst off the windshield, which turned magically to a green glass net and sagged inward. The dog's corpse slid forward, to be halted by the rear seat back.

Dazed, his forehead bleeding, Junior groped for the door and tumbled out of the Blazer to the paved deck of the bridge. The Blazer had opened a usable gap between the guardrail and the fence. The cops had gotten turned around, and he was running out of time. Blood ran into his eyes. He rubbed his eyes with the back of his hands and lurched around to the rear end of the vehicle. Traffic from both directions swerved around him with shrieking tires, and drivers cursed at him and threw him the finger.

Ed seemed to have gotten heavier. Junior staggered and fell and dropped him. On his knees, he got some leverage under the dog and moved him closer to the rail. He pushed and shoved and rolled Ed toward the gap. His ears hurt from the sirens, screeching even closer. He made one last superhuman effort, hoisting Ed up over the rail and through the gap under the fence. Then he let Ed go and Ed disappeared, plunging toward the smooth dark waters of the river.

The sirens were upon him.

The gap in the fencing was like the mouth of a monster, the jagged triangular edges like teeth catching at his clothes as he thrust himself through it. He reached for the blackness of the river with a sense of intense relief.

But all at once he was caught around the knees, then at the hips, and was hauled roughly backward through the dentition of the fence. A muscular blue-clad forearm as hard as a crowbar locked under his chin. Any attempt at resistance, he understood at an instinctive level, would get him strangled. He went limp. The cop knelt on him, one knee on his left kidney, a hand gripping him by the hair.

"Howyadoin', Junior?" the cop asked. "Havin' fun yet?"

Junior started to laugh and the cop jerked back on his hair and slammed his face into the pavement.

Kissy watched a pair of uniforms she knew—Schmidling and Feathers—arrest Dionne. He didn't seem to understand what he had done to draw their wrath. Horgan and nearly everyone else in the *News* building came outside to watch. Though the day shift was ending, people were for once reluctant to go home. Arriving night shift workers joined their colleagues in gawking. Everybody appeared to be having a good time. Good-natured jeering broke out as the local live-TV units with their huge antennae wheeled onto the street. Horgan made a beeline for the blow-dries and the Minicams and helpfully pointed her out.

She beat a retreat into the building, returning to the darkroom to process the film she had been loading. It helped to have to concentrate. As the lowest of the low, she spent half her time processing and considered herself lucky to actually get to use a camera regularly.

After a while Schmidling and Feathers sought her out to ask for a statement.

"What about Junior?" she asked.

The two cops looked at each other.

"Stopped on the Mid-Dance," Feathers said. "Evidently he tried to drive your vehicle off it but couldn't get through the suicide fence. He threw the dog off it, though."

"What?" It was beyond comprehension.

"The dog," he said. "The Saint Bernard. He threw it off the bridge."

Kissy groped for Schmidling's forearm. "I don't understand."

"Me neither," Schmidling said. "You better sit down. You gonna faint?"

Feathers pushed a chair to the back of her knees. "Siddown. Put your head down."

"What happened?" she cried. "Is Ed okay?"

"It's a hundred-fifty-foot drop, miss," Feathers said.

Kissy blinked back the sting of tears. "I have to talk to Junior."

"We'll take you to the station," Schmidling offered. "You can make a statement there, find out what happened."

Junior was not at the cop shop yet. He had been taken to the hospital for a blood test and to check his injuries, which Schmidling and Feathers assured her were minor. She learned a little more, information the cops had extracted, with considerable effort, from Dionne.

It seemed Junior and Dionne had been bingeing for several days.

"They had enough empties in the back of that truck to open their own recycling center," Feathers told her.

It was a relief to know that Ed had been dead before Junior threw him off the bridge, less of a comfort that Dionne claimed Junior had killed the dog himself, though by accident. If they had let Junior jump, she thought, he would have survived effortlessly, paddled around in the river like it was a big bathtub, and climbed out with clean ears and a light heart, ready to go find the next beer. She would like to kick his idiot ass over the moon.

She waited a long time in the office where Schmidling and Feathers deposited her. It appeared to be Chief Cobb's own office. She had an idea she was getting the high-rent treatment. Maybe it had something to do with her connection to the *News*. More likely Junior himself was the decisive factor. His face and name in the sports pages.

A few minutes later, Mike Burke knocked at the door and stuck his head in tentatively. "Howyadoin'?"

She gave him a weak grin.

He closed the door again and she heard him speaking to someone else, softly, and then he laughed. Shortly after, he knocked again and came in, bearing coffee.

"Junior's okay," he said. "I mean, physically. He's got a few bruises, a cut on his scalp. He's got some problems, of course, and so does his buddy, Dionne."

"Screw them both."

Burke didn't seem surprised at her double-barreled anger. "I'd be ripped too. I'm afraid your vehicle may be totaled. Would you like to tell me what happened?"

"What I know. I don't know much."

"Whatever you know. After you give me a statement, do you want to see Junior?"

She shook her head no. She had changed her mind; if she saw him now, she would lose it.

"You want to call somebody for him?"

"No. He can make his own calls."

Burke paused to look at her speculatively. It made her uncomfortable and then she lowered her eyes to the coffee shivering in the Styrofoam cup. When she finished giving her statement, which stuck to the barest facts—she did not tell him why she had broken up with Junior—he asked her if she had a way home.

"Cab," she said, nodding toward the phone.

∽ 10 ∽

With one of the two eastbound lanes closed, traffic moved across the river at a creep.

"I been listening on the scanner," the cabby told her. "You know Junior Clootie? The goalie?"

"No," she said, "never heard of him."

He craned at her in the rearview. "I thought maybe you was his girlfriend. I know I seen ya ta the games. Takin' pitchas. I wouldn't forget your hair, honey. Somebody tol' me you was his girl—"

"Do I look that stupid?" she asked.

They were inching on the bridge. Below them, in the water, she could see men in wet suits in the water. They were rigging something floating there. It looked like a hundred-fifty-pound dead chrysanthemum.

"Damn," the cabby said, "look at that."

Ed was coming out of the water, dripping like a huge mop as he was hoisted toward the bridge deck above.

She shuddered and flopped back against the seat back and stared straight ahead.

"They said he throwed his dog off the bridge," the cabby said. "Whadya 'spose he did that for? You sure you ain't his girlfr—"

"I'm not his goddamn girlfriend!" she snarled. "I hate hockey! Junior Clootie can go fuck himself!"

The cabby was offended. "You don't need to use that kind of language, honey. I was just makin' conversation."

She sat forward to see her Blazer as the cab crept by it.

"Ain't that something?" the cabby marveled. "Hope it's insured."

Insured or not, she was going to be bumming rides for days. She would have to borrow a car from Mary Frances or Latham to continue looking for an apartment. The inconvenience did not equate with killing Ed, but it was going to be there every day for—she could not even guess how long.

At eleven, she was curled up on Latham's couch, her feet in his lap, watching the TV news. Latham had already given her a foot massage and was painting her toes. Mary Frances sat on the floor. Most of the TV coverage was so mortifying Kissy wanted to watch between her fingers, the way she had done when she was little and the news about Vietnam was on TV.

There was the briefest glimpse of Kissy getting into a blue-and-white unit outside the *News* building. She looked guilty, the way people always did in the glare of the lights that made everything black and white. As always, it was startling to see herself, whole and presumably as others saw her, though she did not trust the accuracy of any form of film. And as always, when she saw images of herself, she had that sense of not being quite real, not quite identical with that woman, as if the image was more real than her flesh and blood.

It was hard to believe Junior might really go to jail. It was a first offense—well, several first offenses. At least the first time he had ever gotten caught. That Kissy knew. How many times had he tangoed with the cops before, back in Kingston, or even during the four years he had been a student at Sowerwine, that she did not know about because it had been buried, the cops and coaches and administrators covering up Junior's transgressions like cats burying turds? He was Junior Clootie, after all. Maybe the prosecutor would turn out to be a Spectres fan—maybe the grand jury would all be fans, and the judge too.

Trying to contain all her emotions was exhausting. The silky fibers of the velvet upholstery of the couch reminded her of the place behind Ed's ears where he liked to be scratched, and the treacherous tears welled up again. Poor old Ed, without a mean bone in his body.

Deep in her belly she was knotted up as if with menstrual cramps. It was a distinctly physical sensation. How much was actually caused by the war of microbes in her body, the antibiotics duking it out with the bad bugs Junior had given her, and how much it was manifest misery, she hardly knew.

Earl Fish was waiting for her next morning when Mary Frances dropped her off at the *News*. He whisked her into his office, where he pressed coffee on her, inquired as to her well-being, and expressed his personal regrets. He was a nice man, the managing editor.

"I want you to know, as far as I'm concerned, you have every right to your privacy. Only, please don't talk to the other media."

She laughed.

"And if you decide you would like to make a statement, come to me and I'll set you up with one of the women writers."

"Thanks."

"Of course, you can also tell me anything you'd like, off the record. Give us some inside leads."

Fat chance. She shook her head.

"I understand. Well," he said, "good luck. If I can help you in any way . . ."

She thanked him again and went to work.

The darkroom provided cover from the curiosity of her coworkers, but even there, she did not escape Junior. The night shift had left the film strips from which the front page had been illustrated hanging in the drying cupboard. She examined them with a critical eye. Junior, you jerkoff, she thought, as she studied a negative of Ed coming out of the water, I'd like to back the Blazer over you and throw your dead carcass off the bridge myself.

Junior sprawled in his father's antique barber chair in the kitchen of his parents' home in Kingston. Shaving him with a straight edge, Dunny muttered threats about cutting his throat. "I take a mortgage, bud, you're givin' me a personal note. I'm not gonna eat this. You did the crime, you do the time. Sit up, I'm gonna cut your goddamn hair. You're gonna take that shittin' ring outa your ear and look like an Eagle Scout from now till you get this mess cleaned up."

The old man had bailed him out and brought him home. Junior had been miserable the whole way, shakes and sweats and several times they stopped to deal with spasms of vomiting. Three hours northwest of Peltry, they had pulled over again to take a leak, and it hurt so bad, Junior cried out with the pain.

"What's wrong?" Dunny had asked.

"Forgot the penicillin," Junior mumbled. It was back in the apartment and he could not remember if he had been taking it, but the way he felt, he probably had not.

Amazed, Dunny had demanded, "What the fuck are you taking penicillin for?"

"The fuck is what for," Junior had answered sullenly.

Dunny had to think about it, and then he spat in disgust and asked what the hell Junior thought rubbers were for.

On the road again, Dunny worked it out in his head. "She left you 'cause you picked up a dose."

"I gave it to her," Junior had said.

His father had groaned. "Goddamn." Five minutes later, Dunny had hammered the wheel. "I liked that girl." He had glared at Junior. "So was it worth it, stud?" They were at the Kingston town line before he spoke again. "You better see Doc Hansen, get a new prescription. I knew guys in Vietnam, picked up a dose, didn't take it serious, and spent six months, a year, getting rid of it. It ain't something you want to fuck around with, Junior. Though now I think of it, it might be a good thing, you wind up sterile from it."

Automatically, Dunny handed him a mirror to check the cut. Junior stared at himself. He looked like an Eagle Scout with an earring and a shitass hangover.

"You fucked up," Dunny said. "It's gonna cost you. I come out of the service, all I knew besides killing people was what my old man taught me—cutting hair. You don't have to cut hair, you can do something else. You might even make some money at it. I don't think what you did is gonna stop you, but you can see, can't you, you can't do it again."

Tears slid down Junior's face and wet his shirt collar.

"All right," the old man said, "all right, then."

The lawyer Dunny had hired called to report. "The young woman declined to press charges on the grand theft auto. Then there's the trafficking charge. Obviously, you are not a trafficker. Here's the deal. You'll plead to OUI and simple possession and accept the usual fines and probation, plus counseling and community service. And lose your operator's license for six months."

Junior welled up all over again with relief.

His agent, Spenser Lobel, had to know. But as soon as Junior raised him on the phone and told him he had some minor legal problems, Lobel didn't want to talk to him. He wanted to talk to Dunny.

"Naw," Dunny kept saying. "Naw, don't worry about it. He's got no record, they're gonna let him plead down."

Then Lobel was willing to speak to him again. "It's not the end of the world. You just take care of business from now on. *Capice?*"

Junior *capiced.* He had always done what he had to do. This time he had dug himself a nice deep hole. He had to climb out and fill it up. Starting with calling Doc Hansen and getting another charge of penicillin. And calling Kissy. Not today, his head hurt too much and she'd be too pissed off at him. Tomorrow. Or the next day. When his brains were working well enough to devise something resembling a strategy.

"It's for you," Latham said, his palm cupped over the speaker of the headset. "The Ineffable."

It was nearly time to leave for the graduation ceremonies. Kissy took the receiver and started to replace it in its cradle.

Latham gently arrested her hand. "He said it was about the Blazer."

So she lifted the receiver to her ear and spoke calmly. "Hello, asshole."

"I'm sorry—"

"Yes you are. I'm just going out the door. Say what you've got to say and be quick about it."

"I'm going to pay for the repairs to the Blazer," Junior said hastily. "Soon as I get enough money, I'll pay you back for the stereo too."

"Eat shit and die, Junior," she said, and hung up.

Mrs. Cronin had promised to meet her after the ceremonies on the quad for a personal tour of the still-intact art show. Kissy's mother, Caitlin, had come to attend the graduation, and she and Noah, Kissy's four-year-old half brother, would also join them. Arriving with her mother and Noah, Kissy found the gallery crowded with new-minted graduates and visitors. Caitlin and Noah lived in isolated circumstances and the crowds of the day disconcerted them, so that Noah clung to Caitlin's leg.

Kissy was surveying reactions when a familiar profile arrested her eye. As people do when they sense someone's gaze on them, Mike Burke looked her way. He smiled and waved and turned his attention back to her prints. It was the first time she had seen him out of uniform. He looked like another college student. Graduate student anyway, or maybe teaching assistant.

From the entry, Mrs. Cronin called her name.

Later, after lunch, they all went together to the dedication of Diane Greenan's memorial in the pine copse. With her mother and Noah and Mrs. Cronin at her side, Kissy stood through a short program of prayers and remembrances. It ended with a piper's performance of "Amazing Grace." Mrs. Cronin seized Kissy's hand and held on to it tightly. Beside them, Noah crooned the familiar hymn in his mother's arms. Far back, in the deep shadows of the pines, Kissy saw James Houston, wearing sunglasses, lurking like a murderer in a graveyard.

There was another letter from Junior. Without opening it, she dropped it into the trash.

Her new place was a third-floor walk-up in an even crummier neighborhood than the one where she had lived with Junior. It was cheap, already partially furnished with castoffs from previous tenants, and she could move in immediately. Junior was prompt in paying for the repairs to the Blazer, but it came out of the shop with shimmies and shakes it had not had before.

She settled into the graveyard shift, eleven to seven. She signed up for a postgraduate course, two seven p.m. classes a week. Becoming a graduate student allowed her to retain access to Sowerwine's athletic facilities. Latham lent her the money, against the occasional printing job for him. She slept until two or three p.m. and worked out before her class. She did not mind not having much else in her life. For the moment, she wanted to be alone. Mary Frances had gone off to Europe with her dad. Nearly everyone who had been at school with her had scattered as well, off to start their real lives.

Just off work early one morning, she was treating herself to breakfast at Denny's, when Mike Burke strolled in and took the stool next to hers. Wearing sunglasses against the too-bright too-early light, he was out of uniform, his hairline at the nape of his neck damp. Just off the night shift, too, she figured. She acknowledged him with a faint smile.

He worked his neck and shoulders as if they were stiff and then leaned toward her. "Howyadoin'?"

She gave him a shrug.

"I can never go home and just sleep," he said.

"I like the early light."

He grinned. "You would."

The waitress appeared with coffee for him. The cop glanced at the breakfast Kissy was eating and ordered what she was having.

He sipped his coffee and twiddled with a spoon. "I liked your pictures."

She supposed it was an improvement on "Interesting" or "Nice pictures."

Burke was highly regarded among her colleagues at the paper. Reporters, photographers, editors—they were officially noncombatants at the *News* and professionally cynical to make up for it. But she thought they secretly loved the combatants they covered: the rogue, the athlete, the cop, the politician. Mike Burke was smart, going places, they said, ambitious—a fault more than a virtue to them because it was tainted with power seeking. To seek power was, to their mind-set, antidemocratic. They seemed not to know they had power of their own; except when they were sneering that they owned the ink. But Mike Burke was somebody more like them than the old-fashioned beat cop. Not only was Burke an articulate, attractive young fellow with a college education, he was going to law school in his spare time. He had what they called street credibility.

"I heard the Islanders traded Junior to Denver," he said. "Do you know—did it have anything to do with his being knee-deep in shit here?"

"No. All I know is what I read in the paper."

He gave her a sidelong glance. "You know I was just doing my job when I busted him." He smiled his sincere, intelligent smile. He touched her knee lightly with the tips of his fingers.

"The hell with him," she said. "And to hell with Ryne Kowanek too."

Reminded he had actually busted two of her boyfriends, he reacted with a mock-solemn "Happy to oblige," and pulled his sunglasses down his nose to show the good humor in his eyes as he grinned at her.

"Have you been called?"

"Called?" For an instant, she thought she was about to be proselytized.

"The grand jury. I thought—" He hesitated, then shrugged it off. "I thought maybe you had been called to testify in the Houston case."

"I was once, last fall, about the accident."

Burke waggled his coffee cup at the waitress.

Kissy washed down the last of her own coffee. She wiped her mouth with a napkin. As she reached for her check, Burke covered it with his hand.

She plucked it from under his fingertips. "Thanks anyway."

Over the top of his sunglasses, Burke checked out the view as she walked away.

He had lied about her photographs. He hated them. She had forced him to see Junior Clootie through her eyes, to share their intimate life. Kissy's photographs did not stop with the powerful discreet eroticism discussed in the catalog copy provided by her major adviser. There was a monkey hilarity to them, a brilliant unflinching eye above an upper lip aquiver at the edge of laughter. She had made him feel as if he had never been seen by any but a blind eye, and as if, by the fact of his never having been seen, never been hungry or thirsty or asleep or hard or depleted, never lived as anything but a zombie going through the motions.

She had taken his photograph, too, made him a hero, helped get him a commendation, and probably thousands more people had seen it than had seen the art show pictures. He stared into the coffee cup, remembering the song about clouds in the coffee. The man who was so vain he thought the song was about him. He was vain, he knew it. He wanted people to know his name, his face. There might be a powerful fantasy in Kissy photographing him as intimately as she had Clootie, but he would not want the whole world looking at the results. No wonder the goalie had lost it; she was lucky he had not taken it out directly on her.

Sitting at the counter at Denny's, Burke contemplated his vanity. His pride and ambition. He hadn't been to confession since—since he was confirmed. He snorted at the irony. Now he heard confessions.

It was a dirty job; nobody knew it better or felt the corrosion in his soul more. The only one who really understood was the old man, now retired and on disability after twenty-five years as a cop. The job had nearly killed Dan Burke, driven him to booze and from there to AA; ironically, too late to save him for the job. But he had saved some others. The time his father had once spent on a bar stool he now spent in meetings. There were a lot of other cops in Peltry who owed their sobriety and sometimes their careers to Dan Burke's twelfth-stepping them into AA.

"That book your mother's reading," the old man had snorted, waiting for the coals to go white in the barbecue, in the backyard, "*Why Bad Things Happen to Good People*— I coulda wrote that book. Been shorter, too. It's two things, bad luck and bad actors. Your kid gets sick and dies, that's just bad luck, like getting hit by a truck. God don't have nothing to do with it. We all gotta die, it don't matter to God when or how, it's part of a cosmic crapshoot. But when your kid gets hit by a truck and the truck driver's a drunk who's lost his license for drivin' drunk, that's your bad luck again but it's also the trucker's being a bad actor. He's got himself a hobby, which is getting shitfaced and getting behind the wheel. See, your bad actor doesn't go out and go fishing, or building birdhouses or collecting baseball cards. When he gets a hobby, he gets a messy one. He takes up boozing and cruising, or drugging and mugging, or breaking and entering, or maybe fucking little kids. Your babyfucker is the worst. He ain't giving up his hobby until somebody makes him give it up. Somebody being a cop. We can't do nothing about bad luck. Cop's job is busting the goddamn bad actors with their fucking hobbies. People don't like us much for it 'cause they know in their hearts they ain't got the balls to do the job we do. The way I see it is, anything we have to do, we should do. I don't lose no sleep over the rights of some babyfucker. Asshole gave up his rights when he took up that particular hobby. These days the system is so rotten with the fucking lawyers and the softheaded judges, probably the only punishment the asshole ever sees is what the cops dish out, arresting him.

After that, the asshole's got more rights than his victims. I ever write a book, I'm calling it *When Bad People Happen to Good Ones*."

Burke had had no illusions when he put on the uniform. Thanks to his college education, he knew all the theory too. He knew what the theorists would say about his father and even about himself. He thought he could write a book too, about the bad things good people have to do to protect other good people. His book would be about how the work made you realize there were no good people, just the weak and innocent and the assholes who prey on them. Sometimes you wanted to shake the weak and innocent and scream Get strong, get real. The anger burned in your gut and through your veins, and if it didn't kill you it made you strong. It gave you X-ray vision and you could see right through people, right to the bone.

You became a good actor, walking the walk and talking the talk that shielded other people from the fission inside you. Your petty sins, your envy and self-seeking, the once-a-month beer bust, the occasional hard-on for some juicy piece, humbled you with the insight it gave you into how an asshole finds a hobby. You had to be tempted and fall, and tempted and not fall, to fully understand that the assholes had a choice too. Everybody had a choice.

The waitress put a plate of fried everything down in front of him. The smell of cooked egg nauseated him. Why had he ordered what she was eating, hadn't he noticed the eggs were hard-fried?

"I didn't order this," he told the waitress.

She gave him a look of disgust.

"Bring me some oatmeal."

Sweeping the plate away, she stalked off, her saddle-bagged middle-aged ass jiggling with outrage. Kissy had left a two-dollar tip, easily forty percent of the tab, ridiculous really, but he had better match it. The waitress might be a voter, looking at his name on a ballot someday.

∞ 11 ∞

Since the accident, Kissy had fallen into the comforting delusion it would all be settled with a plea bargain. When she was formally subpoenaed to testify against James Houston, scheduled to be tried in mid-July, she had a moment of panic. But there was nothing to panic over, Kissy told herself. She would testify and, finally, that would be the end of it. But for the first time in months, she had the nightmare again. It was Ruth staring sightlessly up at her.

Ruth's condition changed subtly but only in the direction of becoming more pronounced. She had lost a quarter of her weight at the time of the accident, despite her feeding tube. Her eyes had sunken in their sockets. Though she received regular physical therapy, her limbs had begun to stiffen. Her mouth had acquired a slight rictus. Her body was learning stillness and learning it well. It was changing in a glacially slow mutation, a living mummification.

Kissy was never sure she would be able to summon the courage to go back again. It was too difficult to maintain her distance. She had thought to be a witness, an observer, recording what remained of Ruth's life. Memorializing her. But now it felt part of the cruelty of the accident—somehow sadistic, even blasphemous. Sometimes she wanted to smash the living monument to herself that Ruth had become, to sever the meaningless futile knot that tied Ruth to life. Somehow, to effect the release of Ruth's final breath.

But she returned, regularly, as if it were a religious duty. It occurred to her, as she sat near an open window and the summer breeze stirred the fine hair on her arms, and on Ruth's, that Ruth's room was like a church in its essential quietude. This was the church of Ruth. Wither thou goest,

Kissy recalled the verse, there go I. But no one knew where Ruth was going.

The Friday before the trial was set to commence, there was a message on her phone recorder that it would be delayed until August.

Dunny had taken a storefront downtown—near the cop shop, the central fire station, the courthouse, and the jail—for his barbershop. The rent was negligible, the market for close trims a solid one. Esther had started classes. The Clootie boys were spending their summer as they usually did, in various hockey camps, either being paid to teach younger players or paying to be taught by older players. They passed through en route to somewhere else, bunking a few days or a week at a time at the house their folks had rented. They were occasionally on campus to use the gym or the ice surface, on their own stick or during the periods the Sowerwine hockey program required their presence.

For his sins Junior had done more than his share of the lifting, toting, and sweating as he and his father loaded the rented U-Haul to make the move to Peltry. It was then it began to sink in, as his mother curtly laid one hot and dirty chore after another on him, that she was as pissed off at him as Bernie was. And Bernie had declared war on him. He hardly dared eat for fear his sister had spiked his food with laxative. He was used to occasional impatience from his mother but had never experienced her holding a grudge against him.

One more woman's anger was more than he could cope with. Kissy refused his phone calls and made no response to the letters he labored over. He knew he should go see her, but for the first time in his life, he was afraid of something. He was afraid now that she would not forgive him. Because then Kissy would be gone from his life forever. Her day-to-day absence was painful enough.

He missed Ed as he never had when he had been in college and the dog had been home in Kingston. There was a terrible finality in knowing he was never going to see Ed again, and in the guilt of having killed him, even accidentally. What had Ed ever done to deserve what he had done to him? No wonder Bernie was so wild at him. He could hardly blame her.

Gifted with health, Herculean stamina, a predator's reflexes, youth, looks that encouraged his natural narcissism, and a self-sufficiency that left little room for meanness—who in the world had anything he could possibly want, really, other than a few material goodies?—he was ill acquainted with depression and had few tools to combat it. The only thing he knew to do was what he had always done. He filled the few hours not consumed in hockey camps with volleyball, basketball, baseball, golf—every kind of ball except the one that would do him the most good. The frantic round of distractions wore him out enough to sleep, most nights.

He had always been content to break even for the summer, but this year, Dunny was getting his paychecks from the camps that compensated him, and paying for the camps where he was one of the payees, while doling out a meager allowance. As a consequence, Junior was chronically short. Nothing in his pocket to drink on, let alone date.

At pickup games he tried not to watch the other guys drink, but he could smell it, practically taste it, and then there was the whiff of reefer being passed as the sun set and the unfinished games were called. It left him thirsty and restless and resentful of the doctor who had forbidden him alcohol until he tested clean of the clap. It was weird; he could fuck as long as he used a rubber but he couldn't drink because the antibiotic wouldn't be as effective, his past indulgence the reason he still had the dose.

When not obsessing about reconciling with Kissy, he obsessed about the trade. Spense Lobel insisted it had been in the works.

There was no connection, but it had come suspiciously quickly after the Big Screwup. However much bullshit the agent wanted to sling, the fact remained that Junior had lost exposure in a stronger division and been exiled, in effect, to an expansion team in a part of the country where ice hockey vied for popularity with field hockey. West of Chicago, south of Minnesota. It was mostly football country, except for the square states smack in the middle where the football fans also got worked up over hoops in the winter. High school hoops at that. Given a choice, he would rather play in Canada and take shit for being a Yank. He would rather play in Quebec and take a metric tonne of Franco merde for the sin of not being a frog.

What made everything worse was the proximity of his

brother Mark, kept for the previous four years at a bearable distance. Now Mark was chronically in his face, trying to be just like him. He couldn't stop Mark from connecting with his teammates—former teammates but still buddies, who would be his brother's teammates in the coming season. The little fucker infiltrated his life, the facilities at Sowerwine, even the pickup games he played. Mark not only had a valid license but drove the truck that had been his.

Dionne returned for some summer block courses that would keep him eligible for his final year. Predictably, a party broke out. Junior was clean of infection by then, so he had a beer or three. A girl named Page, a compact little package on the Paula Abdul scale, started to make fuck-me moves on him. For a while he amused himself trying to decide whether her breasts could be described as pert or impertinent. Then it occurred to him that if he went home with Page, Kissy would find out. Somebody, like for instance his dickhead brother, Mark, would regard it as his duty to inform her. He reflected bitterly that people were a lot less likely to let Kissy know he had not slept with some other woman than that he had. He knew perfectly well that even if he had not infected Kissy, she would never have forgiven his screwing around on her. It was the way she was, and when he stopped to really think about it, the way he wanted her to be. The kind of woman who didn't care if he was fucking around was probably fucking around herself, or planning on it. He wanted Kissy to be the kind of woman who would not fuck around on him. He did not want to find out she was already fucking someone else. At the same time, he didn't know how to get her back, and even if he had had a clue how to do that one, he had no idea how the hell he was going to pursue his career and keep her. It gave him a splitting headache and a sick stomach, just thinking about it. Life should be simpler. To punish himself for killing Ed, he told Page he thought she showed early signs of alcoholism and then informed Dionne he was a degenerate moron who had ruined his, Junior's, life, fuck-you-very-much. Dionne blinked in astonishment and invited Junior to blow him. Junior did not deign to reply but trudged off, next-door-to-sober, chaste-as-the-driven-snow, to his parents' house. Where his kid sister, who had cut her hair just like Kissy's, and had one ear pierced several more times like Kissy's, had short-sheeted his bed and run a box knife around the roll in the bathroom to turn it into scotch toilet paper. He left it just as it was so his father could enjoy it.

Next morning he had the satisfaction of being wakened by Dunny's roar and a vocabulary of curses over the flush, the rush of water in the basin as his father scrubbed, and then the bathroom door slamming open and the bellow of "Bernadette!"

Summer in Maine hardly begins before it begins to wane. As the draft of fall began to cool the summer evenings, it felt like a hand at the small of Junior's back, pushing, pushing, pushing him off balance. He would have to go soon. His dreams were full of Kissy, of needing to reach her, talk to her, deliver some important message to her, but always he was kept from her—by a raging black river where a dripping-wet Ed stood guard upon the only bridge. Ed's head hung strangely, but still the dog was able to bare his teeth and bark furiously at him.

It seemed to him that the state of his life was far too reminiscent of the time when he was six and the Atwood boys clipped the belt loops of his pants to the rigging of the flagpole outside the Kingston firehouse and hoisted him. The excitement at the start, the fascination of the view of Kingston below him, had faded abruptly as he saw the Atwoods pumping their bikes frantically around the corner and he had realized they were going to leave him there.

By the end of July, Kissy was on the day shift. She prowled the county fair, taking pictures of the kids on the midway, the horses at the racetrack, people going on balloon rides. One morning she rose before dawn to hitch a ride herself. From the balloon's gondola she had a bird's eye view of Peltry and the bridges on the Dance, the length of the Hornpipe and its valley.

The balloon pilot asked her for her phone number. "Garrett," read the embroidered script on his jacket. He was in his thirties, with a pale band around his ring finger where he had until recently worn a wedding ring. He had nice wrinkles in the corners of his eyes, a receding hairline, and a modest, good-humored mustache.

He was not the first guy to show some interest in her in the weeks since she had broken up with Junior, but she usually saw it coming. As when Zoo, back in town to pick up some furniture Brenda had stored, turned up with a six-pack and a solicitous attitude that became, in short order, an outright pass. She had laughed at him. He had shrugged it off and gone on his way.

In the evening, she went up with Garrett again, to shoot the lights of the fair, tacky on the ground where the missing lightbulbs stood out like missing teeth, but completely magical from above. Then there was the nightly fireworks display blooming gorgeously beneath the spectator moon.

They were settling to the ground again when, as she focused her lens at the near end of the midway, she found herself looking at a boy giving a girl a hand off the Tilt-a-Whirl. Kissy took the picture almost automatically as she recognized Junior. The girl fell laughing into his arms and Junior looked into her eyes and drew her into shadow to kiss her. Only it wasn't Junior, Kissy saw almost instantly, it was his brother, Mark. A sense of the weirdness of it was not the limit of her reaction. Something more visceral happened to her. All at once she wanted Junior again. Wanted very specifically his arm around her waist, his body to lean against in the melting shadows, his mouth on hers.

The knock woke her at once. She knew it was him, unseen, though she could not have said how. It was as if her momentary desire for him had brought him. For a moment she was as paralyzed as in her nightmares, but she was not afraid. Only unsure of her own reaction.

"Kissy," he said, on the other side of the door. It was a plea.

She could see him in her mind's eye, with his fingers fanned against the wood, the side of his face against the door panels, her name falling, in all its ridiculous childishness and yet unavoidably intimate, from his lips.

She sat up slowly, hugging her knees. She had been sleeping naked in the heat.

"Kissy," he repeated.

She groped for a pair of boxer shorts and a T-shirt. Snapping on a small lamp at her bedside, she went to shoot the bolt and unhook the chain. She peeked out the door.

"Kissy," he said again, beaming. Giving off the yeasty smell of beer, the tang of smoke too, and his eyes were a little red.

"I might have had somebody here," she said.

He tried to grin but it fell apart. "I'll kill him." His voice was tremulous.

She flipped back the door, showing him the interior.

"I know he's gone." Junior seized the frame of the door and rocked in it. "Who was he?"

"None of your business. Are you drunk?"

"A little." He stared at the mattress on the floor.

She had been sleeping between the sheets only, and he could see they opened to the left only and were disarranged but slightly. Exactly as he had seen them many times when she went to bed before him. He sniffed at the air.

"Fuck you," she said, crossing her arms under her breasts. "I didn't sleep with him. Yet."

He knew it already, of course. He was just being a jerk because he was a little drunk and aggrieved she had gone out with someone. Without invitation, he came in and closed the door behind him.

"I saw him leave," he said, sheepish and defiant at the same time. "I wasn't spying on you or anything. I wanted to see you." He shrugged. "Mr. Pussy-tickler didn't look like a guy who'd just gotten laid, anyway. I went all the way home and turned around and came back. I had to see you."

"You're looking at me. Now you can go home."

"I'm leaving tomorrow."

It wasn't a surprise. It was time.

"Kissy, I can't go away with you hating me."

"I don't hate you," she replied, but all at once she was shaking with fury. "So go away."

"I love you, Kissy. I hate this. I hate being apart."

"We were going to be apart anyway. Goddamn it, Junior, you gave me a dose! And you were too chickenshit to tell me. When were you going to tell me, ten years from now when I'm trying to have a kid and find out I'm sterile from untreated gonorrhea?"

"I was going to tell you and you were already gone. You never gave me a chance—"

"I gave you a chance to infect me and you took it—"

"I didn't do it on purpose, it just happened—"

"Like catching a cold, huh?"

"I didn't set out to hurt you. I was high. It was Zoo's stag party and there was a hooker—"

"Shut up, Junior, you're not helping yourself. You know

how it makes me feel, sharing the clap with you and a public fucking machine?"

He shut up. But he looked at her with the same miserable abjectness that she had seen in Ed's eyes when he had committed some doggy sin. He fixed her with all his longing.

"Junior," she murmured, and one bare foot groped back uncertainly, in search of safer footing. "Don't look at me like that."

Charmed and besotted, he reached for her and she was not quick enough in her backpedal. He tried to kiss her. Gasping at his temerity, she grabbed his hair to yank his head back. He pressed himself against her. Closing her eyes, she breathed in the smell of his skin, his hair. As at the fair, the sudden ferocity of her desire appalled and bemused her. She hardly heard him, babbling about how much he loved her, how he hadn't been with anybody since they broke up, he was still so crazy about her.

In moments they were on the mattress together. The lamp pooled an amoeba of light on the ceiling. It was pale and insubstantial as the face of the moon in the sky. There was a face between her legs, Junior's face, his nose and lips and tongue. She came hard and while she lay catching her breath, he crawled up her and kissed her tenderly and devotedly. With one hand he dragged at his shorts and then bore her hand to his erection.

"Stop it," she cried.

"Why? It was great—"

"Shut up," she gasped, and then she started to sob, great wracking spasms. The tears surprised her, flowing out of her with such suddenness, as if a seal had been suddenly broken.

Junior cradled her in his lap, rocking her back and forth, shushing her like a baby. He kissed her eyes and began to lick her face as if he were a cat cleaning a kitten. The roughness of his tongue on her skin tickled her throat and she giggled. She was so tired, she thought, anything would be funny, even Junior tugging at his shorts again, drawing her hand to his hard-on.

"Junior—listen to me—I quit taking the Pill when we split up—"

"I'll pull out," he said immediately, and laughed.

"We've been through this before—"

"Please—" He cupped her breast and nuzzled behind her ear. "Please Kissy please I love you it'll be okay—"

She closed her eyes. His palm cupped her pubis and she rocked against it. He kept at it, whispering and pressing and promising and touching her in places he knew rendered her helpless and half out of her mind. This is stupid, she told herself, how stupid can you get, but she didn't stop him. She was amazed at her own heedless desire. She locked her legs around him, sucked his tongue into her mouth.

She was his again, incontrovertibly and totally, and he wanted to be inside her forever and of course he wanted to come inside, did not want to pull out until the last second and it just happened, suddenly, without warning. Too late, she tried to tear herself away from him. She swore at him furiously, but then the anger blinked out of her and her mouth quivered with panic. They were separate again, both of them breathing hard, staring at each other, on the mattress. She rolled over and onto her knees and staggered into the bathroom.

Returning a little later, she looked down at him with dark unhappy eyes. He held up his hands in supplication. She sank slowly, reluctantly, to the mattress, and he pulled her down next to him and snuggled up against her, belly to bottom. He pressed his face into the damp hair at the nape of her neck. She shuddered against him and he closed a hand over hers on the pillow. With the other he cupped her sex possessively.

"I love you," he told her again.

Under his hand, her chest hitched.

"No," she whispered. "You don't. You're a liar, Junior. I hate you."

"I couldn't help it, it's been so long—it'll be okay."

She said nothing more.

She would get over it, he told himself. She was just angry at herself too for not being able to say no to him, but she still wanted him as much as he wanted her. Her hunger had been equal to his own, the best evidence he could have had that there had not been anyone else. They were together again because they belonged that way. He was aglow with the realization of his love for her. It was all going to be all right, she would see.

* * *

The birds woke her. One of the pleasanter things about the place, they infested the tree branches outside her small windows. She did not know what kind they were; she could tell a crow from a robin and a chickadee from a chicken, and that was about the extent of her expertise. A failing she had been meaning to address, to the extent of having purchased a paperback bird guide. It was the false dawn whatever kind of birds they were announced this day, but it was still time to get up if she was going to swim and work out. The warmth of Junior's body next to hers was seductive, though, and she snuggled back against him for a moment. Waking up with him was so familiar, so comfortable. Still half asleep, he was tucked up to her fanny, hard as a crowbar, and she pressed back against the all-too-familiar leverage. With which he moved her earth, planet Kissy. This was the end of it, she told herself, turning toward him.

When they finished, she rolled out hastily and went to the bathroom again, not that she could do anything more than pee, as she had the night before. She was crazy, a goddamn fool who deserved whatever happened to her. She would not let herself look at a calendar and try to remember when she had her last period and whether she might be fertile.

She found some clean clothes and then started coffee. She heard Junior making water in the bathroom. He came into the kitchen still buck-naked, clutching his clothes in one fist, his sneakers in the other. Yawning, he dropped the shoes with a thud. He pulled on his shorts and dragged a chair under his ass.

"I always loved your idea of a wake-up call." He grinned.

Kissy pulled the carafe out of the coffeemaker and stuck a mug directly under the drip to fill. She shuffled another into its place and topped it from the carafe and put it down in front of Junior.

He was stuffing his feet into his sneakers. "The Drovers usually send their top prospects to Allentown for seasoning. We're all going, the whole family, driving cross-country. Taking it easy, looking at everything on the way. Come with me, Kissy—the folks would love having you with us, and when I get my assignment, you and me, we'll drive back east to Allentown together, like a honeymoon—"

"What about my job?"

"It's a shitty one. There's shitty jobs everywhere."

She pulled her mug out from the drip and replaced the carafe. "Maybe I like my shitty job."

"What about last night? This morning?"

"It just happened," she said mockingly. "It didn't fix anything, Junior."

He stared at her. "I don't understand." He licked his lips. His voice came out hoarse and incredulous. "Are you in love with that twink you went out with last night?"

"No."

Relief loosened Junior as if someone had cut a string inside him. "Then what is it?"

"Junior—"

His mouth set stubbornly. "All right, I fucked up. But what's past is past. We still love each other."

"Nothing's changed." She turned her back on him and threw the rest of her coffee into the sink. "I'm going to swim. I'll give you a ride to your folks' if you want to go. Then we say good-bye."

Junior was dumbstruck.

When she turned around, he was staring at her with overflowing eyes. "You can't jerk me around like this."

She grabbed her gym bag and her keys. "You don't own me, Junior. If you want a ride, move your ass." She waited at the door to lock it.

He followed her down the stairs to the Blazer, at the curb. "I woke up with you sucking my cock half an hour ago, Kissy—"

"It was habit, Junior," she snarled at him, out of the guilt she felt at having gone weak-kneed.

"Habit?" Unshaven and with his eyelids red with pending tears, Junior still looked a little drunk. Grappling with the concept of cocksucking as a habit, like cigarettes, he was almost too flummoxed to be sure he was not, in fact, still loaded.

"You gave me the clap," she said through clenched teeth, "you got from a whore."

Which facts were not new to him, or disputed either. At her side as she unlocked the Blazer, his body tense with anxiety, he could not focus enough to deal with what was happening.

"Well?" she asked. "Are you going?"

"Please," he said. "Please."

When she turned back to the Blazer, he grabbed her shoulders and tried to force her to face him. She sucked in a lungful of air and yanked a knee up between his legs as hard as she could.

He let go of her and sat down on the curb with his hands between his legs, and then he rolled over and threw up. She dove into the Blazer and managed to start it, though her hands were shaking. She jerked it into gear. He lifted his head and got a mouthful of her exhaust.

He made it to the corner a few minutes later, banging one shoulder into a lamppost as he scrabbled for support. He got his balance and shuffled on. Before he got very far, a blue-and-white police unit crept up slowly behind and then alongside him.

"Morning, Junior." Officer Friendly grinned at him. "Howyadoin'?"

Junior was not up to chitchat. He just stood there as the cop car stopped and Officer Friendly and his partner, whose name was something like Sergeant Preston, got out to pass the time of day with him.

"You drunk?" Sergeant Preston inquired solicitously.

Junior shook his head.

"You look a little rocky," observed Officer Friendly. "It's early too. You got a paper route now?"

Junior finally managed enough spit to speak. "Just goin' home."

Sergeant Preston took him firmly by the elbow. "Tell you what, Junior, you step over here and let us check you out, and if you're clean we'll give you a lift home. Best deal you'll get today."

Junior did not see that he had any choice. He put his hands on the hood of the unit and spread his legs as directed, and Officer Friendly got very familiar with him. When he winced away from the brush of the cop's hand between his legs, the cops snorted with amusement.

"Junior, what have you been doing?" Officer Friendly inquired with tender concern.

"Nothing," Junior mumbled.

They were kind enough to give him a hand into the backseat.

"So, Junior," Officer Friendly said when they were rolling slowly through the quiet streets, "did you forget the way home last night?"

Sergeant Preston laughed heartily at his partner's wit.

"I guess," Junior agreed.

"In Kissy Mellors' neighborhood, if I'm not mistaken. Rotten block, except for her," Officer Friendly continued. "That was Kissy in her Blazer, wasn't it, come busting around that corner five, ten minutes ago? We could have stopped her, she was up ten on the limit, but the streets are empty and we were having some coffee and we figured she was late to work—what the hell—we gave her a break."

"Kind of you," Junior murmured.

"You weren't bothering her, were you?" Sergeant Preston said suddenly, as if he had just thought of it. "You wouldn't be that stupid, would you?"

"Sure he would," Officer Friendly assured his partner in a bored tone. "Junior doesn't think, sometimes. Gets a little shitfaced, kills his dog, steals his girlfriend's truck, wrecks it, and throws the dead dog off the bridge. Few beers, couple tabs, a toke or two, and Junior's liable to get spectacularly stupid."

"I'm leaving today," Junior said. "I wanted to say good-bye."

"Just had to catch her before she went to work?" Sergeant Preston nudged.

Junior didn't respond. They didn't have any right to ask him anything. He was just trying to get along. He was still sick to his stomach. His balls ached fiercely. He cupped them gently and closed his eyes.

"Answer The Man," Sergeant Preston said sharply. "You might not be leaving today, Junior."

Junior gritted his teeth. "I was at Kissy's overnight. We had a fight this morning. You ever get up and have a fight first thing? It happens."

"Never had one left me clutching my nuts," Sergeant Preston said. "You make her sleep in the wet spot?"

That one sent Officer Friendly into paroxysms of sniggering.

The unit sidled to the curb.

"Hey, Junior," Sergeant Preston said, "no hard feelings. We can't have the public thinking we're giving you any special treatment, you know?" The cop was smiling with apparent genuineness as he held the door open for Junior. He offered his hand, shook Junior's firmly, and patted his back. "Best of luck, son."

Officer Friendly was right there, too, hand extended. Junior looked at it and decided, reluctantly, this was one he had to fake. Not only was he on probation, he had to come back to this town.

Dunny was in the doorway. The cops waved at him, and after a slight hesitation, he waved back. Junior trudged past him to drop cautiously into the nearest kitchen chair. Dunny, watching him closely, poured a mug of coffee and clunked it onto the table in front of his son.

"Nice start to the day, seeing you climb out of a cop car. When you didn't come home last night, I told your mother you had a few too many and had sense enough to stay at Dionne's. Don't tell me you been in the tank."

Junior studied the oily sheen on top of the coffee. His gut still hurt. "Just cab service from the cops. I went to see Kissy. She let me stay but this morning we had a fight. She's still ripped at me over the old shit."

"Shoulda let it be," Dunny said. "Some shit you can't fix, Junior, you know that."

"She's important to me, Dad."

Dunny sighed and shook his head. "You got an appointment two thousand miles from here that's important to you too. You want this thing, seriously, you have got to buckle down. Eyes on the prize. You only got the one career. Don't let your dick run your life, Junior."

Esther caught the last as she came into the kitchen. "Write that down, Dunny. I'll embroider a sampler for Junior and Mark too. Excuse my interrupting your father-son talk, but we've got a long day ahead of us." She drew a glass of water and handed it, along with a bottle of aspirin, to Junior. "Finish your packing, Junior. I want to be out of here within the hour. Dunny, run up and make sure Bernie and Mark didn't just turn over and go back to sleep."

12

The standard motions to dismiss rejected, James Houston, Jr., was required to be tried for vehicular manslaughter and aggravated assault with a motor vehicle. The *News* rehashed the details of the accident in a feature series during the week the jury was being selected. According to the *News,* Houston was an only child, his mother an equestrienne and horse breeder, his father a pediatrician. After learning of his son's involvement in a fatal accident, his father had suffered a nearly fatal coronary and undergone an emergency bypass. Houston's paternal grandfather had been a neurosurgeon of some note who had established a trust for the education of his grandson through medical school. An honors student from his first semester, Houston apparently unequivocally shared his grandfather's ambitions of a medical career for him. He had continued to pursue it while released on bail and had actually graduated summa cum laude from Sowerwine's premed program, as part of the class that included Kissy and would have included Diane Greenan, had she lived, and Junior Clootie, had he completed his requirements.

Twelve days before the trial began, Ruth Prashker entered an acute crisis with pneumonia. When she began to be unable to breathe on her own, she was rushed to the hospital, where she was placed on artificial respiration. Ruth's father sought permission from the court to remove her from the respirator and forbid further heroic measures. Mrs. Prashker and Mrs. Cronin, with the hospital administrators, initially opposed the requested order. The influence of Ruth's brother, Dan, brought the family members together and produced a change of mind: Mrs. Prashker and Mrs. Cronin reversed their positions. The hospital

administrators asked the court to appoint a neutral
guardian. This was granted, leaving the Prashkers and Mrs.
Cronin without any legal power over Ruth's day-to-day
care or her future. Ruth became entirely the ward of the in-
stitutions. The newsroom was abuzz with gossip that if the
court ever granted the order, Houston's lawyers were prepared to enter the case to object to it. If Ruth Prashker died,
it would mean not one but two counts of manslaughter
against their client.

The night before testimony was to begin, Kissy was
sleepless. Her period was coming on. The relief of the first
twinges underlined her folly with Junior. She did not miss
him. It was the flux of hormones that made her dreams
wet, made her weepy and lonely, given to breakage and
inexplicable forgetfulness and aimlessness. She did not
really want a baby. Not now. Nor did she want to go through
another abortion. It would cost money she could ill spare,
for one.

She peeked into the courtroom. Mrs. Cronin and Ruth's
parents, who had reconciled at least with regard to Ruth's
future, and the Greenans too were present, but the two
families made no common cause. With a bare exchange of
civil greetings, they took seats in opposite enclaves. The
Prashkers had suffered through nearly a year to arrive at
last at the decision that their daughter should be allowed to
die. They could hardly console the Greenans with the
thought that Diane was better off than Ruth.

The big old-fashioned courtroom's floor-to-ceiling windows had been opened for ventilation. Outside in the
pocket park, where the courthouse crew ate lunches and
flirted and gossiped in the shade of heavy-limbed old
maples, the grass was deeply green. Begonias edged the
small garden beds with brilliant red and luminous pink.

The defendant, in a dark suit that was too big for him,
had knotted his dark tie so tightly it was like a ligature. His
hands displayed a tremor. He was unwilling to raise his
gaze from the papers on the table in front of him. Very
soon after he sat down between his attorneys, he saw Kissy
loitering by the entrance and paled—if it were possible for
so pale a human being to become any more colorless.

She wondered why did he not just plead guilty and take
the best deal he could get, as Junior had. No one was going

to stand up at the back of the courtroom, as on a TV melo-drama, and shout that they had done it.

Opening statements proceeded. The first prosecution wit-ness to be called was newly promoted Sergeant Michael Burke.

The mountains broke the horizon in stony exultation through the mist of an afternoon shower. Junior, riding shotgun while Dunny drove, sat up straighter. The Rockies rose up from the plains like the mountains of the moon in the sky.

Esther leaned forward from the backseat and squeezed his shoulder in excitement. "Oh, my!"

"We're not in Kansas anymore," Dunny said. "I've driven two thousand miles to say it."

With his license suspended, Junior had not taken a shift behind the wheel. He had slept a lot, while Mark and Bernie had bickered and played with Game Boys and read comic books. Bernie had averaged one good kick into the vicinity of Junior's kidneys through the seat back every time he sat in front of her, until finally he exploded at her.

Wrenching himself around, he screamed, "Jesus, will you get *fucked,* you raving little premenstrual bitch!"

Everyone in the vehicle had been momentarily stunned into silence.

Then Bernie said, "Sounds like you should take your own advice—"

"Enough!" Dunny interrupted. "The both of you cut the shit. Apologize to Ma."

The apologies were duly muttered.

"Now shut the fuck up," Dunny said.

Mark pinched Bernie. She drove an elbow into his ribs. But it was just closing arguments and it stopped there.

He killed the three days before rookie camp being a tourist with the family—going to the zoo, and the Coors factory in Golden, and to Colorado Springs to climb Pike's Peak, where it seemed as if he could see most of the way back to the Mississippi. He saw for the first time what a long goddamn trek home it would be. The last night his folks were there, Spense Lobel flew in and they all had dinner in a pricey restaurant, which made it seem real. Bernie dressed up and the agent actually flirted with her, until he noticed Junior and Dunny Clootie both glaring at him.

When he checked into camp, he found out he was rooming with the kid from the Red Bloc team, last sighted holding his own in Skinner's. The kid had joined a steady stream of defecting Eastern European athletes. Glad to have the hard currency the athletes invariably sent home for their families, their governments were looking the other way now. Rumor had it that some of the financially strapped Communist regimes were even actively selling their athletes to the highest bidder. The kid's name was Evgenny Bezymyanny, but the media had christened him "Elvis" for his effect on the female fans. It was impossible to dislike him. The kid was so naive, so thrilled by the attention, nobody could hold it against him. The young Russian remembered Junior too, even recalling the nickname of "Hooter."

It was like rooming with Mark, except Mark was a total pig and the kid had been raised in the military-style jock barracks of the East and was noticeably fastidious. But his rack went unused; he was touring the beds of the local puckbunnies. Junior envied him to a degree, with a little resentment that the kid succeeded in making him feel old at twenty-two and also because he felt he had to live like a monk himself, under the circumstances. Calling the kid Elvis made him feel smarmy, and when he tried to say Evgenny, it came out Eugenie, which sounded like a name some guy named Eugene would stick a daughter with if he couldn't get himself a son to be Eugene Jr. With more than a little edge of mockery, he took to addressing the kid as Der Kommissar, after the song.

"Hoot," the kid pointed out, "der Kommissar is not being a Russian word. Is being Chur-man."

"I know that. Listen to the fucking song. The guy singing it is German, which is why he says it in German, but he's talking about some Russian asskicker. Actually, he's talking about cocaine, but in his metaphor, cocaine is like an ass-kicking Russian commissar," explained Junior.

The kid was amazed. "Is this being true?"

Junior didn't let on he wasn't actually absolutely positive. He had spent a lot of 1982 listening to the song and contemplating the question. It might be der Kommissar was the coke dealer, or even a narc. But his interpretation was possible.

Then all of a sudden everyone was calling the kid Der Kommissar. And Junior realized he was going to have to listen to Der Kommissar every time the goddamn Russian scored a goal all season. Junior shortened it up to D.K. and then Deker, and a Deke, of course, was a feint, which delighted the Russian. That was the problem: everything delighted him. He was totally indiscriminate. Growing up communist, Junior concluded, it was no surprise that he lacked standards.

Junior knew most of the other rookies—postschoolboy hockey was, like every field of competence, an ever-shrinking circle of expertise—and even the ones he had not actually played against, he knew by repute. Not only were the rookies competing against other rookies, they were all obsessed with who was occupying the roster slot they wanted. Junior, for instance, had a couple of well-established netminders in front of him—both of them in health as rude as his and with money stats—plus the goalies in the Drovers' farm system, who ran from green to hopeful to hobbling. And, of course, every other goalie, up and down, minors to majors, was his competition, because the Drovers could trade his ass in a phone call, as the Islanders had. Nothing new; if he wanted a place, he had to beat somebody out of it. At the end of a week of camp, he was told he was going to the Dry River, Montana, Dinosaurs, the pit of the minor league clubs affiliated with the Drovers.

"What did I do wrong?" he blurted.

Not a thing, he was assured. Nobody faulted his fundamentals, but they didn't want to rush him. The idea was to bring him up to speed, let him acquire a professional game with a little less pressure of expectation than he would face on the Big Pond. He understood it—had expected it, for Christ's sake—but Dry River? The shock made him realize how much he had been counting on going to the Tommy-knockers in Allentown. Not only was it the best of Denver's affiliates, it was East Coast Hockey League, which meant he could get home once in a while; his folks might

actually have a chance to see him play. Playing out of Dry
River, he would have no hope of seeing Kissy for months.
It was like a door slamming in his face. He managed to
hold himself together until the handshaking was over and
then, blinking sweat from his eyes, found his way to a
lavatory and threw up. When he left the toilet stall, the
Russian was at the urinal.

"You are being sick, Hooter?" Deker asked.

"Morning sickness," Junior muttered, and blundered out.

Spense Lobel, over the phone, cheerfully claimed it was
just what he had expected. Junior was beginning to suspect
that nothing would ever happen to him that Lobel would
not claim to have foreseen, and indeed planned.

The front office supplied a bus ticket and the information that he could get a room at the Devil's Backbone
Motel, an easy walk to the facilities. The Dry River Ice
Arena, Home of the Dry River Dinosaurs. He did not
board the bus alone. Deker was among the others with the
same assignment. Another was a big shapeless boy from
Moosejaw, Saskatchewan. He reminded Junior of Dionne,
with less brain damage and a sweeter temperament. Everyone called him—naturally—Moosejaw. Moosejaw was
happy to be relatively close to home. They sat together, as
if the Greyhound were a team bus, and soon were talking
about money and agents and what the assignment meant
to them, to their plans. For the length of the ride, anyway,
they could relax a bit—the decisions had been taken and
there was nothing to do but live with them until they were
on the ice again and had another chance to show their
stuff.

Hockey had taken Junior a lot of places, not all of them
pleasant, but even at first glance Dry River qualified as
one of the least attractive. The favored building materials
appeared to be cement block, mummified wood, and plywood scraps. It only wanted a pair of gunfighters squaring
off on the dusty Main Street. From the bus window he
picked out the bed of the river, a ribbon of rock, scrub,
sand, and rusted, gutted major appliances, as it meandered
through the town. From the three low bridges spanning the
river that wasn't there, he deduced the river must run some
water at least some of the year. Or decade; they didn't call

this town Dry River because the river was wet *very* fucking often.

Though it wasn't a regularly scheduled stop, the bus driver let them all out at the motel, on the outskirts of town. Junior could not see anything that looked like an arena from its ragged parking lot. The desk clerk, a derelict octogenarian of indeterminate gender, grinned gleefully, giving the new tenants the news that the arena was on the other side of town, a three-mile trot away. None of them with rides of any kind. Doubtless they could all pile into the wreck of a cab parked outside, or, Junior sadistically told the gullible Deker, they could use the world-famous Dry River Metro. Along with the fucking prairie dogs. If the locals hadn't eaten them all. Junior was not actually sure what prairie dogs were, other than vermin, and didn't care either.

His single room—like all the motel's rooms—was designed to encourage a steady turnover, say once every half hour. It had a bathroom with a broken-seat toilet that ran all the time, and a mildewed shower stained in a way that suggested someone had used it as an abattoir. The basin's faucet handles came off in Junior's hands when he tried to turn them. A wreath of gummy hair welcomed him in the shower drain, short-and-curlies on the toilet when he lifted the seat.

The bed listed to one side, and the coverlet was mottled by several different mystery substances, including what appeared to be blood. Gingerly, Junior lifted the coverlet and top sheet and studied the bottom sheet for crabs. He was pretty sure there was something hopping around there. Briefly, he considered taping his pants legs and shirtsleeves and collar closed, then figured it was hopeless. Something would crawl into his ear in the night and lay eggs in his brain. Or up his dick. He had a mental vision of his balls crawling with worms. There was a smeared picture window that looked out on the parking lot, decorated with smashed bottles, shredded panties, and abandoned muffler pipes.

The telephone—its plastic body cracked—was on a nightstand next to a bolted-down clock radio that was blinking the wrong time. Junior checked the telephone book; there were no Clooties listed, no long-lost relatives, and nobody had thoughtfully entered his name in the book as a surprise welcome. There was nobody named Fuck either.

That night he walked down the road to a gas station and bought a map of the USA. He couldn't believe the distance between Maine and Montana. The country seemed to sag in the middle from the weight of all those miles. He had been crazy, he thought, to go ahead with a deal that would take him so far from home. Denver was three hours from Boston by air, Lobel had said; he could be home in five hours. Right. *I won't come in your mouth, baby. The check is in the mail. Vote for me; I've got a secret plan to end the war. This'll only hurt a minute.* This wasn't Denver. This was fucking Dry fucking hole River, Montana, and it wasn't three fucking hours from Boston. It was approximately ten fucking light-years from Boston on the wrong side of the fucking moon.

He didn't have to look up Kissy's number in his address book. Her phone rang two thousand miles away. He waited for the recorder to kick in, then he waited for her recorded voice to tell him to leave a message.

When the beep came, he could not remember, for a second, what he had been going to say.

"Kissy," he said, "I'm in Montana."

Then he lost control. Blindly, he groped for the stud on the cradle to break the connection.

The defense tried to cast doubts by inquiring of the state's expert witnesses if the victims' injuries were consistent with the possibility that the other vehicle, a 1984 Blazer driven by Kristin Mellors, had hit them first, and possibly even thrown them into the path of Houston's vehicle. The absence of damage the serious impact of a body would necessarily produce was eloquent, as convincing as the state's black-and-white photographs of the ominously dented T-bird.

James Houston, Jr., was represented by the senior trial lawyer from a well-regarded local firm, and also by a female junior partner, who questioned the witnesses. The junior partner sought confirmation from the expert witnesses that Diane Greenan and Ruth Prashker had been under the influence of intoxicants that included alcohol and cocaine and that Diane Greenan had, in fact, been in possession of some small quantity of cocaine.

Kissy waited outside the courtroom while the woman who had seen James Houston, Jr., drinking behind the wheel testified, and then she was called. After reciting the tale so many times Kissy was sure she could tell it in her sleep. This, she hoped, would be the last time. As she looked from the witness stand at the spectators, she met Sylvia Cronin's encouraging gaze.

She took the oath calmly. She took a drink of water and began her testimony. It was simple enough: she was driving down College Avenue at a certain hour on a certain evening last year. Then she could see Diane and Ruth again in her lights, in their *dance macabre,* and her voice shook. She dug her nails into her palms and told the court about the lights of the other vehicle glaring in her rearview and the sudden appearance of the T-bird beside her, the bodies of the two girls rising and falling and the way the Blazer shuddered when Ruth hit the tire. By then she was weeping and the judge asked her if she needed to compose herself.

In the women's room, she washed her face with cold water. Sylvia Cronin, who had followed her in, offered her aspirin. She took it gratefully.

"You're doing fine," Mrs. Cronin assured her, and gave her a hug too.

Kissy was surprised by how much it helped.

The prosecutor guided her through the rest of it—seeing James Houston behind the wheel, getting out of the Blazer and smelling the alcohol on him.

The woman lawyer opened aggressively. "You almost hit the two girls yourself, didn't you?"

As she answered with a simple yes, Kissy was intensely aware that the defense strategy of using a female lawyer to discredit the female victims also applied to her.

"Let's go back to your description of what the girls did."

Swiftly, the woman lawyer had her repeat what she had already said—in trying to avoid being hit by her, the victims had jumped or staggered directly into the path of the T-bird.

"Did you know either Diane Greenan or Ruth Prashker?"

Before she could answer, the prosecutor objected that it

was not relevant. The woman lawyer said it would be shown to be. The judge, who seemed bored, shrugged and allowed the question.

"I knew Diane Greenan to speak to," Kissy said. "We were in the same dorm our first year. We were acquaintances, not friends."

She didn't tell the court she had not recognized Diane in her headlights, or at the side of the road with her features broken into the primitive geometry of a Picasso profile, but it was what she thought about. She barely heard the next question.

"And did you know Ruth Prashker?"

"Pardon me?"

"Ruth Prashker, did you know her?"

"No."

"Do you visit her?"

"Yes."

"Why?"

For a moment, Kissy's mind was blank. Then she understood. The woman wanted her to admit feeling guilty.

"I went to see her first on impulse," she said. "I met her family. Her grandmother invited me to continue to visit her. It seemed like the right thing to do."

"What do you mean—the right thing to do?"

"It's just—if I were Ruth, I'd want to be . . . acknowledged. I'd want people to treat me as if I were there. If I hadn't been wearing a seat belt, I might have gone through the windshield, gotten hurt too. I've crossed that street, right there, many times. I might have been hit any of those times and be in Ruth's condition. It could happen to anyone."

"Ruth Prashker was legally drunk at the time of the accident. Have you ever crossed College Avenue at that point while legally drunk, Miss Mellors?"

"No."

"Have you ever driven while intoxicated?"

The prosecutor objected again, and this time, the judge sustained him.

"Have you ever passed illegally on the right?" the woman lawyer asked.

Again the prosecutor objected successfully.

Suddenly Kissy was exhausted. The tension in her gut, she realized, was cramp. There was a wetness between her legs that was going to stain her underwear and soak through her denim skirt if she did not do something about it soon. She wanted to be done, now and forever.

"You want me to tell you that I feel guilty because I nearly hit Ruth and Diane myself," she blurted. "The fact is, the T-bird came up beside me, where it didn't belong, and it was the T-bird that hit them."

The judge instructed the jury to disregard her answer and all the immediate preceding testimony and then he reprimanded the woman lawyer. Kissy met James Houston's eyes. He did not flinch but held her gaze for a long moment and then smiled, so faintly and so briefly it seemed an illusion.

"I'm in Montana." Junior's voice on the phone recorder choked and then he cut the connection.

"Good," Kissy muttered, "stay there."

The following day the case went to the jury, and after twenty minutes, James Houston, Jr., was found guilty on all counts. There was no surprise in his drawn features. Kissy wondered if the mystery was explained. It was not the Greenans and the Prashkers and Mrs. Cronin and Kissy Mellors that Houston had forced to endure his trial, but himself.

The judge revoked bail, ordered Houston to jail, and set a date for sentencing three weeks hence. The woman lawyer asked for bail until sentencing, pointing out that her client had observed the conditions of his pretrial bail for nearly a year since he had been charged, proving he was not a risk for flight. Not only had he submitted completely to the authority of the court and led an exemplary life while awaiting trial, but he was destitute and the court held his passport. Granting bail, the judge then invited the statements of the victims' families and character witnesses for Houston in reference to his sentencing.

Kissy doodled in her notebook as the courtroom emptied, glancing up only briefly when Mrs. Cronin touched her shoulder in passing. She ducked the TV crews outside the courthouse. There was nothing else to do, and she felt remarkably useless. It crossed her mind to go see Ruth, but she didn't really want to encounter the Prashkers there or even Sylvia Cronin. What would she be taking to Ruth? We got him, Ruth, we fixed the bastard.

On the computer at the *News,* she pulled up the biographical piece on Houston that the paper had run prior to the trial. The only address for him was Crossroads Farm, a nursery where he had worked every summer since becoming a student at Sowerwine.

It was indeed a farm, unsurprisingly located at a four corners. The farmhouse had been converted to a salesroom and storage facilities. With its low-pitched rooves and several small additions, it gave an outward appearance of shrunken and parsimonious spaces. Though the proportions of the structure had doubtless been dictated by the nineteenth-century necessity of heating with woodstoves, the impression was of diminished old age. None of the angles were true any longer, and the walls and rooves were gently bowed as if time itself had weight. She was reminded of the house her mother had rented for them after her father left. They all lived together in a little crooked house. Its floors had been warped into rough seas under threadbare carpet, stairs uneasy with creak and ominous give underfoot, windows cockeyed in cracked and bulging walls. The house had thrust up nails and splinters continually from floorboard, stairboard, and woodwork that snagged at feet, hands, and clothing like the grasping talons of something wicked and hungry.

The yard was a plantation of rows of potted plants and shrubs and saplings of myriad variety. The sign on the front door read closed. A black Labrador on a chain barked at her pathetically. It was an old dog, white in the muzzle, and rather fat. She spoke to it gently, and it began to wag its tail, all hostility vanished. Cautiously, she approached and it permitted her to scratch behind its ear and then it dug its doggy snout into her crotch. She laughed and pushed it away.

With her gadget bag on her shoulder, she wandered among the plants and flowers at the front and then, growing braver, went around to the back. The farmhouse was built on a rise; the front was level with the road. As the land sloped down toward the back, the foundation was gradually exposed and the cellar became the ground floor. She followed a wide, carefully graded and paved path around the house. There was a horse barn in noticeably better repair than the house, and a paddock with a couple of horses standing in it, dozing, tails whipping at flies.

There were several outbuildings and sheds and an herb garden and two large vegetable beds. Kissy could smell the tomatoes warm on the vine. And beer.

"We're closed," James Houston said from behind her.

∽ 13 ∽

She wheeled to face him. He was at the back of the farmhouse, where a green-painted door with a window in its top half stood open in the stone foundation, a screen door closed against insects. Below narrow windows in the stone wall, garden beds billowed with white chrysanthemums and wild white roses. A ten-speed bike hung on the wall, its wheels making pies of stone wedges. On a patch of lawn, a ratty old wicker rocker sheltered in the shade of a maple. Next to the rocker was a working case of bottled beer and a bottle of Jim Beam. Among dead soldiers littering the soft grass, a battered Panama hat was turtled on its crown. The late-afternoon light was gilding all colors and defining everything with east-lying shadow.

Sunglasses hid his eyes. He had taken off his tie and jacket and unbuttoned his shirt, but he still wore his suit trousers and dark socks and fine leather shoes, polished to a gleam. His hair was disordered and damp, his eyes bloodshot. Transparent red suffused his cheekbones. It was the first time she had ever seen any color in his face.

"What do you want?"

"I thought you might like some company."

"Like Ruth." Mockingly. "You're so kind." He backed up and his knees went loose. He sat down abruptly in the wicker rocker. Booze lubricating his joints.

He started to unlace his shoes. "Want a beer?"

She helped herself from the case. The first cool sip was golden, all the way down. She had thirsted for this, its cold and arrogant funk, without knowing it until it was in her mouth.

"Thank you," she said, "James."

He glanced up with a grimace. "Jimmy, please. James

Houston, Jr., is that no-good drunken bastard who ran down that poor girl and her friend." He finished taking off his shoes and socks. Wiggling his toes, he reached for an open beer. "Want some tomatoes? Good year for tomatoes. Got a ton of them. Liesel let me plant the gardens for therapy. Liesel's the owner. She's very kind too. She let me live here all summer. Me and Groucho, up there on the chain— did he lick your hand?—we're the night watchmen. The caretakers." He pushed himself out of the chair, plucked the Panama from the grass, jammed it on his head, and made for the gardens.

Beer in hand, Kissy followed him.

Among the vines, he pulled off his shirt and used the arms to tie it around his waist like an apron. He wore a sleeveless cotton undershirt. Apparently, it was his usual work shirt, for long hours in the sun every day had burned its outline on his skin. The Panama kept his face unburned. Where he was exposed—arms and the area of his neck and collarbone—the sun had tanned his hide, fried his skin repeatedly until it was a tough, smooth, seamless garment of what was essentially scar tissue. It had the warm dullness of sepia, only it was darker—and made the undamaged skin of his face look naked. He began to pick tomatoes into the impromptu apron. His skin was dewy not with heat or exertion but from the hard liquor sweating him.

She took a swallow of her own beer.

He held a tomato, rose red and very round, out to her. She polished it gently on her shirt before biting into it. It was sun-warm and rich and sweet. It squirted a little, and she wiped a dribble from her chin. He laughed.

As he moved among the vines, picking, filling the shirt, and glancing at her from time to time, she watched the light on his head and face and hands. Framed pictures she would never take. The shades made a depthless dark of his eyes, and the brim of the hat shadowed his face and drew the eye to his mouth, chin, and jawline. He had a manual laborer's muscle but lacked the heavy frame that made Junior solid as a wall. Though callused, his hands were nothing short of sculptured, a musician's, the long fingers tapered, nails short and so clean they spoke of a painstaking fastidiousness in the face of work that must have blackened them daily.

When the fruit threatened to overflow the shirt, he knotted

the arms together and ushered her, with a mock seignorial manner, back toward his booze dump on the lawn. "Guess I'll need this shirt one more time. I'd better find a bag." He picked up his beer on the way into the house.

Depositing her empty in the box, she took another and uncapped it. It had tasted very good in the heat. He returned with a brown bag from a supermarket and folded it ritually. She recognized what he was making as what, in some childish arts and crafts class, she had been taught to call a Spanish box. Into it he carefully transferred the tomatoes.

"There," he said, "kindness rewarded."

She thanked him.

He took off the straw hat and flung it aside. "What did you really come here for? Not for tomatoes. Do you want to take my picture for the paper? The felon contemplating his conviction?"

"I told you why. I thought you might like company."

Sitting cross-legged on the grass, he held the Jim Beam in both hands. He squinted up at her. "Oh. I forgot." He took a long swallow of the whiskey, propped it between his legs, and seized a beer to chase it. "Tell you what you can do for me." He grinned wolfishly. "Take your shirt off, show me your tits."

She sucked beer down the wrong pipe and coughed it back up.

He laughed with childish pleasure at having shocked her. "Don't get your knickers in a twist, baby. They convicted me of manslaughter, not rape."

Staring at him, she had to restrain the impulse to empty her beer over his head.

"Don't tell me you're offended? I thought you were an artist. Isn't it part of the code—no shame about the human body? You hung those pictures of your boyfriend—the goalie. What's the big deal? I showed you my tomatoes, you show me yours. Give the poor bastard something to remember when he's in the slam."

He had been drinking a while before she blundered into his sights. He felt entitled to be a prick. He did not, she reckoned, so much want to see her tits as to score points and drive her off so he could wallow in his misery. It would take a saint to be gracious under the circumstances,

and a saint he patently was not, nor had she come bearing
some redeeming message. Which might make it under-
standable but did not change the familiar feeling of being
the target of some guy trying to bully her with sexual aggression. The same curiosity and defiance that had involved her with Junior made her want to call Jimmy
Houston's bluff.

She scooched down and reached between his legs. He
flinched as she grabbed the Jim Beam. He laughed. The
whiskey was hot in her mouth and hot as she gulped it
down. She followed it with a cooling swallow of beer. Hot
and cold, it made her sweat as if steam were coming out of
her ears, her pores. Then calmly she yanked her shirt over
her head.

He burst out laughing, with the whiskey halfway to his
mouth. Flopping onto his back, he laughed again.

She shook out the shirt, turned it right side out, and
started to lift it over her head to pull it on again.

"No," he said hoarsely. Clutching the bottle, he struggled to his feet.

His gaze behind the shades remained fixed on her breasts.
He moved slowly around her, pausing to study her bare back
and then continuing to her other side. The sensation of sun-
warmed air on her nipples raised them. He reached out with
a shaking hand to touch her. Though she saw him reach and
his touch on her nipple was light, she could not help starting. He traced the color with his fingertip and then turned
his hand to cup the weight of the breast. He nudged her elbow away from her body and his fingertips caressed the hair
in her armpits. He sniffed at his fingers. At an angle to him,
she could see his eyes behind the dark lenses flutter briefly
closed, the better to smell. He took his hand away and
grasped hers, the one that held on to her T-shirt, and he
tugged the shirt free and dropped it to the grass. Stepping
away from her, he sank down into his cross-legged posture.

He stared up at her. "If you would be so kind, I'd like to
see the rest of you. In this light."

If he hadn't spoken of the light, she might have picked
up her shirt and left. Or perhaps not. She didn't know. The
whiskey felt like it was in her head, not so much delivered
there by her blood as breathed in, as if she were drinking
the smell of it from the open bottle. She was curious. It
was all so unexpected. Sitting down on the rocker, she

pulled off her boots and then stood again. She unbuckled her belt and drew it through the loops.

"Wait," he said. "Turn around."

She turned her back to him.

Without haste but also without coyness, she hooked her fingers over the waistband of her short skirt. She pushed it slowly down over her hips. She let it fall on its own to her ankles and then she stepped out of it. And waited.

"All right," he said. "Turn slowly."

His eyes were bright and his skin suffused with color, as if he had just had a transfusion. He put the bottle aside and held out his hands palms up.

Kneeling, she took his hands, and he pulled her down to the grass. For a long time, it was all tongue and mouth, as if they had reverted to that stage of babyhood in which everything went straight to the mouth to be tasted and identified. He thrust his tongue into her armpits and then went back to her nipples. He was hard against her and she unzipped his trousers and played with him, squeezing and stroking. Then she curled over his body and used her mouth until suddenly he moaned and pushed her head away.

His face was flushed and sweating and he was breathing in long shudders. He seized her by the shoulders and bore her down onto her back. The light flared over his shoulder into her eyes and she half closed them. Distracted, she was unprepared for the hard thrust of his penis. She cried out in pained surprise and, as the tip of his cock encountered her tampon, he jerked away from her, his face gone incandescently red.

"Sorry," she muttered, groping for the string, "you surprised me."

With the tampon in her grasp, she was at a loss what to do with it. Impulsively, she stuck it into the neck of the nearest empty beer bottle. He laughed from his belly in a prurient bellow and rolled over her leg again, in as great a hurry as before. He grasped her hips and drove himself deeply into her. She was not ready and it was painful. Hot and dry, her vagina yielded reluctantly to the weight and thrust of his penis. He lifted her hips and fucked her with a crude fury to which she could not respond. She was hardly there, except as an observer, and she remembered the first time, with Seth, when she had been too numbed and confused with drugs and alcohol to react to what was happening. She was startled from her distraction by the hot wetness on his face as he pressed his mouth over hers and drove his tongue between her teeth as he came.

He made no move to withdraw. She was in a kind of daze. The sun was on the tree line and the shadows lengthening across the lawn, the horses black stick figures in the paddock as if the sun were burning them up. After a long moment, he did withdraw and sat up. He still wore his sunglasses. Staring at the line of fire on the horizon, he wiped at the end of his nose and took a noisy swallow of the Jim Beam.

"I didn't think I could do it," he said. "I've had some problems—" he smiled ironically at her— "have I had some problems?" He glanced down at himself and then at her. They were both bloody. They looked as if they were wounded. Siamese twins formerly joined at the crotch, now torn apart. "That was a dirty fuck, you know? You must want to go inside and shower." He had not taken off his trousers, only opened them. He kicked them off and picked them up. "Grass stains and blood, the dry cleaner's going to think I've been out raping virgins."

So it would look, she thought. A figure from mythology or an aberrant tarot card. A man naked but for an undershirt, his inner thighs painted by his bloodied balls, his sagging cock red with blood, stands over a naked woman, her own thighs streaked bloody, on the grass. The woman androgynous of face, her shorn hair mostly white, but fully female of body. The man's hair also shorn close to the skull and his eyes hidden behind black circles of glass. Pale face and body but his arms red from the sun. What story does the picture tell, what does it represent? She could not think, could not work it out. The air on her labia felt strange, as if it were rusting her flesh. She did feel wounded, torn inside. Broken in. Her heart felt as if it were in her hands, pulsing frantically. She tucked her legs, curled up on herself. In a little while he crouched next to her and touched her with rough cloth. She opened her eyes; he was offering a robe. Passively she allowed him to help her up and bring her into the house.

The fullness of light outside made the house a cave. Blind with the contrast for a moment, she stood there just inside the threshold, waiting for sight to return and listening to the sound of the shower he had started for her. The high narrow windows, the screened door, cut swathes of gold light into the darkness but showed her little. The shapes illuminated were too bright and without context. This had been a cellar. It still smelled of damp stone and stored root vegetables, but there was also the musk of the leaves of aster in the air, and the honey sweetness of the milkweed flower.

He guided her toward the sound of rushing water, opening a door on an ordinary well-lighted tiled bathroom. The shower was a tiled stall like the ones at the pool, only rather wide. There were bars inside and out, as if it had been built for someone unsteady on her feet.

"Liesel has multiple sclerosis," he explained. "She has times when she has to use a chair, other times she gets around with one cane or two. She built this place for herself. Then her parents came to live with her and it was too small. The business takes up the rest of the house and it's unsuitable anyway, all corners and tight angles and narrow doors and passages. They have a ranch house half a mile from here, everything on one floor, all fitted up for her, easy on the old folks too." It was as if he were an agent, showing her the house, for rent or sale. Information, ordinary words, fell out of his mouth as if nothing had happened.

Amid the conspicuously utilitarian fixtures, the commodious shower seemed sybaritic. She stood under the water and watched it spatter translucently pink upon the white tiles. Stepping in with her, he soaped a washrag and began to wash her back, disconcertingly domestic. Junior used to wash her back. For the first time, she realized it was dirty from the lawn; torn blades of grass were in the sluice of water down her legs.

"Your back is beautiful. I never saw a woman's back with such clearly defined muscle." He lifted the rag from her skin. Taking her by the shoulders, he turned her around to face him. He soaped the washrag again and wiped it over her breasts and down her belly and between her legs.

She winced.

"That was bad for you out there, was it?" The harsh satisfaction in his voice was crosshatched with a darker shame. He had given her what she deserved and ought to have expected from someone like him.

She backed away from him against the tiled wall and

they kept a wary eye on each other while he washed himself. He was uneasy with her silence. Rather than give him whatever response it was he sought, she chose to give him none. She was still too disoriented at what she had permitted. He finished and handed her the soap and rag as he stepped out and drew the curtain behind him. After a moment she helped herself to shampoo, and washed her hair and then stood there, until the hot water ran cold.

The lights were on against the twilight when she emerged from the bathroom. The apartment Liesel had built for herself was a single large room, with only the bathroom walled off. The kitchen, at one side, was all built in like a ship's galley and low to accommodate a wheelchair. On one counter a plastic milk carton with the top sliced off served as a vase for pink asters, blue chicory, and dusty-rose-colored milkweed in their golden hoods. Desk and chair, bookcase, couch and TV, bed and dresser, and bench and free weights made islands of necessity on a rugless linoleum of the most expensive kind, easy to clean, easy for rolling wheels. The furnishings of mission oak, even the utilitarian chrome-and-leather bench, the iron weights, added to the sense of monkishness. The absence of personal clutter, the boxes packed with books, an open suitcase on the bed, made it clear that the current resident had been prepared not to pass go but to go at once to jail.

While she had run out his hot water in the shower, he had donned a fresh pair of shorts, folded his shirt and suit on top of the laundry bag, and brought in her clothing from the outside. It was neatly folded on the bared mattress, her boots aligned on the floor next to the bed. He had also fetched in the beer and whiskey. Wordlessly, he offered them. She shook her head, thinking of having to drive home.

Momentarily at a loss, he scratched an eyebrow and then gestured toward the out-of-doors. "You need that—?"

"Plug?" she asked, with deliberate crudity. "No. I need my gear bag."

The red stained his cheekbones as he went out. After what he'd done to her, his embarrassment at her bleeding only made her impatient. She wanted to scream at him it was just blood, the same stuff that he had in his own veins, only his was half alcohol. It washed off, whether it came

from a cut finger or a cunt. Whatever his faults, Junior at
least had never shown even a smidgen of male prudery
over menstrual blood. It was all she could do to restrain
herself from snarling that males had their share of hair and
they sweated, bled, leaked, squirted, dribbled, and shot off
at least as many bodily fluids as females did.

In the bag she carried a plastic box of spares. She could
feel fluid beginning to trickle onto the back of his robe.
She didn't care if she stained it. The resentment she could
hardly contain was multiplied by her awareness that he
was sneaking looks at her. Picking up her shirt, she shrugged
the robe off her shoulders to her waist and pulled it on,
over her head. Then she stood and let the robe fall away
from her. She lifted her left leg, rested her foot on the
frame of the bed. Taking a fresh tampon, she tried to insert
it, but it hurt too much. She flung it to the floor. She legged
into her skirt and reached for her boots.

"Are you leaving?" he asked. The words were a panicky
rasp. His Adam's apple worked in his throat. "I hurt you. It
hurt me, you know, the tampon. I felt so stupid and I was
afraid I was going to go soft and it made me angry. I
wanted to hurt you back. You didn't want me, you were
just letting me. I couldn't stop myself wanting it. I felt like
Groucho, the way he goes fuck-crazy around a bitch in
heat, and you knew it. You shouldn't have come out here. I
didn't ask you—" He stopped to reach for the bottle of
whiskey. "I'm sorry," he said, and took a swallow and
licked his lips. "I'm sorry I hurt you. Don't leave yet,
please." He couldn't look at her. As his gaze dropped, he
sank with it, slowly, to his haunches, and then he seemed
to collapse like a broken chair into a sitting position on the
floor. "Don't go yet. I'd like some company." His voice
shook. "I don't want to be alone. I won't hurt you again. I
promise I won't." He was shaking all over.

From the edge of the bed, she hesitated. Her anger faltered. If this were television or the movies, she would slap
his face and tell him to quit pitying himself. An easy dramatic default, she had always thought, simplistic and cruel
as well. She saw him again through the lens of There-but-
for-the-grace.

"Maybe you should eat something," she ventured.

His fingers tightened on the neck of the bottle, and he

snorted something like a laugh. "I just want to drink, okay? You can drink with me if you want."

"I don't want to get drunk."

"That's okay. I won't pass out on you or anything. I've got it down to a science, I can stay where I am as long as I want. All night. Days. Please." He covered his eyes with one shaking hand. "You want me to beg, I will. I haven't got anything left."

She couldn't think what she could do nor was she sure she wanted to do anything at all. While she dithered, she surveyed the room as if it would answer her. Near the foot of the bed, there was a box of books. The titles arrested her and she stooped to take a closer look. Nonfiction or fiction, hardcover or paperback, they were all in some way concerned with imprisonment.

His voice startled her. "I've known since I felt the impact I was going to jail."

She looked up, but he was staring into the neck of the bottle.

"I was raised to believe in books. I bet I could write a thesis, hell, four or five theses, on what I know about prisons." He raised his eyes. "You know what I know?"

She shook her head.

He grinned mirthlessly. "All the fucking books I read won't help me one fucking bit." He tipped his head in the direction of the bench and weights. "I couldn't bring myself to work out in a public gym. I've actually taken night courses in martial arts and self-defense. It's fucking pathetic, isn't it?"

There was no answer she could give that would help him. He wasn't going to ask questions that would yield helpful answers. He didn't want help. His embrace of his suffering was more conscious than she thought she could have managed in the same fix.

"You're staying here a while yet," she said, turning away from him to close the open suitcase and move it off the bed. "Come on, you ought to make up this bed again." She heard him behind her groping his way to his feet.

"Sheets," he muttered.

Together they made up the bed. The spare sheets were ticking striped in royal blue on cream. In the whole place there were no floral patterns, only discreet, well-disciplined geometrics—two plastered walls painted in cream, two papered in pale yellow pinstripes. Everything was a background, she thought, for flowers and plants. Liesel had planned a room green with plants, brilliant with cultivated flowers, but the solitary crude vase of ditch-dwelling wildflowers was all there was.

He moved rustily. "I've been trying to get used to being alone. I thought I was doing okay." She handed him a pillow slip and he stared at it and then reached for the pillow. "I was glad to be alone at the start. I mean, I was glad to break up with Erin. I couldn't stand being around anyone else."

Allowing him to do his half of the work, she waited for him to catch up with her. In the state he was in, it would be easy for him to let anyone who was willing to do everything for him. The more he did for himself, the less empty time he would face.

He stuffed the pillow into the slip and shook it to settle it. "I don't know what's worse, people like Erin and my parents, who look right through me because they can't stand looking me in the eye, or people like you and Liesel, who insist on looking at me and speaking to me and being kind to me, as if I were still a human being to you."

"You're not dead," she said. "You killed somebody and you're in deep shit. You could be dead if you wanted but you're not, so you must have decided you'd rather be alive and in deep shit."

He nodded. "You're a lot like Liesel. She quotes that business about a death sentence concentrating the mind wonderfully. With her, it's the MS. It may not shorten her life span much but there are potholes everywhere for her. It's the same for me—ten years, not a death sentence, but one big fucking pothole. I'm scared—" He lunged for the bottle. "I've been terrified since those two girls jumped into my headlights."

"Me too," Kissy said, and he spun around to stare at her.

The crotch of her panties was damp, she realized. And she felt a trickle. She looked down and a thread of blood showed itself above her knee, inside.

Deep in his throat, he made a noise of distress and then hurried to the bathroom. He returned with a dry terry cloth washrag folded into a rectangular approximation of a sanitary napkin. She took it and pulled up her skirt to insert it into her panties. He turned away, face burning red again.

* * *

The cool cleanliness of the bed linen was somehow comforting as she crawled tiredly onto the newmade bed. A reminder of childhood. Her weariness was as much depression as any degree of physical fatigue but knowing didn't change it.

He took a tentative seat at the edge of the bed. "Are you going to be all right?"

In answer, she smiled faintly and touched his hand on the mattress. His fingers curled eagerly, desperately, around hers.

"I deserve what's happened and whatever's going to happen and I can't duck it," he said. "Only I don't know how to do any of this. I'm faking it."

"You've been drinking," she pointed out, doubting even as she said it he was able to absorb it. "I bet you haven't eaten or slept properly for ages. I think it might be a good idea to put something into your body besides booze and to get some rest. Give your nervous system a break."

"A well-nourished, well-rested, sober felon," he said. "Liesel says the same thing. Clean inside your ears and eat your bran for breakfast."

"Suit yourself." She untangled her hand from his. "You'll get what suits you."

"You read that on a tea bag?"

She sat up and swung her legs over the side of the bed. He put the bottle down hastily and grabbed her wrist and she shook it off.

"Don't go," he said. "I don't mean to be such a shit. Being a jerk has gotten to be a reflex. Please. Let me hold you for a while. Just hold you. That's what I need worse than anything."

His hand moved to her waist as he spoke. She closed her eyes and let him draw her close. He did exactly what he had said, just holding her. The smell of the booze came off him the way it had the night of the accident. It was sweating him, tarnishing the good clean soap scent from his shower.

She wanted to take pictures of him. She wanted the frame to imprison him, to box the tension in him, as he fought to contain the contradictions of his fate. The energies of guilt and remorse, of terror, and of self-destruction at war with the instinct to survive, were like a nuclear pile inside the man. She wanted to contain it by light and shadow into images that would generate an emotional polarity to the pictures of Ruth. First, though, she would have to gain his permission.

Her legs were tangled with his. She tightened her arms around him. Making a machine to hold him, she thought. He shuddered in her arms and clung to her as tightly as she held on to him.

His science failed him. Voice slurred, he begged her to come back tomorrow if she would not stay the night. Again she hesitated, then promised she would.

But in the Blazer on the way home, she counted the cost of the evening spent with him. Her work at home not done. More work not done if she saw him again. She had to balance it against the pursuit of something she might not be good enough to accomplish.

The thick rough texture of the terry cloth between her legs reminded her she had done nothing to protect herself. Odds at the end of her period, she was not fertile. But a risk was a risk, however small. She had taken a greater chance with Junior and not gotten pregnant. Perhaps the gonorrhea had indeed made her sterile. If she kept on taking chances, of course, sooner or later she would have an answer. She didn't care, she told herself. She would get rid of it, in the old ugly phrase fraught with sin and judgment. Or she wouldn't. She didn't know. She was not herself. Roughly she wiped at the sudden infuriating overflow from her eyes. Shit. Her eyes were going to look like hell tomorrow.

The message light was on when she let herself in. Punching the play button, she sat down to take off her boots.

Mrs. Cronin's voice spoke: "Kissy, dear, I'd like to have copies of your photographs of Ruth to submit to the court as part of the family's statement regarding sentencing. If you could call me at your convenience please—"

She flung her boot across the room. It was not a request she could refuse and still continue to ask for access to Ruth. From the beginning it had been implicit the project would not be completed until Ruth's inevitable death. She knew what she had done in those photographs. Unless the judge was heartless, they would have an impact. Sylvia Cronin knew it too or she would not have asked for them.

Blinking away yet more hot tears, Kissy dropped to her mattress in exhaustion. *Matthew Mark Luke and John, bless the bed that I lie on.* Then there was something about *Four angels, four angels 'round my bed.* She couldn't summon up the rest of it. Images of Ruth crowded out everything else.

∞ 14 ∞

That time of the month, honey," the trainer called out to Junior, heralding the entrance of his new probation officer.

Catcalls racketed the length of the locker room.

Responsibility for Junior's probation had been transferred from Peltry to Denver and thence to Dry River. His new probation officer, Mr. Horace, had won the office lottery, for in exchange for randomly administering drug tests to Junior and dispatching the results back to Peltry, he acquired access not only to Junior's personal quarters at the Devil's Backbone Motel but to the Dinosaurs' locker room, training facilities, and all the Dinosaurs' games. He was practically staff, for the duration, and fortunately he was a fan, to the extent he enjoyed the local cachet he derived from his intimacy with the team.

Mr. Horace waggled a urine test kit at Junior and they shuffled off together to the toilet. With the probation officer looking on and offering unsolicited predictions on the upcoming season, Junior obliged. The doctor's swabbing his dick for the clap had been embarrassing—painful too—but no worse than a prostate exam. This was demeaning and made him unnecessarily anxious too. He hated the feeling of being at risk, under some anonymous but overwhelmingly powerful thumb. At least on the flagpole, the view had been interesting. He felt as if he had turned some corner into a grimmer and grayer world. He missed his old teammates, and not just for the joy of playing with known factors. They would have reacted with the same jeers to his being handed a bottle to piss in, but they would, to a man, also have volunteered to slip him a clean sample if need be and they could manage one. Deker and Moosejaw might have, if it had crossed either of their minds, but Deker had culture lag and it was news to Moosejaw that anybody considered cannabis, let alone amphetamines, to be drugs.

"Get out of here," Moosejaw said. "They can't put you in jail for a few molecules of bumper or thumper in your pee. I mean, you could pick up that much bumper riding in an elevator with a bunch of Rastafarians."

"Lotta Rastafarians in Moosejaw?" asked Junior.

Moosejaw shot him a look of disgust. "What would Rastafarians be doing in Moosejaw? I was in an elevator once in Toronto, some hotel, a band got on after me, eight guys, dreads and gold teeth and eyes so red I thought I was in a vampire movie. I was stoned by the time we got to the lobby, I tell you, just smelling those guys."

"So from now on, I better take the stairs," Junior said.

It went right by Moosejaw. "Eh?"

The scrimmage reversed, the puck zigzagging toward him, herded by this stick or that. Deker sliding around to defense him. Moosejaw slammed into Deker as the pill suddenly exploded off the forward's stick. Junior was there, waiting for it, meeting it this time with the edge of his stick, reflecting it off to Deker, who drove it across center ice. Junior watched the action move toward DeLekkerbek. A career minor leaguer of thirty-three, Lek was a gently balding guy with the hangdog look of a high school math teacher who could not seem to avoid zipping his shirttail into his fly. He was at best pedestrian and at worse, according to rumor, too often hung over. He seemed vaguely embarrassed around Junior, leaving him uncertain as to whether Lek found his own or Junior's performance, or even person, defective. Lek's defense intercepted the pass and reversed it toward Junior.

Junior had never felt more focused. He could do this job face first, on his ass, on his knees, on one side or the other, on his belly, his back, with his forehead—standing on his head if need be. Facing the puck with the devotion of Moslem to Mecca, disporting himself in the Kama Sutra of Goalie, attending the elusive Black Spot, the Ding Dong, the period at the end of the very hockey sentence, Junior scuttled in his crabbed stance in front of the net.

The club was shaking out, the way they do, as it became clear who was cutting it and who was not.

Junior filled long days with hard work, honing his body and his skills, determined to be ready for the first opportunity to bail. There were moments of exhilaration even in Dry River. But it was exile he felt most of the time, an exile he had chosen in general if not in its particulars. There was a Gideon Bible in the nightstand of his room, and he looked into it occasionally, as many travelers do, for no reason other than that it was there. He recalled the passage about the rivers of Babylon and amended it to suit himself: *By the Dry River in Montana, there we sat down, yeah, we wept, when we remembered.* The Book of Junior, verse one, chapter one. He did not allow himself to specify what he remembered, beyond another country, another river.

It was not his idea later that he needed a beer. He only went with Lek and Moosejaw and Deker to Rockie's, a favorite club hangout, to be one of the guys. Rockie's differed from Bird's in nearly every way. It was dark to the point of being furtive, and shoehorned into a narrow structure that made it cramped. Everything in it was deliberately rough-hewn to the point of splintery, except for an antique bar, its mahogany worn smooth as a woman's inner thigh. Over the bar hung a bad nineteenth-century painting of a plump blushing female nude. The bartender referred to her as "nekkid" in a tone that made it clear she was somebody's idea of a joke. The music of choice on the jukebox—the only music, in fact—was country, which seemed to be nine-tenths depressing laments about getting wasted or losing women or dead dogs or combinations of the three possibilities. Otherwise, like Bird's, Rockie's offered two TV screens angled to be visible from anywhere in the room, and was unmistakably a place where men drank and watched sports broadcasts. Early as it was, some girls were there already, some by prearrangement meeting returning players they had dated the previous season, some scouting the new talent.

After he heard Lek order a Coke, Junior made a quick decision and ordered the same. He did not want it getting back to management that he was out drinking when Lek was not. He could stick to having a beer or two discreetly in his room. They would still be selling beer in bars when he had secured a place with the club. Technically it was a probation violation just to be in a bar, let alone drinking, but of course, no judge really expected anyone to live like a monk and never socialize, never mind going cold turkey teetotal. He understood the judge wanted him not to get wasted and fuck up again in public for at least six months. To prove he had learned something. The real punishment was no license. Probation was a bunch of bullshit rules that allowed the cops to kick his ass if he looked like he needed it.

He chewed the ice out of his Coke and opened his ears and eyes as wide as they would go. The guys were all scavengers, hyenas out for the pickings the lions had left. Fearful they were going to be trapped in the minors, each of them was driven by self-doubt and insecurity. Nearly to a man they considered thrilling the chance to play professionally at all, never mind the possibility of Big-Time Ice under one's blades, but no one wanted to play long for a team Junior had discovered the locals called the 'Sores. As he listened, the grapevine thrummed with indiscretion as the returning players caught up on the state of injuries, who was on the ropes and who looking better than ever, agents fired and hired, and who had patched up the marriage or busted up, how they were handling it. All stuff it could be useful to know.

"Seen the Rich Girl?" one of the other guys, Kiamos, asked Lek, who shook his head no and discovered something riveting in his Coke. Kiamos shrugged and moved along. Lek's reaction interested Junior with its implications that he didn't care to be the expert on the Rich Girl's whereabouts, and then there was the tingle of the phrase. *The Rich Girl*.

"Who's the Rich Girl?" Junior asked in an offhanded way—just poking experimentally at Lek.

Lek cleared his throat. "You'll know her when you see her." Then Lek suddenly had to tell a joke to somebody at another table.

Deker and Moosejaw had already abandoned Junior and were flirting with some girls. Kissy had always said it derisively as one word, Junior recalled: somegirls. She had always curled her lip at the whole idea of being one of the guys. He had tried to explain how it was numero uno, necessary, and numero two-o, fun, and she had rolled her tongue in her mouth to distort her cheek and moved her curled hand to and fro in front of her mouth in a simulation of cocksucking, which had gotten him laughing too hard to continue serious discussion.

Joining the table-hopping, he worked his way to Kiamos. "Tell me about the Rich Girl. Why is Lek so spooked?"

Kiamos grinned and confided, "She's quite the filly, as the shitkickers around here like to say. Must go six five—you never saw pussy that high off the floor outside of a circus. Monette Daniels. Her old man thought Monette was the feminine form of Money. He owns half the known universe or some such shit. She's actually from Denver, but her best buddy is a local filly and the two of them like to cruise the club a few times a season. Everybody called her Mony, as in Moanie. Maybe she does. I never got that close. Yet. Or else they call her the Rich Girl, just in case anybody forgets. Mony broke Lek's heart," Kiamos said, and laughed. "Meaning she led him around by his tongue for four, five months before she let him get his dick wet once and then she dumped him. She's fun. Kind of girl who'd dance naked in a fountain any night. Her buddy now, Diane, she ain't got the Rich Girl's trust fund or the looks either, but she can suck the black off a puck." Kiamos licked his lips and drained his long neck.

Junior shuddered. Diane. The Rich Girl's friend's name was Diane. Why did it have to be such a common name? He tipped a salute of thanks and looked around for his friends. Deker was gone, and Moosejaw was leaving with some girl. Lek caught his eye from across the room and indicated the door. Lek not only had a rusted-out wreck of a pickup truck, which represented a ride back to the motel, but a license to operate it. It seemed the best course to accept his generosity.

"Where were you?" Sitting outside in the dark, which was alive with summer, too brief and rich to ignore, surely, without committing a sin of ingratitude, Jimmy was petulantly aglow. "I've been waiting for you."

After a long tiring day, she had to struggle not to tell him to go fuck himself. "I had to work late. It happens."

He followed her into the house. "I couldn't stop thinking about last night. All day."

She took a beer out of the refrigerator. He had managed to distract himself from last night long enough to restock his supply of booze. He came up behind her and put his arm around her. His hands groped under her shirt. She closed her eyes and rested her forehead against the cold enamel face of the refrigerator. He nuzzled her ear. His breath was hot with booze. When he rubbed her crotch through the cloth of her Levi's, she rocked into it. He bent his knees into hers, forcing her to the floor as he pulled her Levi's down and undid his own. She was still bleeding a little, but she seemed to have overcome, again, his fastidiousness. Supporting herself on her hands, she let him take her on her knees. He spoke to her obscenely and she let it be part of what was happening.

When she had taken care of herself and came out of the bathroom again, he was still on the floor, the top buttons of his Levi's still undone and his Jim Beam at hand.

"I haven't eaten all day," she said. "Have you got any food in this place?"

He shrugged.

She poked through the cupboards and the refrigerator again. Though he had been expecting to go to jail the previous day, the place was stocked with staples. No doubt he had expected Liesel to take care of it, along with the laundry. Probably Liesel had done the stocking. Probably had to spoon-feed him too. The apparent willingness of the woman to mother him made her mildly curious. There was no sign or signal of a sexual relationship. Perhaps it was a chance for Liesel, in her dependency, to do for someone else.

She found a loaf of bread, then a sheaf of bacon. She sent him out to pick a few tomatoes and some lettuce. He went out and came back wordlessly and stood watching her layer the rashers of bacon between paper towels in a Pyrex dish. She shoved it into the microwave oven.

"I didn't know you could cook bacon that way," he said.

She picked up the tomatoes and washed them and sliced them paper-thin. He seemed to be fascinated. Booze could make a lot of things interesting that weren't. By the time the bacon was crisped, she had bread toasted. She built a couple of sandwiches. He was still studying the construction of his admiringly when she finished hers. She cut his sandwich in two and ate half of it. At that point, he decided to eat the other half.

"Want another one?"

Mouth full, he nodded.

She shuffled it together for him. While he ate, she stacked the dishes into the dishwasher and finished her beer. On top of a restless night and the day she had put in, the combination of beer, food, and sex made her sleepy. She kicked off her boots at the edge of the bed. Next to it, he had opened one of the boxes of books. The titles in this one were all medical reference and nursing texts.

He spoke at her shoulder. "I took some practical nursing courses."

She hadn't been aware of his crossing the room as sleepiness weighed down upon her like a sudden increase in gravity.

Fondling his whiskey bottle, he took a seat on the edge of the bed. "I was worried that you wouldn't come back."

She would have to tell him about the pictures of Ruth and Mrs. Cronin's request for copies. But not tonight. He had gotten too far into the booze. And as much as she wanted to photograph him, that too would have to wait for the intersection of opportunity and sobriety.

The bottle sloshed softly as he put it down on the floor. Then his sneakers thumped softly. She felt him stretching out next to her. He wrapped himself around her. "Stay the night," he murmured. "Stay with me. I'll be good to you."

Trying to duck the near-nightly partying that Deker and Moosejaw wanted to do, Junior resorted to the movies to fill up his evenings. There was only the one theater, the Dry River Cineplex, and the first night Junior found his way, Lek was buying a ticket ahead of him. The third or fourth time they ran into each other in the ticket line, Lek admitted he was ducking the partying too. It only seemed sensible to go to the movies together. It made them friends of a sort. It was as if they had some miserable betrayal in their past they had decided to put behind them but was still like a knot between them.

After they had seen everything on the bill at the movie show, they went halfsies on a secondhand videotape player, rented a mutually agreed-upon movie, and tossed a coin to determine whose room. Chance made it Lek's. Feeling like a guest, Junior brought along a six. Lek paled at the sight of it. And Junior found himself the recipient of a abrupt confession: Lek had decided he was an alcoholic and was going to AA meetings several days a week, sometimes at noon, sometimes early in the evening before the movies. He told Junior he had put together four months of sobriety, the longest he had gone without alcohol since he was eleven.

"Go ahead and have a brew yourself," Lek offered, but he was sweating so hard when he said it, Junior had to conclude it was just heroically good manners.

And then he wondered if it made Lek worse to know Junior could take it or leave it, when he couldn't.

Once the secret was out, though, Lek could relax with him. It turned out AA was the source of the aphorisms that peppered Lek's conversation and were stickered over the bumper and dash of his truck. That discovery was like the lightbulb going on in the thought balloon of cartoon characters—all those one day at a time bumper stickers were explained. Junior felt a little stupid not to have put it together earlier. Not only had he had no idea there were so many reformed drunks out there, he felt a momentary chill of paranoia, discovering the secret society of AA in the midst of the unknowing larger world.

Every week or two he and Lek dropped in at Rockie's for a few hours with the other guys. It was stressful for Lek, but he insisted the world was full of booze and he had to deal with it. Lek said it was important in staying sober not to isolate. With his start secured, Junior allowed himself a beer or three.

They were all sitting around Rockie's soaking it up— except for Lek, sticking to the Co'Cola—on Deker's birthday, and somebody whistled through his teeth and started to applaud, triggering a general uproar, and there was the Rich Girl, in the doorway, holding a birthday cake afire with candles. Junior had no doubt it was her. As Kiamos had said, she had serious height for a woman. Though the proportions were right, her long bones were too well fleshed for her to be a model. Not fat. More like, she was sleek. She was not beautiful by any stretch. Her skin was coarse, her face a little bony and strong, a shade masculine, and her nose was crooked in two places. But she had the model's trick of moving as if she thought she was beautiful, with an athlete's confidence. Junior guessed she had a year or three on him, might even be bumping up on thirty.

At her side was another woman, presumably the Rich

Girl's friend, Diane. This Diane was a blonde, as Diane Greenan had been, and was about the same size and build, but otherwise there was no resemblance. This-Diane had hair enough for two models on her head and wore so much makeup that there was no telling what her face really looked like, which suggested maybe she didn't want anybody to know. This-Diane dressed to show off her slim body, but it was noticeably slack, except for her tits. It was like she was only partially inflated, and for some reason the air had all gone to right there. The guys received her with a warm and genuine enthusiasm that Junior recognized: once in a while a slut was so well liked she got to be almost a mascot.

"Where's the birthday boy?" the Rich Girl cried.

They manhandled Deker to her presence. He turned on his patented thigh-dampening smile. To his surprise, she rolled her eyes.

"Oh Jesus," she said, "he's just a bay-bee!"

Everybody broke up laughing and hooting, and Deker actually blushed. She came up close and kissed him sweetly on the lips, like they were brother and sister, and he stuttered something in Russian. Depositing the cake in his hands, she turned away, surveying the bar for someone. Her casually searching gaze found Lek, standing at the bar next to Junior.

She waggled her fingers and sailed their way. "I'm Mony," she introduced herself, with a little challenge in her tone. Junior guessed whatever amusement value her name had ever had for her had long since been exhausted. Lek cleared his throat and introduced Junior. The way the Rich Girl and Lek were looking at each other, Junior knew he was just in the way. He bailed.

He caught a glimpse of the two of them later, sitting at a table in the corner, hands on the table, threaded together. Not staring into each other's eyes or anything, but Lek looked happy and so did she. Junior felt a little tight in the throat, glad for them and jealous of Lek, and then the misery hit him, the loneliness, and he was furious and depressed all at the same time. What he needed was another woman—anyone would do to break the spell. He looked around at the other women in the place and they were all fatally flawed; they were not Kissy. It was ridiculous. He was disgusted with himself and his moping.

Junior hitched a ride back to the motel with Moose-jaw, who had enough beer in him not to notice the funk he was in.

The Rich Girl didn't hang around.

She spent the night with Lek in the room next to Junior's. They made it three times by Junior's count—she not only moaned, she talked a lot too. It reminded him that was something else he used to do with Kissy. As he finished his breakfast, they came into the motel restaurant, looking as if they had made a night of it. He felt as if he had too. They sat down with him, and he gave Lek the sports page of the local paper and exchanged a smile of connubial warmth with the Rich Girl.

When Lek was at the buffet, she suddenly confided in Junior. "He's not really an alcoholic, you know. It's just the magic formula that's going to make everything work for him again."

Junior was too surprised to know what to say. He had accepted that if Lek said he was an alcoholic, then he was. But she was sleeping with the guy. Presumably she knew the guy a whole lot better than Junior did. And maybe better than he knew himself. In the time he had lived with Kissy, Junior had often had the same sensation about her. It was spooky sometimes. He rarely felt anything like confidence in his sense of Kissy except in the sack, which he did not want to dwell on, considering the situation. Lek came back and the Rich Girl didn't say anything else about it and neither did Junior. Then she was gone again. Lek seemed okay about it. He didn't even seem to mind that outside of team scrimmages and practice, he was almost never in net.

Out more than ever, Junior spread dangerous space between him and the goal. He came spinning out to swat the puck into reverse, to shove oncoming opponents into the boards, the back of the net, other players. He made astonishing saves—blind, out of position, miraculous stops, plucking the puck from the air, the ice, seemingly out of his own ass. This, while the other 'Sores did a heroic job of being in the wrong place at the wrong time doing the wrong thing. Except for Deker. Most nights Junior was protecting the goal on his own while the guys who were supposed to defense him fumbled for position and sometimes, it seemed, to stay on their fucking skates and hold a stick at the same time. He watched lines collapse and tangle on themselves, defensemen provoke ruinous penalties, and Deker craning constantly at peril of his cervical vertebrae, to find someone to take a pass, to set up a shot. Moosejaw was playing as badly as the rest, though he had the excuse of a pulled groin muscle. They lost more than they won, they tied as often as they won, and when the 'Sores actually pulled one off, the wins were slapstick half-assed affairs, comedies of errors on ice.

Nobody was happy with the situation, but for Junior, who had never had a losing season, the frustration was fierce. At the same time he was wracked with fevers and chills and burning urination, possibly because he was playing in equipment that never had a chance to dry out between games. The road trips became hallucinatory. It seemed to him he was always waking up, his eyes and nose running, with a constant ache in his groin and the small of his back, with no idea where the fuck he was. He was not alone in his miseries. Injuries, illnesses, consumption of thumper, and frustration of every kind were rocketing among his teammates.

When in quick succession three women claimed to be pregnant by Deker, Junior was struck with the realization that he had never known the Russian to beg, buy, or borrow so much as a single condom. Unlike everyone else. There was Wynona from Denver, Terrianne from Dry River, and Lisa from Gormly, Nevada, where the Russian kid recalled seven or eight minutes of passion in a bus stop rest room with a woman he had met while buying gum at the newsstand. Deker had to be restrained from immediately dividing what money he had three ways and sending it to the women. As it was, hiring a lawyer to at least get some blood tests done was enough to make the rent he shared with a couple of other guys unaffordable and send him back into residence at the Devil's Backbone Motel. The thought of becoming a father thrilled him.

"I am being the father of mens," he predicted. "I am only making boy sperms."

Like the porn videos on the motel cables and the steady diet of road food that alternately constipated him or gave him diarrhea, Junior found the sexual opportunities on the road as limited in their way as the ones in Dry River—and

nearly as flavorless. Or maybe it was only him, feeling like
the boy in the bubble, living inside a skin of plastic that
dulled the world around him but kept him safe from—he
didn't know what. He had taken enough psych at Sowerwine to suspect he was punishing himself, even as he in-
dulged. Getting head from some girl—in an automobile or
the cloakroom of a bar, once in the back of the bus—ought
to be of the same order of significance as having a beer or
three, the very same few beers that made doing it an attractive option. It was only marginally different from jack-
ing off. But it didn't make any kind of dent in the appetite
that being with Kissy had created in him for something
more. And worse, it felt as if he had lost ground somehow.

At last they were headed home for a pre-Christmas
home stand and then the Christmas break, a stingy four
days, but Christmas nonetheless. An hour out of Dry River,
they were all suddenly giddy. First sight of it, though, and
every one of them experienced a plunge in their emotion,
the bottom dropping out of their guts, as if the bus were
falling off a cliff. In their absence, Dry River had grown
yet more bleary. Every miserable stick and cement block
of it pulsed and throbbed and wailed like a mad prophet in
the wilderness. The wind that howled in their ears was an
echo of their own despair.

The gale had blown the motel's sign down, ripped shin-
gles from its roof, and broken some windows. The long
low beige stucco wall of the building seemed to be covered
with blisters, reminding Junior of a man he had accidentally pissed on. The man had been sheltering in some
bushes outside a bus stop in Nebraska where the toilet facilities had all been stopped up. Whether the fellow was
homeless, mentally ill, or a wino—all three, likely—the
poor bastard wore only rags that left his unclean and dis-
eased skin exposed to the elements. The only shower he
had seen in some time was Junior's golden one. Junior
had given him a stale sandwich and a can of soda from
the cooler on the bus, and the man had asked him for
money. When he refused, the man had cursed him for a
cheap fuck. The bum had changed his tune as Junior
walked away, calling after him pathetically, offering him a
blow job.

The memory caused him to momentarily count his

blessings. But the sight of the motel was like coming over a rise and having the road drop out from under him. He had been looking forward to getting home, and now he was there and it wasn't much. It wasn't just the grunginess of the place but the fact that the room was empty. There was no one waiting for him. Never had been. Not once.

The fossil clerk had very kindly delivered his mail, a cardboard boxful tucked just inside the door. What wasn't hometown newspapers with the sports pages dominated by adulation of his rotten little brother—busy making the Spectres contenders for another conference title and maybe another run at a national championship—was junk. He shifted through the Wal-Mart and Kmart flyers addressed to the ever-popular Occupant. He should change his name, become Occupant Clootie. There was no note, no letter, no postcard, not even a goddamn Christmas card, from Kissy.

He culled the newspapers, piled them on the table and opened the scrapbook. Slowly he paged through the papers, looking for her credit line. His calmness and resolution surprised him. He turned a page and there was a photograph with the tiny print underneath that made the shape of Kissy's name. His breath caught in his chest like a sharp pain and he came abruptly to his feet and kicked over the table.

Sometime later he was standing in the middle of the room, realizing he had destroyed it—thrown the table through the window, torn the doors from their hinges, kicked and punched holes in the walls, reduced the furniture to fragments. It looked as if the wind that had taken down the motel's sign had gotten trapped inside the room. There was a patter of applause, and his eyes focused a little better and recognized his teammates, the ones who weren't sharing rents elsewhere, standing there looking in through the broken window.

"Way to go," Moosejaw shouted over the window.

Deker stuck two fingers between his lips and whistled.

And DeLekkerbek and the Rich Girl and This-Diane applauded. The Rich Girl's sleek old Rolls-Royce Silver Shadow squatted behind them, as if hunkered down against Junior's tantrum.

Junior lurched into the bathroom to get away from them. His fingers hurt, and when he looked at them, he saw the nails were mostly gone and he remembered bloody stripes on the walls, paint clawed away. He looked up at his face in the mirror over the basin. That struck him as wrong. He punched out the mirror.

∞ 15 ∞

Going home less than a success was the same as going home a failure. Of the four days allowed, two would be consumed just getting there and back by air. The cheaper buses would take more time than he had, but if he had a week, it wouldn't matter. It hurt too much to think of spending forty-eight hours in the same town with Kissy. His hands trembled at the thought. He was afraid if he got that close, he might kill her. Surely by now she would have someone else. That wuss, the balloon pilot, or maybe she had gone back to that fucking drummer. He should have killed that bastard when he had the opportunity.

Finding an excuse for his folks was easy; he told them he wanted to save the money. He understood they could not come to him, with Mark's schedule stacked up the way it was. He canceled his flight reservation and mailed home to them the gifts he had picked up on the road. A turquoise bolo for Dunny, squash blossom necklaces and earrings for Esther and Bernie, hand-tooled leather boots for Mark. In the same shop where he had purchased the turquoise jewelry for his folks, he had plunged for another necklace, big silver tubules threaded with turquoise chunks and a bear claw of silver set with a red stone the color of blood. He had been told but he forgot what it was, that red stone. He wrapped it up and insured the package and mailed it to her anyway. She could wear it for her new lover and laugh over what a fool her old boyfriend was.

Once those tasks were accomplished, he had to think about what he was going to do for Christmas. Besides repair the ruin of his motel room. Fix it or pay for it, the motel manager had told him. He had boarded up the windows but otherwise done nothing but clear away the broken glass. What he wanted to do was drink. Get started on it right after the last game, get blind and stay that way till the Fat Man had crawled back up his last chimney and gone back to the North Pole.

But outside the arena, after the last game, the Silver Shadow was idling, the Rich Girl at the wheel, Lek lazing in the seat next to her with the window down. This-Diane with her face hanging out of the window behind him. All of them grinning at him like they knew something he didn't.

"Hoot," Lek said, "let's blow this pop stand."

The Rich Girl popped the trunk on the Silver Shadow and Junior tossed in his duffel. Even with the luggage the women were dragging, and Lek's duffel, there was room enough for Junior in it. He resisted the closet appeal of the trunk and climbed into the backseat next to This-Diane. And they were off, Junior guessed to Denver, where he knew the Rich Girl had a place.

Behind the wheel, the Rich Girl demanded a drink. This-Diane broke out the champagne, and the flutes buried in the ice with it, from the cooler on the floor in the back. Forgetting about Lek's being an alcoholic, she poured him a glass. Lek laughed and waved it off but his cheerfulness seemed forced. This-Diane apologized too much and the Rich Girl told her to drop it. Hunched up guiltily, This-Diane guzzled a lot of champagne in a hurry to get over her faux pas.

Too bad for Lek, Junior concluded, because the champagne in the ice-crusted flutes was like a fairy-tale nectar. He had had it only a few times before but he could tell this was very good quality. He settled back to savor rolling toward Colorado in a Rolls-Royce Silver Shadow with a glass of Roederer Crystal in his paw and a pleasant glow from it in his gut. The Rich Girl, driving, caught his eye in the rearview, and he realized he had been letting his face hang out fatuously. She grinned at him, her eyes twinkling, and he knew it was all right, she wanted him to wallow in it some.

A three-hour run brought them into Denver around two the next morning. During the drive he found why This-Diane's tits stood out the way they did. Implants. It was an odd sensation, sort of like groping his own hard-on. He also experienced what a puck might feel like having the black sucked off it by This-Diane. The last hour, she slept in his lap. Running the silent streets of the city, it felt like they owned it, owned the world. Outside of the movies, Junior had never before seen anyone order up champagne at the check-in desk. The hotel was so fancy all the help had accents, mostly French, some he couldn't identify as anything but European, which he guessed was the mark of distinction from the 7-Elevens, where all the help had accents too but from places like Pakistan or Mexico or Sri Lanka. The manager of the hotel showed them personally into a private elevator that went only to the Rich Girl's penthouse, occupying two stories. It had breathtaking, belly-jumping views in every direction.

She had Lek's duffel taken to her bedroom. This-Diane showed off the other rooms to Junior and invited him to park his duffel in the one she habitually used. With a certain half-loaded wariness, he missed his cue. He didn't want to be her date, let alone her boyfriend, and didn't see why a hummer in the backseat meant he had to be, especially with other bedrooms standing empty. He wasn't at all sure he wanted to wake up in the same bed with her even once.

The next stop on the tour was an indoor pool—and next to it, a Jacuzzi big enough for half a dozen people, exactly the sort of thing Junior fantasized about having when he had the money.

The champagne arrived as Lek and the Rich Girl emerged, a little breathless and rumpled, from the Rich Girl's bedroom. Both women started shucking their clothes. In three minutes they were all lounging around bare-ass in the Jacuzzi. There was something about the way hot water made a woman all soft and pink that made Junior euphoric. Lek was liking it too. Junior wondered if they were headed for a free-for-all.

This-Diane sat next to Junior and cuddled up to him. It occurred to him that if he got el-stinko and started to drown, he could just hold on to her and her tits would keep them both afloat. The steam from the rolling hot water was making her makeup soften and run. He resisted an impulse to push her head under water so when she came up for air he could see what her face looked like. With a trill of panic, he thought maybe she would look just like Diane Greenan, and for an instant, he was on the verge of tossing his cookies. But of course she wouldn't, he reassured himself; if she did, she wouldn't need to wear so much makeup.

The Rich Girl trailed her fingers over a bruise on Lek's forearm. "If I were a publisher," she said, "I'd put out a calender of nekkid hockey and football players called 'Men and Their Bruises.' "

They all laughed and This-Diane fumbled under water for Junior's dick. He pretended not to notice. He was going to have to drink a lot more before he would want to fuck This-Diane. He wanted to fuck the Rich Girl, that was who.

"How 'bout some music?" he suggested.

This-Diane was eager to please. Junior braced himself and presently Madonna was holding forth from the speakers on the wall, wailing that she wanted to keep her baby. Lek and the Rich Girl weren't listening; they were kissing each other. Junior wondered what he was supposed to do now—play with himself to keep them company? This-Diane solved the problem, reappearing with a mirror hatched with lines already chopped and cut. He got his nose right into it. Oh, Jesus. The women did too. Lek looked the other way like they were doing something embarrassing, the three of them. And then he climbed out of the tub and picked up his clothes and walked out. Junior's heart was goose-stepping right along in his chest, and he closed his eyes.

"Oops," the Rich Girl said. She sniffed a few times. "Goddamn it's a drag trying to have a fling with somebody who thinks they're an alcoholic."

"Why don't you go after him?" This-Diane asked.

"Fuck 'm," the Rich Girl said, and then both women laughed, snorting and snuffling, and the Rich Girl repeated, "Fuck 'm," and they laughed hysterically.

The heave and fall of the water was alarming, giving the sensation that the whole building was moving, and Junior opened his eyes to discover This-Diane was getting out of the tub. She winked at him and trotted away.

The Rich Girl sloshed water on him playfully and he sloshed back and she jumped up, shrieking happily, and fell onto him. He caught her and held her; such a big girl. She made him think of his mother's saying when he took more than he could eat that his eyes were bigger than his stomach.

The nose candy had made her talkative. "Last week, I was in the French Antilles. I went out after dinner to sit on the edge of the pool. I took off my shoes and pulled up my skirt, so I could dabble my feet. I noticed a bug, a moth, in the water. At first I thought it was drowning, and then I realized it was lifting itself off the water every few seconds. It was making this loud noise, like a cat purring. It kept riding the surface of the water, beating it with its wings, lifting off, dropping back, and beating the water some more. Then I realized it was over an underwater light in the pool. The moth thought—can moths think?—well, it acted like it thought the light was the moon." She laughed contentedly. "It must have been so fucked up, trying to figure out why the sky had gone all thick and wet."

Her breasts in the water were like drowned moons, Junior thought, and then, Jesus, am I fucked up.

She grinned at him and then she sank beneath the surface of the water. She pushed his legs apart and her head was a shape between them. She nibbled like a little fishy and then sucked his cock between her lips. He gasped and she released him and her head emerged, water running from it. She snuggled up to him and he put his arm around her and weighed one of her tits. He rolled a thumb over her nipple. It was weird; her breast felt like his own erect cock, the skin pliable and soft with a rigid core.

She swung a leg over him and put him inside her. He closed his eyes and she rocked and rolled on him. The Material Girl sang with palpable sadness.

He should have trusted his dick, it really was what he needed. It was almost as good as with Kissy, or so it seemed. But immediately afterward, he felt let down. The rocks-off blues. She noticed.

"What's wrong, baby?" she begged him. "What's wrong?"

He admitted it was the first real sex—getting blown wasn't the same thing, especially not lately—he had had since the last night with Kissy. The Rich Girl was immediately curious and wanted the whole story. While he told her, they lolled in the tub. They had been in it so long, Junior felt as if he could just slough his skin. He would be like the Visible Man, the one in Anatomy, red-meat muscles, bald eyeballs. Occupant Clootie.

"Kissy," she said. "I thought *I* had a silly name."

They sat on the edge of the tub and did up the rest of the powder on the mirror. Then they went looking for Lek and This-Diane and found them in the Rich Girl's bedroom. Lek was licking more cocaine off the tips of This-Diane's tits, while she giggled. Lek grinned and laughed edgily. His eyes had gotten red as if he had been crying. The Rich Girl bent over him and put her mouth on his and he kissed her back hungrily. The two women made love to Lek together, the Rich Girl straddling his knees and curling over him to suck his dick. This-Diane on his face. Junior watched for a while, in a state of detached excitement, then he picked up the phone and the room service menu and announced he wanted to order a lot of food, demanding of his companions what they wanted. They had to interrupt their activities long enough to tell him to fuck off. He told them he would order for them and proceeded to stumble through the menu, pretending to misread the names of the offerings so that they were somehow sexual. Listening to him, the three of them broke up, and sprawled on the bed, laughing. The man trying to take the order seemed unfazed, as if it were not the first time he had had to deal with this kind of behavior.

The air had gone hot and thick and liquid. Yet he had almost reached the moon. He could feel the heat of it burning him, and he understood with a special clarity that though the moon did not generate light, only reflected it, its enormous pale eyeball intensified the reflected light so that it could indeed burn. His whole mind was one great shining white plane and he was nearly snow-blind with it.

He opened an eye and the light, though it made him wince, was degraded, nothing to the shining in his dream. His head hurt with trying to contain it. He groped his way to a toilet.

The Rich Girl was still sprawled in her bed when he came out. So, on her other side, was This-Diane. He had not, he was quite sure, actually fucked This-Diane. The sense that it would be very bad luck, very bad karma, had somehow maintained itself even with all the booze and blow he had ingested. He found his shorts and went looking for hair of the dog.

Lek was sitting naked on a bar stool at the wet bar in the living room, hunched around a cut-glass decanter of some clear fluid. A silver chain around the shoulders of the decanter bore a silver tag that read *Vodka*. There were two other decanters. The one tagged *Whiskey* was empty of all but faint dregs. The other, *Scotch*, had a few fingers of liquid amber in it. There were glasses, but Lek was sucking the vodka straight from the bottle, so Junior had a good swallow of the scotch, standing up. He located a stool next to Lek and backed onto it. He squinted at Lek, and Lek looked at him and made a sort of snorting sound.

The two of them sat there a while. Lek worked at the vodka and Junior finished the scotch. An image welled up in Junior's aching head: a tag on a silver chain draped over a woman's crotch: *Pussy*. Or maybe *Cunt*. *Hairpie*. He thought about telling Lek but was put off by how morose he seemed.

"Merry Christmas," Lek said suddenly.

Junior thought about that for a while. "I don't think it's Christmas yet, is it? I think maybe it's Christmas Eve."

"That's right," Lek said. Then he started to cry. "Fuck it," he said, "Merry fucking Christmas anyway, I can say Merry fucking Christmas on Christmas fucking Eve if I fucking well want to." And then he lurched from the room.

A minute later the crashing and shouting started in the Rich Girl's bedroom, first Lek and then the Rich Girl, and then both of them. This-Diane came bolting down the hallway, pulling a T-shirt over panties. Her real face showed through her molting makeup. He couldn't tell what she would look like at the end of the process. At the sight of Junior, she slowed to a trot.

"Jesus," she said, rolling her eyes. She was glad to see someone who hadn't lost it.

Junior handed her the vodka. She stared at it for a moment and then she knocked back a huge swallow, tipping her head so far back, Junior started to feel a little bit of interest.

The ruckus in the Rich Girl's room quieted down, and Lek came out, fully dressed except for boots in one hand. He had his duffel. He slammed off the private elevator without looking back at Junior and This-Diane.

"Jesus," This-Diane said in a wounded tone.

The Rich Girl did not emerge, and Junior began to think maybe he should check and make sure Lek hadn't strangled her.

When he looked in, she was sitting on the edge of the bed, smoking a cigarette. Looking her age and hangover.

"Lek left," Junior said.

She sucked angrily at the butt and blew smoke out her nose.

"I should go," Junior went on.

She stared up at him, her eyes smoldering with what seemed to be increasing anger.

Junior fumbled on. "Maybe I can chill him out."

The Rich Girl flicked the cigarette at him, and he plucked it out of the air and put it out in the ashtray.

"See ya," he said.

The doorman had seen the direction Lek had gone. Junior doubted he would ever find him but it was easy. All he had to do was look through the window of the first bar he came to on the street. Lek was sitting at the bar and he had a drink in his hand. It was a fern bar, and at two-thirty in the afternoon, empty except for him.

Junior went in and dropped his duffel next to Lek's and took the stool next to Lek's stool. He ordered a beer. When the bartender put it down in front of him, he glanced at Lek.

"Merry fucking Christmas," said Junior.

For a moment Lek didn't say anything, and then he sighed and wiped at his eyes as they watered. "Merry fucking Christmas," he agreed.

The high school hoop tournaments began in the middle of February and continued through the first week or so of March, if no blizzards interfered. At the end of the marquee game at the Civic Center auditorium one night of the Class A tourney, Kissy packed up her gear outside the locker rooms where she had gotten some final shots— the losing team exchanging teary hugs, the winning one pouring cider on a coach's head. Along with the usual gadget bag, she had a big lens that belonged to the paper. The lens was bulky and banged against her thigh. She took the media exit, down a flight of stairs to a side door that let out onto the main stairwell.

Entering the flow of the crowd, she found the steps slippery underfoot with melted snow and grit. She was congratulating herself at having worn sheepskin-lined boots that had a decent tread on them to give her some traction when her feet skated out from under her. Reflex would have her throw out her arms, but she was holding on to her gadget bag and the paper's expensive lens. She tried to turn her body toward the rails in an instinctive search for support. Her belly tightened and her vision blurred as the lights above flared in her eyes. Then there were arms around her as somebody caught her.

She staggered heavily against her rescuer as her watch cap slipped down over her eyes. She didn't need her vision to know it was a man steadying her onto her feet again, her weight against his muscular forearm under her breasts. She struggled to push her cap back up.

She looked up into the shocked face of Mike Burke. He was in uniform—working the security detail. Most of the cops loved tourney duty. They got to watch the games and make overtime simultaneously. The only bitch was drawing traffic duty outside when the weather got ugly.

"Are you all right?" There was more concern in his voice than she cared to hear. He let go of her rather reluctantly, as if he thought she was going to fall down again.

She cleared her throat. "Thanks."

"You're pregnant," he blurted, going red as he realized immediately what a stupid remark it was. Obviously it wasn't news to her. He fumbled for the right thing to say. "When did you get married?"

"I didn't."

The smile on his face fell apart. She almost felt sorry for him. She liked even less the condescending pity that immediately softened his surprise. It had become too familiar to her. She resented it more than she would have being forced to wear a letter *A*.

"I have to get film back."

He was still all anxious solicitude. "I could have somebody give you a lift."

"No thanks. I got here, I can get back across the street." She slipped back into the exiting crowd.

Watching her go, Mike Burke thought of salmon struggling upstream to spawn. She had nearly fallen, but he was the one who was staggered. As soon as he had caught her and registered the round high belly like a small basketball against his arm, he had been thrown off balance. He had felt it tighten against his arm. All the times he had seen her around the courthouse and wherever else their paths crossed, he had not noticed anything. Her face had become a little more full, he realized, but she had succeeded in hiding her rising belly under bulky sweaters all winter. He was glad now she had not responded to any of his warm smiles. The last thing he needed was some woman looking to get her kid legitimized.

Inevitably he speculated who the father might be and recalled picking up Clootie leaving her place just before he left. Pearce would be amused with the possibility that Clootie had left his calling card that night. Burke would have expected Kissy to rid herself without hesitation of an unwanted pregnancy, but in a way, going ahead with it was the kind of in-your-eye choice Kissy had made previously. Just when you thought you had her figured, she messed you up.

A Post-It stuck to her desktop computer screen commanded her to the managing editor's office. Earl Fish was pacing when she knocked. He held the chair for her and patted her shoulder absently, confirming this was the face-off she had been anticipating.

"We've danced around this situation long enough. You're pregnant." He spoke wearily.

Kissy shrugged. "The paper doesn't have any maternity coverage. I took it to mean as far as the paper's concerned, whether or not I'm pregnant is irrelevant."

"We offer unpaid leave to employees past the probationary first year, which you are not," Earl retorted. "You have only a few days of accumulated sick leave to have this baby and then you come back to work or you're fired. You may not care for it, but it's not indifference."

"No," she agreed. "I'd call it hostility." As the remark escaped her, she regretted it. It would hardly do her cause any good. She needed the job. She would beg for it if it came to that. "Never mind. I'm not complaining. I accept the situation. I'm taking care of myself."

He threw himself into his chair, which protested audibly. "I understand you nearly fell down the stairs at the auditorium the other night."

She wondered who had ratted. Not that it mattered. If it weren't that, it would be something else. "I didn't break anything."

"Grace of God."

"Pregnant women fall down all the time. I've heard of women throwing themselves down stairs on purpose, trying to induce miscarriages, without effect."

"Indeed." He grimaced. "The fact remains you're becoming more awkward. You're carrying heavy, expensive equipment. Never mind the possibility of damage to the equipment, you could hurt yourself. You may choose to take risks for yourself and your . . . fetus—but I can't allow you to take risks that might result in a worker's comp claim."

"I'm not looking to sue the paper," she said. "I need this job, Mr. Fish."

His lips pursed. "You may need *a* job. You could work a desk job."

"I could do lab work full-time."

He shook his head. "The lawyers say the exposure to chemicals is too risky—"

"I'm exposed to those same chemicals in my own darkroom—"

"That's your choice, not something I've assigned as part of your work. Look, I know you don't want to do sales—"

Sales. The paper gave you a desk and telephone and you hustled for a commission. She had heard the average commission amounted to the minimum wage, which meant some weeks you ate Hamburger Helper and some weeks you ate Hamburger Helper without the ground chuck.

She blinked back a sudden welling in her eyes. "I'd rather deliver pizza."

"We're not in the pizza business. I'm trying to find a way to keep you on. Help me out a little, will you?"

"I appreciate it, Mr. Fish." Sitting there with her belly in her lap, she felt a lot more pregnant than she did on her feet. "I just don't see why I can't go on shooting pictures— I can still carry my own gear. I'm just pregnant, Mr. Fish, not crippled. I'm strong. I'm still swimming. I can do what a guy can do."

Seeing the hesitation in his expression, she thought she might have found a lever. If he was afraid of her suffering some injury or complication that might become a worker's comp claim, he also had to consider that male photographers did not get pregnant. Letting her go or forcing her inside might be construed as sex discrimination.

He sighed. "The best I can do is let you continue as a regular shooter until the end of your seventh month. You're not to go to emergency scenes. You cover the Rotary luncheons and charitable events and that sort of thing—indoors and sedate. You're out of the lab right this minute. After your seventh month, if you want to continue to work through to the end of your pregnancy, it will have to be inside at whatever I can find you and at the appropriate wage level."

He knew she had no choice.

After a little silence, he worked up a smile. "What are you going to do, Kissy?" He wasn't asking whether she would accept what he was offering. Gently, with concern softening his angular features, he was asking her the larger question. It was as close as he could come to the fact she was unmarried and gave no sign of changing her status.

"I don't know," she said quietly.

"For Christ's sake." His voice shook with frustration. "Don't you think you'd better figure it out soon?"

"I've got three and a half months."

Maybe. Or maybe three or maybe two and a half. There was no way Earl Fish could find out for sure.

The tension went out of him and he shook his head. "It's your life. I certainly have no business in it. But if you'd care to talk to me about it, I'd be happy to listen. If you think it might help."

Getting out of the chair was more of a struggle than she would have liked. "Thanks. I'm all right."

"Are you?"

She nodded and left the office, but the heavy sigh behind her suggested he didn't believe her.

Beyond doing his job for the paper, protecting its interests, Earl meant well. She could hardly hold the paper's antediluvian policies toward pregnant employees against him personally. The *News* had successfully fought every attempt at unionization that might have resulted in such revolutionary benefits as paid maternity leave or insurance coverage of pregnancy. In fact, few employers offered anything more and nobody offered anything if you were pregnant when you started with them.

For a while she had anticipated a period. Her breasts had ached, she felt bloated, she had the occasional cramp. Then she had begun to wake up nauseated. Neither food poisoning nor intestinal viruses caused swollen breasts or missed periods. She had bought a test; the bead had turned blue. It was just a drugstore test, she had told herself. No need for panic.

Her symptoms made it hard to think at all. The morning sickness declined to confine itself to the forenoon; she had it all day long. With no appetite, she lost weight and felt attenuated—disconnected. She lost any interest in sex and looked back on her former behavior with bemused disgust. She was lonely and would have liked to be held and cuddled, but the thought of intercourse revolted her.

Her body had changed slowly. The tenderness in her breasts diminished without ever completely going away. When the nausea stopped, she quickly regained the lost weight and began to gain. Her waist thickened and her stomach rounded gently. Her face was puffy in the morning, particularly around her eyes, and she had to pee all the time.

Early on she had begun to photograph herself. She squeezed off the shots by remote, thinking if she aborted the pregnancy, she would have a record of how she looked for as far as she let it continue. The weeks had passed until she arrived at the second trimester and abortion became an increasingly risky and complicated option. But at some nebulous point, she had stopped considering abortion. She was fascinated to watch the changes in her photographs of herself. It was as if her body was developing like a photograph. She did not want to interrupt the process.

Nothing else was settled. She had no idea if she would keep the baby or how she would pay for it. Or how, if she kept it, she would support the two of them. Who would take care of it while she worked? She did not, in fact, know who the baby's father was. Jimmy Houston, she had been convinced, until she finally did go to a doctor. After examination, the obstetrician thought it was possible the conception had occurred in August rather than September. It seemed bleeding was common in the first month and often mistaken for a period. The period she had had during the trial had been a week off schedule and therefore suspicious. So Junior might be the father. It was depressing to consider and impossible to settle without blood tests. She shoved it into the same mental closet as the question of keeping and paying for a child. Like her belly, the closet bulged now, threatening to burst open and spill its contents onto her head.

But she had another three months. Or two and a half. Or two. She could not help but giggle at her own misty-eyed dithering.

∞ 16 ∞

Ruth breathed again on her own, but even before then, she had been returned to her grandmother's care, under a court order that heroic measures would be taken if needed. Of the hours Kissy spent with Ruth, by no means all of them were with an eye to the lens. Like Mrs. Cronin, she read to Ruth—usually the newspaper, as if having the ephemera of the times recited at her might somehow suffice for experiencing it. Mrs. Cronin had once told her Ruth had had little or no interest in sports, but Kissy read her the sports page too. Occasionally there was some report of Junior's progress, and somehow, sharing it with Ruth allowed her to feel a certain rueful affection for him. Like Ruth's mother, Kissy helped to groom Ruth's unresponsive body—brushing her hair, trimming her nails, rubbing lotion into her skin. She brought a tape player with her and a cassette of the luminescent music of Vivaldi, or of reggae, warm and easy and full of the joy of life. She also told Ruth the jokes she heard in the course of her daily rounds, at work, at the *News*, in the coffee shops, and in the courthouse and around the Babbittry she was now allowed to cover. It felt strange at first, and then she decided it was only what she would have done had Ruth been Mary Frances.

One night as she framed Ruth and her grandmother—the older woman with her lively, emotional eyes and animated expression, Ruth with her slack face, her eyes turned up in a mockery of sculptured saintly ecstasy, or the unsanitary sexual kind—Kissy had her first serious contraction. A wave of tightness girdled her belly. She nearly dropped the camera.

"Are you all right?" Mrs. Cronin came quickly to her feet and to Kissy's side. "Sit down."

Responding to the authority in the older woman's voice, Kissy sank into the nearest chair. The tightening continued until she was nearly breathless before it began to relax. Mrs. Cronin took the camera from her hand, and Kissy spread her fingers cautiously over the curving bulk of her belly. There was a sudden ripple under her fingertips as the baby moved, seemingly in response to her touch.

For weeks now the baby had been active. She had come to regard it as a parasite, using her body for its own purposes. She was like a balloon, blown up around this being that had tethered itself inside her, but she struggled like no balloon against gravity. It was only when swimming that she had some relief from the sense of gross fleshiness—and only then did she feel the least bit sensual anymore.

"Something's happening," Mrs. Cronin observed anxiously.

"Just a contraction. I'm okay."

The older woman drew a sharp, impatient breath and her arms crossed under her shapeless bosom. "No, you're not." She glared at Kissy fiercely, seeming on the verge of stamping her feet. "Do you know you have never mentioned the fact of your pregnancy to me? You just keep getting bigger and more silent. I've actually wondered if you were one of those girls who convince themselves they're not pregnant and then leave the baby in a trash can. I don't believe it, though. You're tougher than that. I think you're just shutting everyone out. Kissy, why? Has everyone let you down so badly in the past? Or is it a kind of tantrum because whoever fathered this baby has evidently abandoned you?"

"I'm not abandoned." Kissy pushed herself from the chair. "I just haven't made any decisions, that's all."

"But you have. You didn't terminate your pregnancy."

Kissy clutched at her camera. "True. I made that decision. I don't know what everyone wants from me. I didn't think an announcement was necessary. It's just a baby, Sylvia. They get born by the millions every day. This one will too, and I'll give it away or keep it and everyone's life will go on, whatever I do."

"Let go of the damn thing," Mrs. Cronin said, tugging the camera from Kissy's hands. "It's an addiction, I swear."

Kissy gave it up.

The old woman drew her to Ruth's side and they stood there, staring down at her. "I remember when my daughter was carrying Ruth. I remember Ruth as an infant." Mrs. Cronin seized her granddaughter's limp hand and pressed her lips to it. Then she moved it to Kissy's belly and held it there. "Listen to me, you stubborn, contrary girl. You're standing there on two feet and strong legs with a new life inside you. I'm an old woman with more of my life gone than I have left, and I'm telling you, every second of it should be seen with eyes wide open. I look at you with your face crammed up against that camera, blinkering yourself to everything but a tiny rectangle of existence, and I want to kick your bottom."

Kissy laughed.

Mrs. Cronin smiled. "You've having a baby, dear. Making a new human being. Maybe millions do it, but you're not going to do it millions of times. Please try to experience it as something more significant than having a plantar wart."

The older woman's scolding pleased Kissy in an odd way. It wasn't just how Sylvia Cronin looked—as if she wanted to hop up and down on a branch and caw at her—or even the fact Ruth's grandmother cared about her. The older woman had spoken her mind with a passion that testified to her continuing vitality. Mrs. Cronin's words were a candid snapshot of Kissy from a new point of view, forcing her to reconsider the situation.

She didn't think she even liked babies—drooling, snot-glazed, leaking little monkeys, so far as she could see. "What if I'm no good at it?" she blurted.

And to her surprise, the older woman burst out laughing.

"I worried about that too," she confessed. "It's only the first one. By the time you've been a mommy for three months, you'll be the world's biggest expert. Just remember to take care of yourself as well as the baby, and that shit washes off, and you'll be fine. That's if you keep it, of course. More urgently, how are you going to manage, Kissy? Have you got any money?"

The old woman's bluntness took Kissy by surprise. Her blank reaction revealed everything.

Mrs. Cronin sighed. "Oh, dear. We are going to have to have a talk."

Kissy thought that's what they had been doing. But she knew what Mrs. Cronin meant. Mrs. Cronin had been a schoolteacher. She was going to want to know who the daddy was and why wasn't he helping her and did her mother know her situation. And unlike Earl Fish, Mrs. Cronin would get answers. Not because she had taught school for thirty years or because she was an old woman but because it was time for Kissy to start dealing with the questions.

On the movie screen, a nervous teenage blonde, entering the kind of house any sensible person who had ever seen a horror movie would never dream of approaching, tried to reassure herself, saying aloud, "Be calm, Kristen."

The audience, including Junior and Lek and most of the rest of the Dinosaurs, spoke her line with her, in the same tense tone. The bill at the Dry River Cineplex did not change very often. A movie like *Nightmare on Elm Street Part 4* was the manager's dream, for it filled the house night after night for weeks as the ticket buyers came back, like Freddy Krueger himself, over and over. The movie had become an event, a kind of ritual in which the audience participated, having learned all the dialogue and all the incidents of the story so that everything was anticipated and relished in the most minute detail.

Next to Junior, Lek sucked vodka through a straw, his paper cup emptied in the men's room of the 7-Up purchased at the concession stand and refilled from the bottle in his jacket. Junior's Coca-Cola cup contained only Coke. After leaving the Rich Girl's penthouse on Christmas Eve, he and Lek had toured Denver's bars and gotten invited—at least he thought they had been invited—to some bash in the suburbs where they had passed out in somebody's living room under the Christmas tree. Wake-up call had been leftover eggnog from squirt guns in the hands of some pissed-off little kids with an apparent resentment that Lek and Junior had opened, and played with, their toys before they had. It had been a long hike back to Dry River on their thumbs, and they had lost their duffels to boot.

Then, of course, he had to face the mess he had made of his room. Santa's elves had not repaired it in his absence. Every little chore—replacing the plywood in the window with glass, patching the walls, painting them—was a reminder of his own irremediable stupidity. Wielding the putty knife, the paintbrush, he accepted it as his own fault.

If Lek had heard from the Rich Girl, he had not mentioned it to Junior. He was concentrating on his drinking. Junior had reverted to serious training, no more than a beer or three, since Christmas. They had seen *Part 4: The Dream Master* once a week for three months, either in Dry River or wherever they found themselves. Part of its fascination for Junior was that the heroine's name was Kristen, though she looked a lot more like Diane Greenan than Kissy.

On the screen, a dog named Jason pissed fire, to moans and laughter from the audience.

"I had a piss like that once," Junior announced. The laughter swelled to a clamor, and he ducked a sudden but not unexpected hail of popcorn—a sequence of events immediately adopted as part of the script of watching the movie since the first time Junior had said it.

The flamethrower of dog piss opened Freddy's junkyard grave. Freddy's scattered bones and rotted tissues gathered themselves, and Freddy chased a doomed teenager through the automobile graveyard, as the wrecks themselves revived, until it seemed as if the kid was caught in a massive ongoing pileup.

"You shouldna burned me," Freddy yelled, "I'm not dead."

Lek bellowed the lines along with everyone else. Pleased with his reading of the line, he settled back into his seat, chuckling. Not only Lek and Junior but the lot of them spent long hours dissecting the movie, on the bus, in the locker room, at meals. Lek talked about having a mask made up that looked like Freddy. The thought of it gave Junior the creeps. It was a good thing Lek was drinking as much as he was; passing out every night; there was no way he could know Junior, his roommate on the road, was having nightmares. Freddy nightmares. Too many viewings of *Dream Master,* Junior reckoned, shrugging it off. Freddy preyed on teenagers, particularly girls in their nightclothes. Junior didn't qualify by age or gender and didn't have a nightie to his name. And, like any healthy viewer of a horror movie, he believed that if he ever found himself facing Freddy or Jason in the old-style goalie mask, he would be the one to survive.

"Lighten up," he said with Kristen's boyfriend on screen, "no one died." And as always, the line made him want to get up and leave. But he didn't move. He sat there, assuring himself if he were one of those teenagers, he'd be out of fucking Springwood the day before yesterday. Never mind fifty ways to leave your lover, you needed fifty ways to leave your monster. Straight out the back, Jack.

The 'Sores pulled it together after the holidays and played well enough to make the playoffs, but they lost their division in the final. With Junior in net, the other guys playing the upgraded defense, Moosejaw and the offense proved unable to make up for the offensive loss of Deker, called up to Denver ten days earlier.

At least it wasn't a losing season, and he had played brilliantly himself. Junior allowed himself considerably more than a beer or three by way of consolation. The next day, with a paralytic hangover, he packed in slow motion and groped his way onto a bus to Denver with most of the rest of the guys, who were in the same shape as he was. In Denver he connected with an eastbound bus. As he waited in a terminal coffee shop between buses in Chicago, he was paged to take a message, which turned out to be to call the Drovers' front office. Going into the divisional playoffs, the Drovers had one goalie on leave to attend his mother's deathbed, another out with his spleen blown up by a runaway case of mono, and the pick of their minor league pool was a guy named Junior Clootie.

"I'm headed to Edmonton," he told Dunny from a telephone kiosk at O'Hare, waiting to board a flight. "I've been called up for the playoffs."

"We'll be there." Dunny's voice crackled in his ear. "Can't wait."

Two hours later, he was on a jet climbing out of O'Hare, headed for Alberta.

Deker met him at the baggage carousels with a bellow of "Hoot!"

He was hand in hand with the Rich Girl, This-Diane at their side in the maid of honor position. Junior grinned and kissed the Rich Girl. She kissed back playfully.

He murmured, "Isn't Deker a little young for you?"

She threw back her head and laughed bawdily. "You bet," she drawled. "We were just waiting for you to make the party complete."

Junior glanced at Deker, beaming back at him. "I'm working, Mony. My folks are coming into town too. Maybe when it's all over—"

The Rich Girl nibbled at his ear and kissed him again. "If you need a little distraction, just give me a call."

Junior threw himself into preparing for the playoff games. The coaching staff was relieved at how he looked. He was relieved himself that he still had anything left. He had been living for weeks on the stamina, sheer physical strength, and coordination that came from having chosen his parents well and then working like a sled dog all his life. He thought he might be close to pure sled dog now, nothing but instinct lunging against the harness. There was a certain flagellant ecstasy in the sense of being tested, in discovering just how much he could reduce himself to pure goalie. He could not imagine the day would ever come when it was not exciting, let alone that he might actually not want to be there.

Then he was on Big-Time Ice, on the fabled Big Pond, making his major league debut before the largest crowd of his career in a playoff series. He had to fight his eyes' welling during "The Star-Spangled Banner" and then, during "Oh Canada," nearly threw up. The Oilers smelled fresh meat and came at him hard. So what? he kept muttering. So what? That was just Wayne Gretzky out there. It was a relief when the Great One wrapped the puck around the corner and put the first one past him. Junior tapped the posts to center himself and settled in for a long game and a short series.

His folks were waiting for him outside. Mark pounded his back and slapped his face in violent affection. Bernie actually hugged him, the first sign of affection she had given him since he had killed Ed and broken up with Kissy. Dunny had tears in his eyes. Esther flung her arms around him to kiss his cheek. Then she had to daub at her eyes with a hankie. Junior borrowed it to wipe his own suddenly moist eyes, and then Dunny borrowed it for a big honk. Junior hustled them into his rent-a-dent to return to their hotel. He had his license back and felt like he had at sixteen with a brand-new one.

It was not a luxury hotel, let alone the Rich Girl's penthouse in Denver, but it was several cuts above the Devil's Backbone. He had taken a room for himself too, for the convenience, and to get away from the partying. He was scared: he couldn't think of anything but being ready.

Mark was noisy, full of the game and the night to come— he had invitations to go out on the town with Deker. Though his folks urged him to go too, Junior declined. His folks had come a long way for him, not just from Peltry but from Kingston, and through years, to reach this pinnacle. Only his parents could truly share the satisfaction of having achieved, if only for a little while, his goal of playing in the NHL. Kissy might have. For the first time in weeks, he wanted to call her, to hear her voice, to find out if she was happy for him.

As his brother departed, he sensed that both Esther and Dunny were relieved to see the back of Mark. It seemed perfectly reasonable; Junior had found Mark exhausting since Mark was about two. Hanging out with Deker would eventually bring Mark to the Rich Girl's suite and maybe This-Diane would suck him to death. Failing that, he might get lost and not be able to find his way back to the hotel. Or maybe fall in with devil worshippers and be sacrificed in Satanic rites.

It did not require much consultation for the four of them to elect to stay in, ordering room service into his parents' room because they all preferred this first meal together in a long time be private, and also, because they could.

"You looked good," Dunny said after they had called down the order. He had already said it once, hashing over the game on the ride to the hotel. "I think you could win the next one."

"Introduce me to Deker," Bernie begged.

The day Deker had a sex-change operation, Junior promised himself.

Bernie threw herself onto one of the double beds and pouted a minute, then grabbed the TV clicker. She found some late sports news and they all focused on it, waiting for clips of the game.

Dunny kept looking at Junior's head.

Junior found himself actually looking forward to the

inevitable haircut—indeed, savoring Dunny's struggle to
stay away from the kit in his suitcase on the luggage rack.
He wondered if, given the occasion, he could jolly him
into something with some spike to it. At last there was a
clip of the night's action that showed Junior, and then it
was over and Dunny exploded from his chair and rum-
maged for his kit. Esther and Junior exchanged a grin. Junior got up and arranged a straight-back chair in good
light. Then he undid his tie and unbuttoned his shirt.

"I was going to ask," he told Dunny.

"Alla you guys," the old man said, "you look like
you're trying to pass for Jane Fonda in that movie, what
was it, *Klute*? Shag down the backsa your necks all sweaty,
it's a wonder you don't have acne and boils. None of you
got time for a decent cut?"

"You loved that movie," Junior teased. "You got a little
hot for Fonda, didn't you?"

"I did not!" Dunny protested.

Junior was down to his undershirt and was waiting patiently. "Close but ragged, okay? Some spike—"

Esther straightened in her chair. "Junior, there's something I have to talk to you about—"

Bernie clicked off the TV and tossed the remote control
aside. From her pursed lips and her half-closed lids, she
knew what was up.

Dunny's scissors and comb stopped in midair. "Mother,
it's none of our business."

Whatever it was, by the set of his mother's mouth and
the warning in his father's tone, Junior could tell they had
chewed it a while—probably all the way to Edmonton.

"We saw Kissy last week," Esther said.

Dunny sighed. The comb and scissors resumed their
dance around Junior's head.

"At the movies," Bernie chimed in.

So far it wasn't exactly riveting.

"She's pregnant," Esther finished up.

The word seemed to hang in the air like a balloon. For a
second, Junior was totally stunned.

Dunny knuckled the back of his head impatiently. "Jesus, Esther, I told you, you'll throw him off his game! And
we shouldn't be talking about this in front of Bernie—"

"Bernie knows how babies get made, Dunny," Esther
snapped.

Bernie smiled knowingly at Junior.

Esther's chin jutted accusingly at Junior. "I can't make you two get married, but if she's having your baby, the least you can do is acknowledge it and support it. You know all you have to do is say so. Maybe you don't want it, but if that baby's my grandchild, Junior, I want to be its grandmother. I want to be able to see it and hold it. I don't want it growing up thinking it had grandparents that didn't care about it—"

"You don't even know if it's Junior's," Dunny burst out. "I say wait till you get a look at the kid."

The lights in the room had gone a little blurry for Junior. He closed his eyes and pinched the bridge of his nose and then he drew a long breath. When he had heard nothing from Kissy, he figured they had gotten away with it. In the silence, the snip of his father's scissors made him think of castration.

"Junior," his mother said sharply.

His eyes snapped open. Esther was still there, spine rigid, her hands primly in her lap.

"I didn't know," he said. "She never told me."

"Well, she's big as a house."

"She didn't look so big to me," his father said.

"Dunny Clootie, I've seen my share of pregnant women," Esther cried. "She's in the last three months, that's for sure." She jumped up and bent into Junior's face. "Are you going to tell me you can't be that baby's father?"

"Maybe he can't," Dunny said. "I keep telling you, for all we know, it isn't his. He hasn't even been home since September, and they split up months before he left. I told you he didn't even know. He woulda told us. Why wouldn't she tell him? 'Cause it's not his, that's why—"

"It could be," said Junior.

Dunny snorted in disgust.

"I knew it," Esther said triumphantly.

"You don't even care if this kid is Junior's, do you?" Dunny went on.

"Not much," Esther admitted.

"Trust me, Mom, I'll find out," said Junior.

Esther beamed at him. "Good."

"She's buying baby clothes," Dunny said. "Sees your old girlfriend with a big belly and the first thing she does is goes right to Sears and runs up the credit card like she was going to be the only guest at the baby shower."

"I can give a few gifts if I want," Esther protested mildly, and then laughed quite happily, as if she had bested Dunny in some game only the two of them were playing.

Bernie slid off the bed. "You're such a jerk, Junior, I wouldn't blame Kissy if she didn't want to marry you."

It was a huge relief to have room service turn up just then. Distracted by the news, Junior struggled to fake his end of the dinner conversation. He guessed his parents understood. Bernie didn't speak to him, except for the occasional searing look of scorn she'd probably practiced to get just right.

That Kissy had kept it from him was beyond comprehension. What was she waiting for? A better offer? She could not really have thought no one would ever mention it to him or that he would never come home again, never seek her out, never happen to notice she had a baby. No question—Kissy had some s'plainin' to do.

He had never paid any attention to pregnant women. He could imagine her with her belly swollen up, her breasts heavier, but what about the rest of her? Didn't a woman's ankles sometimes swell? And what if her ass had gotten wide? All of a sudden the Kissy inside his head looked like the Pillsbury Doughboy.

He left his parents and Bernie as soon as he decently could. In his own room, he went directly to the phone and dialed Kissy's number. It was far too late, with the time change, but he didn't care if he woke her up. She was due for a wake-up call as far as he was concerned. He was denied the satisfaction: the number had been disconnected. He sat at the edge of the bed staring at the phone. He could call directory assistance and locate a number for her mother. Who would probably have some way to get in touch with Kissy but might very well not know much else. Kissy and her mother weren't exactly tight. It occurred to him that one of the things he might very well learn from Cait was that Kissy had married someone else since encountering his folks.

Maybe it wasn't his kid. But he knew they had taken a chance, and he also knew Kissy had had a bad experience taking a chance. He might flatter himself he was the only one who could persuade her to take the risk and that was why she was having the baby. Because she loved him. But she could have screwed that guy with the pussy mustache, she could have gone back to Kowanek, she could have put out for the entire straight male population of Peltry. Including his brother. She hadn't exactly been hard to knock over the first time, or any other time. Not for the first time, his stomach churned at the thought a woman who liked it as much as Kissy Mellors was not going to do without for all the months he had been away.

He swung his feet to the bed and with one arm under his head, stared at the ceiling. Then he rolled over and called the Rich Girl. This-Diane answered the phone, party babble in the background. If he was not mistaken the music in the background was "Der Kommissar." *Sha sha wuh oh oh.* Deker carried his own copy now. When he asked for the Rich Girl, This-Diane sighed dramatically but went to fetch her.

"Your brother is here. He's like you, four years younger. Pete and Repeat," she said.

"Come see me," he said to the Rich Girl.

"Why should I?" she teased.

" 'Cause I want you."

She laughed with pleasure. "Oh, all right."

He liked the idea of summoning her, of having the power over her to take her away from Deker, from his own brother. The champagne he ordered arrived before she did. Though he was already over his limit after two glasses with his parents, he had another. It was ginger ale for grown-ups as far as he was concerned. He wouldn't do any blow, if she brought any with her, he promised himself, and then when it turned out she had, he decided he could do a little, just a line or two. And immediately after he did it and his blood was thundering in his veins, he wished she was a little more into ganja and a little less into this shit. The jolt made him talkative and he broke another promise to himself: he wasn't going to tell her about Kissy.

"My girlfriend's knocked up," he announced.

The Rich Girl laughed and squeezed his dick as if in congratulation.

He asked her if he was better than Deker, and she laughed and said that was funny, when he called she had been wishing he would, she was tired of the kid not having a clue. It was just what he needed to hear.

Later on, he came back to the subject of Kissy, as Mony was lighting a postcoital cigarette. It was a habit he could come to dislike intensely. She wasn't a real butthound, a chain-smoker or anything like it, but apparently couldn't get fucked without a Marlboro to celebrate it. The tobacco smoke made his head and chest ache.

"It might not be my kid," he said.

Mony snorted. "Jesus. What is this? A fucking soap? I can't believe you give a shit. If she didn't want it, she could get rid of it. If she does, it's her choice."

He knew then he should have kept his mouth shut about it. She was there to get high and fuck, not to listen to him bitch about how some other woman was treating him. Fine. She could take it up the ass while he was in the mood.

When the blasting powder wore off, he was goddamn tired but not particularly eager to sleep either, afflicted with a twitchiness that was undoubtedly a little bonus from the flake. No amount of flake or firewater or getting his rocks off was going to stop him dreaming of tending goal, as he did nearly every night. Sometimes the dreams had a euphoric quality but not lately. No, not lately. Some nights, it was Freddy trying to stuff a puck past him. Eventually he did drift into troubled sleep. When his aching bladder woke him in the early hours of the next morning, though, he had been dreaming not of the net but of Kissy. She had been standing before him, stark naked, holding out a newborn baby. If the baby had a sex, he couldn't remember it. As he reached for the baby, it seemed to come apart, so that he couldn't get a grip on it. And then he realized, in the dream, that the baby was Kissy, newborn Kissy, white-haired, rings in her ears. Her face floated before him, round and waxy and pale. She smiled at him, sadly, with the mouth of the man in the moon.

17

Too late into Boston to make the late commuter prop jet into Peltry, Junior opted for the road. Sleep had failed him the night before as well as on the cross-country flight. He was too tense to see any point in checking into a motel when he could, driving, be home before the first flight boarded in the morning. It took an hour after landing to rent a car and recover his gear from the airline, so he didn't actually get out of Logan until nearly midnight. At the speed limit and in the light traffic of the small hours, it was a four-and-a-half-hour run. With eighteen-wheelers blowing by him at ten and fifteen miles an hour faster, he gritted his teeth and stayed legal for the sake of the license restored only weeks earlier. The drive gave him another dose, like the jet flight, of time alone with his head, his tired, wired brain spinning like a wheel in a gerbil cage, radio cranked to keep himself awake.

Not unexpectedly, he had gotten shelled in the last game. The Oilers were probably headed for another Stanley Cup, Gretzky another Conn Smythe Trophy. While the Drovers lapsed into defensive ineptitude, he had been tight as a drumhead, tired and distracted, and had played one of the worst games of his career. He could blame the meth, what Moosejaw had always called thumper, that he had been doing to compensate for the hangovers contracted with the Rich Girl in their little late-night romps. He called her; she came to him, they fucked like minks, and she slipped away before dawn—the pattern set by the first night. He didn't know why he had wanted it that way, but she had gone along with it, as if it suited her as well. His folks—and probably Bernie, whose narrowed eyes were daggers in his back—had figured out that though he wasn't going out with his brother after he said good-night to them in the evenings, he had something going. He didn't talk about it. Dunny and Esther got quieter, their mouths tighter. He guessed they thought, since he didn't introduce them to a woman, that he was hiring whores. He couldn't explain the Rich Girl any more than he could have explained a hooker. And he resented even having to consider explaining himself—he didn't want to acknowledge it was a reaction to the news about Kissy. All that aside, his performance on the ice was going to hurt him, he feared, for a long time to come.

Before he had tried and failed to sleep on the plane, he had read the papers and waded through the postmortems. The kindest thing written was that it was a lot to ask a rookie goalie and a nineteen-year-old Russian defector fronting an expansion club to perform the miracle it would have taken to beat Wayne Gretzky and the Oilers with Grant Fuhr in net. There was speculation the Drovers, in search of a decent defenseman or two, already had Junior Clootie on the blocks. Weeks before, the Utah Pioneers had been sniffing around after him and might still be interested. The Pioneers had a farm club in Baptistville, Kentucky, which did not sound like hockey country to Junior. It sounded like the major sports would be snake handling, lynching, and incest, and the only ice would be in the shape of improbably endowed naked female torsos, in the drinks at the VFW Hall.

Nor was the Utah club his heart's desire, though he suspected Salt Lake—maybe even Dry River—was gay Paree next to Baptistville. Like the Drovers, the Pioneers were an expansion club that in its best season had fought for last place in the division like a wet-brain wino for the last dry patch under the overpass. Junior consoled himself with the thought that the columns were wrong as often as they were right. Probably it was bullshit, start to finish, and even the Pioneers did not want him. At the moment that part of his life was out of his hands.

Just before five in the morning, Peltry rose out of the mist from the river that was so high it quivered at the top of its banks. The town was a pale vision, as if it were not a real place but the land of the dead, where even the red brick and the granite and the old elms and maples and pines were but ghosts of buildings and the bridge passed over something blacker, deeper, more divisive than a mere flood of water. If he fell into that water, surely he would forget everything and, crawling forth from it, would go about the business of living the life he had already lived. Walk the streets and breathe the air, go to classes, run through the Valley, work out and drill and scrimmage and play great games for Sowerwine. Eat and drink there, sleep and shit and shave and shower and do his laundry. Surely he would find Kissy there and they would embrace, kiss, make love to each other. And never remember anything or know that they were dead.

Crossing the Mid-Dance, he felt the bridge straining against the enormous weight of the river tugging at its piers and realizing the Dance was in spring flood. He had never seen it run so high. He could see its shiny nemetite surface that was like the back of some immeasurably large alligator. Upriver it must be over its banks. The suicide fencing where he had knocked it out of true had been bent back into place. Rust was at it where it had been stressed. And he was suddenly choked, grief-stricken for Ed, for himself.

The rain rattled ghostly knuckles against the windows of his room, in contrast with the empty quiet of the house around him when he woke. Eleven by the clock radio. Dunny at work, Esther and Bernie in class. It was like being home from school with bronchitis, the one time in his childhood he had ever been absent for illness. He felt frozen in time. Though he had been in bed since six, he did not feel as if he had done anything more than close his eyes. But now he was awake, very awake, except for the sensation of pressure behind his eyes.

Finding a change of clothes, after a long shower and a careful shave, was no mean task. He had been dressing from his laundry bag for a week. Everything in it had achieved the same level of what he had learned from the Canadians to call pong. Though he distinctly remembered having left some well-aged Levi's in his dresser, his brother must have ripped him off, for there was nothing in the drawers now but shorts and well-ventilated T-shirts. He tried a pair of Dunny's khakis, but they were too short in the leg and too big in the waist. Too early or not, it was going to have to be shorts. For socks he raided the clean laundry basket for a pair of Dunny's. No sooner was he decent that his armpits were wet with nervous sweat, his stomach queasy. It was worse than facing Gretzky again.

The rain was light but steady and cold, and he shivered with it and turned on the heat in the rent. Same old Peltry outside, as he poked the rent through the slow-moving traffic. It was as if he had never been away. Dry River and Denver and all the isolated mean little western towns strung along a thousand miles of lonely road had happened to him in an instant or never. In early spring, when the river swallowed the ice and was swollen by snowmelt and rain, and the dead leaf, garbage, and feces unfroze and began to rot again and the new vegetation shoved and burgeoned and flowered, the smell of Peltry was of the opened earth.

As he crossed the Hornpipe downtown, he saw that its black roil was nearly level with the cement dikes that contained its entry to the river. A fair number of the citizenry were engaged in watching it, among them cops and firemen in brilliant yellow slickers, with emergency vehicles parked everywhere. Waiting for an emergency. Waiting to evacuate downtown. Peltry rose steep from downtown and the occasional overflow of the 'Pipe was always localized in the few blocks of downtown and the gorge of the Valley itself.

Kissy's Blazer was in the *News* parking lot. In the copies of the paper his mother had continued to supply him, her credit line had become rare, the last one two weeks previous. It was nearly lunchtime, and if she was still working, she might be leaving the building then, to eat somewhere or buy a take-out meal or maybe go have a look at the 'Pipe. If he didn't see her come out with the other employees on their way to lunch, he would go into the building and try to find her.

Just as he was about to give up and try inside, she emerged from the side door. With a watch cap over her hair, she looked tired. Her face was a little more full and she was visibly pregnant—well along, even to the most indifferent or ignorant eye. Even knowing ahead of time, it was a shock to see the change in her body. The reality of it hit him harder than he had anticipated. There was no mistake. She was knocked up. To the moon.

Without any memory of opening the car door and getting out, he was out of the rent and moving toward her. A car horn squeaked at him as he stepped into traffic without looking and tires screeched and threw up water from the wet pavement in a violent spray. A bumper shuddered a couple of inches from his leg and somebody was hanging a choleric face out to swear at him. He barely noticed the fuss, but Kissy spun around to see what was happening.

Eyes widening, she took a step backward. He broke into long strides, hurrying to her.

"Are you all right?" he asked.

"What do you want?" she cried.

Concern for her had momentarily erased his mission from his mind. He struggled to recover it. "You. The baby. I guess."

"It's not your baby."

"What?"

She shook out her keys and managed to unlock the Blazer.

"Kissy—"

With the extra weight in front, it took effort to get into the Blazer, but she did it and slammed the door behind her. Gunning the engine, scooting away from him like a pigeon being chased by a small boy, she fantailed out of the lot. The roostertail of water from her wheels drenched Junior squarely. He did not react but stood there, dripping and blinking, for a moment, and then he turned and set off, sneakers squishing, for the rent. He stepped out into traffic, aware this time he hadn't looked but not giving a shit, and as it happened, crossed without incident.

Sitting in the water that quickly accumulated under him, he drove aimlessly. She said it wasn't his. He should be relieved. He was relieved. Except that meant she had let somebody else fuck her. Which made his hands shake and his gut ache. He felt like he was sitting in a puddle of cold piss. While he was out there breaking his ass, she was being somebody else's piece of ass. He wanted to tromp the accelerator.

Emergency vehicles, detour signs, and yellow police tapes blocked access to the Valley. Junior took a detour through some side streets, slipped onto an interstate exit, and got a look at the 'Pipe from the overpass. The fury of the water was tearing whole trees from the banks. It would take the strongest of swimmers in a matter of seconds, he thought. Even Kissy.

A horn blatted behind him, and he realized he had come to a complete stop in the middle of College Avenue. It felt like fate. He needed a workout. He could throw his wet clothes in the equipment manager's dryer while he did it. It was a lift to walk into the Sowerwine gym and cause a flutter and be welcomed. He borrowed shorts from a trainer and did his regular routine.

Some guys were shooting hoops in the gym, so he spent an hour playing with them. By four o'clock he felt good again, physically, and that always made him feel like anything was possible. Something about sweating made his head function a lot better.

Esther hunched over her books, spread in front of her on the kitchen table. She had an ink smudge on her chin.

"Mom," he said, "I saw Kissy. She says the kid's not mine."

For a second, she looked so disappointed, he took a step forward to hug her, but she glared at him.

The house smelled of fresh ironing, a dry clean smell that made him feel wetter. There was a basket of clean laundry on the bottom step of the back stairs and the ironing board was still out.

"Thanks for doing my stuff," he said.

"Take it to a commercial laundry next time, Junior. You're too old to bring me your dirty clothes. I'm telling myself I should be thrilled I've got a healthy boy I can do his laundry for him but the minute I thought it I realized what a crock it was."

Esther, it came to him, was pissed at him. Big Time.

"I'm sorry about the laundry, Mom. I didn't think."

"You're old enough to give thinking a try any time now, Junior."

He realized he was dripping on the floor. He was cold too. He hooked a beer out of the refrigerator and trudged upstairs to hit the shower. At the top of the stairs he turned around and came back down and picked up the basket of laundry to take up. She never even looked up at him.

In the shower, watching the muddy water swirl around the drain, he thought of the way the river had looked when he crossed over it. The surface like alligator hide. "Alligator pie, alligator pie," he croaked softly, taking himself in hand, "if I don't get some I think I'm gonna die. Give away the green grass, give away the sky, but don't give away my alligator pie." It was oddly comforting to sing the nursery song to himself. There was a verse about alligator stew too, but he skipped it for the one that had always been his favorite. "Alligator soup, alligator soup, if I don't get some I think I'm gonna droop. Give away my hockey-stick, give away my hoop, but don't give away my alligator soup." He watched his alligator soup spatter into the water around the drain.

Bernie had left him a present on his pillow—a foil-wrapped suppository.

Warm for the first time all day between the sheets, he drifted into a doze. He woke at the sound of Esther and Dunny in their bedroom, some mumbled argumentative exchange as the bedsprings creaked with them, settling in, and the light clicked off. And then his mother's voice, rising in anger, was perfectly clear. "So what, maybe he's got a career. All the work, all the sacrifice, and he's a bum. That's what he is, a bum with a career."

Dunny's response was exasperated enough to be audible. "Girl says it's not his."

"He's been such a fool she doesn't want him, don't you see it?" Esther said. "Would you want him married to your daughter?"

Dunny's silence was eloquent.

The crest came in the very early morning. Wakened by his parents and Bernie as they hit the ground running at the start of their day, Junior went out to look. The 'Pipe had spilled its banks downtown and the water stood in great shallow sheets as placid and flawless as ice in the thin silvery light. The sky was still low, the fog rising from the water mingling with ground-grazing cloud so heaven and earth were indistinguishable, restored to the Chaos before Creation. The mist condensed from the damp air off the river floated on it like lost souls in trance. It recalled the night's dreams to him, drowning dreams, sexual dreams, Kissy, swollen and beautiful, tangled with him in waters neither had the strength to resist.

Junior went home again and made himself breakfast. Kissy was living on James Street with Mrs. Cronin, Ruth

Prashker's grandmother, he knew—his mother had told him as soon as he got in from Logan. It had been as much a surprise as the information that Ruth was there too, still comatose, in the care of her grandmother. His mother had explained the legal maneuverings. It was disturbing news: Kissy was still in the thrall of her obsession with Ruth, which he had never considered very healthy.

He put the clothes he had worn the previous day into the washing machine, along with the towels he had used and the things Dunny and Esther and Bernie had left in the hamper upstairs. Then he set the load running. It made him feel ridiculously competent. That was the unfair part. He had done his own laundry for years, in Laundromats, when he was in college and since. Piece of cake. Alligator pie.

The clouds were breaking at lunchtime, and he had fallen behind schedule, baking a cake for Bernie—her favorite, angel food. He thought about frosting it with chocolate laced with Ex-Lax but decided to stick to a peace offering. So he had had to go into the *News* building and find out Kissy had gone out.

Somebody said the park on the river to get a look at it, so he went that way. The park on the river was a little patch at the confluence of the Dance and the 'Pipe that was too small for building. On the grass, the city had stuck some benches and planters and a trash can and a sign so discreet it made it instantly forgettable that it was Charlie Howard Park. Everybody just called it "the park on the river."

Kissy was sitting on a bench, staring at the river. And all at once, he felt unprepared. He ducked into a pharmacy in the line of shops across the street from the park. Idling there, pretending he was having a crisis of choice between the Big Red and the Dentyne, trying to think of a way to approach her that wouldn't result in her slamming a door in his face, he noticed a cheap point-and-shoot camera in a display case. And the place sold batteries and film too.

In her gleaming yellow slicker, her feet in matching yellow rubber galoshes, she looked, she thought, like a rubber ducky. Kissy drank up the scene: the 'Pipe hitting the broader Dance in a wild snarl of muddy foam and debris. The marauding water tore at the banks, beat upon the rocks, swept everything before it. Pleated into its mud-colored skein, it carried branch and twig, both dead and minutely abud, drowned vermin and varmint, a midden slew of human artifact, boot, gimme cap, mitten, rags of orange and blue and black and green plastic, shards of planking, fragments of shingle. It carried boulders of ice and drowned trees and branches like bundles of wet black bones and other flood-borne materials—bits and pieces of things and lots of out-and-out garbage—well above its banks and left them there like trash. It stank like an open grave as the first glitter of sun cast its net of diamonds up on the water. Gulls were everywhere, shrieking with excitement at the pickings. Though she was warmly dressed, the air was still raw. But all exactly as it should be. She was even content not to have a camera in her hand.

Then a click drew her gaze and there was Junior, camera to his eye, taking a picture of her. Reversing their old roles. And her passing as Rubber Ducky and behind her, the surreal detritus and the flooded river. She shouted with laughter. Coming to her feet, she flapped her arms.

"Quack!" she cried, and stamped her feet in the puddles. "Quack!" It only took a little stomping about to cause a contraction before she had to sit back down.

Slipping the camera into a jacket pocket—he was more sensibly dressed this time—he sat down next to her and put his arm around her shoulders. "You okay?"

She nodded and he gave her shoulders a gentle squeeze. She settled back against his solidity and he took one of her hands in his. It was a good feeling, a good time. They sat there looking at the river and only occasionally each other.

"I missed you," he said with a catch in his voice.

She guessed she was supposed to say she had missed him. She had, of course. And after all the months, her anger, when she poked it, was little more than cold ashes. The most she could work up was irritation that was as much with herself as him. The only thing fierce was her confusion.

She felt his chest expand as he took a deep, appreciative breath.

"There's more wet in the air than I've breathed for months," he said. He laughed with pleasure. "This is the most real place, isn't it?"

The gulls screamed as if in agreement.

She began to gather herself for the push off the bench. "I have to get back to work—"

He moved with her easily, as if in a dance, taking her weight and lifting her to her feet. She filled his arms and laughed, as she often did, at the change in herself.

He kissed her. She had forgotten what lips felt like against hers. He had always been a good kisser. In the last few weeks, desire had returned with an ironic strength. It was strange how the contractions went so deep. At the same time her uterus was flexing, doing the reps to prepare it for pushing out the baby, she would be aching. There was nothing girlish or bodice-ripping about it. She had a sudden impulse to tell him but instead she struggled to her tiptoes to kiss him again. And with a giggle at her own boldness and awkwardness, again, until they were kissing deeply and a huge contraction startled Junior, with his hand on her stomach, right out of the kiss.

"Wow," he said reverently.

She pushed his hands away. "I really have to go to work." And pee, she didn't say. I'm going to pee myself any second.

"I'll walk you back."

It was only three blocks, and it really helped, having his hand to dig her nails into, and he caught on immediately she needed to get back without saying why. He kept giving her worried looks. "See you tonight?" he asked. "I'll take you out to eat—"

Distractedly, she shook her head.

"Afraid you can't resist me?"

"I don't think that's up for debate," she shot back, and then, "Twenty-two James Street, seven o'clock," over her shoulder, as she hurried through the door he held for her.

∞ 18 ∞

From Mrs. Cronin's open door Kissy looked out doubtfully at him. Her hands went to the opposite elbows and she smiled at him, still distractedly. No suburban baby machine, circa 1957, in a car coat and a Donna Reed bob—she must be the first heavily pregnant woman Peltry had ever seen with an ear full of studs and a butch cut of white hair, never mind rigged out in a pair of forest-green satin overalls over an electric-blue lace T-shirt, silver hightops on her feet.

A white-haired old lady appeared in the foyer, to be introduced as Mrs. Cronin. She and Junior recognized each other instantly as natural antagonists. She was an old lady schoolteacher with the eyesight of an eagle, the hearing of a bat, and a bird dog nose, the natural enemy of rambunctious small boys, a species she could not fail to identify on sight, even grown up. He was stricken with guilt for whatever he had done, or not done, and felt an immediate tingle ghosting across his knuckles. For old bitches like her—doubtless once called Cronin or Old Lady Cronin—with their rulers always at the ready, a boy's knuckles were merely the convenient, socially approved substitute for a boy's stiff little pecker. Her gaze on him was cool and ironic, alert to the failure of nerve that would reveal his guilt.

The foyer had a plain elegance of golden hardwood floor and Persian carpet and antiques. It declared a house without children, of someone educated, conservative of taste, and with a certain amount of money. Once Mrs. Cronin carried away the roses he had brought, to arrange them in a vase, there was a slight medicinal odor that reminded him that behind one of the closed doors, one of

these high-ceilinged tasteful rooms housed the unresponsive existence of Ruth Prashker. He had no desire to go
farther into this dwelling. With a distinct sense of relief, he
accompanied Kissy out the front door and heard it close
behind them.

"Nice place," he said.

"Sylvia's been incredibly kind to me," said Kissy. "She
won't take money from me. I'm supposed to be helping
her with Ruth, but it's nothing to what she's done for me."

Unlike himself, Junior thought. "You look good," he
said, because she did. "Still swimming?"

"For a while longer," she said.

"It must be strange, living in the same house with
Ruth—"

"I feel very close to her now. It's been one of the most
interesting things I've ever done."

With her obsessive, pack rat curiosity, Kissy could find
almost anything interesting, he reflected. Anything she
could put a frame around. Fortunately they did not have far
to go—nothing in Peltry was all that far from anything
else—and he did not have to pursue the subject of how interesting Ruth Prashker was.

He had made reservations at Matty's, the best restaurant
in Peltry. They had never been able to afford it as students.
The maitre d' recognized him, though, or had been alerted
by his name on the reservation list, and was obsequious.
Kissy seemed amused.

He was suddenly conscious of being in the company of
a very pregnant woman, of people looking at them, recognizing him, making connections in their minds. He wasn't
embarrassed by it, but it made him realize she must have
had a lot of people looking at her since she started to show,
she must have had to deal with a certain amount of shit, no
wedding ring, no man. But holding her hand going to their
table, he felt coupled to her and surprisingly protective.
She had that belly, and he was no high school romeo but
her attendant male, indistinguishable for the moment from
a young husband.

Before they could open the menu, Matty, the owner-
chef, bustled from the kitchen. Though Junior had only
met Matty as a Sowerwine booster, and Kissy knew him
chiefly from Chamber of Commerce and Rotary and that

kind of civic event, Matty greeted them as if they were long-lost children.

"Look at you!" he exclaimed, and patted her belly.

"And look at you!" she returned, patting his belly.

It was nowhere near as big as hers—no more than the comfortable over-the-waist-spillage of middle age—but he did laugh uneasily.

He punched Junior affectionately in the shoulder. "You weren't listening, kid. I told you, you couldn't be good, be careful—"

Junior laughed it off, in hopes the man would go away faster. There was nothing else he could think to do. Kissy was embarrassed enough without his denying paternity in public.

When Matty finally left them alone, Kissy leaned toward him. "We should have gone to Denny's."

"I'm sorry."

She shrugged. "It's okay. I've gotten used to people presuming on my belly."

Then Julius Horgan blew in from the bar, trailing the *News* sports editor.

"Heard you were back," said the editor, Rex Mortensen, and there was a round of handshaking and more bullshit to endure, though Mortensen at least refrained from publicly congratulating Junior on knocking up Kissy. For Junior, it was reflex to gladhand fans and the media alike, and he threw off clichés about his rookie season effortlessly. He hardly noticed Horgan but Kissy found Horgan's twitching sneer nearly as irritating as being groped.

"So buddy," Horgan said when Mortensen had shaken Junior's hand again and begun to move away, "you going to make an honest woman of our Kissy?"

"Excuse us, sorry to bother you," Mortensen interrupted hastily, clamping a hand on Horgan's forearm and hustling him away.

"Hey, Julie," Kissy called after them.

Horgan craned around and Kissy flashed him a bird. Mortensen caught the rude gesture and shoved Horgan back into the bar. A ripple of amusement passed through the room, along with some shocked snorting and head-shaking among the other patrons.

"Prick," Kissy muttered.

Junior apologized again. She shook her head and

laughed, and he squeezed her hand, sharing the sense of being beleaguered.

She asked about his time away. Halfway through the appetizers, they were in conversation the way they used to be, leapfrogging between subjects, finishing each other's sentences. He found himself staring at her, conscious he was falling in love with her again.

"Now you know what I've been doing—tell me how it's been for you," he said.

She told him some stories about shooting pictures for the *News*. She spoke of her graduate school classes. It was like a first date, he realized, all the personal stuff discreetly skirted.

"It's been tough for you, hasn't it?" he said.

For a moment she didn't say anything, just twiddled with her pasta. "I'm okay," she finally said, "I'm getting by. I have friends—"

"I'm one of them. I want to be—"

"That's nice." She put down her fork. "I guess that's what we're doing here, trying to be friends—"

"I love you."

She crumpled her napkin on the table. The people at the next table were looking at them.

"We had good times, wonderful times," Junior said quickly, quietly, afraid she was going to bolt.

Her jaw worked with stress, and she blinked at him. "I want to go home now."

There was no graceful way to get to her feet. Junior was right there, as before, by the river, his hand under her elbow, making a difference.

"I'll get the check," he mumbled.

She went into the ladies' room, she had to, anyway, she always had to. And there was privacy, if only in the stall. She shut the world out and collected herself.

They didn't speak again until they were in his rented Ford. "Whose is it?" Junior asked abruptly. "That guy Hewes?"

She had nearly forgotten Garrett Hewes. Once her belly had started to show, their friendship had diminished to his nodding at her in an embarrassed way when they happened to run into each other. "Jesus, no."

"I didn't know Jesus was a candidate," Junior joked.

Caught by surprise, she grinned in spite of herself. And then she made herself be stern. She didn't know why but she didn't want him to know about Jimmy Houston. She didn't want anybody to know about him. It was her secret. And her baby.

"I don't know who it was."

Junior winced. Thought a bit and found the door she had left open. "So it might be mine."

"No! That's impossible. It was just some guy. Some guy I picked up. I don't even know what his name was, that's what I mean. I was drunk."

Her face was hot and she knew she was blushing, and he glanced at her by streetlight. And she saw the change in him, the rejection of her lie, the anger at her for telling it, the hurt that she would lie to him at all. He looked harder and bigger.

"I haven't even made up my mind if I'm going to keep it," she stumbled on.

They were already on James Street. He curbed the car with a jerk and reached past her to slam down the door lock. "You are not giving my kid away like it was an old coat. I'll sue you, Kissy, I'll get a lawyer and sue for custody myself if you don't want it—"

"Fuck you!" she cried, fumbling for the door handle and the lock release. "This is not your baby, you have no rights—"

"Easy to settle," Junior said coolly. "All it takes is a blood test."

For a moment they glared at each other.

She could see it now: the first paternity case in the history of professional sports where the putative father sued the mother, instead of the other way around. It would be Junior Clootie who set that bassackward precedent. But the thought of being forced to surrender the baby even to Junior, in the event a blood test confirmed his paternity, made up her mind for her. She was going to keep it. The most he could force on her was the blood test, and if it was positive, then she would have to give him some visitation rights. He wouldn't use them much—he couldn't. He would be away too much.

The urgency of getting out of the car slipped away in the heat of argument. "How are you going to take care of a baby? Leave it on the bench or the top of the net while you're on the ice?"

The question appeared to shake him, but he rebounded onto the offense. "What about you? How are you going to take care of it?"

"I can take care of myself—"

"The way you are now? Sylvia Cronin is taking care of you—never mind that shit, anyway. Raising a kid is no joke. You need help—"

"Plenty of women raise kids alone—"

"Because they have to. It's not right, those kids miss having daddies—"

"Plenty of kids wish they didn't have the daddies they've got—"

"But they still want a decent daddy, goddamn it, Kissy, I'm willing to be this kid's daddy—" An assertion he believed with the suddenness of revelation, with a conviction that could not admit the slightest doubt.

"Sure, you'll be gone half the year, you can mail the kid videotapes of your games and I can point out who Daddy is—"

"It's my living, the best I can earn, and you and the baby can come with me—"

"And the hell with my career—"

"No! You won't have to work a shitty minimum-wage job and do your serious work in a bathroom at two in the morning—"

"I don't want to be supported by some guy—"

"What's wrong with a guy supporting a talented wife who happens to have a career that pays like shit? How many wives put husbands through school?"

They realized simultaneously their voices had risen to shouts and for a moment sat in silence, staring out opposite windows, recovering their self-control.

Kissy covered her face with her hands. "Junior, you've gone from suing me to assuming we're going to get married."

He didn't say anything for a moment. The muscle in the corner of his jaw popped and writhed.

"All right," he said. "If you don't want to get married, then at least let me put my name on the birth certificate and give you financial help and be there for the baby."

She moaned softly.

He reached out and tugged her hands from her face. "Are you okay?"

"Yes, yes," she insisted. He moved close to her and fanned his fingers over the curve of her belly. The baby writhed inside her, seemingly in response, and Junior, wowed, laughed softly and took her hand and kissed her palm.

She shut her eyes and let his embrace enclose her. He had been sweating hard sometime during the afternoon, and even a shower hadn't obliterated the faint saltiness of it on his skin. His hand moved from her belly to cup her head and hold it against his shoulder. She could hear his heart. Her throat tightened. Her belly tightened too. She opened her eyes and he was staring at her, his eyes dark with delighted heat. He started for her mouth and she twisted out of his arms.

"I can't think straight. I'm too tired—"

"All right." He sighed. "I'm not going anywhere. We don't have to sort this out tonight. I'll see you tomorrow, okay?"

He helped her from the car and took her to the door and kissed her again, gently, and she let herself in. Ruth's mother's wagon was in the driveway. Sylvia and her daughter would be performing the nightly routine of care for Ruth. Kissy went to the kitchen and put the kettle on, to make tea for herself and for Mrs. Cronin and Mrs. Prashker.

She had messed up so spectacularly, she thought, she was probably wrong about everything. Sparring aside, what if the baby was his? Whether Junior had a right to have some involvement with a child he had engendered, did the baby have some right to know its daddy, no matter how feckless he might be? Did the baby have some right to some sort of daddy? She needed to do a lot more thinking about it.

They sat in the parlor with their teacups and inquired after Kissy's health and evening. It was apparent to Kissy that Mrs. Prashker thought she had been at a class. Perhaps Sylvia Cronin had regarded Kissy going out with an old boyfriend nobody's business but her own. Mrs. Prashker— and Ruth's brother, Dan, too—had been a little askance at Kissy's presence in Mrs. Cronin's household.

They informed her of the events of theirs, which chiefly

consisted of attendance on Ruth. Ruth's doings were very limited, but highly significant to her mother and grandmother. Each day was a prescribed round, designed to maintain the tone of unused muscles, the flexibility of unused joints, and the integrity of skin that suffered from her incontinence and her profound inactivity. Her hair wore off in patches if her head was not moved often enough, and since she was unable to attend to her own teeth and gums, someone had to floss and brush for her or she would suffer caries and thrush and periodontal disease. The input of her nutrition had to be maintained and the output monitored. A shortage of urine could signal inadequate fluids, a kidney stone, a bladder problem, a rise in her blood pressure. The evening was when Ruth would move her bowels, if she was going to, as her feedings of a liquid nutritive were timed to produce a nightly result. If she failed to do so, then concern rose that she might be constipated or impacted. Immobility made Ruth fragile; her caretakers obsessed over every aspect of her physical existence like soothsayers over auguries.

Sylvia insisted, since Kissy had brought them the tea, on returning the tray to the kitchen.

Bundling up her knitting to leave, Mrs. Prashker asked, "How are you? Still working?"

Kissy grinned. "You bet."

"All that bulky equipment. You wait till you have to manage baby and all of that too." Mrs. Prashker crimsoned. "Oh, I'm sorry. I've put my foot in it. You're giving the baby up, aren't you?"

"No, I'm keeping it."

"Now I feel even stupider." Mrs. Prashker glanced at Ruth. "I'll refrain from offering advice. I leave the dispensing of wisdom to my mother. She's much better at it than I am." Her smile was pinched. She buttoned her coat and fluffed the collar. "The only thing I know for sure is you can't imagine how it will work out. And while I'm minding your business for you, I'm going to come right out and say I admire you for not getting an abortion." Again she looked at Ruth. "And here I am petitioning the court to let Ruth go." Her dark eyes, so like Ruth's and Sylvia's, returned to Kissy. "It's not the same though, is it?"

"No," Kissy said. "It's not the same."

The abrupt nod with which Mrs. Prashker departed suggested she did not quite believe it herself.

"I'm going up," Sylvia announced from the door. "Good night, dear."

Kissy set up and then sat down—she never went right to work photographing Ruth, and these days, she needed to catch her breath first. She made a point of talking to Ruth first. She described the weather and ran through a few events of the day. All the while intensely aware that she was carrying a child possibly fathered by the man who had put Ruth into this condition.

"Did you hear your mother?" she asked. "She's not happy about asking the court to let you go. She knows you aren't going to get well, but she still wants you to recover. She doesn't want the possibility of some miracle eliminated. It's a hard decision. You know, if this hadn't happened to you, you might have one day had to make the decision for her. More people must make it for their parents than for their children."

Of course, Ruth did not respond. There was no flicker of eyelid, no twitch, no gurgle of tubes. From time to time, one of her attendants would shift her around a bit, turn her face in one direction or another. For the moment she was showing Kissy a three-quarter profile and would not have been looking at her if her eyes had been open. Her hair was quite short, in a boy cut, and the upside ear was prominent and vulnerable. Her skin was like marble, veined and translucent, her hand on the bedsheet a minimalist fiction over the bone.

Kissy cupped a hand over Ruth's. "Junior's back."

A contraction wrapped her belly like a girdle. The obstetrician was still fence-sitting—one week he said sooner; one week, later. It hardly mattered. Jimmy Houston was not getting out of prison until this baby was halfway to grown up. And if it was Junior's baby, the fact remained he would not be around on a day-to-day basis to help her raise this kid either.

Marriage to Junior would be an endless sequence of departure, absence, and return. She would be lonely and he would be lonely and every time he came home she would want him—as she did now—and every time she went to bed with him she would be afraid he was infecting her with something he had picked up from some whore or groupie and she would hate herself for being so weak as to take him back. Still, she wanted him and it was very difficult to have a baby alone—no one could tell him better than she. It was she who had gone through morning sickness and hurting breasts and cramps and the ache of softening ligaments in the pelvis, sleepless nights, the tyranny of her bladder. Who had people looking down their noses in condescension at her, people assuming her belly was proof she didn't know what she was doing, so they should feel free to tell her. Junior was one of them, really, and worse—and because he might just be the guy who had knocked her up, was licensed, somehow, to impose his will on her.

She pushed herself out of her chair.

Ruth's thin chest rose and fell. Her mother had exercised her, leaving her legs slightly bent and angled to one side. Her hipbones tented her flesh and the thin sheet over them. From the hollow that stretched from the bottom of her ribs to below her groin, the small mound of her pubis rose pathetically. There was a chortle in the breathing tube like the sound of air trapped in the line of the dentist's saliva drain and then it cleared.

Whatever was going on in Kissy's life, Ruth's half-life continued like the sleep of a hundred years imposed by an evil fairy godmother. Presumably Ruth felt no desire and no pain—but how could anyone be sure she did not? No one could say if she heard and saw everything around her and knew exactly what her situation was. Did she live a real enough life in dreams or on some other plane? Perhaps she was in a special kind of utero, waiting to be born into another existence.

Kissy reached for her camera with the hope it would show her some clear and unmistakable vision of Ruth.

"Oh, it's you," was Mrs. Cronin's greeting the following evening, her hand on the door as if she was thinking about closing it on Junior. "She's gone up." She glanced at the stairs behind her, and he looked up them too. "They get higher for her every day."

"I'll go up," he volunteered, as if there was some expectation Mrs. Cronin was going to fetch Kissy. "She's expecting me—"

He didn't give the old lady a chance to react but ducked by her and took the stairs two at a time. On the second-floor landing he picked up the bass from Kissy's music above and kept on going. It was as good as bread crumbs, not that the third floor was large. It appeared to be a converted attic. The door was ajar. She looked up from her book when he peeked in. She was in bed, reading in the circle of warm light thrown by her bedside lamp. Her face brightening, she pulled down her headphones and let the book fall to the counterpane. He hung over her to kiss her, and it was a very welcoming one that he pursued long enough to get her giggling.

The music whispering from her headphones had died. She had a boom box on the dresser next to the bed—he jumped up and started rummaging in her music. There was a tape marked casually with the word *boot* that looked from the handprinted list on the sleeve to be live recordings of Boston bands. He dropped it into the slot and reeled it back to the leader and punched play. The Neets began to pump a weird numerology that sounded like the son of "96 Tears." Kissy laughed. He climbed back onto the bed on all fours, made it shiver and shake, and then flopped onto his back next to her.

"I miss living with you. Sleeping in the same bed," he said. "I was never happier."

Though she snickered derisively, her eyes were suspiciously bright. He kicked off his high-tops and stretched out next to her to make spoons, the only way to hold her and accommodate her belly. She sighed. He hesitated to touch her belly; it seemed safer to rest his hand on her hip. The music went on and they didn't speak, and when it was played out, he glanced down at her and she had dozed off. Reaching over, he snapped off the lamp.

Her bladder woke her, as it did several times each night. It was nice to wake up in his arms. She crept out and back again without his seeming to notice. The next time she had to pee the dark was letting go. She was backed up against him the way they used to sleep, with Junior hard against her. It was pleasant and disturbing. Again she slipped out. When she came back, he was awake too.

"Look at this," he murmured, taking her hand and putting it on him and trying to kiss her.

She turned her face away.

"Let's make love—" he urged.

"No."

"We don't have to fuck—"

"No!" It was eight months late to be trying alternatives.

He sighed and rolled over. After a moment, he got up and found his high-tops. He crouched to kiss her ear before he left.

He crept downstairs to the front door and sucked air into his lungs like a drowning man. The paperboy was coming up the street. The kid was fat and slow and he jiggled as he walked. Junior held out his hand and received the rolled-up *News*. The fat kid blinked at him.

"Hey," he said, "you're Junior Clootie. Can I have your autograph?"

Junior held out his hand and the kid fumbled in his jacket and came up with a thoroughly chewed pencil stub. Junior wrote his name in a corner of the front page and tore it off and gave it to the kid.

"Thanks," said the paperboy, staring at it. "You live here?"

"No."

The paperboy squinted at him. "Right, this is Old Lady Cronin's. She was my dad's first grade teacher. Her grand-daughter's the one in a comber. There's another one living with her—" He cupped a belly in the air inches from his own.

"My girlfriend," Junior said.

The kid snickered. "She let one in the five hole, huh?"

"Fuck you," said Junior.

The front door opened behind him and Sylvia Cronin looked out in astonishment. "What are you doing here? Is that my newspaper?"

Junior handed it to her. "I was just leaving. Dozed off last night."

The paperboy's eyes widened and a prurient grin stretched his features into lumps.

Mrs. Cronin's mouth clamped like a tourniquet. "Get out of here," she told the paperboy, who obeyed, hustling down the path. She turned to Junior. "You too." She closed the door in Junior's face.

Sylvia was reading the paper. She had coffee on, and melon sliced and oatmeal cooked.

"God, that smells good," Kissy said, glomping oatmeal into a bowl.

Sylvia folded the paper and set it aside. "I met your friend going out."

"Oh," Kissy said. "I'm sorry. He dozed off."

"I thought that he had left. Next time I'll look to see what's parked out front."

"It won't happen again."

"Kissy, I don't mind him staying over—I mean, it's none of my business, you're an adult." Sylvia's eyes were twinkling. "Now I've shocked you—"

"No." Kissy grinned over the oatmeal.

"I don't expect you'll let him move in or that I'll be tripping over young louts every morning. This is the fellow you were living with, the one who killed the dog, isn't he? What interests me is his coming 'round at all—"

"He wants to marry me, he says."

Sylvia nodded. "I thought it might be that. You're a bit far along for dating. So he wants to do the right thing—"

"It's not his kid, Sylvia."

For a moment Sylvia Cronin digested the information. "Well, he evidently cares more about you than that one detail, which certainly would put off a lot of men."

"I know."

"I love having you here, dear," Sylvia said. "I would love having a little one here. You're part of my family now. I just want you to know that, whatever you decide."

❧ 19 ❧

J unior had a busy day before he fetched up on Mrs. Cronin's stoop again. Once again, Old Lady Cronin herself loomed in the doorway. Just an old woman, a hundred-ten pounds of dried-up pussy that probably leaked every time she sneezed—nothing to be intimidated by. "Good evening," he squeaked.

She smiled.

She would, he thought, coughing to cover his chagrin.

"She's gone up," she said. There was something going on with her mouth, making it twitch. She was laughing at him. "You'll have to go up."

He nodded with all the dignity he could summon and concentrated on not tripping as she watched him take the stairs.

"You again," Kissy said when he let himself into her bedroom, but she was smiling. She was wearing overalls again, denim ones, a white cotton Henley underneath.

Being casual, he poked around in her music. "Bought a car today, a used Saab. Guy threw in a car seat for the baby."

"Really." She seemed to be amused.

He slotted *Abbey Road* and set it to loop through, which would give him the length of the album to get back to the first cut, the important one.

Kissy rubbed the back of her neck wearily as she set aside her book and headphones. There was body lotion on her dresser. He picked it up in passing and sat down at the edge of the bed and took her by the shoulders. She knew right away what he was doing and cooperated. He turned her around and went to work on her neck. She had always carried all her tension there. He worked his fingers up and around her scalp to her temples and her face. Cry of guitar, pleading, Lennon pleading, and she shuddered at his fingertip tracing the outline of her mouth and then the sweep of his palm down her throat. He undid the buttons of her shirt and slipped his hand inside, snubbing his fingertips against the edge of a bra. And then, inside it, her nipples were rigid.

"Junior," she whispered, "don't do this to me."

He covered her mouth with his and her tongue told him another story, the one he wanted to hear.

Her breasts were much bigger, of course, the skin milky and traced with blue veins so they were like some extraordinary marble come to life. The nipples huge and sable. Her smooth belly like a huge opal cabochon set between breasts and bush. She was like the bellied Venus emerging from the sea. He could see her on the spread wings of the shell, naked, except for the white socks she wore now. Though intensely aroused by the exposure of her body, he was also moved by it and more than a little hesitant. The bodies of women had always seemed vulnerable to him, even Kissy's, muscular as she was. Still tender at the breast, still wounded between the legs. Now the existence of the baby in her womb rendered her fragile and precious, like one of those jeweled eggs the Russian czars had collected. Lie about it though she might, he had done this to her, and she had allowed it to continue. It meant something, didn't it? She reveled in his touch, preening, writhing. As he oiled her stomach, the baby moved within, creating waves and dimples and asymmetry on the surface.

"Golden Slumber" 's lullaby bled into "Carry That Weight" with its disconcerting warning. "Boy, you're going to carry that weight." "The End" began "Oh yeah all right," McCartney sounding weirdly like Eric Carmen.

Kissy gasped. "No." And then, more steadily, "We can't."

Next to her, up on one elbow, his fingers on the buttons of his fly, he was feverish and disbelieving. "Why not?" Then suddenly worried. "Are you okay?"

"I don't need another dose, thank you," she said.

He flinched.

The music kicked in again, the coda of "Her Majesty" that he had never liked anyway. And now the timing was blown. He rolled off the bed and killed the tape as the leader ran out.

"For Christ's sake," he said. "We weren't together."

She just looked at him with that X-ray vision women turn on men when they suspect infidelity.

Instantly he discarded the impulse to stonewall it. Admitting to too many would make her think he was hopelessly promiscuous, but if he said only one, it might look like some other girl had really given him pause. "You went with other guys. I had a couple girls. Nothing serious, Kissy—"

"That's just it, nothing serious."

"I'm clean, I was careful, Kissy."

She turned her face sharply from him, clenching her eyes against a sudden stinging. It still hurt, hitting the wall of his life. It was impossible not to imagine the acts. Nothing to him, he would say. The casual insertion of his cock into the mouth of some strange woman, some woman whose name he never caught, or if he did, promptly forgot, a quick shoot off and it was over. The woman spit out his semen or swallowed it, according to her taste. He went his way, presumably feeling some relief or satisfaction not achievable by his own hand, and the woman went hers. To make a note in her diary, to brag on a rest room wall or to her friends, to award herself a gold star—I blew him, the goalie. An autograph won't do, gotta suck his dick, get a mouthful of the guy's come.

How would he react, she wondered, if she told him she had taken up blowing strangers as a hobby? Or seeking them out for anonymous cunnilingus—she supposed there were men and women too who sought that with the eagerness so many men seemed to have for fellatio.

"You left me," he said, "you wouldn't take me back. Don't punish me for being honest with you."

Honesty was not the problem. But totting it up, the sums of their guilt were nearly identical. How could she judge the women he had fucked? She was one of them. She had done everything with him he might have done with one of them, and at the beginning, he had been nearly as much a stranger. And then there was Jimmy. She turned back to him slowly and he kissed her wet face.

He got up again to fix the tape and push play. And came

back to her, to make spoons with her, to *shu shu* again. A wash of heat triggered a mild contraction. He drew her back against him to stroke her tight belly until it relaxed, and then he put his hand between her legs from behind.

"No," she whispered. "No. Not without a safe."

He sucked air. "I don't have one. Please, Kissy. It's been forever and I'm dying, please, don't yank me around. I don't have anything." He kissed the back of her neck. "At least this time there's no chance I'll knock you up." His hand was on her, fingers probing and caressing. "Please."

She moaned. He pushed a finger into her and rested his thumb behind it. Shuddering, she tried to move away, but he held her back against him. She was breathless. He kept at it. Then he was inside her, drawing her up onto her knees and sinking into her in one easy motion that made her cry out. He moved gently. It was so easy, letting go, falling into it with him, and he sighed in her ear and she closed her eyes.

His heartbeat slowed and settled and his breathing slowed too. It was hypnotic; she was tired. The next thing she knew it was early in the morning. About three, by the pressure in her bladder. Stealthily she eased from his embrace—it was more like a net of arms and legs in which she'd become entangled—and went to relieve herself. On her way back to bed, because it was a little shivery, she slipped into a nightdress. The dark was fraying and she had her night vision. Sitting on the edge of the bed, she glanced at him.

All at once she hoped the baby was his and had his ears. She would lick them incessantly like a mother cat. She crawled up against him and began to trace the outline of his ear with the tip of her tongue. He twitched in his sleep and began to come out of it. His hand groped for her, and she put the tip of her tongue delicately into his ear as if she were a hummingbird and he sighed. She felt the flutter of his eyelashes and lifted her head to watch him open his eyes and focus on her. His hand cupped the back of her head and he raised his mouth to hers.

He liked the nightdress, liked pushing it around to expose parts of her. When the lovemaking was over, he drew it down reverentially and tucked it around her ankles.

She snuggled into his arms. "This doesn't change anything."

He was quiet for a while, thinking it over. Then he muttered "Shit" at the ceiling and sat up and seized her by the jaw and made her look at him. "Stop it, Kissy. Just stop the shit right now. You've dicked me around long enough. I'm done apologizing. I took my punishment."

They glared at each other and he let go of her. She sat up and saw them, darkly, in the dresser mirror. Her hair was standing up all over and so was his. He reached over and snapped on her reading lamp, and their images leapt up in the mirror like fish to the flawlessly still surface of a pond.

"It'll be okay," he said. "I promise."

In the silence as they looked at each other, she heard each word all over again with absolute clarity. *It'll be okay. I promise.* It wasn't the first time she had heard them, she thought, not even from him.

"I can't go into this without telling you," she began. It was phrased to make him uneasy. Junior did not want to hear it, but she did not give him any choice. "There wasn't any one-night stand. I was involved with somebody for a while after you left. The baby's as likely his as yours."

Junior was relieved the news was no worse. He had tortured himself enough, imagining her with someone else. He was not going to pursue it any further for fear of where it might lead. "Over-done-with-tout-finis. I don't care."

Kissy took a deep breath. "What if it doesn't work? What if I just can't live your kind of life?"

"It'll be okay," he said quickly. "You ever want out, just say so."

It was easy to say. He pled with her silently not to challenge him, not to remind him aloud how he had behaved when she left him with just cause the previous time. Letting it go, going along, it felt like speeding up to take a bump fast enough to leave the road and fly over it. They were both sweaty and pale with it.

"All right," she said.

The image of the still pond remained in her mind. Now she saw pebbles skipping on the skin of the water, wrinkling it, vanishing beneath it. She saw, suddenly, a baby's car seat, settling slowly through the depths of the water. The surface stilled again into perfect reflection and she saw there, smiling down at her, lovingly and foolishly and unreachably, the face of the man in the moon.

* * *

Though it was short notice, this time of year none of his teammates were tied up with superconductor experiments or emergency brain surgery, and attending Junior's wedding looked like a good excuse to golf, eat lobster, and make jokes at his expense. Junior and his brother, Mark, made several trips to the airport to pick up various past and present teammates. The last to arrive were Deker and Moosejaw, manfully shouldering golf bags and suit bags as they piled off a connection out of Boston, where they had rendezvoused from different departure points. In front of a group of high school basketball players returning from an AAU camp, Deker dropped his gear, seized Junior by the jaw, and kissed him passionately on the mouth, sending the other two into hysterics.

Moosejaw engulfed Junior in a bear hug and planted a slobbery kiss on his mouth to match Deker's.

A flutter of applause and some whistles broke out among the AAU campers.

"I never met any of these guys," Mark said loudly.

Crammed into the Saab with the golf bags tied to the roof, the visitors rolled down the windows and gawked at Peltry.

"What am I telling you, Moose?" said Deker, "This is no Dry Hole, Montana. I am telling them all the way from Denver, Junior, this is just like Ukraine, only with no queuing up for the lobster and the toilet paper in every store and the music of the headbanging."

"Kissy would have been here but she had to see the obstetrician today," Junior told them.

"She gonna make it to the wedding?" Moosejaw asked.

"We'll move it to her, if we have to." Junior grinned. "Maybe you'll be here for the baby as well as the wedding."

"A hum is less expensive." It was an observation Deker offered pensively, no doubt borne down by the legal and financial complications of an ever-increasing number of paternity claims, some from back home in the USSR and dating back to when he was jailbait. If they had jailbait in the former socialist paradises. It had begun to occur to Deker that he could not afford to pay them all off and that some of them might even be opportunistic. His enthusiasm for sowing his seed, while not totally checked, did appear to be faltering.

"Goddamn," Deker breathed suddenly, "is that being the golfing course?"

Junior confirmed it, and a long reverent silence followed as they craned at it. Then they broke out whooping and screaming and slapping each other about the head and shoulders.

He decanted them from the Saab directly to the clubhouse to allow a brief stop for restorative libations before they hit the links as a foursome. All the other guys and Coach were already out there, some of them nearly through thirty-six holes, others reaching eighteen. A day on the greens had struck him as a great way to stop sweating the wedding, which his mother and Old Lady Cronin were organizing. He had his haircut and his clothes. They had blocked out the ceremony last night at the chapel, so all he had to do was entertain his guests and show up and hope Kissy didn't go into contractions. She was having them off and on all the time.

Dionne had wanted to do the bachelor party, but Junior had checked him, asking Coach Stannick to do it. Coach had been flattered. What with Junior's teammates flying in, and the return of former Spectre teammates for the occasion, it was a chance for Coach to revel in the celebrity and the nostalgia of past glories. The whole event thus acquired an athletic banquet cast. It would doubtless have some raunchy moments, but there would be none of the strippers, hookers, and stag films that Dionne would regard as essential, and any doping would be discreet. Junior didn't care how stupid Dionne might get; he was determined to show up for his wedding without a hangover, a police escort, or a dose.

While they waited for Moosejaw and Mark to tee off, Deker slung an arm around his shoulder.

"You are making one woman happy," Deker said, "but so many others sad. One of those sad women is being Monette. She is calling me, asking for your phone number here."

"You didn't give it to her, did you?" Junior asked, horrified.

Deker laughed. "Am I looking stupid? I am not being the fool so much as that!" He slapped Junior on the shoulder. "If she is calling," he said gaily, "she is not getting a number from me." He changed the subject. "I am looking forward to meeting Bernie again. For being your sister, she is hot."

"My sister's fifteen—" Junior said.

Deker frowned. "Fifteen is an excellent age. This I am not understanding. Only in America is everyone believing fifteen is too young for love."

"You better. You stay the fuck away from her too." Having said it, he knew at once he had been too vehement.

"Sometimes it is not being my choice, Hoot," Deker smiled.

Junior watched the lying idiot horny fuck step to the tee. Deker stroked it beautifully. Junior fished a Titleist from his pocket. He examined it closely. Deker was strolling down the fairway after the other two, no doubt thinking about his next shot. Junior teed the ball. They all turned to watch him. He grinned and waved. He took a long careful gander down the fairway. Then he took a prodigious stroke. Half a second later, Moosejaw screamed—but it was Deker collapsing, hands on his crotch.

Junior fixed his face in an expression of horrified concern. "Come and keep your comrade warm," he muttered as he hurried to his wounded teammate.

"Monette called," Esther told him when he blew in from the golf course. She was ironing, this time with a religious enthusiasm; the air smelled scorched. On her ironing board, his suit was taking a pressing. It was cream-colored, express-delivered from Paul Stuart in New York, and she had done the spot-tailoring for him—tightening the waist, hemming the pants, letting down the sleeves.

He wasn't seeing Kissy that evening; he had the bachelor party. Bride and groom weren't supposed to see each other until the wedding, a custom he suspected proceeded directly from women wanting the men out of the way while they got the thing organized.

"Oh," he said, feeling deeply unclever.

"She said she was an old girlfriend," Esther went on, thumping the iron down heavily. "She said she wanted to wish you well. I told her not to call again. The slut."

"Thanks, Mom," Junior said faintly.

"You're a goddamn idiot sometimes," said Esther. She

lifted the iron. "But Kissy knows that and she's willing to marry you anyway, and I'm not going to let you screw it up, Mr. Stiff Prick. Her and that baby are your best chance of making a man of yourself. You had your fun. You're old enough to run your pecker instead of the other way around."

The iron thumped down again.

"Okay, Mom," Junior agreed. Considering the grim set of his mother's face, he didn't want to think where that iron might thump down next if he gave her any argument. He had visions of iron-shaped scorch-outs on his beautiful linen, his boxers on view to the congregation. He sidled past her. "Gotta get a shower."

She sniffed. "Gotta is right."

"Goalie Marries *News* Photographer." The picture had been taken on the steps of the campus chapel as the newlyweds left. The white Kissy wore was not conventional satin and lace but an Indian sari over leggings, and she had gone veilless. In a white linen suit and a white shirt with the collar unbuttoned and a white bow tie stuffed into the breast pocket of the unbuttoned jacket, Clootie looked as if he were just escaping his First Communion. White hightops on both bride and groom. The bride had given herself away, the *News* reported. The groom's brother, Mark, stood up with him; his sister, Bernie, with the bride, in a double-ring ceremony. Along with the groom's brother and some other present and former Spectre teammates, several professional hockey players, including the Russian defector, Evgenny Bezymyanny, a.k.a. Der Kommissar, Deker, were in attendance. Private reception in the bride's home.

The paper reprised the known history of the couple, using the euphemism "college sweethearts." It was the breakup of the relationship, the *News* reminded anyone who might have managed to let it slip their consciousness, that reportedly sent Clootie on a binge, accidentally killing his own dog, and resulted in his arrest after a high-speed chase. The paper advised readers that if not for the indulgence of the legal system, Clootie's professional hockey career might have been derailed by the incident. The last line of the article noted that "the couple expect their first child momentarily."

Burke snorted and threw the paper down on his desk.

He should be glad for Kissy, he guessed, that Clootie was legitimizing her kid. It was probably even smart of her to hook up with a guy worth divorcing. Still, he found himself unexpectedly irritated. People were such fools. He decided to go find Pearce and see if there would be any money in organizing an office pool on how long the marriage would last.

Junior looked down upon the small round face, eyes and mouth and nose seeming no more detailed than the features of a gingerbread man—uncooked, of course, pale dough upon the cookie sheet—as he cupped her head in his palm. Blinking, her small mouth rubbery as if she were trying to make it work, his daughter jerked like a fish out of water. Her tiny hands grasping uselessly at the air. She was impossibly real and not quite human, her eyes little more than slits. The small throbbing life in his hands terrified and exulted Junior. Then her lips closed and a smile shaped her mouth, a tiny ironic smile. For all the world, she looked as if she were going to laugh. Junior laughed aloud in delight, and a small arm jerked, a tiny hand clawed the air, as if in a salute or a wave of greeting.

"Show her to Mom," someone said.

Kissy was a husk, limp and exhausted, wet with sweat and blood. She had had back labor and stayed on her feet until nearly the end, leaning against him, first with her fists clenched against his chest, then actually beating on him. It had been like one of those clumsy fights on the ice that are all above the waist, two guys punching furiously at each other while simultaneously clinging to each other like a couple of drunks as their skates slide their lower bodies in opposite directions. He had been nothing in the final act. It was Kissy who had truly made the baby from her own body and suffered its birth, and she had been nothing in it too, a slave to a process her body was running on its own. So physical, so violent, so gross—the baby forced itself from her body like a wild animal, like the chestburster in the movie *Alien*.

Kissy's lashes fluttered down over her glazed eyes.

A nurse guided him in placing the baby on Kissy's chest.

"Mom," the nurse said, speaking to Kissy in a firm,

loud, you-are-an-idiot voice, "you've got a girl." They had already told her once but she had not responded.

She was tired and cold—shivering—by the time Junior put the baby in her arms. It was small and nearly weightless and she did not feel very connected to it. She was not terribly interested in it. She wanted to be allowed to go to sleep. But there was the baby, very quiet, very small to have been so much trouble. Her skull was capped with thick black hair that swirled from two asymmetrical crowns, one off the back, the other off the front. The little fists clenched, the small limbs jerked spasmodically. Her skin was mottled and waxy. One ear was strange.

Kissy touched it. It was folded over against the baby's skull. Carefully, she spread it. The ear flopped back when she let go of it. She wondered if it had gotten broken somehow and if it could be fixed.

It had been the hardest physical work she had ever done. Trapped in the intensity of pain and effort, it seemed to her that she had been tricked. No one had ever told her that this was what it would cost her. She did not care about the broken-eared baby. It did not bother her that she had no maternal feelings for it. She just wanted them to leave her alone and let her sleep. She closed her eyes.

She struggled from a doze that had settled over her like a coffin of glass. The hospital room was full of dusty summer light coming through the glass wall where the curtains had been left open. It was like floating in an aquarium. The heat in the light was heavy in her lungs and her head and her thoughts were small slippery fish flashing away from her grasp.

The first day when she woke, Junior had been there, sprawled asleep in a chair. The light had washed the detail from a quarter of his face and cast defining shadow in the rest and picked out the stubble of his beard and his eyelashes and eyebrows in gold. Struggling toward wakefulness, she half expected to see his face hanging there still, reflecting the light, as serene and untrammeled as a stone in the sky.

Someone came into the room. People did that. They didn't even knock. They came in and did things—emptied the trash and cleaned the toilet of the little bathroom, or poked at her or the baby. Sometimes it was visitors or Junior. He always made straight for the baby's crib to peer into it, like a little kid at a pet store window full of kittens.

But it wasn't Junior bending over the crib. Blinking, rubbing her eyes, she got up on an elbow with her heart jerking in her chest. It was her mother.

Kissy pushed herself up on her elbows. "Mom."

Cait looked up. "She's gorgeous."

Kissy slid from the bed and went to the crib to check the baby. She was on her belly and sound asleep. The ear was perfectly normal. It always had been. Just gotten folded over and pressed down in the birth canal. The baby was distinctly female, the rare infant whose gender was readily apparent without removing a diaper. She had long beautifully shaped hands. She was not squirrelly in the cheeks or rolly in the thighs. No longer mottled, her skin was flawless, without the rashes and pimples Kissy had seen on the other newborns in the maternity wing. Kissy picked her up. Her hair was all thick ringlets. Esther Clootie said she looked just like Junior as an infant. Kissy had already taken the first photographs. And sent one to her father, though he had made no response to the wedding announcement that had included a photograph of herself and Junior.

"Dynah," Kissy cooed.

"After Junior's team?" Cait asked, amused.

"No. I just like it."

"She looks just like you did—"

Kissy took the baby back to her bed with her. Her breasts hurt. She hoped Dynah would wake soon and make another try at nursing. So far it wasn't working very well for either of them. She was sore and Dynah was hungry. Dynah stirred. Kissy unbuttoned her nursing bra.

Cait sank into a chair to watch. "I don't know how I feel about being a grandmother—"

Dynah mouthed Kissy's nipple wetly and then, whimpering, chomped down on her. Kissy winced.

"How's Noah feel about being an uncle?"

"At five?" Cait laughed. "He finds it very funny."

Noah found nearly everything funny. He was very bright, with the self-sufficiency of a child often neglected by a distracted mother who nonetheless adored him.

"I've been feeling guilty," Cait continued. "You were

out on your own at such a young age, and I can't help thinking if I hadn't had Noah—"

"You wanted him," Kissy said. "He's a terrific kid. Yes, the fact you had a baby on your own and you've raised him by yourself, it had some influence on me. But Mom, I'm not alone now. I'm married."

"In the nick of time." Cait laughed.

Kissy raised her eyes to her mother. Cait had had Noah with a younger lover, who had since wandered off. It seemed to Kissy that the divorce from her father had freed Cait to become herself, a very different woman than she had been as Ken Mellors' wife. She had blossomed as an artist as well as a person.

"You don't think much of our chances, do you?"

Her mother smiled. "I know you don't. I suspect some of that is a legacy from your father and I. I see what you see in him, baby"—she burst out in a laugh— "and I see all the problems too." She shrugged. "All you can do is play your hand. You have a lovely baby, whatever happens."

20

B ernie sobbing in her arms was ironic. She was all
Bernie had for a big sister. In comforting her, she
comforted her own chagrined, panicked fifteen-
year-old self.

"It's not the end of the world, baby," she murmured,
feathering Bernie's hair, massaging her scalp, just as she
did Dynah's.

Outside, a motorboat throttled up on the lake, and kids
water-skiing shrieked and bellowed. Kissy, on a wicker
chaise with Bernie, could see Dynah in her playpen next to
them, blinking in her infant puzzlement at a mobile of
nursery rhyme characters Cait had made for her in bright
shining fabrics.

"Yes, it is," Bernie whispered.

Feeling her breasts tightening, her milk letting down,
Kissy patted the teenager's shoulder gently and nudged
her upright.

Bernie sat up, sniffling. "You must think I'm an idiot."

Kissy laughed. "I'm living in a glass house, honey."

"Box out!" Junior bellowed at the five hapless Summer
Leaguers skidding over the parquet.

The point was a girl, Fiona, the only one of them who
showed any real talent, and she had even less confidence
than the rest of them. She flailed in the face of the heavy-
set kid playing point for the other team. While the others
milled around in confusion, Fiona slipped and landed on
her ass. The opposing center hooked the ball out of the air
and shouldered his way to a rebound.

"Shit," said Junior, and made a *T* with his hands. The instant he did it, he remembered he had no more time-outs.

The ref spun around and hit Junior with a technical. With the opposition up four points and eighteen seconds left on the clock, there was no chance for a miracle from this bunch of wussies. The shooter knocked in the freebies, eighteen dispirited seconds drained away, and it was over.

"My fault," Junior told his team.

Relieved that it was over and they had not lost by an embarrassing margin, they were less disappointed than he. The little idiots still thought he was God. He suppressed his own disappointment and said as many positive things as he could think up. Babbled. Then he signed off the hours in the office, another six down on the total of his community service debt.

Just for the summer, they had taken a little three-room cottage on a lake forty minutes away from Peltry. It meant some commuting for him, but the quiet and cool were worth it. With Dynah belly down on her abdomen, Kissy was asleep on the daybed on the screened porch. The baby looked so much like Kissy, it was as if she had been cloned. Mother and child continued to sleep in frequent shifts, as if recovering from the arduous labor of Dynah's birth. Sleep, wake, nurse, bathe, sleep again. His mother assured him that was the way it was supposed to be.

They had weathered a dose of her family—Kissy's mom and half-brother, Noah, for a week. Caitlin wasn't hard to take, a reassuring preview of how Kissy would look someday, and evidently unconventional herself. The kid was what you would expect. A little brainiac. In the interest of turning the kid on to a more balanced life, Junior had taken Noah to Sowerwine, put him on the ice for the first time, taught him how to skate. The kid took to it so enthusiastically, Junior was fairly sure he had saved him from starting a serial killer scrapbook in a year or two.

He crept to the fridge for a beer. His ambitions for the evening were modest and domestic—sitting on the porch and listening to the ball game on the radio while he had another brew or two and held Dynah. She seemed to like stretching belly down across his knees. And maybe later he would get some nookie. But there was a piece of paper stuck under the key of the nearest can of beer.

"Call Spense," it said, and there was his agent's number, which he knew already by heart.

The beer in one hand, he went straight to the phone. It only rang once.

"Fella," Spense said genially. "Been waiting to hear from you."

"What's up?"

"You are," the agent said. "They traded Mickelson's ass. How'd you like a chance at being the man in Denver?"

Junior took a deep breath. "What's the money?"

"Two hundred and a quarter, with another up-and-down. This is a good deal."

Better by a long shot than the one he had had last season. If he didn't play up to demand, he would be back in Dry River at the minimum. Or maybe Allentown. Incentive he scarcely needed.

"I don't mean to be unappreciative," he said. "It's just I got a wife and kid now—"

"You and everyone else," the agent said. "The wife and kid is good. Management likes wives and kids. Good motivation. The name of the game is performance, son."

With the baby against her shoulder, Kissy appeared in the door of the living room. She blinked a little sleepily and he held out his hand. She came closer and he wrapped an arm around her as he hung up the phone.

"Denver," he said. "Two and a quarter."

Her eyes widened and he grabbed her and kissed her. Then he filled her in on the ifs. They had already talked out the possibilities. Nodding, she handed Dynah to him and took a macaroni salad and a jar of sun tea out of the refrigerator.

"It'll be okay," he said. He got another beer out for her. Her mother had told her a beer was good for her, and Esther agreed, but Kissy hesitated anyway. For someone who had not been sure beforehand she even wanted to keep her baby, she was a very serious mother. She was so involved with Dynah, she had very little energy for anything else. Or anyone. Like him. "You don't have to drink it all. It's just to celebrate."

He knew she did not want to leave Peltry, but it was a big deal in his life and she beamed at him and took the beer and laughed and let him hug her. It should have been champagne, he thought, and then no, this was exactly the way it should be.

Mouth full, surprised, he asked, "This Ma's macaroni salad?"

"Your mom's recipe. Actually, Bernie made it. She was here today quite a while." She pushed her salad around the plate and then fixed him with an ironic eye. "There's something you should know. She's pregnant."

Junior coughed macaroni salad back onto his plate. "Ma?"

"No, of course not. Your mother's in change, I thought you knew. Bernie's the one who's pregnant," she went on. "Your golf ball didn't slow your buddy down much at all."

"Deker? Come on, it's not possible. The guy's nuts looked like plums. He had an ice pack on them all weekend."

"Not all weekend."

"I don't believe it," he said. "Bernie's pregnant? She's sure? Jesus Christ. She's just a kid. It must be some other guy."

Kissy shrugged. "Whatever. She is pregnant."

"She's saying Deker? No way, baby, he couldn't have. Why would she say it was him? Whoever it is, I'll kill the son of a bitch. I'll cover the cost of a scrape myself. Mom and Dad don't need to know anything about it."

"She's decided to have it, Junior—"

"Aw, shit, that's just nuts. She's too young to have a kid—" He stopped. "Ma's gonna be mad at us for giving her ideas."

Kissy shrugged. "Probably she should be—"

"Come on, there's a big difference, we're not teenagers—does Bernie know about you? I mean, when you were fifteen . . ."

"No, of course not."

"Goddamn it—" This was supposed to be an occasion and it was down the toilet, just like that.

Six weeks, the doctor had advised, and Dynah was seven weeks old and he had no complaint. Kissy had taken care of him when he had gotten amorous, made him happy, if all she got out of it was a little kissing and cuddling. The news about his contract ought to have qualified if anything did as deserving an old-fashioned straight-up connubial bang. And there was Kissy, broody over her supper, which she needed to eat if she was going to feed the baby, and both of them upset about Bernie, and with somebody's hard-on the root of it, and Bernie being a dizzy fifteen-year-old going on sixteen, and Kissy with her history. It took the starch out of him too.

He got up and went to Kissy and worked her shoulder muscles, her neck, her scalp, and felt her let go, the way she did, trusting him, working with him. And she smiled up at him and they kissed each other softly and she said, "Eat your supper," and he picked up her fork and wrapped her fingers around it and said, "I will if you will," and she laughed. Everything was going to be all right. They would take care of the Bernie problem. It was just a shock to think of his little sister knocked up.

He put away her beer for her and stopped himself there. Between plays, he allowed himself to drift into sexual fantasy. It helped with the anxiety. He was afraid having the baby might have changed her. It had been rough enough on him and he had only had to witness it. He was not even sure that when push came to shove, he might not go soft.

He kept sneaking looks at her, until she caught him, which made them both chuckle. Her eyes like the lake when wind ruffled its surface and the sunlight bounced off it as chips of far-flung diamond. Love was great, he thought; he was so fucking lucky. He could even deal with the Bernie mess.

"Hey, Eu-genie," Junior greeted Deker, who was already ensconced in the hotel bar with some girls. Just off the road, half an hour or so, after a three-day marathon drive in the Saab, Junior had seen no one else yet.

"Hey, Hoot," the Russian crowed.

Until he spotted Deker, Junior had been almost euphoric—glad to be off the road and full of anticipation for the new season. Things were different this year, everything better, not least because Kissy would be joining him. Of course, he would have to earn the slot, but he was eager for the fray and the feel of the ice under his blades that was like riding a wave, herding a power outside of himself the way he wanted it to go. There were few things so *enough*.

"I am buying the beer," Deker told him.

"Oh, maybe more than that," Junior said, dropping a heavy arm over Deker's shoulders. "Bernie says hello—"

Deker laughed. It was a laugh Junior had heard before, Deker pleased with himself, the prick.

Junior nodded toward the men's room. "Go to the girls'

room with me, I gotta tell you a secret." He put a knuckle to his nose and sniffed.

Deker lit right up and trotted along, promising the girls he would be right back. "Mony, she is looking for you already," he told Junior.

"I'm not looking for her," said Junior, ushering him into the men's room. The door wheezed shut behind them. There was a guy taking a leak at a urinal and another guy in a stall.

Again Junior flung a friendly arm over Deker's shoulder, as if to gather him tight to whisper a secret or maybe reveal a stubby little vial with a tiny spoon chained to the cap. "Bernie's pregnant with a boy," he confided, and Deker's eyes widened, his mouth curved in delight, and Junior stiffened his arm instantly into a vise around the Russian's throat and drove his fist into Deker's face. The Russian's reflexes were as superior as his own, but the shock of the arm-lock across his windpipe and the leverage Junior had was overwhelming. Deker was unable to get his fists up before Junior hammered him twice in the face, and then Junior drove a knee into his crotch, and Deker collapsed with a small sad bubble of protest. It all happened so quickly, the guy at the urinal barely had time to say "Hey—"

Junior let Deker drop. "I lied, she doesn't know whether it's a boy or not yet, but it's gonna cost you about half a million bucks and maybe a sex-change operation if I let myself think about it too much—"

The guy at the urinal was already zipping up, hurrying out. The guy in the stall was very very quiet.

Deker writhed on the floor, clutching himself.

Junior walked out. His knuckles hurt. Four of the other guys had arrived, among them Moosejaw, and taken up the attention of Deker's girls. At the bar, he bought a beer and watched the men's room door. Deker eventually came out, white of face, trembling. The girls waiting for him gasped and hurried to his side.

"The fuck?" Moosejaw said in amazement.

Deker was a mess. His eyes swollen, his nose spread over his face, his mouth split open. What showed of his eyes was full of fear and pain and disbelief. He stopped at the sight of Junior, loitering at the bar.

"Shot of brandy for my friend," Junior said to the bartender, who was frozen in place, staring at Deker. "Looks like he tripped on his dick and hit his face on the urinal."

Moosejaw glanced down at Junior's knuckles. "When'd you change your name to Urinal?"

Junior didn't laugh. Neither did Moosejaw, who went to help Deker from the bar.

Deker on his bed later would not lift the ice bag from his face to even try to look at Junior. "I am doing what you want if the blood test is correct," he said, his voice muffled by the ice bag and swelling. "You are not needing to be bushwhacking me. Now we are not being friends. Be fucking off now, Hoot."

The tone of righteous injury inflamed Junior again. He had only come by to say they had to work together, they had to keep their differences between them. "If you were *being* my friend, you'd have stayed away from my sister. I ought to have you prosecuted, she was *being* jailbait, you dickhead."

"Hey," Moosejaw said, "take it easy, Hoot—"

"We have to play together," Junior continued. "I'm not going to let the personal shit get in the way. You take care of business and I won't give you any more trouble."

There was silence.

"He's right," Moosejaw advised Deker. "You can't let personal shit get in the way. Remember Kiamos—you heard the story how he played three years with a guy who stole his wife, after the guy did it. On the same fucking line."

"Yes," Deker muttered. Then he lifted the bag and peeked at Junior. "Someday," he said with much injured dignity, "you are telling me why it is being okay for Hoot to be knocking up a woman, but for me it is bushwhacking offense."

"I told you, asshole—"

"Go on," Moosejaw said, urging Junior to the door. "Damage is done, go take a shower."

Returning to Peltry by air, Junior packed up Kissy and Dynah and Bernie in the Blazer and set out again, in a morning fog, leaf color wet and blurred and delicate, the crackle of fall in the air. Though her eyes were fixed on the river, Kissy was aware of him checking on her reactions.

He was tense with barely suppressed exhilaration. She was afraid if she looked back, it would all be gone. All just disappear into the fog.

Crossing the bridge always reminded her of Ed. One day Ed had been woofing around, being Ed, and then he wasn't. She did not know when she would be back again, beyond tentative plans for Christmas, and it was silly to suppose nothing would change in her absence, besides the leaves come down, the seasons turn. Leaving Peltry, where she had lived longer than anywhere else, distressed Kissy more than she admitted, especially to Junior. But it excited her too, and she was clammy as they crossed the Mid-Dance, her armpits wet with a sharp nervous sweat.

In the time Junior had been securing his position with the Drovers, she had been out shooting again. Carrying Dynah in a Snugli strapped to her front, she had been forced to reconsider the burden of equipment. She switched from her medium format Hasselblad to a lighter, smaller 35-mm Minolta. The shift in format and the necessity of pruning the amount of gear she dragged with her had the happy result of forcing her back to basics. The results were not just satisfying, they were exciting. She was refocused, she thought. Dynah's doing, the total experience of pregnancy, birth, and motherhood, the presence of her warm little body against hers, that was Dynah's gift to her.

On Kissy's last visit, only a few days previous, Ruth had been fighting a urological infection. It was difficult to believe she could go on much longer. Yet the courts were so far as inconclusive as Ruth's own existence. It bothered Kissy to leave the project incomplete, but perhaps it was nearly so, or as near as was meant to be. She was in an accepting, go-with-the-flow mood. Those maternal hormones turning her into mush.

Tearing her gaze from the river, the skyline of Peltry, she stared at Junior's profile. He had been sailor-horny since his return. She had to resist the suspicion he might be faking it to reassure her he hadn't been cheating, wasn't going to infect her again. The nagging distrust was a worm in her heart, eating at the reality of being with him. She still found him funny and unpredictable, she liked and loved and desired him, and he was a relaxed and adoring daddy to Dynah. But when he told her he loved her, she could not allow herself to believe him.

* * *

The house Junior had found for them was in a declining middle-class neighborhood of a small town northwest of Denver. Crammed with the Victorian furniture of its late owner, an elderly piano teacher who had resided in it some sixty years, none of its rooms were on the same level but meandered up and down around corners. The kitchen sported a slate sink, and there was no shower, only a claw-foot tub in the bathroom. Among the furnishings was an ancient, one-eyed tomcat, ten bucks off the rent if they would care for it.

The teacher's daughter could not bring herself to break up her mother's household. Uncertain that she wanted to sell the house—one of her grown children might want it, one of these days—she could not absorb the furnishings into her own house, or part with them either, so she put it up for rent fully furnished. And she had cats of her own and was quite distracted with what to do about old Samson. It was a considerable relief to find a nice young couple with a baby to take the house for a year or two. The old tom was so mangy and arthritic, he looked as if he were already dead and only refused to lie down and stink.

There was a ground-floor back room that had been the old woman's bedroom when she grew too crippled to go up and down stairs easily. Bernie claimed it, falling behind the house tour to explore the closet and peer out the windows.

Touring the lopsided little rooms of the crooked little house, peering up the narrow uneven stairs, Kissy had to laugh. "Whoever built this place was drunk."

Up the stairs ahead of her, Junior grinned back at her just as the cat twitched between his legs. Though he caught himself easily, he swore loudly at the cat. Old Samson laid back his ears and hissed and then bounded away, exhibiting remarkable speed and agility for a beast of his age and decrepit condition.

Upstairs as down, the place was all corners and eaves and tiny windows, some of them jeweled with stained glass. Once the cat hair was vacuumed up with the piano teacher's antique Electrolux and the place had been given a good scrub, Kissy guessed it would be more than livable. Its odd corners would bend light in interesting pleasurable ways.

In the bedroom upstairs a brass-framed double bed squatted under the eaves. Junior caressed its metal curves lightly. "What do you think? Are we going to have some fun tying each other up?"

On the road or off, Kissy knew already, how much the members of a club saw of each other socially was largely a matter of personal taste. While living with Junior, she had recognized the similarities of the social dynamics among his Spectre teammates to those of military families. Some players worked together but always maintained a degree of distance. Others seemed never to really take off their uniforms—eating, drinking, and breathing as a member of the team. She discovered quickly that, like military people, some professional athletes—and their families, if they had them—avoided becoming too attached to one place, one set of friends. Others achieved superficial friendship for the duration. A fortunate few made lifelong friends that might even include their families.

There were some initial social events that allowed her to meet all the other players, some of their attachments, and other people in the Drovers' organization, but with an infant, she had every reason to stay home otherwise and she did. Bernie had to go to school, of course—they had found her a private religious school, all girls, at her request—but made easy company the rest of the time and was eager to baby-sit and help around the house. To Kissy's surprise and pleasure, Junior seemed to prefer to stay home with them.

"Why don't you ask some of your friends here?" she offered one night toward the end of camp.

Junior brightened at the prospect. "You wouldn't mind? What about Deker?"

He and Deker were playing together without any problem. They were even speaking. Deker claimed to be in love with Bernie, and interested in her welfare, and the child, if it was his.

Before bringing Bernie with them, they had talked—all three of them—about how Bernie would handle crossing paths with Deker.

"I'm not in love with the guy," Bernie had said. "It was just stupid. Three beers stupid." She said she had no interest in seeing him again, but if it was unavoidable, she could handle it. She didn't want his money and would be damned if she would take a blood test. But when she learned Junior had beaten him, she was angry with Junior. And Deker's phone calls clearly piqued her.

"What would you do?" she asked Kissy anxiously.

"I'm not you," Kissy had replied. Having been a fifteen-year-old girl once herself, she suspected Bernie's motivations were a mix of fantasy, calculation, and contradictory desires. "If you're old enough to be a mother, you have to take responsibility for the other stuff too."

Quietly, Bernie stopped taking his calls.

"Go to it," she said to the idea of the cookout.

"We don't have to invite him," Junior said.

"Don't let it be a problem. You guys have to work together."

The nights cooled rapidly but the afternoons were still often hot, and so they had a cookout that filled up their small backyard. Déjà vu all over again, Kissy thought; it was like seeing the Spectres together. The age range of the men wider but still young, and there were some girls. She was one of a handful of wives present, though many more than a handful of the players were married somewhere and many of them, admiring Dynah, spoke of their own little ones. Bernie hung back, in her role as mother's helper. They all knew who she was, of course, and that Junior had beaten up Deker over her, and that she was pregnant, but she wasn't showing and she looked her age. The unease her obvious youth caused quickly evaporated with a few beers. DeLekkerbek, the goalie Junior had told Kissy a little about, arrived drunk and grew drunker. Everyone seemed relieved when he crawled under the piano and passed out. There was much shaking of heads over him, all of them knowing—as he knew himself—he was going to be cut.

People were beginning to leave when Deker arrived. Bernie, in fact, had taken Dynah up to bed earlier and not come back downstairs. She was probably half asleep in Kissy and Junior's bed. It was past midnight but he was conspicuously bright. Cocaine, Kissy guessed, to go by the constant rubbing at his nose and his antsiness. The two women with him were even higher than he was. They could hardly speak for giggling. Monette Daniels, Deker introduced the tall one, and the other one, a woman who cried when she was drunk if ever there was one, as Diane

Salterton. There were two just like them in every high school, clubbing together to sneer at everyone else and incite each other's empty-headedness. The tall one fixed a mascaraed Gorgon stare on Kissy, allowing the shellac to crack into horrified amusement before turning it on Junior. With several more than three beers in him, he glared at Deker and ignored the two wenches so vehemently, he might as well have taken out an ad.

Kissy thought about it a moment, and then dug around in the melted ice at the bottom of the beer cooler for the last couple cans of beer. While the two women strutted around Junior, red-faced and looking trapped, and the oblivious idiot boy Deker, she shook the beers behind her back. Walking up to them, she held them in her palms as if in offering.

"Good night," she said, flicking the tabs with her thumbs and smiling warmly as the two women shrieked in the spray of beer. Deker took it for fun.

Kissy handed the cans to Junior and went into the house. Upstairs, Dynah slept peacefully. Bernie struggled to her elbows, rubbing her eyes.

"You missed Deker," Kissy said.

Bernie yawned. "Like I want to see him in the middle of seventy-five people."

She looked younger than fifteen. Kissy ruffled her hair. "Honey, I take back what I said. I think the guy's a disaster."

Looking up at her, Bernie blinked and her eyes welled. Kissy sat down hastily to hug her. Bernie had a good bawl. She was averaging one a week, which Kissy figured was probably about right for a pregnant fifteen-year-old two thousand miles away from home. Then Bernie blew her nose, accepted a last hug, and crept off to her room downstairs.

The last car doors slammed, the last engines ignited. It was quiet outside, quiet enough to hear the shuussh and spatter of Junior taking a piss on the shrubbery. Then the screen door behind him. The cat yowled as Junior threw it out, and she listened to him stumbling around downstairs.

He couldn't seem to navigate the house without banging his head, his knees, his toes, his elbows—or else tripping over Samson, swiftly renamed the Fucking Cat. There was no doubt the cat hated him: it stalked him with undisguised maliciousness.

Creeping, crawling, working out the mechanics of standing up, Dynah delighted in first rolling over and then climbing the one or two steps between the rooms. She regarded the tom, naturally, as a particularly fascinating variety of stuffed toy. Yet ugly as the old cat was with Junior, it tolerated Dynah's casual poking and clutching at it. Junior suffered nightmares in which the cat crept into Dynah's crib and suffocated her. He reminded Kissy repeatedly that cats were dirty fucking beasts liable to infect people with blood poisoning and cat scratch fever. He examined the baby daily for cat scratch but though he never found a one, it never had any effect on his paranoia.

The door closed, the tumblers fell. Then the front door, and Junior trudged and bumped his way up the stairs. He avoided her eyes.

"Charming people," Kissy said.

Junior kicked off his shoes. "I didn't invite them. They took Lek with them. Had to pour him into the car but at least he's gone."

She sat up and punched the pillows up behind her. "You partied with those women." Her use of the code word, *party*, was sarcastic.

"This isn't a good idea, getting started on shit like this, right now," Junior said. "I'm half loaded, baby. All I want to do is sleep."

"You can be married or you can be divorced," Kissy said. "What *I* won't be is the wife you fuck around on."

He sat down on the edge of the bed and met her eyes. "I'm married. I haven't had anything to do with anyone else since we took our vows."

It was in her court to believe it or not. Sick to her stomach, she turned her back on him. Welcome to your life. This was how it was going to be. You went on not knowing until you did.

21

"**I**s Hoot there?" drawled the woman on the phone. "No," Kissy said, and as she dropped the phone into its cradle, the woman's jeering laughter reached her like an echo.

The phone rang again immediately. "Have him call me," the woman said. "He knows my number."

"So do I," Kissy said, and hung up again.

She scrawled a note to Junior. "Woman called. Says you know her number." She spread open the telephone directory to the yellow pages, and placed the note on the pages headed "Lawyers."

Bernie looked at it curiously and then at her. "Everything okay?"

"Some old girlfriend of Junior's—don't worry about it."

Bernie picked up Dynah and swung her around. The baby shrieked with glee. Bernie took her outside to play.

"I'm sorry," Junior said, arriving home. He crumpled up the note and threw it away.

She glanced out the kitchen window into the backyard, where Bernie was rocking Dynah in a baby swing, then turned her attention back to the salad she was making. She shook out damp lettuce leaves and broke them into a bowl. "I'm having the phone number changed. Tell your buddies not to give it to her or else don't give it to them. If she calls again, I'm leaving—"

He stood in the doorway to the kitchen, watching her. "For Christ's sake, I can't control some wacko bitch—"

Her only reply was the sarcastic chop of her knife slicing through a cucumber.

He took a bottle of beer out of the refrigerator and spun

off the cap. His throat worked as he swallowed from it. "It's not fair."

"No it isn't." She shoveled cucumber slices into the bowl. "It's not fair to me to have to take phone calls from some wacko bitch you diddled and it's not fair for me to have to get treated for gonorrhea because you fucked some whore—"

He spun on his heel and walked out. She listened to the door of the Saab slam and waited for the sound of the engine, the gears ripping, the tires squealing, but instead there was quiet. And the car door opened and closed again, the front door, and his footsteps through the house again, and again he stood in the doorway, holding the beer in one hand.

"I am sorry about all of it," he said. "You've got a right to be angry. I promise I'll do everything I can to make things right. But you have to let go of the anger, Kissy, sooner or later. It'll kill us if you don't."

Her hand shook slightly and she put down the knife. Bernie stood in the back door, Dynah on her hip. The baby stretched and gurgled toward Junior. Bernie looked anxiously from Junior to Kissy and back again. Junior crossed the kitchen to take the baby. She grinned a wet, toothless baby grin, drool glistening on her lower lip. Kissy reached out and rolled a finger over it, gathering it up like dew.

The bitch would get bored and stop calling, he thought, if she didn't get any reaction. But there was no talking to Kissy. He sought out Deker, flagging him in the parking lot outside the facility where they practiced, climbing into Deker's Porsche to have a chat.

"Mony's calling my wife," he told Deker flat out.

Deker's happy face slipped. Worry clouded his eyes. He had become very eager to stay on Junior's good side. Not because he was afraid of a beating—if he could be intimidated, he would be dead as a hockey player. But the language of physical intimidation was one he grasped in his bones. He was taking Junior very seriously because he knew Junior had restrained himself from killing him. And there was the political side of it that was ultimately the money side of it. Everyone else in the club was acutely aware of how Deker stood with Junior Clootie.

"If you've got any influence with her," Junior said, "convince her it's not funny, she's got to stop—"

"Yes, yes," the Russian agreed quickly. "She may not be listening," he confessed. "She is doing her own thing."

Junior couldn't think of what else to do. He got out of Deker's car, patted the roof of it. "Thanks," he said.

Deker hung out the window after him. "How is Bernie?"

Junior looked at him, all the anger welling up in him again. He thought he could beat him all over and it would not change anything. Deker would just regard it as the price of admission, the price of manhood, or whatever he called it. Deker was truly still a kid, only twenty, Junior reminded himself.

"Pregnant," he said. "She's still pregnant."

Deker nodded soberly. "She is not speaking with me, Hoot. I am trying to do the right thing. Moose is explaining to me—Bernie is your sister, I am respecting her. She is a nice girl—"

"Jesus, Deker, how the hell could you screw, the condition you were in?" Junior blurted.

Deker laughed, eyelashes aflutter, a fine blush suffusing his skin. Convicting himself, again. Full of pride that he had managed to fuck after taking a golf ball in the basket. "Ah," he said modestly. "Bernie is being so hot, it is not being all my fault, Hoot—"

"It was *your* dick," Junior said.

Walking away, he realized he sounded like Kissy.

The next day when he came out of the facility, the Rich Bitch's car was parked next to his and she was in it. This-Diane, too, the pair of them sitting there, smoking cigarettes and laughing, like a couple of wives or girlfriends legitimately waiting for some guys. He couldn't believe it. He swore and strode up to it and rapped on her window. She rolled it down.

"What are you doing here?" he demanded.

"Waiting for you," she said.

In sight and sound of half the club.

"This is bullshit," he said. "I don't want anything to do with you. Don't call my home anymore either."

"That'll go down well with Kissy." She made a kissing sound.

This-Diane laughed.

He walked away from them, unlocked his car with shaking fingers, and threw his duffel into it. When he looked up, over the roof of the Saab, she was still there. Smiling lovingly at him, amused with him. she was doing this to him on purpose. This was part of her game. He was in a cold sweat and she loved it.

"She's a psycho bitch," he told Kissy. It was the last thing he wanted to talk about with her, but he didn't know what to do. "She's having a good time making me nervous, making you angry." It was like walking into a cloud of midges. All he could do was flail. He groped for something reassuring. "Maybe she'll get bored tomorrow and move on to some other hobby."

Kissy listened quietly. They were in the backyard, sitting on the back stoop, watching Dynah staggering around after the old tomcat, the beast positively kittenish in a feline second childhood. Bernie was out at her after-school Driver's Ed class. Everything perfect, except there was this little problem, and it made him feel even angrier and more helpless.

"Maybe," Kissy said at last, and let it go.

Soon enough she understood. The notes started coming, and the Polaroids of the Rich Girl, and it was all too obvious that Monette Daniels was a psycho who scarcely needed any encouragement from Junior. A nutcase was a nutcase. He couldn't be expected to be able to make a nutcase go away. Anybody in the public eye was apt to attract one of them. His only fault was ever having been involved with her. Sickeningly, through her notes, she was supplying the details, fantasized and real, to Kissy.

"Who ever said letter writing was a lost art?" Kissy asked sardonically. "The tradition is alive and reaching new heights in Looneyville."

The Minnesota forward threw Junior into the net as the right wing drove in the puck. To Junior's amazement, no interference call was made and the goal counted. He exploded from the net, tearing off his gloves as he threw himself onto the forward's back. He managed to pound a fist into one of the fucker's ears before being dragged off and finding himself in the middle of a donnybrook. He couldn't get at the forward—two Drover defensemen had taken over for him and were pounding the bastard enthusiastically. The

Minnesota goalie raced down the ice and Junior shot out to meet him at the blue line and throw him into the boards. Crouching to get a shoulder between the other goalie's legs, Junior levered him over the boards and into the Drovers' bench, where another Drover dragged the goalie down and cleaned his clock for him. Somebody else jumped Junior and he struck out furiously.

Getting tossed was a rare event for him. He was still violently pissed as he glided past his replacement, Damien St. Louis, on his way to the runway. This game, the second in a five-game road trip, was in Minneapolis. He had given up a hat trick to one guy and two to a rookie hotshot. And the third period was only half over. As much as the official's blindness, it was frustration that had sent him hurtling onto the guy's back, a frustration beyond the confines of the game.

With one eye on the monitor as he shed his gear, he watched with his gut knotting as St. Louis immediately let in another goal. This game was going down the toilet and it was his fault. He hadn't been able to come up with any better defense than getting thrown out. His head ached with disaster. How much worse did he have to be before they sent him down? The thought of having to call Kissy to tell her to pack for Dry River made him sick.

It seemed significant that once the game was over, nobody gave him a hard time. Like a funeral, he thought; the locker room was like a wake, and he was the dead man. They didn't look at him, reminding him of how many times he had avoided eye contact with some guy in deep shit. Bad luck to look at a dead man.

Deker sat down next to him on the bus and slipped him a flat glass bottle, a pint of Old Jock, cheap and nasty. Junior knocked back a mouthful and it seared all the way down and made his eyes water. When they got off the bus, Deker was at his elbow, nudging him into the bar. Most of the other guys were right behind him. Just the one, he promised himself, just the one. To be polite, to be one of the guys, to get past a bad night.

A couple hours later he was still deciding just one more, and This-Diane was suddenly in his face. He had not known she was there; he had not seen her around, and no one had mentioned seeing her. It was extremely disconcerting; he looked around anxiously, certain that where she was, the Rich Bitch would be too. And there was Mony, perched on a bar stool, watching avidly.

This-Diane grabbed his arm. She was drunk, her face choleric with it. She had a beer in one hand.

"You suck," she said loudly.

Junior was a little too numb to do anything but laugh. From her, it was too much.

"You suck," she repeated, "like a cocksucking faggot." Then she spit in his face and dumped her beer in his lap.

Reflexively, Junior threw his beer into her face.

This-Diane howled in outrage, and all at once he was in the middle of his second donnybrook of the evening, people shoving and pushing, throwing punches and screaming and shouting and swearing almost randomly. He ducked and dove his way through it. Once he reached the periphery, though, a wide boy stepped into his way.

"Hey, asshole," the wide boy said, and started to swing on him.

Junior stepped into a scissors kick and flipped the wide boy ass over teakettle. Then it came to him the wide boy looked like a bouncer. Another set of huge arms locked around him from behind and bad breath hissed around his ears.

"Quiet down, asshole," his captor growled. "I'd love to pound your fucking face into the fucking floor."

Junior expected to be dumped onto the sidewalk. Instead, the second bouncer shoved him into a cloakroom, and in a little while, some cops appeared and took him away.

He had to admit he knew her. She had gone and told the cops she was a girlfriend of his. He knew he should keep his mouth shut, he should wait on a lawyer. He had had sense enough to use his dime first thing to call the manager, Ed Toth, to bail him out. But while he was waiting, they wanted his side of the story. That was the way they put it and he thought, goddamn it, he had a right to tell it. All he had to do was tell the truth.

"She's a groupie, a freak. I was single then," he told the cops, who arranged their faces in sympathy but asked increasingly nasty questions.

Then Ed got there, with a lawyer in tow, and the lawyer told him to shut up, and he did. And they got him out of there.

As soon as he was back in his hotel room, he called Kissy.

"Baby—" he said, but before he could ease the presentation he had worked out, Dynah fussed querulously not far from the phone.

"It's one in the morning," Kissy said groggily. "Hold on."

He listened to the flap of bedclothes and her shushing Dynah and then the baby cooing, getting tit, the lucky kid.

"Are you all right?" Kissy asked, her attention back on him again.

"I had some trouble—"

"Oh?" The single word coming from some really cold airless planet in some very unfriendly universe.

"I didn't start it. Don't worry, we'll get the charges dropped." The faraway silence lengthened into light-years. "Kissy?"

"I'll be here when you get back," she said, as if maybe that had been in doubt. "We'll talk about it then."

Three more road games. Then one at home, before the Christmas break. When at last they were headed back to Denver, the weather was bad, air traffic all across the country affected. A couple of drinks turned into several more, just to numb the boredom and the stress, the shit he had had to wade through from the media since the incident in the bar, but he was okay, he practically sobered up on the fucking runway at Stapleton, it was so fucking long. After that, keeping the Saab on the road through the sleet finished the job, sweating out whatever was left of the alcohol in his system. He expended a lot of energy cursing too, especially at himself for not having the sense to have a four-wheel-drive like everybody else in Colorado. He picked up a take-out coffee at a drive-through, poured half out the window, and emptied two nips he had pocketed on the airplane into it. It helped ease his headache and the tension in his chest that was like a block of stone under his breastbone.

He swung the Saab around the Blazer, which looked as if Bernie had left it where she had been practicing parallel parking, halfway up the driveway, well to the right. A hard glaze of sleet encased it. The Fucking Cat twitched from the shadows as Junior put his key in the door. Junior curled his lips at it and hissed and it spat back and bounded past him into the house, where it disappeared again. Only a little light spilled down the stairwell into the darkened downstairs. The Fucking Cat curled like smoke out of nowhere between his ankles. He tripped over it, cursing, and it was gone again.

"Junior?" Bernie stood in the light from her room. She was wearing a flannel nightie that cloaked the fullness of her body but not her face.

"It's all right," he said. "I tripped on the Fucking Cat."

"Are you drunk, Junior?" she asked.

"Go back to bed, cookie." He kissed her cheek.

With her arms crossed under her breasts, she backed into her room, doubt in her every move.

The bedside lamp was on, Kissy sitting up waiting for him, a paperback she had closed and put aside on the bed. Dynah fussing faintly in her sleep.

"Sorry," he said, "the Fucking Cat." He checked the baby but she had not wakened fully. He sat down on the edge of the bed. "They were both there. The psycho bitch watched, her bitch buddy started it." Kissy just looked at him, as if she thought maybe he was describing something that happened in a motel room. It was irritating, to say the least. "Don't look at me like that."

"How am I supposed to know one way or another?" She spoke softly, without accusation, just stating the facts. "You liked them being there well enough once upon a time, didn't you? For all I know they're always there. So this time you were in some bar and they were there too, and you got loaded. You got into a fight and got busted— that's what I know, that's all—"

"Does this have to be a big deal? It won't happen again. It's over-done-with-tout-finis." He took her hand but it was limp in his, like something dead. "I'm going to take a bath. Join me?"

"No." She closed her eyes. Her lashes were wet. "I'm not going to let you fuck me stupid."

It took a minute to sink in. Then it was like falling, a rope breaking, only it was inside. And all the words were stopped up below his breastbone, roiling and burning, eating at him. Fuck her stupid. All the crawling and begging he had done, he could tell her who was fuck stupid.

"Fuck stupid?" he shouted. "That's in the dictionary after the word *marriage*, right?"

He stormed down the stairs and out the door, where he

sucked in great freezing lungsful of air, so cold it felt like
it was full of splinters, as if he were sucking in the stars
with their jagged edges. The heavens the mountains nearly
touched reeled above his head. The crooked little house
tipped away from him and he found himself on his ass on
the cold ground. He picked himself up again and got to the
car and into it and jammed the keys into it with witless fingers. He stomped on the accelerator but the hand brake
was still on, it was still in parking gear, and the engine
roared in impotent fury and the tires pawed up the icy
gravel. Kissy stood barefoot in the open door, hugging herself, the light behind her outlining her in her pajamas,
haloing her hair. Bernie was at her side, her face white as
moonlight.

"What are you doing?" Kissy shrieked. "You're not fit
to drive!"

"Junior, you idiot!" Bernie wailed.

Yanking up the hand brake, shifting the protesting gears,
he threw the car into reverse and it bucked backward violently and was suddenly out of his control, feeling like it was
sliding out from under him, like a wave going from under his
feet, taking the sand with it, and then it hit something, and as
he was thrown forward, into the sound of the glass crack-
ing, the thunk of his own bonehead skull, his cervical vertebrae compressing, he remembered the Blazer. And then he
slumped back, half conscious, knowing he had done something really stupid and hurt himself enough to make him see
red, and then he did see red, running in his eyes and over his
fingers as he looked at them in astonishment.

To add to his humiliation, he had pissed himself. It had
not felt like anything except this sudden gush of hot fluid
flooding out of him that he couldn't stop any more than he
could stop his head from driving into the windshield. He
was on the ground, Kissy holding him, Bernie cursing him
hysterically, and he knew he had somehow opened the
door of the Saab himself and fallen out into her arms and
from there his weight had taken them both down. There
were other people around, neighbors drawn by the noise of
the impact or her shouting, after. A distant shriek of police
siren grew louder, headed their way.

Whiplashed, the EMT said, and put him in a collar
brace, and spoke of stitches for the cut on his forehead,
contusion, maybe concussion, meaning a night in the hos-

pital. He tried to tell them he had hurt himself worse on the ice more than once but they treated him like some drunken fool who had busted his head.

The cops all looked like cowboys. He thought they smelled like cow shit. Maybe it was the concussion. Maybe it was the aroma of the cat shit he had seen the Fucking Cat burying all over the yard, scratch up a teaspoon of the sandy soil and splurt and scratch again, delicately, not too much effort, and then flop back and lick the old asshole, oh yeah, that tuna fish was good the first time around too. And his baby played with the goddamn thing in the goddamn shit-mined yard. Be funny if cows buried cowpats. If cops buried cop shit. He should bury something, he should bury the shitass cat. Deep. With that psycho bitch and her bitch buddy.

One of the cops wanted to know if he had been drinking.

"Not enough," Junior mumbled. It was true: he felt as sober as the air was aching clear, and it hurt in his head the way it hurt in his bruised nose and in his lungs and he hated it. It felt like a gutful of broken glass.

The phone rang through a confused dream. Kissy lifted her head and blinked. The clock said three. Dynah was drooling into her armpit. She shifted herself free of the baby and picked up the phone on the third ring.

"Kissy," he said in a choked voice. She closed her eyes. "Kissy, I'm sorry—"

She dropped the receiver into the cradle. They had left him in the ER. She had ducked the media by leaving through a parking garage and taken herself and Dynah and Bernie home by cab. For a long time she had lain in bed with her angry thoughts chasing each other like tigers around the tree until they all melted together and she drifted off again.

Dynah woke her next, or rather the fact that Dynah had wet through and the bed was damp. She rolled out, stripping the baby, herself, and the bed in passing. The bad night had not troubled Dynah, who was delighted to be in the bathtub with Mommy. Once changed into warm dry clothing and with coffee making and dry toast on the table, Kissy herself was surprised by an unexpected calmness.

Bernie crept out of her room, gave her a silent hug, and slumped at the table. "What happens now?"

"We were going home for Christmas, last I knew," Kissy said. "I'm thinking I'll stay right there."

Bernie nodded, a flicker of relief in her eyes. She missed her folks more than she had ever wanted to admit.

Kissy watched without the slightest tinge of alarm as a cab pulled up and deposited Junior on the sidewalk. Unshaven and in yesterday's clothes, head-bandaged and wearing a collar brace, he trudged warily up the walk to the back door.

Dynah in her high chair screamed happily at him and banged her spoon and her cracker on the tray. He grinned at the baby and kissed her on the head. He kissed Bernie on the head too.

"Way to go, bro," Bernie said sarcastically. She gave Kissy a meaningful look and stood up. "I'm going to get dressed."

Kissy said nothing until the door of Bernie's room shut firmly behind her. It was painful to see him, to be upset again. The smell coming off him shook her with its derelict hint of old piss.

He got himself coffee and sat down in the chair opposite her and held the mug in both hands as if for the warmth. "I'm all right." He looked down into the mug and then glanced up again sheepishly. "I'm really sorry." He cleared his throat. "It was all just an accident." She let him take her hand and knead her palm, her fingers. "I love you," he said.

She sighed. "I love you too, Junior." His body slackened with relief. "I'm going back home early," she said, "as soon as I can change the reservations." Junior's smile froze and his fingers ceased to work hers. "I'm not coming back."

"I don't understand," he said humbly, but she knew he did understand she had said she was not coming back.

She eased her hand free of his. "I can't live with you anymore."

"Because of last night? It was an accident—"

"Yes I know. It's always an accident."

He blinked, his eyes beginning to redden and water. "I've admitted when I was at fault—shit happens! Happens to everybody—"

"Happens to you incessantly. I don't want to live the life you've chosen, Junior."

He stared at her for a long moment. Then he cleared his

throat and squeezed his eyes. "I was wiped out. I'd had a few drinks and you knocked me on my ass, what you said—" She was looking at him again, with that look of hurt that was like a kick in the slats. "Kissy, we only got married seven months ago, you're not giving it a fair chance—" He groped for her hand again, and she snatched it away and got up and walked to the sink and looked out the window, with her arms crossed tightly under her breasts.

"You're wiped out," he said, "you're not in any shape to make rational decisions—what about Dynah?"

"What about her?"

"She needs a father—"

"You can be as much of a father to her as you want—"

"When she's with you and I'm here? That's ridiculous—"

"It's up to you where you are."

For a moment he was speechless. He came to his feet abruptly. "Is that what you want? You want me to quit playing?"

"Yes," she said, and even as she said it, she knew she couldn't ask it. "No. No." Except sooner or later he would have to stop, and why did their lives have to be ruined, waiting for injury or age to end his goddamn career? "Yes!" she cried.

Her confusion was disastrous, or perhaps it was only that quitting was a solution beyond his imagining. His body stiffened and he wiped at his mouth. "No. You can't ask me to quit. I worked too hard to get here. It's all I know. I've got to make a living. We can't live on your pictures. I'd never ask you to quit taking pictures, you know. I never would."

She pressed her forehead to the glass of the window and closed her eyes.

"It's not forever," he insisted. "That's the whole point. It'll be over and we'll be able to have a more normal life. I just need you to hang in there with me—I've tried so hard, Kissy. I don't know what I've done to deserve you leaving me—" His voice broke and the chair scraped and she looked around to see him sinking back into it, his head going to his hands in grief and defeat.

She made herself move, touching his shoulders lightly. He turned around and buried his face against her stomach. She stroked his hair and then she broke away from him as gently as she could. Silently she made more toast and cut some grapefruit and put it in front of him, while he watched her with feverish obsession. He looked at it a moment and then he ate it, all of it. She made herself eat too. She gave Dynah another crust to chew on and a bit of banana and watched her mess it around on her tray.

"I'll clean her up," he volunteered.

When she went upstairs after cleaning up breakfast, Dynah was in her crib and slamming a ring of keys against the bars of her crib. Junior was in the bathroom, shaving—awkward work around the collar. He looked at her in the mirror. She shucked her clothes and got into the tub. He finished shaving and wiped his face with a towel and climbed into the tub behind her. He put his chin on her shoulder, his arms around her, and she leaned back against him with a sigh.

With the media reporting Junior's collision with his wife's vehicle in his own yard, Kissy wanted to call Esther to reassure her, she was all right, the baby was all right, Bernie was fine, Junior would live. Playing with Dynah on the bed—she was climbing him laboriously, using him for a mountain range—Junior listened to Kissy talk to Esther. Telling his mother she and Dynah and Bernie were coming back early.

Past the first shock that brought him up on his elbow, he could see it made sense to get her and the baby out of town. And Bernie was homesick; he knew it. She said good-bye to Esther and called Bernie to come talk to her mother.

Then she started packing. After a while it hit him she was emptying the baby's dresser, she was packing all her things. He was totally confused. They had shared the bath, gone to bed together—everything was supposed to be all right.

"What are you doing?"

"Packing the Blazer to drive back." She did not look at him. It was like she was going to the supermarket.

"You don't need to take everything. Goddamn it, it's got a loose bumper and the headlight's busted—"

It was as if she did not hear him. Either she had gone blind and deaf or he had gone invisible and lost his voice.

He slammed out and came back an hour and a half later

with a six-pack temporarily inside him and begged her for
forgiveness. Got down on his knees. And she said "Stop it,
Junior," and kept on packing and then started dragging
bags out to the Blazer. Furious with her, he helped, grabbing everything in sight, lamps and antimacassars and shit
that belonged to the house and heaving it all into the back
of the Blazer any old which way.

"Take that too," he kept saying.

The phone rang, someone from the *Denver Post,* and
Junior told the guy to fuck off and then it rang again and he
told the guy from the *Rocky Mountain News* to fuck off
too. He left again and came back with more beer and gave
Kissy the silent treatment, sitting in front of the TV and
bending his elbow. Each beer he finished, he crushed the
can and threw at the TV until the rug in front of it was littered with them. It was cartoons on the TV but he didn't
know what the hell was going on in them.

Bernie came into the room and kicked the cans around
idly, arms crossed, staring at him. Finally she burst out,
"Why do you have to be such a flaming asshole?"

"It's my karma," he retorted, trying to be sarcastic, and
to his horror, began to cry.

Bernie did too, and pitched a box of Kleenex at him and
stormed out.

Ed Toth called to say he was getting some calls from the
media that someone answering Junior's number was
telling callers to fuck off, and Junior said they must be getting some wrong number because he hadn't gotten any
calls, but he guessed now he knew why. There was a silence that meant Toth knew goddamn well Junior was
weaseling and was debating what, if anything, to do about
it. A little cautiously, Toth ventured that if anyone should
happen to call, a no-comment would be in order. Then he
said once the medical people cleared Junior, he and Coach
Gerrard didn't see any reason he shouldn't be in net for the
game, day after tomorrow.

"Me either," Junior agreed, and belched loudly.

"How's it going?" Toth asked.

"Like shit," Junior said. "I can still play. In fact, that's all
I can do, I fuck up everything else—right, Kissy? Bernie?
You got an opinion, don't you, Bernie?"

They both ignored him.

"You drinking?" asked Toth.

"Just Coca-Cola. Makes me burp."

The manager sighed. "I don't want to have to bail you out again, Clootie. It's getting old—"

"No shit," Junior interrupted. "Older for me than you, Ed." He hung up. He stared at the phone a moment and then he gave the line a good yank, disconnecting it from the jack. He crushed another can and pitched it at the TV.

It was nearly noon the next day before he got himself up and showered. He came into the kitchen and picked Dynah out of her chair and pressed his cheek to hers.

"It's nuts for you to drive cross-country with a baby by yourself," he told Kissy. "Go by air. You and Dynah and Bernie fly when you're ready and I'll drive the Blazer for you and get in a little later."

It was the sensible thing to do. And it was also a gesture she could not mistake. Not of surrender. Junior did not give up, or at least for long. He was trying to find a way, any way, to please her.

"All right," she said.

He strapped Dynah back into her chair. "You won't leave before I get home, will you?"

She shook her head. "We'll stay for the game."

A faint smile threatened to break out on his mournful face. It was a gesture to equal his offer to drive the Blazer back to Peltry.

22

"**D**addy's home," Kissy told Dynah, who grinned wetly at her. She let go of the sheer curtain she had tweaked, far too many times, to check the street. Sweeping up the baby, she hurried to the door.

Junior came up the walk of his parents' home with his duffel bag on his shoulder, open at the top to show Christmas presents inside, and he was laughing at the sight of her and Dynah, wildly excited in her arms. Catching Kissy by the waist, he hustled them out of the damp and into the house, dropped his duffel, and engulfed wife and baby in a passionate embrace.

"Muffler fell off," he explained, and then he kissed Kissy and she returned it. There was uncertainty in it, and the awkwardness made them laugh, and then he kissed her again and it was full of wonder and trepidation.

"You must be hungry," she said, easing out of his arms and changing the subject, sort of.

He ate with the baby in his lap. Dynah shoving her fingers into his plate and then his mouth in pursuit of his food. He told Kissy about the fan belt and the muffler. Then he ran down. He was careful not to look at Kissy as he wiped the baby's chin with a tissue. "Sorry I'm so late. You'd probably like to be tucked up by now."

They had not talked about where he was going to stay. She was occupying the second bedroom with Dynah, and Bernie had the couch, and Mark was on a mattrress on the hall floor while the dorms were closed.

"You can stay here," she said.

"You sure? I can get a motel room—"

"I'm sure." She held out her hands to Dynah and the baby came to her immediately.

Her eyes were on the baby and maybe she didn't hear the involuntary intake of his breath. He glanced at the clock, and sure enough it was past midnight, it was Christmas.

"Look what Santa brought," Dunny greeted Junior and Dynah on Christmas morning.

Junior let Esther take Dynah, who reached out eagerly for her. "Kissy will be right down," he told them. He poured himself coffee and sat down at the table to watch his folks make of the baby. Bernie sang snatches of carols as she made waffles.

Mark wandered into the kitchen in his shorts, scratching and yawning and looking for coffee. He pointed a finger, gun style, at Junior and made a popping noise. "You ever notice that kid looks just like me?"

Junior showed him another way to point a finger.

"Hit the shower!" Dunny ordered.

Mark obeyed, with the deliberate lassitude that made it clear he was doing it because he felt like doing it, not because his father had ordered it.

Unexpectedly, Dynah pushed her legs straight against Esther's thighs and babbled angrily, scolding Dunny and Mark.

Dunny cleared his throat. "Kissy says she's staying in Peltry after the holidays. That'll be great, the baby around where we can see her oftener."

"It's just a separation," Junior said. "We're not getting divorced or anything."

His parents nodded simultaneously with uncertain understanding.

"It won't take her long to get a place. She wants to go back to work, part-time anyway . . ."

Esther and Dunny rushed into the pause to assure him they would help Kissy and look out for her in his absence. He thanked them and then he ran out of bullshit.

Dunny jumped up. "Come see Winston, Junior. He's out back."

Esther surrendered Dynah with a sigh. "I've got to get the turkey in the oven. Don't you let that dog scare the baby, Dunny."

In the backyard, Junior and Dunny and Dynah admired Dunny's leggy black retriever pup. Dynah jumped in Junior's arms with excitement and the dog responded, recognizing, as dogs always do, that human babies are just another variety of puppy.

"Is this about what happened out there?" Dunny asked. "The woman in the bar, the paper said she was a girlfriend of yours, you get home and bang your head on the windshield—"

"It's a misunderstanding."

"Your mother's not here," Dunny said, "so quit shitting me."

"It was an accident. I told you I'd been drinking, I lost control of the car, that's all—"

"What about the woman?"

"She was drunk. I had too much myself but she started it—"

"You on drugs? You doing those fucking steroids?"

"No, I'm not doing ster—"

"You act like it. I read they make people nuts. Maybe it's something you were born with, like brain damage, or you cracked your head on the ice too many times, but for Chrissake, Junior, you gotta do something about it, your life's turning into shit—"

"All right, all right. I heard you, Dad."

The yammering was a measure of how upset his father was, of course. The old man ragging on him made him feel like maybe things were worse than he had thought, maybe he was walking around with some kind of mental fly open.

Dynah gurgled and rammed a finger up his nose. Tears sprang to his eyes in reflex. He laughed so she wouldn't know she had hurt him, but he could feel a snail's track of blood slipping out of his nose onto his upper lip. She had a talent for kicking him in the nuts too. Took after her mother. To his horror, he was on the verge of tears.

"I'm getting blood on my shirt," he said, handing Dynah hastily over to Dunny and heading for the nearest bathroom.

Ruth seemed unchanged. Not having seen her since August, Kissy was struck with the realization that Ruth's condition had become her normal state. The withered, stiffening body, the bones that were so close to the skin they appeared to be trying to work their way through it, the slack breasts on the prominent rib cage, the unseeing yellowing eyes—this was Ruth, the real Ruth, the only Ruth.

Sylvia Cronin had had a mild stroke in September. Wearing a patch on one eye, she greeted Kissy with speech that was slightly slurred and effortful. There was a cane within reach, and she struggled unsteadily into motion. Her illness, which she had not disclosed to Kissy in their occasional correspondence, had necessitated hiring nurses to help care for Ruth.

Mrs. Cronin snorted. "Take some pictures, Kissy. Get some before I'm drooling around a lot of tubes."

Mrs. Prashker brought Kissy up to date on Ruth's condition and the status in the courts of the request to allow her to die, which was essentially unchanged on both counts. Kissy might have left yesterday or never been away. Then, politely, Mrs. Prashker inquired after her. How was she doing? How was the baby? She confessed apologetically she had forgotten the baby's name.

Kissy showed a Polaroid snapshot. The women appraised it in the manner of women, finding Dynah as beautiful, flawless, and as much the spit of her mother as they had declared her to be as a newborn.

When Ruth's mother had left, Kissy told Sylvia casually, "We're staying here, the two of us."

Settled into a rocking chair, Sylvia tugged at her eye patch. "Would you like to live here again? I would certainly love to have you."

It was an appealing solution. And a regression.

"You've done so much for me. It would be an imposition. And you have no idea how busy Dynah is—"

"Oh, yes I do. Think about it, dear."

Just as Kissy was leaving, Mrs. Cronin pressed something into her hand. Under the Blazer's map light, Kissy examined the snapshot of a baby girl, an infant, in the lap of a Mrs. Cronin younger by two decades. Ruth had been a bald baby, blond and fat in the face and thigh. Nothing like Dynah. Nothing like Dynah.

There was no full-time position for her at the *News*—the best she could wangle was a freelance assignment to shoot the Spectres at home for the paper. The road games were out of the question. Getting a baby-sitter on the road would be impossible, and she could hardly shoot a game with a baby strapped to her front. Dynah was all legs now anyway and never stopped moving.

There was nothing anywhere except minimum wage, no benefits. She could not pay rent and eat on minimum, let alone pay a baby-sitter or take classes in pursuit of her MFA. Latham would give her a job as a lab assistant in Sowerwine. Working at her MFA, she might be able to edge her way into a teaching assistant's slot. The hourly wage for TAs was a little better than the minimum a lab assistant got, but not by much and with no benefits.

As long as she and Junior were married, of course, she and Dynah were covered by his insurance, so that aspect of her finances was not as important as it would be when she was truly on her own again. Junior denied she ever needed to be. They fought over it furiously. He saw providing for her and Dynah as a test of his maturity and an expression of his continuing love and commitment. Admirable as his intentions might be, as his generosity certainly was, she feared accepting his support unfairly encouraged hope of reconciliation. The frustration, anger, and resentment that she could not make it on her own was sharpened by the humiliation of having to accept his paying the rent on the apartment she had taken, providing her with an allowance, and putting her through graduate school. The only way she could live with herself was to promise herself that one day she would pay him back.

Going back to classes in January, she could complete her master's classes in four semesters. If the thesis committee approved her series on Ruth, she might collect her MFA at the Winter Commencement two years hence. And unlike the paper or any of the local professional photography studios or labs, the campus was baby-friendly. She could take Dynah with her whenever she wished, which was nearly all the time.

Though only eighteen months had passed since her graduation, it was like time travel to go back. The campus was a little shabbier than she remembered and somehow smaller, like a childhood home revisited, but still serene and dignified— redbrick, granite, thick-trunked, rough-barked old trees, frozen paths, sheeted snow covering the quads. It was she who had changed, of course. Now that she was marginally older than the run of student, the undergraduates seemed immature to her. In turn, she was all but invisible, like almost everyone out of their immediate peer group, to them.

January thaw was happening just then, the world melting all around them. The air outside was nectar for a week, sweet as the spring that was still such a reach. As the filthy snow, the impacted ice turned to slush underfoot or under the Blazer's wheels, was rained away or evaporated, fog softened everything and the willows glowed, burnished brass in the mist.

On impulse, between classes with Dynah riding her back, Kissy ducked down the path to the copse of trees where the memorial plinth to Diane and Ruth had been erected. She sank gratefully onto the bench and undid buttons strategically to allow Dynah to burrow under her shirt and jacket. Her milk let down heavily. There was also the lightest caress of the cool damp air. Lovingly she feathered her fingers through Dynah's hair, the moment worth everything that had gone before it.

There were still remembrances at the memorial—sorority badges, a winter wreath of dried moss and berries, some half-burned sticks of incense in the vase attached to the granite, a plastic box containing folded sheets of paper, and one of the mint-flavored rubbers that could be obtained free of charge from a basket at the reception desk in the student clinic. Jimmies, the kids were suddenly calling them.

When Dynah was replete and Kissy was all buttoned up again, she rose to stir the contents of the plastic box. Some of the notes quoted lines from poems and eulogies, some addressed Diane or Ruth directly and were signed from some friend. Someone had inserted a laminated column from the *News* detailing the death of a male student in a climbing fall the previous semester. There was an obscene cartoon that appeared to be entirely irrelevant. Candy and gum wrappers.

Dynah's small fingers imitated hers, grasping after the bits of paper. Kissy was suddenly hollow with a sense of abandonment. But just who had left her she was not sure.

The place she had found, near the University Medical Center, had one bedroom, a living room and kitchen in a converted carriage house behind a Victorian mansion that had been renovated into doctors' offices. A quiet neighborhood at night and a safe one, it even had a little park a few blocks away for when it was warm enough to take Dynah out. Though living with her parents, Bernie visited often, just for company or to baby-sit.

Nearly every day—sometimes twice a day—Junior called, ostensibly to speak regularly to Dynah, for the occasional reassuring reward of a thin little cry of "Da." If she didn't say it, he told Kissy, at least she was being reminded of the sound of his voice. Often he called late at night just to speak to Kissy, the conversations drifting from the tribulations or triumphs of the day to where their hands were. She felt his absence most often just after he had called and wondered if it was the same for him.

He did not falter in his performance for the Drovers. His reliability between the pipes made him one of their stars, but he was unlikely to earn an All-Star spot—of the fifty-four goaltenders in the league there was room for only two starters and their backups in an All-Star game—and so he told her, every time he called, he would be home for the break.

Junior counted down six weeks of separation, six more weeks as a Drover, six weeks of living, when he was not on the road, with the Fucking Cat instead of his wife and child. Still renting the crooked little house, still being harassed by the Fucking Cat, which he tolerated now with a kind of superstition—feeding the goddamn thing, changing its shitbox, might somehow appease the gods that had taken Kissy and Dynah away. He hired the kid next door to feed the cat while he was away, but the little peckerhead was too fastidious to change the box. The first time he came home from five days on the road, the Fucking Cat had filled the box and moved on to shitting everywhere else. The stench made the house nearly unlivable. Mean as cat dirt, his mother had always said, and he discovered the truth of the saying, cleaning it up. It made the contents of Dynah's diapers look like a box of Godiva chocolates.

Swamping the house with his bucket of Mr. Clean and hot water and rags triggered vague memories of the mess Ed had made of the apartment and the bigger mess he and Dionne had made of it and then the clearer recall of what he had done to the motel room in Dry River. The shitbox of his life, he reflected morosely.

Junior told Dunny that Kissy would pick him up at the airport. Dunny just breathed over the phone. Junior blundered on. "Kissy and I just need to be able to pay total attention to each other."

"Whatever," Dunny said. "While you're paying total attention to each other, don't forget the baby at the airport."

"Thanks. But I need to see her too."

Dunny agreed he probably did. It was the most awkward conversation Junior had had with the old man since he had informed him one day in the week between Christmas and New Year's that he was resuming control of his money.

"You sure?" Dunny had squinted at him as if he couldn't quite make out who he was. "You can't get careless now, not looking at a divorce—"

"We're not getting divorced. This is just a temporary separation. I know what I have to do. I'm going to take care of Kissy and Dynah."

He had tried to ease it, showing Dunny the numbers he had put together, all on his own. The only number he had been sure was bullshit was savings; he figured most of it would get eaten up traveling back and forth to see each other. Dunny had not been able to help being interested but he also could not resist pointing out it was thin ice, predicated on the high end of the high-low contract. True enough, but Junior was currently earning the high end and he couldn't see banking it while letting Kissy live with Dynah in some dump in the Barnyard, struggling and scrimping on the minimum wage.

"So," he asked Kissy with deliberate casualness as she drove them home from the airport, "you seeing anybody?"

She laughed derisively.

"Me neither," he assured her, but she didn't even seem to notice.

The apartment she had taken was strewn with baby junk, camera gear, books, and tapes. He was heartened to see that she had not piled quilts and pillows into a discreet hint on the couch. He saw nothing that was not identifiably Kissy's or Dynah's—no cigarette or ashtray, no bottle of wine in the fridge, strange brand of booze in the cupboard, man's first name with telephone number scrawled on the pad by the phone in the kitchen or the bedroom. Under cover of taking a leak, he checked the bathroom for the unfamiliar blade, somebody else's toiletries. The bathtub was a built-in unit that was also a shower stall, serviceable but

coldly unromantic. A surreptitious peek into the drawer of
the nightstand discovered no rubbers. That was reassuring.
It had occurred to him she might be seeing women, but he
knew that would be a lot more difficult to discern. Recognizing the panic in the idea, he dismissed it. Mary Frances
was in Chicago, not that there had ever been anything to
that but Muffie's tortured novice fantasies. A peek at
Kissy's most recent pictures would tell him something, except she wasn't developing or printing at home; she had
twenty-four-hour access to the darkroom at Sowerwine.

The smell of her cooking—the onion, garlic, spice in
whatever it was—the scent and softness of Dynah's skin,
the baby wriggling in his arms, the sound of Kissy laughing, combined to make him a little dizzy. Though he had
never lived in this place with them, by the time they finished eating, he felt as if he had never left. He felt married
again.

They did the dishes together and then bathed the baby.
As he toweled Dynah dry, he dried the Rubber Ducky she
clutched.

"Gotta put down the ducky," he advised her, "if you
wanna play the saxophone."

She studied him solemnly as if she understood the
advice.

They put her to bed in her crib, only a few feet away
from the side of the bed Kissy habitually took.

In the bathroom for a whiz, he heard Kissy in the bedroom, doing something, and then Janis Joplin's voice tore
loose from the stereo in "Down on Me." He didn't button
up again but sat down on the commode to untie his boots.
Kissy appeared in the doorway. She had abandoned her
nursing bra in the bedroom and her shirt was wide open.
Stooping past him to flip the lever from shower to tub, she
flashed her tits at him. He grabbed and she jumped away,
laughing. He caught up with her and manhandled her into
the shower, both of them still mostly clothed. The water
sheeted over her breasts, slicking her shirt to her skin and
rendering the cloth transparent. She went down on her
knees, down on him, just as she had promised over the
phone, the water breaking over her head, her face, her
shoulders. Her mouth was too much. He could not savor it
long enough, could not contain the violent surge of orgasm.

Rising from her crouch, she wiped her mouth and

backed out, her eyes still locked with his. She kept on backing and he followed her, dripping wet, with only a blind fumble at the water to turn it off. The wet shirt, the water-slick denim of her Levi's, excited him with the strange texture and weight of their resistance as he peeled them off her in the bedroom. It was like peeling the bark of a tree and finding a woman inside. She was shivering when he spread her at the edge of the bed and gave her head until the dew on her skin had changed to sweat and she cried out in exultation. He offered his mouth; she licked at it hungrily. She liked it too much and that aroused him all over again. He shifted over her, his hand between her still-trembling thighs. And his cock, nosing at her. She reacted immediately, laughing and heeling her palm against his chest. "You forgot something."

"Let's make a baby," he pleaded, lifting her a little, pushing forward, the tip of his cock finding heat, finding the way. She hit his chest harder and twisted to close her legs and get out from under him. It was let her go or get hurt. She hugged her knees and stared at him.

Resting on his side, he breathed deeply. He got up slowly and poked around his suitcase and came back with a rubber in his hand. She looked at him and held out her hand, and he gave it to her and let her put it on him. Her touch was not without its own particular reward but he closed his eyes, near tears with longing for contact with her unprotected flesh. She straddled him and took him and he watched her face contort with orgasm.

"You'd finish the semester," he told her when she came back from the bathroom. "You'd only be five months gone in June."

The way she yanked her nightdress over her damp head made it clear he was not making a sale.

"What's so terrible about having another baby?" he wanted to know.

With a little moan, she threw herself face down on the bed and punched the pillow in frustration. "You don't live on this planet, Junior Clootie. You live on the moon somewhere, on moonshine and ice cream pops."

He laughed from his belly. "Sounds yummy. You're funny."

"You're nuts."

"Don't be angry," he soothed. "Look how fast Dynah's growing. She's almost not a baby anymore."

"Junior." Kissy sat up straight and spoke slowly and clearly, as if she were explaining something to a small child. "We are separated. We are not living together. Aside from the insanity of having a baby when I'm not sure we should stay married, you told me you were sorry you missed being around while I was carrying Dynah. If I got pregnant now, you'd miss that too—"

"I'll be home for the summer—"

"Except for a bunch of camps. And anyway the baby would be due in what, October, and I'd be here alone—"

"Or wherever I was, you could be with me—"

"With you on the road half the time and the folks a couple thousand miles away—"

"All right, forget it," he conceded abruptly. He rolled onto his back to stare at the ceiling.

She got up to check the locks and turn off the lights. When she came back, he was still staring at the ceiling, with his arm behind his head, still steaming.

"Ever since we've been back together," he said, "we've used rubbers. I agreed to it because I was the one who fucked up and infected you. After Dynah it was the safest thing—but now we're married and I've been faithful to you, totally faithful, and you're still making me use those things. It's stopped being fair—"

"I take enough chances—"

"Just because you don't like the taste of rubber and you do like the taste of cock—"

"Thank you very much," Kissy said. "I trusted you once and you gave me the clap—"

Dynah cried out and Kissy jumped up to rush to her crib. She took Dynah to the rocking chair handy to the crib and opened the front of her nightdress for the baby. Through the open door, she and Junior could see each other and converse. Voice strained with the effort to speak calmly, she went on. "You're two thousand miles away. You're on the road half the time. How can I believe you when you tell me you're not fucking around?"

"It would be a fuck of a lot easier if you lived with me." Junior rolled out of bed and picked up a pair of shorts. "A whole lot easier for me not to fuck up and a lot easier for you to know it." He hopped into them as he spoke. "It's ridiculous, Kissy."

With one eye on a naked man climbing into his shorts, she thought so too, and hastily dropped her gaze to the baby's head for fear of giggling at him.

"You don't have any assurance I'm not cheating by making me use rubbers," he said. "All you do is prevent me giving you anything. Or you giving me a dose. You could be cheating on me too. Maybe I deserve to be punished once, but enough's enough, Kiss."

"So much for wanting a baby," she shot. "You're just tired of rubbers. You're lucky to be getting laid at all—"

"Bullshit, you want it as bad as I do. The rubbers don't change anything for you."

The giggles had vanished. She smoothed Dynah's hair, watching the way the fontanel pulsed under the silky coils.

Junior crouched next to her, his hand on her knee. "People make mistakes. You're not going to find anyone who doesn't. The only real problem we've got is trust. Let's start fresh. Take all the same-old-same-old and heave it off the bridge."

A humiliating gush of tears washed her face. "I can't!"

He winced. "Kiss—"

"I can't!"

Dynah rolled her eyes up sleepily at her mother. Her small fingers dug worriedly into Kissy's breast.

Junior rose, returning a few seconds later with a box of tissues. He made cocoa for her, which she took with a fresh flood of tears. Dynah was soundly asleep again; he lifted her away and took her back to her crib. Kissy could not stop crying and nothing he did or said seemed to make any difference. In the privacy of the bathroom, with the door closed between them, he sat on the closed commode and fought his rising gorge. If he made her so unhappy, he thought, maybe they were better off apart. There must be something he was not doing, something he could do. He clenched and unclenched his fists to keep himself from tearing the place apart.

23

Blades cut the ice with the scree of nails on chalkboard. Junior watched his brother, circling idly, getting ready to try to put a puck between his eyes. Esther liked to joke that it was nice how her boys played together. Her way of coping with the fact they broke lumber on each other's faces with relish. Mark wheeled easily as if he were just dicking around. Junior knew his brother's habits like he knew his own and he was ready when Mark pulled his little blitz, dropping a puck at the hash marks of the left-hand face-off circle, and another one, immediately, aiming high on him as he expected, the bastard. Junior stopped rubber with his glove, the other with his stick mitt.

"Fuck you," he called out cheerfully.

The guys at the other end of the ice, current Spectres grabbing the ice time for a little extra work while they could, laughed and jeered.

Mark worked him a while and then they joined a scrimmage and after, he hung on to skate. Mark lingered to put in some more time skating too, which made Junior grin at the thought he had had his influence on his brother.

In the locker room later, Mark scratched his balls thoughtfully. "Bernie's having contractions. Maybe she'll have the baby while you're home. You really think it's Deker's kid?"

"You got any other candidates?"

Mark shook his head no. "Someday I'm gonna break his face—"

"I did already—"

"That was for you. I want to do it for me—you know, the son of a bitch calls every couple days. She talks to him by the hour—"

"No." Junior was stunned.

"He wants to marry her, she says. She hasn't told Ma or Dad. I think she's thinking about it—"

"Over my dead body."

Mark grinned. "Yeah, my feelings exactly."

Back at Kissy's apartment again, where the light was richer and the warmth warmer, Dynah welcomed him with her usual wild excitement. She put her little feet on his and he walked her backward on them while she giggled.

Kissy dipped the tip of her finger in the dressing and tasted it, and he bumped the baby close to her and smooched at Kissy and she let him suck some dressing off her finger—vinaigrette: olive oil, lemon, pepper, salt, simple stuff—that he decided he would like to lick off her whole body. Then she let Dynah have a suck of it, and the baby's startled sour grimace made them laugh.

"Mark told me Bernie's having contractions."

"I know, I talked to her."

"She tell you she's talking to Deker about getting married?"

"No." She sighed, then threw herself into a sudden flurry of activity, whipping the plates onto the table, spilling a stew from a crockpot into a tureen.

He strapped the baby into her chair. "Let me help."

Silently she gave up the tureen and he put it on the table for her. She handed him corn bread and the salad and they sat down. He gave Dynah her spoon to bang on the tray of the high chair while he mashed a little potato from the stew on one side of his plate to cool for her.

"How could she see what's happened to us and even think about it?" Kissy said suddenly.

"We could fix us. And I'm not Deker, Kissy—"

Kissy shook her head.

"You're the one who wants to stay here—" He stopped to shovel a little of the warm potato into Dynah. "I'm not bailing out on you—"

"What's the difference? We're still apart, we'd be apart as much as not if we were living together," she said, and there was an accusation and anger in her voice that brought his eyes back to her.

And infuriated him. "There's a huge difference and I'm here to testify to it. I'm paying it—paying the bills, jerking off over the phone and collecting a little rent-pussy when I'm in town—"

Kissy jumped up and stalked out.

"Shit," he muttered.

He followed her, baby in arms. She had thrown herself face down onto the bed. One of her favorite things to do in a snit. He sat down next to her, letting Dynah loose on her other side. The baby crawled up alongside her and poked curiously at her hair. Kissy turned her face to Dynah and the baby cooed.

He touched Kissy's ankle. "I'm sorry. I love being with you two." He hesitated. "Even the fights."

He caught her by surprise. For an instant he could see the struggle going on inside her and then it was gone again, the door closed. He had shaken her and at the same time seen the depth of her resistance. And for an instant he knew jubilation and terror.

Despite the nagging tension, the fear of saying or doing something that would again result in tears and recriminations, the remaining time with her was much better. Kissy clung to him. One part of the trip home almost met his fantasies. He told himself it was enough. That's what his mother said sometimes. If it's all you're going to get, it better be enough.

Like an entrancement, a storm locked up Peltry in ice. Though the skies cleared, the temperatures stayed below zero for several days. Kissy photographed the trees branched out in crystal, the power lines that tied the town in glassy ribbons. At noon, the ice flashed hard and bright, and as the light waxed and waned, it shimmered prismatically. Then came rain that sheeted the ice and sopped the snow. Kissy woke to a rumbling like an earthquake and a whump like the sound of one man hitting another hard into the boards that she identified sleepily as an avalanche of rain-punky snow from the roof. Then the phone rang.

Junior's voice clarified into Mark's, tripping over the words with excitement, telling her Bernie had had a boy.

Mike Burke spotted Kissy Mellors shooting through the peephole in the plexi. Wedding ring still on her hand, he noted, but everybody knew she and Clootie had split. Burke would be a hundred bucks richer from the office pool when the divorce was finalized, but she had not even filed yet—the clerk was in on the pool. Maybe she was still wearing the ring the way some women did to discourage unwanted attention.

There were rumors around town Clootie's little sister had had a kid by that horny Russian. If so, she was nearly the only unwed mother in the country who had failed to file a paternity suit against the hard-on.

As a team, the Spectres were nearly as good as they had been with Junior Clootie in the net—the conventional wisdom was they would make the regional playoffs again and contend strongly for another national title. Burke saw no reason to disagree. Clootie's brother was a standout. Burke himself had minimal interest in hockey. He followed basketball. But he was there with his boss on a pair of comps, the kind of invitation that was compelling. His attention drifted back to Kissy Mellors, in Levi's and a heavy sweater that held the swells of her breasts with authority. As she angled for position, the sweater rode up over her bottom. It was as fine a bottom as it had been before the baby and more interesting at the moment than even the mayhem on the ice.

At the end of the second period, he left his seat to punch quarters into a pop machine and catch the can of Coke it burped out. The guys working security were off-duty cops and knew him, so he did not have to flash a badge to obtain access to the secured area immediately behind the plexi, where the arena crew and the media worked around each other.

"Howyadoin'?" He squatted next to her and offered her the can of Coke.

She looked at it with a flicker of distracted smile. "Thanks. Can you hold on to it a sec?"

"Got a minute?"

She glanced at a wristwatch. "Fourteen, actually."

Securing her gadget, she rose and accepted the pop.

He put a friendly hand on her elbow. "Howyadoin'? I heard you and Junior split."

"We're separated." Her tone, the avoidance of eye contact, made it clear the subject was off limits.

"Hey, it's terrific to see you again," he said.

Her mouth tightened at the hint of approach. "Yeah," she said curtly.

He made himself scarce. She was working, newly separated. He was just trolling.

Her daily round consumed her. Baby, pool, baby, class, baby, work, baby. Kissy paid weekly visits to Ruth and saw Bernie daily. Esther imparted the lessons of practical motherhood with a firm hand and a confident expectation that Bernie would grasp them, and Bernie gained rapidly in confidence. Though she provided snapshots to Deker, she returned a quantity of baby gifts to him when he balked at paying her medical bills without a blood test. Their courtship, if that was what it was, came to an abrupt standstill.

Dynah had become too heavy to carry constantly and too restless to tolerate it. An umbrella stroller became part of their gear, along with a harness and leash. As her teeth erupted, Dynah liked the bright curl of the telephone-cord leash for an occasional chew, and otherwise seemed to take comfort in being connected to Kissy's wrist. Diapers, changes of clothing, water bottles, toys, and books to distract and amuse—the amount of baby baggage seemed to increase daily, until Kissy felt like a bearer on safari. And with the constant increase in Dynah's mobility, the baby was a constant distraction. Kissy struggled for time, for energy, and just to keep her thoughts together long enough to frame, let alone take a picture.

During spring break, she packed up Dynah and traveled to Junior. For a few days they were together in the little crooked house again and then they joined him on a road trip.

There were hours that he was involved in working out, practices, and other team activities. Idle in unfamiliar places, Kissy made adventures for herself and Dynah, tramping around to museums and zoos and whatever caught her eye. She discovered it was possible to live without cooking. And while waiting on room service, she could shoot from the open windows or balconies of hotels, sometimes situated in a downtown, sometimes sited by suburban mall or interstate. Interesting things went on in hotel parking lots. Hotels themselves were full of pictures. And most hotels seemed to have swimming pools, so she could leave Dynah with Junior first thing every day. She could get to like this life. His life. A learning experience, she thought; an insight about him, about her.

Since the jaunt took them to Chicago, Kissy had a chance to spend a day with Mary Frances, whose eagerness to see her was muted by tension over her visit between Kissy's old friend and the woman with whom she was living. Once Mary Frances and Kissy left the apartment the two women shared, to take in a photography show at a gallery, Mary Frances was defensively apologetic. "Inga has a hard time relating to straight women, especially married and with kids. She's political." And lowering her lashes. "I've gotten a lot more political myself."

Maybe it wasn't just home you couldn't go back to, but old friends too, Kissy thought. Nobody stood still, waiting for you.

Made all the more uncertain by her experience with Mary Frances, she went ahead with her decision to see her father when the road trip brought them to D.C. Renting a car, she strapped Dynah's portable seat into it and ventured into Maryland.

The address she had obtained through the air force turned out to be a secluded and very lovely large house. In the curving driveway, a recent-model Corvette cuddled up to a classic of the same make so beautifully preserved it also appeared to be fresh from the showroom floor. She was unprepared for this level of opulence. If her father lived here, he must be doing very well for himself. She unbelted Dynah, sleepy from a ninety-minute nap on the road, and carried her on her hip up a paved walk to the wide-paneled front door.

The woman who came to the door appeared to be in her mid-twenties. She was rather thin, except for high round breasts, and intense intelligence enlivened her narrow face. Her smile broadened at the sight of Dynah. "Yes?"

"I'm looking for Ken Mellors," Kissy told her.

The young woman's smile faltered, as she registered a degree of surprise. "Oh. I thought you might be lost." She peered more closely at Kissy and Dynah.

Kissy's own gaze shifted to the young woman's ring finger, which bore a wedding band and a large diamond as well. The young woman followed Kissy's line of sight.

"I'm Mrs. Mellors," she said in a suddenly cool tone, "Angela."

Dynah was heavy on Kissy's hip. She lowered her gently to her feet and took her hand.

Angela Mellors was studying Dynah closely. Suspicious, Kissy grasped, that Dynah might be her husband's get by this woman standing on her stoop. But the intense gaze raked Kissy too, and whatever resemblance she saw in Dynah, she saw also in Kissy. The unease in her features gave way to puzzlement.

"My mother was too. Ken's my father," Kissy said. "This is my daughter, Dynah. I'm Kissy."

The young woman was dumbfounded. It was obvious from her stunned expression she had not known her husband had a daughter named Kissy, let alone a grandchild. And yet there was no questioning it.

She cleared her throat. "Come in, please."

Inside, she led Kissy through an elegant foyer and past a room where patterns of color wove across a computer monitor. "I work at home," Angela Mellors said. "I'm a software designer."

My stepmother, Kissy thought, the software designer. It reminded her of the mother in the movie *Kramer vs Kramer* who had abandoned her child for a career in sportswear design. In the novel, it had been nothing that compelling or socially vital. Somewhere between book and film, someone had decided to try to make the abandoning mother more sympathetic. Only in the movie business would a career in sportswear design be perceived as liberation. She checked herself. There was no reason to be resentful of this young woman.

Angela Mellors was equally disconcerted. She gestured wordlessly at the facing pair of marshmallow-creme-silk-upholstered sofas in the flawlessly decorated living room. Kissy sank onto one sofa and Dynah crawled up onto her lap and clung to her, her wide eyes roving over the unfamiliar territory.

Angela Mellors picked up a phone and punched an intercom button. "Ken, there's someone to see you. We're in the living room." She put the phone down quickly. "So I'm your stepmother," she said to Kissy with a nervous little laugh, and sat on the edge of a chair at an angle to Kissy.

"Dynah's stepgrandmother, too," Kissy said, and Angela Mellors sucked in her breath. An instant grandmother at twenty-whatever.

Dynah whined softly and yanked on Kissy's denim jacket. Kissy hushed her. The little girl pushed out of Kissy's arms and slid off her mother to her feet. She wandered around the room, carefully keeping an eye on where her mother was.

Kissy's father appeared in a doorway and stopped there, the curiosity in his face instantly darkened at the sight of Kissy to something else. Fear. Anger. Resentment. He had grown older, of course, though his hair was without a single thread of gray, and he was as slim and fit-looking as ever. The age was in his skin, in the webbing and slackening of the flesh around his eyes, and on his neck. He had to be fifty, she thought, and it struck her how much he looked like Kevin.

Kissy was suddenly a teenager again, her stomach aquiver with fear of her father, his cutting words, his rejection. And furious with him. He had married this young woman and never bothered to tell her he had a previous wife, children. It was possible he had married and divorced other women since her mother, without mentioning the existence of his first marriage or his children to them either. Maybe she had other siblings she didn't even know existed.

"Hello, Daddy," Kissy said evenly. "I was in town, I thought I'd bring Dynah by so you could meet her. I sent you some pictures—"

"You're only here to cause me embarrassment. Mission accomplished," her father said, "you can leave now—"

"What did I do?" Kissy cried.

Angela jumped up, her face flushed with upset and confusion.

"You know nothing about this," he told her. "Stay out of it."

The young woman threw back her head as if she had been struck. She turned to Kissy. "I think it's time I did know."

"I have a brother," Kissy said quickly, "Kevin, and my mother's name is Caitlin. She's a textile artist who lives Downeast and she has a little boy—"

The flicker of shock in his eyes at that piece of news was satisfying.

"That's enough," her father said. "I will tell Angela anything she needs to know."

"I'm married to a professional hockey player—"

Her father strode forward, and Kissy grabbed Dynah almost instinctively.

"If you want to go to the game tonight, I can leave tickets at the will-call window," she blurted, her voice breaking, and she realized she was making a fool of herself. "Why do you have to be such a bastard?" she cried. Dynah began to wail. "I'm sorry, I'm sorry, I didn't mean to scare you," Kissy tried to comfort her.

"My daughter is good at ridiculous scenes," her father said to Angela, "a technique she learned at her mother's knee. I was married too young. I put fifteen years into the marriage and finally realized it was an irremediable error. I put it behind me—"

"Seventeen years," Kissy said.

He ignored her, continuing to address Angela. "The children were teenagers, all but grown—"

"You should have told me," Angela burst out.

Kissy stood, shifting Dynah to her hip. She walked past Angela.

"Kissy," Angela said.

"She's done what she wanted," her father said.

"What I wanted," Kissy said, "was to see you. What I wanted was for you to see Dynah. I've grown up. I thought maybe you had."

She turned on her heel, striding to the door and out of the house and to her rental car.

Angela tripped after her. "Kissy, please, give me a phone number and an address. I'm not going to let this end like this."

"It's hopeless," Kissy said, strapping Dynah into her seat. "Maybe you shouldn't push him anymore. You might find out some other unpleasant surprises about him."

Angela wrapped her arms around herself as if she were cold. "He's harder on himself than anybody—"

Kissy shook her head. "He's a real hero, I know. We were the ones who let him down. That's why he's never paid any support and why I went to college on a scholarship and why we never hear from him and why he kept us a secret from you. Don't feel too bad. My mother's not a stupid woman either, and she was married to him too."

Stricken, Angela Mellors backed away. "Go away," she whispered.

* * *

"What a jerk," Junior said.

Dynah was sleeping. He had drawn the whirlpool bath. The suite was costing him extra, but it had a bedroom for Dynah and the Jacuzzi he needed. It was nearly midnight, the game played and won, and he was aching and bruised physically as Kissy was emotionally. "I can't believe he wouldn't even talk to you. New wife just out of college, huh?"

She rubbed her face against his shoulder. "I was stupid to try to see him—"

"No," Junior said. "You don't know how it will come out. Maybe he'll think about it or maybe Angela's good-hearted and she'll talk some sense into him."

"I just don't understand how somebody could just not care," Kissy muttered.

Junior didn't either. He couldn't fix it for her. Though he would like to kick the guy's ass. He sighed and tipped her chin gently and rubbed noses with her and got a faint little tremulous smile for his trouble.

At season's end, Junior had delivered what his agent called a "money performance." He returned to Peltry trailing rumors of a trade—clubs with real playoff potential giving him serious consideration. A tentative arrangement for him to take an efficiency near campus evaporated in the face of Dynah's frantic searches for him as soon as she woke every morning. It seemed best for him to simply live with them. And silly for him to sleep on the couch when the sexual relationship had continued through their separation.

For a few weeks, they rented another cottage, this one on a lake three hours from Peltry. Kissy filled boxes with negatives she would print later.

Dynah, naked, little legs pumping, tearing shrieking through the cottage with a little plastic bucket in one hand, shovel in the other, with Junior giving chase.

Junior sprawled in a hammock with the radio tuned to a ball game, Dynah like a small quotation on a blanket in the shade he cast.

Dynah in mid-toss by Junior in the lake.

Dynah examining with a doubtful expression a catch of fish displayed by Junior.

Bernie and Casey, visiting. Dynah wide-eyed over Casey.

One day on the beach, Dynah discovered Junior's nipples. He was on his side, reading a magazine, and the toddler was digging in the sand near him. Looking up, she surveyed her surroundings in a squint. Kissy saw her eyes pause on Junior's bare chest, studying the topography with its tangle of red hair. Then Dynah beelined for him. Curious little fingers groped a nipple and Junior started and laughed. Then Dynah's small lips parted and she glommed onto it eagerly.

"Ow! Jesus!" Junior yelped. "Ow!" The little mouth was suckered so tightly he had to work the tip of a finger into a corner of it to break the seal and peel her off. "Hey, baby," he told her, "that's a dry udder. Doesn't even give skim milk."

Dynah grinned and laughed. Anything Daddy said was funny.

"Jesus," he said as he handed her to Kissy. He touched his reddened nipple. "How do you stand it?"

"Mine are toughened up."

"Mama?" Dynah gave the top of Kissy's maillot an urgent tug.

Hours later, as they were going to bed, Junior wanted to talk about it. "It felt like a vacuum."

She didn't have to ask what it was.

He stared at the ceiling, waiting for her to finish undressing. "It was weird. It hurt but it was starting to feel— okay. Good."

As she turned off the lamp she caught the reddening of his cheekbones in the instant before the deepest dark that follows the extinction of light.

He turned toward her, his hand going to her hip. "Is that sick? Getting a tingle from your baby daughter sucking your tit?"

She touched his nipples lightly. "You didn't go looking for it. It's just some kind of automatic response. Like when you have one of those prostate exams and you get a hard-on—"

"Never," he protested.

She giggled. Cuddling up to him, she told him, "Sometimes it makes me feel—not exactly horny, but very . . . sensual. It's not about her, you understand. I wash her and rub her all over with lotion and I'm always holding her and smelling her and kissing her—but it's not sexual. She's my baby, not my lover. The strongest feelings I've ever gotten from her suckling are nothing to what I get with you."

"Yeah?" He was as pleased as he was interested. "It made me wish I could nurse her."

"Nurse me," she said, and flicked her tongue at his nipple.

It came to her that she and Junior were no longer separated. Somewhere along the way they had reconciled. Dynah needed Junior. She needed him too.

❧ 24 ❧

"**T**his isn't working," said Junior. It was in Saint Louis, third stop of a road trip, three weeks into January. He sat on the closed lid of the toilet next to the tub, holding towels. In the bathtub, Kissy held Dynah between her legs while she lathered shampoo into her hair. "Nobody else's wife follows the team everywhere. Let alone with a camera."

Kissy tipped Dynah's head back and scooped clear running water from the faucet with a plastic cup to rinse out the soap. Dynah rolled her eyes back and waggled her tongue at her mother.

"Good girl," Kissy soothed. "Close your eyes, keep out the sting."

Dynah clenched her eyes fiercely and thrust her jaw out, showing the picket fence of her baby teeth in her lower gum. Kissy held out her hand and Junior put a towel in it. She wrapped it around Dynah's wet hair and began to rub it gently.

"They're worried I'm going to get a picture of them with some girls and their wives will see it—"

"Sure, and it's their business, Kiss—"

"I haven't printed any of the pictures yet, let alone sent them to anybody's wife."

"And some of them don't want their wives getting any ideas about tagging along on the road with us."

"I don't give a shit," she said, passing Dynah to him. This was about some of his teammates accusing him of being pussywhipped. She was getting a certain amount of shit from some of them herself when his back was turned.

He took Dynah off to the bedroom to finish drying her. By the time Kissy emerged from the bathroom, he had snapped Dynah into her Dr. Dentons. She slid off the bed and padded off in search of her toys.

Junior picked up the camera Kissy had left on the dresser. He swung the lens in her direction. She was naked, pulling a T-shirt over her head. It just cleared her bottom when she was standing still. When she moved, she flashed bush and cheek, depending on whether she was coming or going. She fanned her fingers over the lens and he pulled the camera back.

"Turnabout's fair play," he said.

She flopped backward onto the bed and spread her legs defiantly.

He put down the camera. "I don't want to fight."

She closed her legs, sitting up and hugging her knees. "Then tell the guys you're not their errand boy. They can make their complaints to me directly—"

"They're trying to be diplomatic."

"Oh, I thought they were telling you to get your bitch in line. Covering their asses—"

"Speaking of which, if you've got any ideas about going into the locker room, forget it—"

"Nobody has any problem if some shooter from a local paper or *Hockey World* or *Sports Illustrated* comes into the locker room. I'm just as much a pro as those guys—"

"Those guys are guys," he pointed out, like she was an idiot and hadn't noticed.

"They protect you—"

"And you're my wife—"

"Meaning what, I'm a cunt on a leash?"

"Could we keep this in rational terms? The other wives aren't going to like you shooting pictures of their husbands in their jocks."

"Oh, for Christ's sake—"

"No"—Junior sat down next to her—"for mine. I'm not asking you to stop taking pictures. I'm asking you to give the guys their privacy. What happened to getting the permission of the subject?"

"I'm doing photojournalism and you guys are public figures—"

"And you have an edge, and you're taking advantage of it."

"*S.I.*'s interested—"

"Jesus, Kiss, you didn't tell me you were shopping it."

"I think I could get a book out of it, actually."

"Write one, you mean?"

"Yes, of course, pictures and text about the pictures. I'll make a deal with you," she said. "I'll tell you how to protect the net and you can tell me how to do my job."

Junior jumped up and paced angrily. "You use that my-job shit every time you know you're wrong and you're gonna do it anyway."

Kissy jumped up and got into his face to hiss, "Fuck you, Mr. Hockey-Is-My-Life."

Seizing the camera, he opened the back and ripped out the film.

"You shit!" Kissy cried. "Dynah's on that roll!"

Junior turned red. "Hide behind Dynah—"

Kissy snatched the camera back with shaking hands and then she shoved it into her gadget. She started packing, stuffing her things and Dynah's into their bags.

"Stop it," he said. "This is ridiculous." As she grabbed her Levi's from the floor where she'd dropped them, he tore them from her hands. "You're not going anywhere," he told her.

Kissy scooped up Dynah, who was watching them closely with troubled eyes, her lower lip tremulous. He caught Kissy by the shoulders and she stood still, her spine stiff with resistance. Dynah writhed in her arms, whimpering in alarm.

"Let me go," Kissy enunciated through gritted teeth.

He pointed out she was bare-ass. Kissy pulled away from him and he let her go. She put Dynah on the floor again and pulled her T-shirt off over her head. With a defiant glare, she picked up Dynah again and reached for the door.

"Jesus Christ," Junior said.

She opened the door and he surged past her and slammed it shut. And threw the bolt and hooked the chain while he was at it. "Very funny."

Lowering Dynah into the crib the hotel had provided, Kissy dressed with more calm.

"You're not going to leave," he said.

"No," she agreed. "not tonight. Tomorrow."

"I want you to stay." His voice shook. "I'm sorry. I shouldn't have taken the film out of your camera." She

didn't respond. In frustration he stumbled on. "You're being totally unreasonable."

Actually, she was being totally silent. She finished packing, except for her toothbrush. Then she nursed Dynah to
sleep. He usually returned Dynah to her crib for her but he
was so upset, all he could do was sit in a chair and stare at
them, Dynah in her arms and Kissy with her eyes closed
because she might go blind or turn into a pillar of salt or
something if she looked at him. After a while he turned off
the lights and crawled into bed next to her and Dynah and
closed his eyes. But he didn't sleep and he knew Kissy
wasn't sleeping either. The last time he looked at the clock
radio, it was 3:57. And he had a game that day.

Sudden thunder on the door startled him awake, and for
an instant he was back in the old place, Kowanek at the
door, adrenaline jolting his heart and his balls contracting,
fear and fury tensing everything for killing.

"Clootie," the trainer called, "the bus is running, we're
waiting on you."

The bed was empty and Kissy's suitcase and gadget and
the baby's bag were gone. The impression of Kissy's body,
of Dynah's small form, remained on the sheet and pillows
next to him.

There was no answer and the trainer rapped at the door
again. "You in there, Clootie? We gotta go."

"Fuck off," Junior said.

After a brief silence the trainer said, "Yeah, back to you,
Hoot."

Junior turned over and punched the pillow. Then he
erupted from the bed, dressing hastily and grabbing his
duffel. The bus was gone when he reached the lobby. He
jumped into a cab and told the cabby to haul his ass to the
facility where they had gym and ice time booked. As they
passed the bus, his teammates hung out the windows,
yelling shit at him. He rolled down the window and offered a finger to them.

She had not had time to get home to the little house they
had rented again, but he left a message on the tape machine apologizing and begging her to call. He was grateful
to be occupied through the day and in net that night. Conscious that the manager was watching him, the coach, the
trainer, all of them knowing somehow that Kissy had

bailed out, and nervous that he was not going to be able to concentrate and do the job. But he did. It was easy. He just pretended the puck was a call from Kissy he was not going to take.

But as soon as the game was over, he called again. There was no answer except the tape machine. He called his folks to find out if they had heard from her, some message maybe that Kissy was headed back east. He got Bernie, just home from school and day care, and both she and her baby, Casey, were tired. He pretended Kissy had gone back to Colorado because she was tired of traveling with the baby. "I think maybe something's wrong with the tape machine. I thought maybe she'd talked to you or Ma."

"No," Bernie said, "she hasn't. What did you do this time, asshole?"

He nearly hung up on her. "Take a Midol, Bernadette. If she calls her mom tonight, could you pass on the message to call me?" He gave her the number of the hotel, the number of his room.

And Bernie crashed the phone down in his ear.

He called Cait, though calling her mother, let alone running to her, was not something he had ever known Kissy to do. Cait asked him bluntly if they had had a fight, and when he admitted it, fell silent for a moment. She did promise, with a sigh, that if Kissy called she would urge her to contact him.

But Kissy didn't call and there was never any answer at the house except his own voice telling callers to leave a message.

He rang the landlady, who was feeding the Fucking Cat and watering the plants in their absence. She went to the house and called back to inform him, with some excitement, that it appeared to her that Kissy had been there, packed her things and Dynah's, and left. The Blazer was gone.

"I hope you work it out," she said. "I really do."

That made two of them. Only it was the wrong two.

Chicago was an easy reach.

"Of course, you can stay the night," Mary Frances told her, having taken the phone from Inga, who had answered. Inga had not been happy to hear Kissy's voice. "Stay a few days—I'll take some time off—"

"Thanks, it's just tonight," Kissy said.

Not until they sat down to a meal of Chinese take-out did she tell Mary Frances why she was headed back east. Inga watched and listened so closely she was hardly able to eat. Learning that Kissy had left her husband did nothing to relax the woman. Kissy had no desire to share the details, especially not with Inga, and Mary Frances did not press her. Or baby her, as she might have without Inga's lowering glare at her every attention to Kissy to keep her in check.

Kissy thought of opting for a hotel, with Dynah and the fussing she might do as a handy excuse, but she wanted the time with Mary Frances, even if it was constrained by Inga's presence. Her old friend had changed in significant ways—Inga the most obvious—but it was apparent her fastidiousness had been modified a little, and there was a substance to Mary Frances now, a certainty or assurance, that came from knowing, finally, who and what she was, at least as much as anyone ever does. But the old nearly telepathic empathy remained between them. Mary Frances was a friend, closer once than her own mother had ever been, and her home was a home, not a hotel room. There was something private and safe and warm in it, and between them, yet.

From Chicago, she plotted her route directly but without momentum. Once on the road, the white hot flare of anger cooled rapidly, not only because it took too much energy to sustain but also because her eye distracted her. There was so much to see. Of course, Dynah was a restless companion and took a lot of attention too. Because of the road trip schedule, she had ten days before Junior would be free to track her down. There was no mystery about her destination, but at least she would not have to deal with him, even over the phone, for a little while.

This time she wasn't going to let him stay with her. She wasn't going to let him back in her bed again. They were finished. She had tried to share his life, and when it came right down to it, she wasn't really welcome in it. What counted to Junior was the other guys, the team, its cohesiveness or whatever he wanted to call it. They didn't call it a club for nothing. He seemed baffled when she tried to tell him what it was like to be dismissed as a kind of camp follower. If she had not been his wife, if she had been another guy, they wouldn't have been half as perturbed at the intrusion of her camera.

One night when she had checked into a hotel that had cable, as she clicked her way to the Weather Channel to get an idea what conditions were on the road ahead, a hockey game flickered on the screen. It wasn't Junior's team, of course. But Dynah ran toward the screen and patted it frantically. "Daddy!" she cried with excitement. "Daddy!"

Kissy sat down on the floor and held Dynah in her lap and let her watch the figures moving over the ice. She had allowed Junior to become Daddy, she thought. It couldn't be undone.

It was a stop-and-go journey, the kind she had always wanted to make. There were pauses not only for rest rooms and meals but also to get Dynah out of the Blazer so they wouldn't go crazy from being cooped up together, mile after mile. She let picture taking just happen. Refusing to be unhappy, to linger on the complications of leaving Junior or the frustrations of staying with him, she let the whole trip just happen. Someday, she thought, she would look back on her cross-country dawdle with Dynah as one of the times she had been most alive. She and Dynah were eating up the country together. It was a time, a time-out, like summer, when the passing days were sufficient unto themselves.

For ten days Junior did not know where she and Dynah were. Presumably she was somewhere between Denver and Peltry, and when she reached the eastern terminus of her journey, maybe someone, perhaps her mother, would be kind enough to inform him. Daily, Junior restrained himself from jumping ship, mentally tying himself to the mast.

It was no secret that Kissy's departure had not been amicable. The guys who had grown impatient at her presence regarded his distracted red-eyed misery as proof he was as pussywhipped as they had previously judged him to be. Another faction was more sympathetic but clung to the conventional wisdom that the wife's being around too much caused trouble, and wasn't this exactly proof of it. The precious sense of connection Kissy had disturbed had to be reestablished. If he would just go out and have a beer or three with them, it would be a start. But he was close to inert, paralyzed with the fear of doing something that might make things worse. If he gave in to the impulse to drown his sorrows, he might get into some mess that would confirm to Kissy she had been right to leave and that would give management reason to think he couldn't handle his personal problems. After she left him during the last season, he had impressed the right people with his equanimity. He had kept his play steady and stayed sober. Spense had found him a lawyer who succeeded in persuading This-Diane's lawyer to remind her how many guys they both knew who could be classified as her boyfriend by the definition she was using. It had taken Junior a lot of self-discipline and loneliness to get to where people thought of him as reliable. He would be goddamned if he would blow it now. For one, he couldn't afford it. Fucking up now meant the money contract would evaporate.

There was a hole in the schedule at the end of the road trip that would allow him to follow Kissy to Peltry. He ceased to ask for messages. None came anyway. He told Ed Toth and Coach Gerrard he needed to take care of personal business and had to miss a couple of practices to do it, and they agreed to it.

Finally free to leave the team, when he boarded the first plane east, he was in a state of emotional exhaustion. When the attendant offered him a drink, he took it gratefully. Sometime later, when the plane was on the ground again and he was getting off to change flights, he couldn't quite get out of his own way. So he was a little bit stupid and would still be when he arrived. Why should he care? She couldn't even be bothered with letting him know she'd gotten home, if she had. She must have. It had been ten fucking days without a word—she could crawl cross-country in ten fucking days.

He hadn't called ahead to tell anyone when he was arriving, so there was no one there, and when he tried to pick up a rental car, the clerk bald-faced fucking refused him, and then the supervisor wouldn't let him have one either, because he was a little sloppy. They were nice enough about it—the supervisor wanted to put him in a cab personally. He put himself in a goddamn cab, he wasn't too fucked up to get a goddamn cab, the airport was the only place in goddamn fucking Peltry you could just walk out and get into a cab and not have to call for one.

He had the cabby stop at a convenience store for a six.

He couldn't hide the shape he was in, so he might as well be in it all the way. And the stupider he was, the better, if he wasn't going to strangle Kissy on the spot for the incredibly high-riding, bitchy, junior-high-school-twitch punishment of refusing him the simple adult courtesy of letting him know she and Dynah, his only child, were still among the living. Peltry was in the bone-cracking cold grip of January-going-on-February, which was also what he had come home to, the walk-in freezer of Kissy Mellors' chesty fucking heart.

Looking travel-worn, the Blazer was in the driveway at his folks'. It sure was fucking grand of nofuckingbody to not fucking call and let him know his wife and kid weren't road meat in fucking Indiana.

Dunny met him in the hallway, the newspaper he had been reading in one hand. He took one look at him. "You're drunk," he said.

Junior barged past him. "Kissy!" he bellowed, and from somewhere above there was a sudden explosive patter of little feet and then a small excited voice babbling and Dynah was at the top of the stairs, on the landing, Kissy behind her and scooping her up.

"Dynah!" he called.

In Kissy's arms, Dynah squirmed and wriggled and held out her arms plaintively, called back to him, "Daddy!"

Esther emerged from her bedroom and Bernie from hers, her little boy on her hip, and they looked at Kissy and Kissy looked at them. Knowingly, resignedly. It was grand, he wanted to say to her, if he could get his mouth to work, being married to someone you could count on disappointing.

The neon graffiti of Bird's was far more welcoming. Junior paid off the cab with some effort—the money had become obstinately slippery—and looked at his gear, which the cabby had thrown down on the sidewalk without interest. He left it there. Maybe someone would steal it and put the cap on a day in which his own parents had told him he was going to have to find himself a motel room because there was no fucking room at the inn. Inside it was wonderfully overheated and smoky and everybody was glad to see him. He signed some autographs before he insisted he had to have a beer. The first one was on the house, and people were lining up to buy him a bottomless draft. Eventually he worked his way to the bar. A guy jumped off a stool so he could have it. And three guys down the bar, Officer Friendly was renting a stool and watching him with contemptuous eyes. Junior grinned at him because he could see Officer Friendly was just as blurry as he was. Amazingly, from somewhere deep in some sober cache of cells in his brain, he summoned the name the asshole's mother had hung on him.

"Hey, Burke," he called cheerfully.

Officer Friendly thrust his chin out in wordless backwoods greeting and didn't fall off the stool, so he still had a way to go. The guys between the two of them jumped to the mistaken conclusion they were buddies. The one nearest Officer Friendly gave up his stool and gestured to Junior to take it. It was too funny so Junior did, giving Officer Friendly an affectionate buddy poke in the biceps as he settled down next to him. He raised his beer mug to him and Officer Friendly did the same.

"Welcome home," said Officer Friendly.

"Yeah, right," Junior agreed. He tapped the bar. "This is my home tonight. I'm fucking homeless. My wife—"

Officer Friendly raised his hand dismissively. "Fuck your wife."

"Not fucking likely," Junior said, and they both laughed.

"She boot you out again?"

"Right the fuck out. I can sleep on the fucking sidewalk, you know?"

Officer Friendly nodded gloomily. "Bitch. They're all bitches. Fuck you over every time."

Junior groped for meaningful conversation. "Hey," he said, "name me five guys with names ten letters long who hit over forty homers in one season."

"Kluszewski." Officer Friendly took a meditative swallow to help his memory along. "Tony Conigiliaro. Yaz." He grinned triumphantly. "Petrocelli."

"And?" demanded Junior.

"And? That's five—"

"Fuck it is, it's four. Ain't you got enough fingers to count that high?"

"You want to get personal, I hear when you want to count to twenty-one," retorted Burke, "you have to drop your pants."

"That reminds me about the Jamaican with the tattoo on his dick."

"What? He had it ruled off in meters or something? I know, he had ten letters in his last name and hit forty homers in one season, right?"

"I never heard of a Jamaican playing major league ball, just Ewing playing hoops," said Junior, trying to get the conversation focused again. "Hint, all right. Italian-American, 1953, hit forty dingers for the Dodgers—"

"DiMaggio—"

"The Dodgers, you numbass. Seven, eight," he corrected himself, "letters in DiMaggio, you really can't count, can you?"

"All right, who's the fifth guy?"

"Campanella."

"The fuck, Campanella was black—"

"His dad was Italian."

"So what? Campanella was black. Whole bunch a black people would take exception to you calling him Italian." Burke waxed philosophic. "There's something about you that irritates somebody else enough to get you lynched, under certain circumstances, then that outweighs all other identifying factors." He waggled an empty beer mug at the bartender. "My round," he said, diverting Junior from arguing the point. "What brand are you, Clootie, Irish? Jamaican?"

"You heard about my tattoo? Probably I am Irish, some. My dad says French, but don't take it seriously, on account of the French have never been particular—"

Burke snorted. "You know what Irish birth control is?"

Junior made some guesses. "Famine? Pubs? English rule? Bomb in a baby carriage?"

"Not bad," said Burke. "Irish birth control is the men waiting till they're fifty to marry. Then they die as soon as the family's big enough."

Junior laughed.

"I'm headin' out, pard," announced Officer Friendly. "You want a ride someplace?"

"You're pretty shitfaced," Junior pointed out.

Getting off the bar stool for Officer Friendly required grabbing the bar and then Junior. "Right, right. I'll get us a right." Junior knew he meant "ride," but it was a kick to hear him fuck it up. Officer Friendly lurched off to the

public phone and the next thing Junior knew, he was back
again, plucking at his jacket sleeve. "Come on."

They made their way into the night that was as frigid
as Kissy's heart, to where Junior's gear was still on the
sidewalk.

"Ride's coming," Officer Friendly promised through
chattering teeth.

The cold hit Junior's bladder and he had to pee. He
leaned against the wall and unbuttoned. His dick didn't
want to come out in the cold but he finally got it going. Officer Friendly turned his back to the street too and unlim-
bered. Junior wrote Kissy's name on the brick wall and
Officer Friendly laughed. Tires crunched on the road and a
unit pulled up at the curb, bleeping them with its bubble
lights and siren, as they buttoned up with fingers made
clumsy by cold and haste. Sergeant Preston climbed out to
hold the back door open for them.

"Your limo, gents," he said.

Officer Friendly nose-dived into the backseat. Junior
had to stow his gear in the trunk before following him.
Sergeant Preston had a new pal, a big boy, who slouched
so as not to hit his head on the roof and made the whole
unit list to the right with his weight. He twisted around,
grinning at them, offering Officer Friendly a low five. He
made Junior think of Moosejaw, back in Canada now,
probably destined to be a career minor leaguer.

"Hey," said Officer Friendly wittily.

Sergeant Preston took the wheel. "Where to, guys?"

"HoJo's for Junior," Officer Friendly told him. "The
missus is pissed at him."

He and Junior found it extremely amusing.

"What about you?" Sergeant Preston inquired of Officer
Friendly.

He pointed at himself. "Me? Why would Junior's old
lady be pissed at me?"

That was pretty funny too. Junior had to wipe tears from
his eyes.

"'Member arresting me on the bridge?" he asked.

Officer Friendly and Sergeant Preston were both con-
vulsed with nostalgic hilarity. The sergeant's new partner
was a little more dutiful in his merriment, but he hung in
there.

They were at the HoJo's downtown. Peltry had two Ho-

Jos and they had picked the one nearest the cop shop. He had to wonder if it meant anything. He stumbled out, shouldered his gear, and waved good-bye to the cops. There was something wrong with this picture, he told himself, when the cops were friendlier than his wife.

Next afternoon the only vehicle in his folks' driveway was the Blazer. He had called ahead. Kissy admitted him with all the enthusiasm with which she would greet a pair of Seventh-Day Adventist preachers. Arms crossed under her breasts, never a good sign.

"Hi, Junior," he said. "It sure is good to see you. Sorry I didn't call from the road but you know how it is, you get looking at the scenery and the next thing you know, it's ten fucking days—"

She turned her back on him and marched down the hall. He kicked the door shut.

"It was a shitty thing to do," he went on.

In the kitchen, she spun about again. "I'm sorry, it was a shitty thing to do."

His sails sagged with the sudden loss of wind. He was hung over, of course, and he wanted to close his eyes and fall down, but then he would just have to get back up again. So he stayed on his feet, but it took effort. "Where's Dynah?"

"Napping."

"Oh." It was a disappointment not to see her. "I feel like shit."

"You look like shit."

He dragged a chair out at the table and slumped into it. "All right. I was an asshole. I am an asshole. Let's call it even."

"Sure," she said. "I'm not coming back."

He pinched the bridge of his nose. He had been just fine until she said that and now he was springing a leak.

"You don't trust me, Junior. You don't trust me to know what I need to do in my work. And you're scared shitless the other guys might think you like a girl—you might bring a girl into the fucking clubhouse." She threw up her hands in defeat. "What are we talking about? It's over-done-with-tout-finis."

"No," he protested. He pushed the chair and it fell over behind him in slow motion so he was able to catch it effortlessly. He set it in place and turned back to her. "We're a family, we belong together—"

"It's your idea of belong, not mine."

He stared at her blearily for a long moment. He was flat. He didn't have a goddamn thing left. His eyes stung and then he was blind with tears. She disappeared. He could not see her anymore. It was like he was drowning, or she was or they both were. He groped his way to the back door, fumbled for the knob, and let himself out.

Her eyes were a mess, her whole face puffy. She had no idea why she was crying. She had not cried once all the way home. Only nursing Dynah seemed to help. She was going to have to wean her if she was going to get a job. Numbered days, she thought, feathering Dynah's hair, enjoy it, kid. They had had a good run. Few babies got to suckle as long as Dynah had.

Esther and Dunny arrived at the house with Casey, having picked him up at day care to allow Bernie a trip to the Y. They looked in on her anxiously but she didn't want to talk and they let her alone. It was too much to hope Junior would too.

He turned up again after dinner—timing it, apparently, so there was no question of his being invited to join them. He avoided her eyes. Dynah screamed joyfully and made straight for him and he made straight for her. Leaving them alone, Kissy cleared the table and did the dishes. He took Dynah upstairs to bathe her. When she followed them up, she found them sitting on the landing, Junior reading to her from an old children's book of his own, Dynah listening raptly.

> *So toss in the puck, for the players are set,*
> *Sing ho! for the dash on the enemy net;*
> *And ho! for the smash as the challenge is met;*
> *And hey! for a glorious night!*

Casey wailed somewhere downstairs and Bernie cried out, "Ma! I've got to study!"

"Again," Dynah demanded.

Kissy picked up her camera. These were shots she had taken before, different only for the change in place, the changes in Dynah. Junior was the same. She closed in on

Dynah, on her face raised to giggle at Daddy, lowered to study the pictures and follow Daddy's moving finger under the words. Dynah's little finger curled around his big finger. Then close on Junior, and he lifted his eyes from the page and looked into the lens, straight down the lens at her, and she closed the shutter as if it were her own eyelid. She lowered the camera and his voice had stopped and he was still looking at her. Dynah yanked impatiently at his shirt. His gaze fell again to the page and he began to read aloud again. Eventually Dynah began to droop; Kissy held out her arms and Dynah crawled into them. He watched them nursing and when Dynah had fallen asleep, took her and tucked her into her crib in the living room, where Kissy was sleeping on the fold-out couch.

"Talk to me a minute," he said.

She followed him to the front door, where they faced each other tensely.

"I'm going back to Denver tomorrow," he told her. "I have to go. I want to stay together. I'd like you to come with me. Or, if you want a week or two here, follow me. We owe it to ourselves and Dynah to work at this. See a marriage counselor and all that shit. We're both too close to this. We're having the same arguments over and over. Maybe an outsider could help."

"I'm staying here."

He blinked tearfully and looked everywhere but at her, the way Dynah did when she was angry at Kissy. "How are you for money?"

"Okay." She had none and they both knew it.

He took out his checkbook and started writing a check. "This is just walking-around money. You set up a checking account here and I'll wire money into it."

"I'm going to get a job."

"Fuck getting a job," he said with only a little rancor. "Spare yourself the starving artist shit. It won't make your pictures better. I'll support you. You can't make enough to pay a baby-sitter, let alone rent. Stay home and take care of Dynah while she's small and do your pictures. It won't be for long. Never mind wasting your time and energy taking pictures of some old fuck who just snagged the first fucking salmon of the year. Shoot on your own and print in your own darkroom and get an agent to sell your stuff."

She bristled at his casual dictation of how she ought to organize her life. "Don't tell me what to do—"

"Take the fucking money, Kissy. You think I want you eating cat food and living in some dump in the Barnyard while I tool around in an expensive car and wipe my ass with ten-dollar bills?" He folded her fingers over the check. "I refuse to be your enemy." He licked his lips. "I'd like to kill you, but I refuse to be your fucking enemy."

He looked so bleak she could feel herself weakening, the hairline cracks starting in her heart. She did not know how she was supposed to make it work if they could not be enemies. She did not know how she could ever be free of him. His reflexes were too good, his patience engulfing, smothering. He held her close, rocking her gently from side to side. Comforting her, refusing to be her enemy. Telling her how much he loved her. It was going to be a long time before anyone else touched her that way.

∞ 25 ∞

He could smell it from the doorstoop as he slid the key into the lock. He opened the door and stepped into it, a stink so fetid he could practically see it. He wondered when the landlady had last been in the house. The soil of the nearest potted plant—sansevieria; Kissy liked it because it was impossible to kill and made a strong graphic in pictures—was dry and crumbly, and the plant looked desiccated too. His eyes watered from the stench. He followed it upstairs.

The Fucking Cat was on the bed. Various puckerstrings had let go when it gave up its evil ghost to its Master, so it reposed in a dark puddle of its own excreta. Its swollen tongue had pushed open its jaw to protrude, and its tiny sharp teeth pierced the enlarged tissue.

Junior bolted downstairs and out the door. There he sucked in several deep breaths. Lungs filled, he dove in again to take the stairs two at a time. He seized the opposite hems of the coverlet, pulled them together, and then stumbled down the stairs again and out the back door to the garbage bin. Knocking off a lid, he stuffed the bundle into a garbage can and slammed the lid back on.

The house still stank horrifically. He went up and looked at the bed again. The stain had sunk right through the linen into the mattress. He dragged it all out, linen and mattress. Still the faint odor of dead Fucking Cat loitered in the air like the devil's own worst fart. Muttering imprecations on the landlady, he rang her phone. A daughter-in-law informed him the woman had had a stroke and was hospitalized. Said daughter-in-law had had no idea her mother-in-law had been looking after the house.

He went outside again to sit on the stoop. No way could

he stay inside and breathe that stink. He was on Eastern
Standard Time, three hours later than it was here, and he
was tired, but it was only six in the evening, and cold, with
a snow-heavy cloud ceiling. He wondered what the Fucking Cat had died of. Fucked to death by demons maybe.
The house was uninhabitable. He locked up again and
headed out to find a motel.

The choices were limited—Hojo's or Hojo's. It didn't
matter to him. He just wanted a room with a bed and a
bathroom and cable that he turned on right away, for the
company. He was in luck; the first *Nightmare on Elm
Street* was screening on some old movie channel. There
was something comforting about the sight of Freddy capering and even the sound of Freddy's cackle.

He could go for booze and drink himself to sleep. He
could call Kissy, tell her where he was, but maybe he
would hold on that, ten days or so, let her find out what it
felt like. He sat on the bed and checked the room for someplace strong enough to hold a rope, which he didn't have,
he would have to use a belt. The room lacked the requisite
beam or hook but that didn't matter because he wasn't going to do anything anyway.

Third time she had bailed out. He kept thinking that,
with the emphasis on *third*. Three strikes, you're out. He
refused to believe it. She had basically sent him down to
Dry River again, that was all. He was three years older and
they had Dynah and he wasn't going to jump off a bridge
or anything else. He was going to do his job and be the
best father he could be to Dynah at this distance. And wait
for Kissy to come around. She had let him stay with her at
his folks'—Bernie heroically taking Casey to the fold-out
couch in the living room—the night before he left and hadn't
made him use any protection, which had to mean she
halfway wanted him to knock her up again. Which desire
he would be glad to oblige. And hey, for a glorious night!
First thing in the morning, he would talk to his agent, ask
him to sound out the East Coast clubs. There had to be
some way to work a trade to get him closer to home.

The book was kangarooed into the pocket of the backseat, forgotten or abandoned by a previous passenger. Junior noticed it, settling in, belting up, but it was just a
detail. The plane was a last-minute replacement for equip-

ment that had developed a problem, and the cleaning crew had not had much time on board. He had other things on his mind—the first game in a series, the twinge in his right elbow he was worried might be tendinitis, the way his left knee was grating, and whether either one would get bad enough to affect his reflexes.

But later on he pulled the book out of the pocket just to see what it was. *Women Who Love Too Much*. He knew about it vaguely—it had had a talk show vogue when it first came out and subsequently the newsstand book racks were full of *Women Who* titles: *Women Who Love Men Who Treat Them Like Boogers; Women Who Love Men Who Borrow Their Lingerie; Women Who Read Psychobabble*—shit like that. There should be one, he thought, called *Women Who Want Every Goddamn Thing Their Own Way*. Dedicated to Kissy. He snorted at the thought and then he opened the paperback, curious as to what kind of bullshit had made it so popular.

"When being in love means being in pain, we are loving too much," read the first sentence.

"No shit," he muttered.

His seatmate, Jameson, the kid who had come up from Allentown to dress with him and wish him ill, stood up. "'Cuse me, Hoot, I gotta pee—"

"This isn't kindergarten. You don't have to announce you have to go Number One or Number Two," Junior snarled as he shifted in his seat to allow Jameson to pass and his knee did its thing; it felt like a small rabid nasty animal was sinking needle fangs into him.

Jameson looked wounded. It was something he did well and constantly. He wasn't a bad kid but he irritated Junior. He didn't hurt anywhere, or if he did, it didn't bother him, and he had a brand-new wife about whom he was totally misty-eyed and who thought he was Santa Claus and Jesus Christ and Mel Gibson all wrapped up in one package and with a hard-on. Worse, he was three years younger than Junior. He played out too far, though, and until he figured out when he should be out of the door or in it, he was going to play doorman for a lot of fast-moving rubber.

When the plane landed, Junior was still reading and had begun to underline passages. There was one about kids in dysfunctional families being damaged that really bothered him; he kept thinking about Dynah.

"Good book, Hoot?" Jameson asked him as they yanked carry-on out of the overhead compartments.

"Yeah," Junior said, "I'll read it to you sometime."

The other guys laughed and Jameson looked wounded. "I can read—"

"With one hand," Junior said. "It's not that kind of book, and if it were, I wouldn't volunteer to read it to *you*."

"I was thinking," he told Kissy over the phone, "we could be messing up Dynah."

Kissy didn't say anything for a second and then she said, "She seems okay to me, Junior."

"Yeah, to me, too," he admitted, "but what about later, when she gets grown up? What if she can't live with a guy who's around all the time or something?"

"Maybe she'll grow up and be a lesbian—"

"Whatever. If she does, maybe she won't be able to live with another dyke who's around all the time—work with me on this, Kissy, please?"

Kissy sighed. "I don't know, Junior. Your dad was home all the time."

"Which has to do with what? Barbers don't usually spend six months of the year on the road. I'm talking about Dynah—"

"You're talking about you. You're the one who's away half the year. Your choice—"

"I'm not all-powerful, baby, I can't make the league play all their games in Peltry."

"We've had this discussion."

And they had. He gave it up for that conversation but he came back to it, the next time he called.

"What would happen to us if I quit and cut hair for a living or something, Kissy? Would you be able to stand me being around?"

"Let me know when you're gonna do it," she said, obviously not taking him seriously.

That was it, he thought, she didn't take him seriously. She picked him because she didn't have to take him seriously. She could just ignore him.

"Your mother," he said, in a third phone call, "she's ignored you since she and your dad broke up. From everything you've ever said about it, she did before too. She's all wrapped up in her work and maybe Noah, for ten, fifteen minutes a day or something. You don't know where your brother is or even if he's still alive, and your dad is a total zero in your life. Wouldn't you say you come from a dysfunctional family?"

Kissy laughed. "Sure. That's why I picked up a dose from a hooker and gave it to you and then I got wasted and stole my Blazer and killed Ed—"

"You like flinging that shit at me, that's what I'm talking about," he said, getting mad in spite of everything he had figured out. "You get to feel virtuous and I'm the shithead of the world, what about you getting pregnant at fifteen and again when you knew better—"

"Fuck you, Junior."

"Fuck you too, Kissy, fuck you too, I'm trying to break us out of this shit we're in—"

She hung up on him.

"There's a book you should read," he told her a few days later, after they had several carefully polite and distant conversations.

"Read my ass," she retorted.

"I have, it's my favorite nighttime story," he said, and she laughed. "I want to make a deal, baby—"

"Uh huh."

"I'll go into therapy if you will."

She was silent a moment, twisting the phone cord, he didn't doubt, she did that, he had watched her do it, he was nearly in tears with the desire to watch her twist the fucking phone cord for a while.

"Christ," she said, suddenly angry. "When? I don't have any time, I'm a single mother, Junior—"

"Please," he said. "I'm going to do it anyway."

Another silence and then, "I'll think about it, okay?"

"You seeing anybody?" he asked.

He always asked it. Sooner or later, usually sooner. In their phone calls or leaving some airport or other, every day, every other day—he asked it as often as he said he loved her. And as soon as he asked it, he announced he wasn't seeing anybody either. And as often, he asked her if they couldn't please get married again.

Occasionally someone did ask her out, or someone else tried to fix her up. But why would she want to see anybody? Where would she get the energy? She was—despite having proceeded with the divorce—another hockey wife, her days consumed in child care, work, hiring someone to mend the roof or paint the trim, waiting for Junior's calls or the next time they could be together. Letting herself be elated at the rumors that Junior was on the trading block, rumors that never did come to anything. In a trap of his own making, Junior had made himself too valuable, preventing a trade to some East Coast club that would allow him to be home oftener.

She asked around, collected a few names and numbers of therapists, but did not make an appointment. Junior had found one in Denver; he went twice a week, and they had their biggest fights over the phone right after every session. He was full of questions then, all of them pointed at her like so many scalpels. The implication was she was broken and he was going to fix her, Junior and his therapist. Sarah Rupert.

Occasionally she spent time again in Junior's world. Sometimes she met him on the road, or she visited him in Colorado. At one home game she met Sarah Rupert, and was relieved to discover that Junior's therapist was a pleasant middle-aged woman with a linebacker-size husband in tow, the pair of them as comfortable together as a big dog on a favorite sofa.

Professional hockey was a tribe, like any other group of people with one big thing in common—the very thing she had wanted to capture with her camera—but like any tribe, the people in it were individuals. Some of them she liked, some she did not. Some liked her, some did not. She could not bring herself to like Deker. There was his history with Bernie and his obsessive interest in Casey, his eagerness to claim him if—and only if—he was his son. But there was also an immediate sexual tension between Deker and herself. He was a more extreme make of Junior, more narcissistic and predatory and careless, much too appealing to what she thought of as the mattress in herself. He always greeted her by asking her if she and Junior were married that day or not, as if he found their situation amusing. He flirted with her in a way that made it clear he assumed she was his for the taking. He offered her unsolicited confidences, confessing how flattered he was at the ceaseless importunities of women who wanted and claimed to be having his babies and how much in love with Bernie he was—how he would marry her in a minute if she would only allow a blood test on Casey.

"For Christ's sake," Kissy said once, listening to him bemoan the cost of daughters over breakfast in a hotel coffee shop on a road trip, "haven't you ever heard of blow jobs? Hand jobs? Masturbation?"

To her amazement, Deker crimsoned and stuttered and found an excuse to leave.

"It's not sex," Junior tried to explain to her later, "it's making women happy, which he thinks means dicking 'm, and it's his duty to his DNA—that's what he says, anyway. He thinks blow jobs and hand jobs and beating off are a terrible waste of seed. I don't," Junior added with a grin. "You lose it whether you use it or not, you know." And then it was his turn to turn red. "There's nobody but you."

Nobody but you. Nobody. But. You. Sometimes she was nobody at all, a qualification, in Junior's life, a nameless second person singular, with no other identity to him than the intimate *you*. Excluded from most of his life, a world of struggle, of passion and defeat and triumph, and between the pipes, jazzy sweaty riffs and caesuras when the scrape of the puck receded from him. It was not that he could not share it; he did, but not with her. He had put his hand over the lens of her camera, he had blinded her to his life. Then she would start to get angry at him again. And what good did it do? Just what good did it do to get angry at Junior?

"Seeing anybody?" he had asked the very first time he had come back to Peltry after their third separation, as they drove home from the airport.

"Yes. I've joined a swingers' club and only last night I was gang-banged by twenty guys."

He went pale and then laughed it off.

"Yes," she said, another time, over the phone. "I have to tell you the truth. I've been sleeping around for years. I go to Bird's or Skinner's and pick up some guy and do him in the parking lot."

A moment's silence and then a nervous chuckle from Junior.

"Yes!" she screamed at him once in Detroit, the time she didn't bring Dynah with her so she and Junior could have some time alone on his birthday. "I've got a boyfriend with a dick the size of Godzilla's and whenever he's screwing me, I'm thinking of you and what a limpdick asshole you are!"

And he put his hand gently over her mouth and said "Jet lag" to the bellman, who was backing away with his eyes bugged out. And then to her, "It's all right, baby. I just gotta ask."

Ask away. She was as much his wife as if they were not divorced. He paid most of the bills, had bought the small stucco house near the campus and his folks that she picked out—in fact, kept her. The money her work brought in was minuscule in comparison to his income, and irregular to boot. He was as much her husband as he chose to be—which was, so far as she could tell, what marriage meant to most men. Whether he in fact "saw" anybody, she had no idea. Like a good hockey wife, she did not check his collars for lipstick, his pockets for notes, telephone numbers, receipts for dinners or expensive gifts. She didn't even make him use a rubber. She went to bed with him at different times and in different places and in different moods, but always with an underlying sense of recklessness. She risked pregnancy along with everything else and could not explain why. She wondered sometimes what she would do if she became pregnant. He would love to have another child. He would want to get married again. It might be funny, actually, another big-bellied wedding. Proof positive: once a fool, always a fool. But perhaps she would merely go out and get rid of it and never mention it to him. Or maybe she would have it and give it away—though if there was one thing that really would anger Junior, it would be that. He would sue her, as he threatened to sue her over Dynah.

What did Junior mean by "love"? Nothing she did or did not do had any significance in the global shine of his love. He beamed down at her with loving irony through her bedroom window, content to look at her, a self-satisfied voyeur hanging in the void miles and miles away. The thin gilt whisper of his love fell over her, invaded her every pore and crevice and orifice and seeped into her womb. She received him. That was all he asked. God hates a coward, she murmured in her sleep, but she didn't know what the hell she meant, what the hell an alleged divine loathing of chickenshitedness had to do with the fact that fucking Junior, in a mysteriously and perversely Catholic way, just did not count. After all, his love was sterile. She didn't get pregnant.

In the fall of the year she divorced Junior and the office pool went not to Burke but to the redheaded legal secretary who had been taking dictation from Burke's boss for several months. The *News* published a photographic series Kissy had done of the Valley, illustrating its seasonal changes. In nearly every shot, the natural beauty of the gorge was tarnished by evidence of human degradation and vice. A debate ensued in the letters column in the paper as to whether she ought to have photographed the garbage and the cardboard hooches, the used condoms and needles and pipes. Through the winter months, she answered with more photographs—of the daily lives of prisoners in the county jail, of kids making coke buys at the 7-Eleven near the high school, of street kids and homosexuals working the dark streets of downtown late at night, leaning into the windows of automobiles, of addicts shooting up in a deserted playground and the litter of their needles amid the crenellated towers of the playground by dawnlight, of young businessmen in suits and ties smoking weed in a downtown alley during their lunch hour, of brawls outside dives on Saturday nights, of beaten women and children in a shelter, of a group of eleven-year-old boys drinking in a cellar.

Mike Burke studied the outpouring of her work in the pages of the *News* with more than passing interest. Kissy Mellors' new subject was the ugly underworld in which he worked. He knew she had been working, and where and when, of course; he could scarcely not know of it. He was impressed by the quality of the published work. It was implacable in its grittiness and beautiful in her mastery of light. And it established that she was the goods. His sources in the media told him she would be winning prizes for it and not just locally.

On the lookout for her, several times he drove by the house she had bought near the campus. Corner lot, the stucco house set across it, big dark pines skirting it that made it broody. Kiddy junk on the porch—trikes and a net and kid-size sticks for street hockey. Late one afternoon, on one such drive-by, he spotted her in the backyard, pushing her little girl in the swing of a sturdy jungle gym.

Mother and daughter were similarly garbed in jeans and heavy sweaters against the chill of early spring. Leaving his Jeep at the curb, he waved at her. She waved back.

"Howyadoin'?" he called.

She grinned. The little girl twisted in the swing to see him. It seemed strange for a moment, to think this small person had first been known to him as a basketball-sized distension of her mother's abdomen against his arm. It made him feel as if he could hear the whoosh of time being sucked away by some universe-size vacuum cleaner.

"Hiya, kid," he said, stooping to her.

"This is Mr. Burke," Kissy told her daughter.

"Mike, please. You're Dynah, aren't you?"

"Yes." Dynah stared gravely up at him. "Absolutely." She launched herself athletically from the swing and raced toward the slide.

Kissy took the swing Dynah had vacated. It was too close to the ground, so she had to stick her legs straight out in front of her, or else tuck them underneath. She opted for straight out. Burke checked her hand, curling around the rope. She still wore a wedding band.

Clootie had signed a million-dollar contract. A feature in *Sports Illustrated* had followed the money as the night the day. In it, the event was cast as a Solomon's choice, forcing the goaltender to swap his open desire to play for some East Coast club in reach of home—Peltry—for all that money. Tough fucking choice, Burke thought. But for Clootie it had been a struggle between his career and his private life. He still loved his ex-wife and desired nothing more ardently than to remarry her. He didn't date, he told *S.I.*, and remained committed to his vows though they were, in fact, legally dissolved. Kissy had declined comment, but the magazine feature detailed continued domesticity, reporting Clootie returned as often as he could to his former wife and their daughter, residing with them in the home he had bought them and spending much of the summer with them. It was all a crock, Burke thought. The bastard had exactly what he wanted, a big green pile of money, a red-hot career, and first-class pussy waiting at home. A kid too.

"When are you going to take a picture of a kid eating cotton candy at the fair?" he asked.

Kissy laughed. "I already did. Two kids. Dynah and her cousin Casey."

He lowered himself into the swing next to her, stretching his legs stiffly and digging his heels into the dirt. "I got a problem."

She raised her eyebrows quizzically.

"You." He was careful to keep the tone neutral.

She let go the ropes and clasped her hands between her thighs. "I run a red light or something?"

"You're wandering around no-man's-land, the DMZ. Taking pictures of people breaking laws—one of these days a bad guy is going to take exception to you pointing a lens at him—"

"It's my job." Remembering the young cop she had first met the night of the accident, she thought how much he had changed. She had heard through Dunny Clootie, who heard all the courthouse gossip in his shop downtown, that the former cop turned chief investigator for the District Attorney, Butch McDonough, was on the fast track to be DA himself someday. And that he was as hard a man in the courthouse as he had once been on the street. The boyishness in his face had gone, and he had a lean and wolfish look.

"You carry?" he asked with a startling abruptness. "You strapped?"

"A gun?" She laughed.

He didn't. "Ever taken a self-defense course?"

She rolled her eyes.

Dynah shrieked happily as she dove headfirst down the slide, like a little otter. Burke tensed, expecting to see her land on her face, but at the bottom she flipped herself over gymnastically and landed solidly on her feet. Like a cat twisting in midair. Must be the Clootie in her. If Clootie ever fell out of an airplane, he would land on his feet. In a pile of money probably.

"I want you to take one," he told Kissy. "I want you to buy a .22 and learn how to use it. I'll get you licensed to carry."

"You're scaring me."

"I mean to."

She was quiet a moment, watching Dynah clamber back up the ladder to the top of the slide. "What happens if I don't get a gun or take a course?"

"I'll put a couple cops on you and scare off your subjects—"

"You shit!" She jumped up.

He grabbed her wrist to stop her stalking off. "Wait. Cool your jets, lady. I'm not trying to stop you doing what you want to do, I'm just trying to give you an edge if anything goes wrong."

She stared down at him and he released her wrist.

"All right," she said.

He took a card from his wallet. "This guy's a little less full of bullshit than most of the brickbusters around here—"

"Brickbusters?"

Chopping the edge of one hand against the other, he mimed the common martial arts stunt. She laughed.

"You want me to take you to a gunshop—"

"I can do it myself."

"Take somebody with you who knows guns so you don't get ripped off."

She nodded.

Watching her stuff the card into the hip pocket of her Levi's, he wished briefly it was his hand. "Come see me once you've bought it and we'll take care of the licensing." He hesitated. "I admire what you've done. The pictures."

He wasn't bullshitting her. She had listened to him. He had had dealings with several women lawyers, one in the office, the others public defenders or private practitioners, and she was that caliber of intelligent woman, quick to see her own advantage. A woman like that might cry and call him a bastard at the end of an affair, but she didn't snivel when she lost a case.

Her body, her looks and vitality, heightened his sense of his own virility. The sudden brightening of his sexual wattage was tonic. But there was no pressure. He could check her out without any compulsion to do anything. Even if he were looking for an involvement—and he wasn't—the little girl was a chiller. Single moms, he had discovered, made for easily distracted lovers. She was clearly a stubborn, mercurial, demanding woman, a better fantasy than a conquest for a prudent man. But still, a little juice in the coffee never hurt.

* * *

Dynah's white-eyelet skirt ruffled over Junior's forearm as he held her so her long legs were exposed to the edge of her panties. Kissy reached over and tugged the skirt down a little. It was overcast and humid, the air thick with gathering storm. Even in summer dress, the mourners in the graveyard for Esther Clootie's committal service were sweating. Dynah wriggled restlessly and buried her face in Junior's shoulder. She did not understand, Kissy thought, but she knew everyone was very sad. Kissy had considered letting Dynah see Esther before the coffin was closed. In the end she had decided death and funerary cosmetics had rendered Esther so nearly unrecognizable, it would only confuse her. It added to her own grief that Dynah was so young, she would almost certainly forget the grandmother who had loved her so intensely.

Dunny grasped Kissy's hand tightly. It was almost over, and he was starting to come apart. He blamed himself because he had thought Esther was choking on a piece of apple. He had applied the Heimlich maneuver. He had himself convinced he had at the very least caused Esther more pain, if he had not actually killed her, though two doctors had assured him it had been one of those cataclysmic coronaries, an embolus blocking the artery to the brain, nearly instantaneous death.

Kissy herself was very still inside, like a leaf on a tree in the thick air. In the time she had been herself a mother, Esther had been more of a mother to Kissy than her own. It was to Esther she had resorted when Dynah spiked a fever for the first time and when Dynah suddenly decided she would only eat marshmallows and when she announced she would answer only to the name of Chiquita Juanita Juniorita.

Like Mark, Junior was inchoate in his bereavement. He and his brother had been boys gifted with attributes their world admired, and everything worked against them putting away their childish things. As their only female authority figure, their mother had been, and remained, powerful and feared. Early on they had learned to isolate her authority by treating her as a ridiculous and eccentric pet, and any obedience rendered to her as an act of indulgence on their part. Guilty, resentful, confused, they nonetheless adored her and were shattered by her loss.

Kissy tried to be fair. Mark was only twenty-one.

Fatherhood had done a lot to mature Junior; his focus on his family was not public relations bullshit. Despite the fact they were divorced—perhaps, she sometimes speculated, with no credit to herself, because they were divorced—he was a very attentive father to Dynah. And faithful to her, to the best of her knowledge—and some of the other hockey wives who had become more or less friends said Junior was, he had that reputation, but then, they believed it about their own husbands. Junior had become the professional he had always wanted to be, professional not only in his game but in his attitude, his demeanor, in more ways than he could ever have imagined, or knew.

At home, when everyone had left and Dynah was in bed, she and Junior made love, turning to each other with an instinctual need to be close. And then he cried his heart out.

"I'm all right," he told her, blowing his nose. "I'm supposed to feel like this. I'm allowed to feel like this."

Therapy speak, she thought. Of course he was devastated. No one expected him to be anything else.

"I love my work," he said. In the light of the single lamp they had left on, he sat hunched, arms around his knees, and his face was drawn and haunted. "I'd be miserable without it. Life's too short to be miserable. I'm entitled to satisfaction and accomplishment and to be happy about it. You make me feel guilty about it, Kissy—"

"Oh," she said, stung and instantly furious that he did not seem to know or care that she too was grieving. She turned on her side, her back to him.

"And you turn your back on me."

She shifted again, onto her stomach, and buried her face in her pillow.

He stroked it lightly. "You got a great ass—"

She snorted into the pillow.

"My mother's dead," he said, "and what you offer me for comfort is your ass, what you always offer me. It's such a great way to fake it, isn't it, Kissy?"

She lifted herself on her elbows and tipped her head back. "Fuck you, Junior—"

"Thanks, Kiss. Listen to yourself, you mean it literally." He flopped back down again and stared at the ceiling. "I've been thinking about making this real. I've been thinking the best thing might be for me to quit. Not come back. Dynah could come to me—"

Kissy slammed her fist into the pillow. "Fuck you! You could have told me before you got your dick wet, you heroic, selfish prick—"

He rolled his head to look at her, stunned, seeing it that way for the first time. But she believed he had been thinking about it; it had been on his mind a while.

"You've got somebody else," she said.

"No." He said it wearily. "It would be a fuck of a lot easier if I did."

"Do what you want," she said harshly.

She got up and went into the bathroom and turned on the shower. Watching the water spattered over the tiles, listening to its gush that drowned out the renewed onslaught of his weeping, she wept herself. She had not asked him the immediate question: if his feelings and happiness were valid, were not hers? And if they were both right, then what was the answer? There was no answer except the separate lives they led. It would be easier if he had someone else, he had said, with no awareness of what it implied. He wanted her to go into therapy, and they could be wrapped up in him together.

It was ironic: Esther had been suddenly taken, but Ruth still lived. Ruth was changed, too, her changes subtle but continuing. More and more she resembled the character in the fable who had been granted the wish to live forever but through the years shrank to the size of a cricket. Flesh mummified upon the dry sticks of bone, spirit faded to a mocking dry and distant and insane laughter. Kissy spent time with her obsessively in the immediate aftermath of Esther's death, and the mystery engulfed her, death in life, life in death, until she thought she would never feel anything again.

Not very much later a court consented at last to the cessation of life support for Ruth Prashker. Kissy was on hand, prepared with the family's permission, to photograph Ruth's last moments. But when the breathing tube was removed, Ruth breathed on her own. She did not die. After a week of waiting and debating, her parents had the feeding tube reinserted. As long as Ruth breathed on her own, they could not bring themselves to allow her to starve to death. They seemed, at last, profoundly relieved to discover they did not really have the power of life and death over their daughter.

∽ 26 ∾

She liked shooting a gun, she discovered—it was very similar to shooting with a camera. She suspected bashing an attacker with her camera would be of much more use to her than the simple self-defense methods Burke's brickbuster taught her. But Burke obtained a license to carry for her and she locked the thing in her glove compartment.

He called occasionally to ask what she was doing. At first she was hesitant to confide, but he never interfered. She began to trust him. It probably was a good idea to have someone know just what anthill she was poking with the stick of her camera lens. Several times he invited her along on undercover surveillances or gave her tips on anthills he thought might interest her. He was cultivating her, she realized, in his relentlessly political way, and it made her a little uneasy.

And then very late one night he called and gave her an address. She bundled up a confused and sleepy Dynah, delivered her to an equally sleepy Bernie at the Clooties', and raced to meet Burke at the command post where a bust was being coordinated. He had given her a scoop over the *News*' regular shooters on the biggest drug bust of the year. His reward was a front-page shot of himself, unshaven, a duster flapping around his long legs, a gun in one hand and a little boy, shivering in only a pair of dirty underpants, riding his other arm. Burke looked like a gunslinger. The bewildered child was one of five taken by the state from the pot-farming parents.

"My mother loves it," he told her over the phone. "My boss loves it even more. I owe you dinner. Champagne."

"Too much." Kissy laughed, covering her own second

thoughts about the shot and the propriety of their unspoken backscratch.

"Linguine and dago red at Matty's, then?"

"All right." She might not even eat the meal, she thought, if she could work out her ethical quandary by then. She thought she would just tell him, No more.

Burke was late, apologetic and distracted. He left the table twice to make phone calls and once to take one. In between was a constant parade of people table-hopping to shake his hand. It was impossible to keep a conversation going with all the interruptions. Kissy repressed an impulse to bail.

"I'm sorry," he said as he signed the check. "This hasn't been much fun, has it?"

She shrugged. "I like the food here and I didn't have to cook it. I really wanted to talk about—" As she hesitated, considering whether to use the word *ethics,* she realized he wasn't listening to her. He was looking at her directly, fixing her with the gaze men used when challenging a woman to bed. Her response was immediate, a hard lurch of interest that bemused her. He hadn't really been cultivating her just for that, had he?

"Baby-sitter," she said with a resigned smile.

He smiled too, as if he had never had the slightest interest, and rose to pull out her chair for her.

At home, she checked Dynah and said good-night to Bernie, who thought she had been at a dinner at Latham's. It wasn't comfortable, lying to Bernie, but the bottom line was Bernie was Junior's sister. Bernie might take Kissy's side in a fight, but she would not like Kissy dating one bit. Though she lived with her dad, she often stayed overnight. It got her out of her dad's house and the kids liked it. Kissy had even put bunk beds in Dynah's room to accommodate Casey.

"If you don't mind the water running a bit," she told Bernie, "I'm dying for a soak."

"'Right ahead," Bernie said. "I'm going to watch the rest of Letterman."

In the bathroom, Kissy opened the hot water tap and flung in a handful of bath salts. As the mineral scent rose with the steam, she kicked off her boots and stripped. In the mirror, she looked at herself. What would Mike Burke

think of her body? What would it be like to go to bed with
him? She grinned at her own horniness.

Time to pay a surprise visit to Junior. He had been hangdog over his behavior the night of his mother's committal.
Never meant it, he had insisted; it was just the shock and
grief. A sudden unannounced visit was fraught always with
the possibility she would walk in on him with some other
woman, of course. She wasn't sure what her reaction
would be anymore. She thought it might even be a relief. If
you couldn't trust someone, she had discovered, sooner or
later you didn't care what he did. You couldn't afford to
care. You split yourself down the middle and led your
separate lives, taking what you had while you had it. And
then you didn't think about it, didn't worry about it.
Numbness set in. Any fucked-up thing, large or small, can
become normality if it goes on long enough.

She slipped gingerly into the steaming fragrant bath.
Relaxing into it. Taking care of herself. Junior talked about
it. It was one of the big insights about therapy. He had
to take care of himself, not just physically, but emotionally. She had to take care of herself too, he advised. She
thought she had gotten good at it, herself.

Burke caught her off guard in the course of one of their
casual phone contacts.

"I'll meet you there," Burke said.

She had been telling him she was going to shoot some
pictures at Skinner's on the impending Saturday night, and
her mind had been on the project. She worked alone. The
last thing she wanted was someone looking over her shoulder. Nor did she need the DA's pet nark scaring people out
of the place.

"People dealing drugs in the toilets is not my major concern," she told him, "I'm interested in the scene there—"

"No problem. I just want to check the place out, be seen
there, so nobody gets the idea I don't care. It's part of
knowing my patch."

He would be there on his own, she told herself. Not with
her. She would be working, and if he got in her way, she
would tear his head off. The way he operated, he was just
as likely to cancel out or never show because something
else had come up.

At first a lot of the clientele took her for a party

photographer and wanted to pose for her and get copies of
the pictures, but gradually the crowd got more loaded and
ceased to pay any attention to her. She was beginning to
get what she had come seeking when she noticed he was
there, sitting at the bar. He raised his glass to her and she
nodded and went back to what she was doing.

Later, she was working the corridor to the lavatories,
shooting a couple necking, three solemn smokers engaged
in an emphatic argument, a weaving shouting drunk who
thrust his face into the lens. The air was tangy with pot
smoke fanning from the lavatories every time anyone went
in or out. She thought she caught a chemical whiff too—
she had heard rumors of a flood of amyl nitrate poppers in
the area. She began to feel a little hyperreal—the pot getting to her or the poppers, if that was what that sweaty
sneaker odor was.

And Burke came out of the men's room. He had had a
few more drinks, she guessed, from the loopiness of his
grin as he sighted her. Breathed some passive, secondhand
weed, too, maybe some of that locker-room-in-a-gelcap.
He dropped loosely into the rickety chair by the pay phone
and caught her wrist as she edged by him.

"Hey," he said. "Howyadoin'?"

She glanced down at him and he smiled up at her. He put
a hand on her inner thigh above her knee where the frayed
denim was mostly lateral shreds and moved it upward. She
stopped his hand an inch from her crotch.

"I've been wanting to do that all night," he said.

"I remember my first beer too," she cracked.

He laughed, and she moved away, back to work, with a
tremble in her stomach and tightness in her groin.

He was still at the bar at closing time. She took some
shots of the crew cleaning up and then started to pack
her gear, which meant a certain amount of dipping and
crouching, and an awareness of the man watching her
every move.

"Hey," he said, spinning the stool next to his invitingly,
"it's closing time. Have a nightcap." He called to the bartender, "Lady needs a brandy, Neil."

"I have to drive home," Kissy protested.

"I'll drive you home."

She laughed and shook her head. "You're the one who
needs a driver."

"Well?" the bartender asked. "What's it gonna be? You gonna have a brandy and go home with him or not?"

Kissy stuck her tongue out at him. It was childishly provocative, she realized immediately, but she was tired and she guessed she spent too much time with a little kid.

"Got the wrong guy." Neil plunked a snifter down in front of Burke, who handed it to Kissy. "Stick it out at him."

She rolled the glass gently and sipped it gingerly.

"So are you going to go home with me?" Mike Burke asked.

She burst out in a laugh. Neil pursed his lips in mock prudery, and Kissy remembered, all at once, in the small hours of a night some years ago when she had been at Skinner's with Ryne, a drunken Neil had confided to her that all his favorite movies had *cheerleader* in the title.

"Nope," she said, handing the brandy back to Burke.

"Another triumph for virtue," Neil declared. "I still have a chance to get laid if I get my ass in gear, so would you two please leave and let me lock up?"

Burke scoffed the brandy in two quick swallows.

"Ouch," said the bartender. "Better let her take you home, Mike. I wouldn't like to read in the morning paper the assistant DA got busted for driving drunk after boozing it up on my license."

"I'll drive you," Kissy said from the door.

Burke grinned back over his shoulder at Neil.

The hour was a melancholy one. Nearly the last vehicles in the lot were her Blazer and Burke's Jeep, only the bartender's and crew's wheels still remaining, seeming abandoned. A rumor of dead leaf tinged the chill air and the gravel underfoot felt harder, as if whatever moisture was in it was beginning to freeze.

When Burke told her his address, she was surprised to realize how close he lived to the Valley, though she had been vaguely aware he resided on that side of town. She had a police scanner in the Blazer now, installed under the tape player, and he flicked it on.

"I can't believe you still run this old wreck," he muttered.

Junior had tried to replace it on several occasions but she wouldn't let him. She didn't bother to explain what it meant to her.

Burke cocked his head back and closed his eyes and listened to the random traffic on the police band while she drove.

"I want you," he said. He opened his eyes to fix her with that predatory gaze again. "I wasn't joking."

She glanced at him sidelong. "You've been on the hard stuff all night—"

"I've wanted you a long time."

As if she should give him points for long-running lust. He spoke lightly but still focusing on her intently. She didn't know what she wanted to do.

The small house was tucked away down a long winding drive on one of the steepest slopes of the Valley. The site was wooded, secretive. She couldn't help wondering what the views were from the windows of its second story that peeped above the tree line, dropping toward the 'Pipe.

"Come in, have a nightcap."

His theme for the night. She didn't want a nightcap, but he left the door of the house wide open and she got out to close it. What she saw inside was austere, almost monkish—a slate floor in the foyer, polished hardwood spreading away from it. Curiosity brought her, almost unconsciously, the rest of the way into the living room. The furniture was Shaker or hand-crafted contemporary, the throw rugs reproductions of Native American or craft designs. White walls and careful lighting set off paintings and photographs.

She took a closer look. The paintings were brilliantly colored abstractions, originals, by someone of real talent whose work she had never encountered previously. The photographs were black-and-white prints, some of them hers, sold through a local gallery. It was flattering to discover he had some respect for her as an artist, and she liked it even more that he had never mentioned it to her. She didn't know what she had expected—an ex-cop, never married—handcuffs and citations on the wall, she guessed. Maybe bachelor debris: unwashed socks and jocks and athletic equipment and dirty dishes. She would also bet his mother found the place barren, in need of the woman's touch. Meaning some ersatz Victoriana of the kind his mother sold in her gift shop.

"Those paintings," she said. "That's some good stuff."

He glanced up from a cupboard he had unlocked for a

bottle of brandy. That itself was interesting—he locked up his booze, as if maybe he didn't trust his cleaner. "Yeah. I get 'm for cartons of cigarettes from the guy does 'm. I put him away, six years ago now, I guess, for offing his old lady. He was so drunk he couldn't remember doing it, which is typical, as you probably know—he'll probably get out next year."

He gave her a snifter and put music on a component system. She was relieved to recognize Peter Gabriel's *Red Rain* and not some men's magazine's recommendation for make-out cuts. And then she was bemused at herself, her own lazy reflexive prejudgment.

He put a hand on her hip and bumped hipbones with her. "In a dance club all night and you never danced—"

"You don't want to dance—"

"Yes I do, the horizontal bop." He grinned. Leading her a couple of steps, he pulled her tight against him.

His hands moved down over her bottom and then to the small of her back to press him against her. She could feel his penis thickening. He moved against her slightly, studying her reaction. The challenge in his eyes. She slipped her hand between them and he inhaled a long, shaky triumphant breath and pressed harder against her. She closed her eyes and felt his thumb passing over her nipple in her shirt and then his hand working under the shirt, under the bra she wore, to bare skin, bare nipple. His knee thrust between her legs to her crotch, his mouth was on hers at last. He didn't smell or taste or feel like Junior. He didn't touch her the way Junior did. That was all right, that was fine. His fingers undid her buttons, opened her shirt and pushed it off her shoulders, down, until her breasts were free. He couldn't raise his eyes from them.

"Jesus," he said. "There is a God."

The skylight over the bed framed a rectangle of the night sky, the void, presently a milky obsidian pavilion where the moon hid its face behind curds of cloud. He watched her undress from the edge of the bed where he was taking off his shoes. He had switched on a small lamp, and it lit her body softly from the side. Her tits made him think of the round full-moon shapes of a Balinese or Indian dancer he had seen in a travel magazine once. A goddess or sacred whore on a temple somewhere, he couldn't remember. What he remembered were the tits that made flesh out of stone. And in this instance, stone out of flesh. He was so hard he thought he would shatter.

"You'd better have a jimmy," she said.

Bet on it. At this point he would wear a feather boa or a saxophone on his dick to get it into her. He covered her pussy with his hand to feel the heat that was like a beating heart. She jerked against him at the intrusion of two fingers and he kept at her, feeling her open to him until he could not wait, could not wait. He lifted her knees higher, taking him deep into her. He fucked her hard. He knew she was getting it but good. He could see it in the sweaty shadows under her eyes, feel it in the way she lifted her box to him, wanting more.

His pupils dilated, a pinpoint of reflected light in each, a glittering splinter, as he stared down at her. Tightening her legs around him, she cried out with the kind of orgasm, wide and deep, that she never seemed to be able to achieve on her own. He tucked his head and she felt the pulse of his orgasm inside her. For a moment he stayed on her, moving once or twice. Then he pulled out and slid down a little to rest his head on her breasts. She closed her eyes.

"I knew it would be good," he murmured.

A little while later the bed shifted and he left it. A door clicked closed behind him and a light switch clicked too, and shortly, she heard him making water and then the flush of the toilet. Suddenly she was cold. She groped for the sheet and pulled it up over her.

She was glad to have his body warmth when he came back. His hardness inside her had been so satisfying and a relief too—he had been drinking all night and she had thought he might come up limp. They held hands in bed. His fingers worried at the ring on her left hand.

"Nobody can figure out what's going on with you two," he said.

She let go of his hand. "Nobody has to. It's between us."

"You're not married to him anymore—"

As if she didn't know.

"Is that it, you've got an arrangement?"

She turned onto her side and her back was hint enough he was out of bounds; he didn't push it. He drew her closer, kissing the nape of her neck. She kissed him and then she freed herself from his arms and slipped out of bed.

He sat up and watched her dress. "You aren't staying?"

"My baby-sitter's expecting me to be late but not out all night."

He could guess her baby-sitter was Junior's sister and he could make of it what he wished.

He swung his legs out of the bed and pulled on pants and a pair of loafers and followed her out to the Blazer, where he kissed her beguilingly and tried to coax her back to bed with him.

She looked back at him in her rearview as she drove away, and he was still standing there, staring after her, the house light washing over him. The light making his faint smile ironic, his skin almost stony.

She wished she had lingered long enough at Mike Burke's to shower. Much as she wanted to now, she could not, for fear Bernie would wonder why she needed to shower at three-thirty in the morning. It took a while to go to sleep. She kept thinking about what she was going to say the next time Junior asked her if she was seeing anyone.

The question distracted her, off and on. She saw Burke once, as she left the public library and he was on the courthouse steps down the street. There was a TV camera pointed at him and a thin woman with a lot of hair was holding a microphone for him. Kissy recognized her, though she couldn't remember her name. One of the network wanna-bes who passed through various Peltry TV stations on their way to somewhere else. There had been a rumor about her and Burke a few months earlier, or maybe it had been one of the other thin young women with lots of hair and a microphone in her hand. But there had been more than a few rumors about Burke and various women. A moment later, swinging the Blazer out of the library parking lot onto the street, she passed him striding down the sidewalk. He glanced at her, nodded, and strode on.

She didn't hear from him. It had been a simple hit-and-run. She was interested to discover no particular pain. A little chagrin, a sense of having been a bit too convenient for him. But no sense of loss or hurt. On the contrary, it was fine with her.

Her own motivation was as deficient and narcissistic as his, nothing more than an idle stew of curiosity about Burke and resentment at Junior. The important insight might be that this was what men meant when they said it didn't mean anything. Of course, that was bullshit—it was highly meaningful behavior—but they meant it was driven by impulse and did not represent a new emotional commitment at the expense of a previous one to a mate.

"Seeing anybody?" Junior did ask over the phone, after days of not asking.

She thought about it a moment, considering telling him what she had done. And then she thought of something else. "Junior, are you?"

And he had laughed. "No, baby." He had had to chortle a little more. "I'm gonna be able to work miracles when I'm dead, I'm so close to sainthood." And then he sobered. "It's not easy sometimes, but I found out I can do it. You gotta sort it out some way, you know. Some of it was being around Deker. All those women—it sounds like some kind of stroke book dream, you know, but the reality is he's got herpes and an album full of pictures of little girls who are all 99.8 percent probably his. 'What you think,' he says, 'Molly's the prettiest, isn't she? No, I am making the mistake, that's not Molly, that's Michele.' And then there's Bernie and Casey. I'm more of a father to Casey than he is, and look at me, some dad I am. I feel sorry for him. He never makes a goddamn call home, Kissy, he hasn't got a home. He gets a message, it's call your lawyer, call your agent. You see guys all over this business, no life but the game. Some guys got a girlfriend here, a wife there, a girlfriend in another place, and you know somebody's not getting much of a deal. I don't know how to have a girlfriend and you too and not feel like a pig. I got you and Dynah. I don't want to lose you."

The way it poured out of him, she thought he had been waiting a long time for her to ask. It sounded like maybe he had tried to have a girlfriend, maybe more than once. He didn't say he never had. She had her secrets too.

The waters rose and receded and this year left behind a body, a suicide, a woman in postpartum depression who had thrown herself into the 'Pipe where it squiggled through a village on the outskirts of Peltry back in early December before everything iced up.

Junior was home again and a big old Victorian came up for sale and they bought it and set about restoring it. He insisted on her having a darkroom, and they had an addition with an indoor swimming pool built for her, and on the other side of the house, an indoor rink for him. They rented the cottage again and talked about buying it, maybe for next year. Before the work was done, it was time for him to go to camp.

Mark was going too, having run out his eligibility at Sowerwine. Dunny was seeing a thirty-five-year-old, Ida Damrosch, a divorced nurse who had been in school with Esther, and it made Bernie as uneasy as her occasional date made him. They needed some space from each other, they agreed, and Bernie and Casey moved from Dunny's house to the apartment over the garage of the new house.

Dynah fussed and threw tantrums and wept at night and tested all the rules twice over and refused all comfort, even having Casey handy to boss around. Casey was equally disturbed, partly by Dynah's upset and partly because he was old enough to grasp the change in his life—a new place, Grampy not with him and Mummy anymore, Mark and Junior leaving.

Kissy did not hold Dynah's distress against her; she felt much the same way herself. The proximity of Bernie and Casey only mitigated her loneliness mildly, for Bernie's parallel singleness emphasized her own. Having graduated high school, Bernie plunged into the pursuit of a degree in physical therapy at Sowerwine. Just as she had found in her struggle to finish high school, she felt older than her classmates because of her lack of freedom. The guys she met were not particularly entranced by the fact she had a child.

Kissy noted a multiplication in the small lines at the corners of her eyes. She was only twenty-six. It was all that squinting into viewfinders. Someday she would look like a goddamn turtle, or maybe Yoda, eyes like boiled eggs set in poached wrinkles. Junior was missing great chunks of her best years. The thought made her snicker. The other side wasn't so funny. She was giving her best years to somebody who wasn't there to take them. Who would rather play hockey. Goddamn him. All the money in the world couldn't buy back time. He could stop a thousand pucks but he couldn't stop a second of time.

Bernie kept the kids one evening while Kissy hung prints at the School of Fine Arts in a show of her thesis project—a series of elegiac platinum prints of places in Peltry. *A public basketball court on what had become over the years a busy intersection, so the fencing around it had the look of a cage. The interior of a small church that had been converted to a florist's shop, its fitments of choir loft and altar, stained glass and paneling, become a gracile background to a jungle of greenery and exotic blooms. The interior of a sandwich shop, narrow and crowded, where an old man with knotty fingers folded white waxed paper around subs with an origami precision. The landfill that was the first sight of Peltry from the interstate driving north, a mountainous midden and monument to trash, dwarfing the heavy machinery that shaped it into a barrow, the flag flapping on its pole stamp-size against its bulk, as if it were being mailed into the future, an unpaid bill. The second-floor dance hall where the line dancers in their western costumes sported middle-aged bulk or the creases of old age. Another dance recital in the same space; a flock of little girls in leotards fluttered and kicked, with a charming gracelessness, over the worn boards. The narrow brick front of the oldest firehouse in Peltry, on the occasion of the funeral of a young fireman who had died of cancer, his helmet, shield, and gear posed empty and traditionally in the open bay. An uneven march of gravestones down a steep hill toward the 'Pipe, a patch of interstate highway arcing skyward over it. A laughing grizzled man, an airport maintenance worker, sliding, on a square of cardboard, down a vast dirty berm of snow plowed off the runways. A teenage girl in practice tunic and shorts, perched in the basket of a collapsed goal, her long legs splayed like a giraffe, grinning into the camera as the playing floor was being laid at the auditorium prior to a state championship game. A stretch of the Hornpipe in winter rendered as a snake of some mythological species, water and ice gone nemetite and mother-of-pearl. The decorative fountain downtown, dry for the winter and littered with trash, a young couple in passionate embrace on its edge while a mangy bristling dog barked at them.*

The showing was a kind of announcement of the award of her Master of Fine Arts degree next June Commencement.

Savoring the uninterrupted time for herself, when she finished the hanging, she treated herself to a stop at Denny's, to loiter over a decaf and idle her way through *American Photo*. The pages of images overwhelmed her with a familiar mingled excitement and revulsion. The power of images was something she knew viscerally. Photographs were not merely reflections of reality, the flat irrefutable truth. Somewhere in the funhouse mirror tunnel of the camera and its lens, and in development and printing and now computer manipulation, reflection was altered. Photographs were subtle metaphors that could be and often were lies, flip-flops of the splinters of truth the camera was capable of catching, like an errant quark. And there was so much the finest subtlest image could not express; she struggled every day with her limitations and the boundaries of the medium.

Preoccupied, she did not notice Mike Burke until he slumped onto the stool next to hers at the counter. His face was drawn with fatigue.

"Howyadoin'?" she asked.

He blinked at her and then passed a weary hand over his face. "Like shit."

The waitress appeared, and distractedly he ordered coffee and a hamburger plate from her without looking at the menu.

"I almost called you a couple of days ago," he said as the waitress filled his cup for him. He picked up a napkin and began to tear it into smaller pieces. "I noticed a while ago—a year anyway—my dad was forgetting things. About three weeks ago he put a package of cookies inside his jacket at the supermarket and got caught and I got called. He was very angry and confused and kept insisting they were his fucking cookies he'd brought with him to the supermarket. Anybody could see he wasn't all right. The supermarket people let it go. My mother admitted he's been having memory problems and weeping spells and tantrums for some time. I put him into the hospital for tests. He's got Alzheimer's. He understands what it means too." The napkin was a heap of confetti. He stirred it with his forefinger.

Kissy said the only thing she could, that she was sorry.

"Me too," he said. He leaned forward and blew at the confetti of napkin and it fluttered here and there over the counter. "I had to take his gun away from him. He had it in his mouth, and when I grabbed it, it split his lip. He cried and cried." He look up at her. "I don't know if I did the right thing."

Kissy was silent a moment. "Who ever knows? You did what anyone would have reflexively."

He nodded. Then he seemed to notice the coffee in front of him. He picked it up and drank down most of it all at once. "Ask you a favor?"

"Ask," she said.

"Would you take a picture of him for me? Right away, before he gets sicker. I'll take you to the house and you can do it there. I want one in front of all his citations and pictures. It's not just for me, it's for him. Something to help him hold on to his identity as long as he can."

"Yes. Of course I will."

"I'll pay whatever you want."

"No," she said. "There won't be any charge."

He didn't argue the point. "Thank you."

The waitress brought his hamburger plate. He ate it quickly, ravenously, without saying anything more. Once in a while, he knuckled moisture from the corner of one eye, seemingly without any awareness of what he was doing.

∽ 27 ∾

In one of the oldest neighborhoods in Peltry, the Burkes'
liver-colored bungalow shouldered other modest houses.
The structures stood so close to one another, they made
narrow alleys where the sun did not seem to reach.

The small rooms, crowded with the effects of nearly
forty years of the Burkes' married life, seemed dark and
depressed. The wattage, Kissy realized; the place was lit
exclusively by low-wattage bulbs. Someone's obsessive
little economy. The contrast with Mike's place was striking; she could not help thinking his taste reflected flight
from a sense of suffocation in his parents' home. His
mother ushered them to the living room, where his father
was ensconced in a well-worn reclining chair in front of a
television set.

"Mike's here!" Mrs. Burke announced loudly.

Mr. Burke averted his gaze from the tube to stare at
them. "I see he is." His lower lip thrust out. "I'm not a
rutabaga yet." He glared at Kissy. "I'm turning into a goddamn rutabaga, you know."

"No, you're not," said Mrs. Burke, as if she could talk
him out of it.

"Shut up," Mr. Burke said sulkily.

Mrs. Burke smiled at Kissy with embarrassment.

Patting his mother's arm reassuringly, Mike ignored his
father's hostility. "Dad, I'd like you to meet a friend of
mine, Kissy Mellors."

Mr. Burke's lips separated in an odd, awkward, and
cheerless smile that made Kissy think of the lips of a
mummy, shrunken, exposing teeth and gums, only Mike's
father's teeth were clearly false. He looked at her without
interest and then turned his attention back to the tube,

where a woman in bike shorts was leading an aerobics class.

Mrs. Burke offered to make coffee, though the smell of fresh coffee was already strong in the house. Kissy accepted and Mrs. Burke escaped to her kitchen.

"Dad," Mike said, "come show Kissy your citations."

Mr. Burke's gaze shifted back to her again. He grunted and then he pushed himself out of his recliner. He was a tall man, an inch or two over six feet, but his flesh was slack. From the way his clothes hung, he had lost ten or fifteen pounds recently. His clothing was clean and neat, though, and he was carefully shaved, and his hair, thinned and gray, was combed. He did not shuffle, and Kissy noted he wore polished hard shoes, not slippers.

His citations were displayed in a little room that was evidently his den. It had another, older TV, a couch, and a small desk and filing cabinet in it, and the decoration was mid-fifties masculine—plaid upholstery on the couch, plaid wall-to-wall carpet, knotty pine paneling, a mahogany bookcase, a stuffed fish among the photographs and citations, a swimsuit calendar on the wall. Miss July's implants were still falling out of her orange bikini though it was nearly Thanksgiving. The room smelled of old cigars.

"There they are, girlie," Mr. Burke said. "Look away."

Kissy examined them, seeing not Mike's looks—he took after his mother in features and coloring—in the images of his father at a younger age, but Mike's bearing, his temperament. Among them were also pictures of Mike and his father, Mr. Burke's pride in his son—in graduation robes, newly in uniform, receiving citations, displaying new stripes, another graduation—ever present. Mr. Burke stood next to her, breathing a little heavily, his gaze shifting and fixing, from one to the other picture or citation. His shield was framed too, and mounted prominently with the other trophies of his career.

"I was a cocker," he boasted. He glanced back over his shoulder at Mike. "Now I'm a rutabaga."

"Kissy's a photographer," Mike said, trying to ease things along. "She'd like to take your picture."

His father frowned. "Don't want my picture taken."

"It'll only take a few minutes." Mike arranged the desk

chair with its padded leatherette seat. "I'll get your gear," he told Kissy.

Once he was gone, Mr. Burke backed into the chair and sat down abruptly. He rocked in it a little, his gaze coming unfocused. Mrs. Burke brought a tray, coffee and a plate of little Pepperidge Farm cookies arranged on a paper doily. Mr. Burke grabbed at the tray as she bore it to the desk. She jerked it out of his reach.

"You'll get dirty," she cried. "You'll get chocolate on your clean shirt."

"I just want a cookie," he said. "One fucking cookie."

"Please don't say that word." Mrs. Burke fussed over the cookies, rearranging them.

He fixed his stare wolfishly on the cookies but he didn't reach for them again.

Mike arrived with Kissy's gear. Together they set up a couple of lights and Kissy made a few quick preparations, metering the light and locking the camera on the tripod. Using a Polaroid back, she took a couple of test shots. Mr. Burke grimaced at the camera each time, showing his teeth in that peculiar apish grin. Mike noticed it and gave her a worried look.

"Get him talking," Kissy murmured.

Mike took the cue. "Dad, tell Kissy about the time you arrested the guys who vandalized the high school—you remember—"

"'Course I remember," his father said irritably. And launched into a coherent recitation of events that had occurred thirty years ago. It wasn't until he had completed the tale that he stopped and asked, anxiously, "Did I get that right?"

By then, Kissy had gotten more than one shot she was sure was a keeper. And when Mr. Burke looked at Mike and asked the last, fretful question, she caught that too—the old man's desperation, his utter trust that Mike would tell him the truth, and something more—Mike's great tenderness toward his father. Kissy made a quick inclusive gesture and Mike grabbed his mother and hustled her into place behind the chair. Mike's hand went reassuringly to his father's shoulder and the old man raised a hand to meet it. The shutter closed on the final formal family portrait of the Burkes, the one that would be displayed next to Mr. Burke's bier in the funeral home.

"Now can I have a fucking cookie?" Mr. Burke asked plaintively.

Kissy offered him the plate, and he smacked his lips and took two and settled back, with a huge sigh, to nibble at them. As he ate them, he brushed the front of his shirt continually, and his eyes never left his wife's face.

As Kissy packed her gear, Mrs. Burke murmured thank you and took the coffee and cookies away. Mike disassembled the lights for her.

Mr. Burke got up and went out, back to the TV in the living room.

Kissy stopped on her way out to say good-bye.

Mr. Burke flapped his hand at her again. "Howyadoin', girlie?"

Mike came to the house to see the prints after Dynah was in bed and Bernie had taken Casey off to her apartment. They viewed them one by one, almost ceremonially.

"They're really terrific," he said. His eyes were watering and he stopped and wiped them and blew his nose. "Thank you."

"How are things going?"

"The way they do. A little bit of deterioration every day. Can't take him out anymore. He grabs at girls, unzips his fly to show them his hose. That'll pass, the doctor says. It's the part of the brain that governs social inhibitions unraveling. He's still eating well, though Mom says she has to watch the cookies like a hawk. I told her to let him have the fucking cookies and she gave me some crap about his blood sugar and I yelled at her, asked her what the fuck she was buying cookies for, if it was such a big deal, him having them. And who gives a shit about his blood sugar. He's had a cookie jones since he quit drinking, for Christ's sake." He shook his head. "He has some bright times too, when he's all there. That's harder, in some ways. He wants to tell me about his funeral, how I have to take care of my mother."

"It's tough—"

"I think about him becoming bedridden and having to be bathed and diapered like an infant—sometimes I think the way your mother-in-law went was the best. I really appreciate this, Kissy—" He took her hand in his. And then he tried to kiss her.

She stepped away from him quickly, both palms up in silent warning off. Then she began to pack up the prints, layering them in tissue, placing them in a box for him.

"Maybe you're right," he mused. "Maybe we're better off just friends."

"Whatever."

For a moment there was only the rustle of tissue.

"You're pissed at me," he said. "You think I was a shit. Excuse me, Kissy, you're a big girl, you knew what you were doing and you knew what was I doing."

"That's right," she agreed. "And I can feel any way I want about it."

He twitched as if he wanted to touch her again, to make another try. "I want us to be friends."

"Sure," she said, and smiled at him.

And he let it go at that.

She didn't see him again until his father's wake, less than a month later. Mr. Burke had had another gun, hidden in the carved-out center of a book on guns.

"All the books were out of the bookcase," Mike told her in the privacy of an alcove outside the viewing room at the funeral parlor, which was full of cops and ex-cops and Mike's own courthouse associates. "He was looking for it. He must have had a sudden memory of having hidden it. My mother was still sleeping. He's been waking in the middle of the night; she's used to his wandering around the house at odd hours. He found the gun and then he went to the kitchen and ate all the cookies—three boxes torn open on the kitchen counter. Then he went into the bathroom and climbed into the tub. That picture you took—him, in front of his citations and shield—he'd been carrying it around with him, looking at it a lot. He put it on his chest, in the bathtub, before he did it."

Mike was calm. His lashes fluttered down over his eyes as he spoke but she caught a glitter of relief. He groped for her hand and held it in both of his. "Everything I ever did, I did for my dad. He was the one who cared about what I did. Who do I do things for now?" He met her eyes with sudden intensity. "Who do you do things for? Your work, I mean."

"Myself, to start. The satisfaction of it. I know what you mean, though. I want my mother's pride in what I do, her approval." Kissy smiled crookedly. "Not my dad's—I never had his approval, never will."

Mike shook his head. "My dad was so important to me. I wanted to be just like him. I was thinking I'd coach Little League this summer, like he did."

"Junior's that way about his dad. His dad put skates on Junior when he was four. Junior had skates on Dynah as soon as she could walk. First she loved it because he was paying attention to her. Now she just loves it. He's got her out there with him, poking pucks at him, or she's in net and he's poking them at her. He tells her she's going to be hell on blades in the NHL someday."

They both laughed softly, and then she covered her mouth in chagrin. "Oops."

Mike leaned closer, his cheek at her ear. "It's all right. Dad liked a good laugh too."

She pulled away from him, wanting to keep her distance, to give him no mixed message, or for that matter, to let anyone who might see them jump to conclusions.

He smiled ironically, as if he read her exactly. But he took her hand again and squeezed it. "The mess—I had to take care of it. I had to look at my dad after and I didn't cry. But it creeps up on me and takes me by surprise. I went to your show," he said. "I know every one of those places. It was as if I had words for them on the tip of my tongue and you spoke them. I cried."

She didn't know what to say.

He released her hand. "Thanks, Kissy. I owe you."

"No," she murmured.

He left her to return to the viewing room. She watched him work the room, shaking hands, accepting condolences, holding up. It seemed to be his job in her life, to teach her over and over that she judged too harshly, that she needed to be more compassionate.

There wasn't much more to Burke's share of his father's estate than the price of a new car. His mother continued to work, but her income from her shop was modest. She needed the supplement of pension and insurance. He had insisted she stay in the house in order to be independent, as if they both didn't understand he'd be goddamned if she'd live with him. So she'd changed all the lightbulbs, forty watts for sixty, and she'd given his dad's worn-out old recliner away, along with his clothes. Burke had taken the citations and photographs and his father's shield. He didn't expect he'd ever see much of anything else. His mother was robust and would live for years; the little money would be gone and there would be nothing but the house, not much in a not-much neighborhood, for an inheritance.

She was—he found the word repulsive—dating. A sixty-three-year-old woman, dating. It was disgusting, and he had to pretend he thought it was just wonderful, her shopping around for companionship in her old age, when it wasn't companionship she was hunting, she was looking for cock, and finding it, old men, guts and wrinkles, and her with bright red whore's lipstick and her hair dyed and her tits to her waist. Christ.

He thought of calling Kissy. He had not been able to admit he had actually returned several times to look at her pictures and they continued to haunt him. Somehow her talent, the power she had to make you see through her eyes, had gotten all mixed up with the desire she had always provoked in him.

He had been a little bit insane, he thought. Days of dividing his time between work and his parents' house. The horror of what was happening to his father and how long it was going to take—it had just driven him insane. He had taken the book from his father's shelf, hollowed it, put into it his own throw-down that he had carried when he was in uniform, and slipped it back onto the shelf. But not before showing it to his father, as soon as the old man had a lucid period. He hadn't said anything. Nor had his father. He had just taken it off the shelf and opened it in the old man's hands. The look in the old man's eyes—he was so grateful. It made up for the mistake Burke had made, stopping his first attempt.

He had his own key. His mother was used to his coming in and out of the house at odd times, late at night when he left work to check on his father, make sure the furnace was running okay and that the old man wasn't out on the sidewalk in his pajamas. She was there but she had to sleep some time, and she seemed to understand that Burke needed to check for himself.

It had been no surprise to find his father in the kitchen with an open package of cookies, stuffing them down. Burke had found another two packages, let the old man have all of them. His father had understood. When he had finished, Burke led him to the book, then to the bathtub. He had given his father the picture, sat there on the closed commode next to him, letting him study it, and then he had said, "Okay, Dad, it's time," and the old man had nodded. Burke had kissed him and helped him with the gun, and picked up a towel and shaken it out in front of himself so as not to get any splatter on him and he watched it happen, the jerk of his father's body, the ballooning of his face. And then left, swiftly, before his mother could see him, slipping out and down the block to where he had parked his Jeep and home to await the call. He had taken the towel with him and put it into his own laundry. He still had it, washed and dried and folded neatly in the back of the cupboard.

So it was over and his father was out of it and his mother wasn't beggared by years of medical bills. The nightmares he had, the weight he had lost, the graying of his hair since, the fact he was drinking a lot, by himself—he figured everybody had to understand, his father had just died. He didn't need anybody to cut him any slack. He worked harder than ever, and if he wasn't the life of the party—well, everybody knew.

Butch's wife, Narcissa, came around to his house to offer her condolences personally, which he accepted, personally, acquiring in the process a new understanding of the term *jumping her bones*. Bony she was, and the implants stuck up off her chest like doorknobs, and all in all, it was like fucking a door, jamming his cock into a keyhole. He had trouble getting it up for her, and she twisted his tits painfully and scratched hell out of him and he paid her back. It got a little rough. She liked it that way. It wasn't very smart, he knew, even though they were careful as hell—not smart to fuck the boss's wife, though refusing her might make himself a powerful enemy. He hadn't even been very interested. His mother running around, acting the way she was, had cast sex in a new light, as ridiculous and disgusting and compulsive. He did not like being run by his cock, which had proved susceptible to the machinations of a randy cunt like Narcissa.

He would cut back his drinking—which had never affected his work and was nothing more than self-medication, to get to sleep, to deal with grief, and had never affected his work anyway. He would get to the gym and eat more regularly, take a little better care of himself, and he would be okay. Grief was natural, everybody agreed; you had to let it run its course.

Twice a month, Kissy continued to visit Ruth. The resulting images fascinated her. Irrationally—perhaps because she had no experience of it—she had not expected Ruth to age. But Ruth *was* aging. She was no longer twenty— she was twenty-five and she looked it, the twenty-five of a woman who had, say, married at sixteen and divorced at nineteen with three babies, and lived hardscrabble, hand-to-mouth, possibly literally fist-to-mouth, forget getting the teeth replaced. It was her mouth that was aging most. In fact, she had lost teeth in the accident and had a couple more die later from the trauma. Though she had careful dental care, there was little point in replacing teeth, and her gums had shrunken and her remaining teeth fallen out of true.

Otherwise, the normal process of leaving behind youth was occurring in Ruth—like her classmates, her face and body were no longer those of a young girl fresh out of her teens but of an adult woman, and one in poor health, with all the aging effect that had. The lack of animation, the slackness of her flesh, and the stiffness of her joints undoubtedly added to the perception; she was aged the way the catatonic mentally ill are.

The change in her had become increasingly difficult for her mother. Mrs. Prashker had had some weeping binges, some terrible outbursts, and been forced to give up her participation in the care of her daughter. At the suggestion of a therapist, she was trying to reclaim other aspects of her life, planning that summer on a long camper tour of the country with her son and his family.

Sylvia Cronin had introduced Dynah to the concept of the tea party. The two of them regularly entertained each other. Sylvia in her antique-furnished dining room, with Dynah perched in a throne of a Victorian chair, and Dynah in the front parlor of her own home, serving Sylvia from the thimble-size china cups Sylvia had given her. It made amusing photographs as Dynah regarded her hockey uniform, the jersey sporting the name Clootie and Junior's number, as de rigueur formal wear, and sometimes she also

wore her skates—guards on, of course. Casey was sometimes invited, and twitched through the parties in a state of
agonizing excitement, watching Dynah for his next cue.

He was Dynah's slave. Like any slaveholder, Dynah was
corrupted by the sheer power over him into a constant de-
termination to humiliate him. She saved stick-on bows for
his hair and insisted he wear an apron and that was just to
attend a tea party. Dynah had chopped her hair to match
Kissy's and Junior's in length, but beyond a bright-red
slash of lipstick, used Casey for her canvas, not herself.
Excursions into Kissy's or Bernie's cosmetics resulted in
Casey, not Dynah, wearing a clown's mask of mascara,
blusher, and lipstick, and it was Casey who got his hair
dyed with Jell-O powder in giggling secret sessions in the
bathroom. It was Casey Dynah led downstairs to her tea
parties wearing ensembles of lace panties and satin halters
and the flashy junk earrings Dynah picked out for Kissy
when Junior took her shopping.

Mrs. Cronin might be Sylvia to Kissy and Junior, but to
Dynah she had become Nana. Kissy was intrigued to discover that by some process of confusion and conflation
and leaping imagination, Dynah had decided that Mrs.
Cronin was Kissy's grandmother and that Ruth was Junior's mother.

Between her work and Dynah and mothering Bernie and
Casey and daughtering Dunny, and keeping the house from
falling down, burning down, freezing up, or being con-
demned, keeping track of Junior and his financial interests, which he delegated to her during the season, Kissy
often felt she was barely keeping her head above water.
She was grateful to have Dunny and Bernie and Casey
making up her family, with Mrs. Cronin as an honorary
grandmother. There were opportunities to travel, to pack
up Dynah and visit Junior, and she took them. The trips
provided opportunities to visit galleries and museums, to
refresh her eye with new sights. She acquired an agent, in-
state, but with good connections to the galleries in New
York and Boston.

Her busy life did not mean that she was not lonely
sometimes. There were many nights after Dynah was in
bed when Junior called again and somehow it was worse,
she was more alone. Sometimes she tried to distract herself
with late-night work, but she could not work all the time. It

was bad for the work, for one. Junior coming home, or she and Dynah visiting him, did not result in instant paradise either. There was always a period of adjustment to each other. There were excitement and expectations inevitably too great to be fulfilled, particularly for a small girl, and often for a grown man who had too much opportunity to fantasize about how perfect his child was, when she wasn't, and what great sex he was going to have with Kissy, who sometimes turned out to be exhausted, or having her period, or distracted by the aforementioned imperfect kid. Her own expectations she could and did tailor. Sunday dinner with Dunny and Ida and Bernie and Casey, a visit to Ruth, happening upon her work prints of Mike Burke's father—she had plenty of reminders of what a sin ingratitude is.

Summer's greening came again. The crowns of the trees thickening and leafed out first in moonlight and then the tiny leaves, like the fingernails on a baby, and the horse chestnuts budding phallically and bursting into white rockets, and the evergreens, old growth dark and thorny, tipping out in light soft green.

Then Junior home, weeks at the cottage with sand in the sheets and a little girl with chattering teeth from staying in the water too long. Mark was doing well in Portland, where he had been traded, and had even gone up for a few weeks during the past season for a major league debut with the Caps, with expectations of making the big jump soon. As an investment, he bought a house in Peltry and asked Bernie to be his housekeeper. In August, Bernie moved, leaving Dynah inconsolable for Casey's company.

Casey missed her too. The first time he came to visit again, when Dynah tried to reassert her old hegemony, he punched her in the nose. And then he begged hysterically to be allowed to stay, to sleep in Dynah's room with her. He hated his mummy, he only loved Dynah and Kissy and her daddy and this house and not that other one that didn't even have a swimming pool.

Without Bernie and Casey, Kissy was a little more alone when Junior left again. She often invited Bernie and Casey to stay over in bad weather, as much for company as some real need to batten down the hatches. Since Casey was at a stage of being impossible in supermarkets—he had to have everything—Kissy often shopped for them both while Bernie took the kids.

One night at nine-thirty, a snowstorm imminent, she left Bernie with the kids and dashed out to the market to stock up. It was nearly as chilly as the out-of-doors, the air more stale, of course. Kissy paused to admire the pears, which had a delicate blush and made her imagine pale thin slices in a Pear Tatin. She hadn't made one in ages. She was bagging pears when Mike Burke came around the corner, pushing his cart into the produce section. He had some gray in his hair he never used to have. She couldn't say how much she might have herself, as she was still bleaching her hair. Junior had asked her once when pubic hair started to gray. How would I know? she had answered, you're my old man and you haven't got any gray there yet. Better check right now, he had said, the old man can feel one growing in. It's a big one too.

The thought made her grin to herself, and she was fighting a giggle when Burke pulled up next to her, like one cop chatting to another from side-by-side units.

"Howyadoin'?" she asked, and laughed, unable to repress herself anymore.

"Fine." His cheekbones reddened and she realized he thought she was teasing him. He watched her tying up her bag of pears. "I miss being friends."

She felt sorry for him. "You like Pear Tatin?"

"Like Apple Tatin?"

"With pears."

"Never had it."

"Come by for dinner—not tomorrow, we're liable to be snowed in, but day after—and you will." The moment she issued the invitation, she decided it had better be a dinner party. Not a tête-à-tête.

"I will. What should I bring?"

"If you mean a bottle, let's go decide between meat and fish right now."

They settled on lamb chops. "Dynah loves them." Kissy laughed. "She coats them in mint jelly."

"Yummy," Burke agreed.

Bernie teased her. "You aren't hot for that pig, are you?"

"Jesus, Bernie, where would I get the energy?" Kissy arranged the pears in a basket. "Are these beautiful?"

"Luscious," Bernie agreed. "Don't change the subject. How much energy does it take to just lie there—"

"Is that an insight into your sex life? Now that I think about it, don't answer that."

Bernie sniggered. She picked up a pear and twirled it by the stem. "What sex life?"

Kissy took the pear away from her gently and put it back in the basket. "You can't have that. I'm making Pear Tatin."

She was quite sure, in her own mind, she was not hot for that pig, not anymore. Going to bed that once with Mike Burke, for such a little voodoo pincushion of reasons—curiosity, piss-off at Junior, to prove she could—had immunized her. Inviting him to dinner might revive the memory but not necessarily the possibility. They were both a little more dug into their own lives. He had taken up coaching Little League, as he had said he would, and he seemed somehow less the hard-driving young Turk, more subdued and substantial—or maybe it was only the touch of gray in his hair. First sign of a pass, though, she would boot him out the door.

She was seated at the head of the table, knee to Burke's, with Latham opposite. Burke had actually taken a course from Latham, a decade earlier, and aced it. They could share dinner conversation as equals, Latham gracious and grateful for cops like Burke, who left him alone as long he was discreet, confining his chickenhawking to his coterie of students, who also took the risk of buying his dope for him. Burke was more interested in Bernie Clootie. She looked like she would be a romp. A little young for him, regrettably.

And there he was himself, at table with a faggot art professor and this motley collection of Kissy's in-laws—or ex-in-laws; she was divorced from Clootie, for Christ's sake, and what sort of relation to her was Dunny Clootie's girlfriend? It made Burke feel like some off-brand variety of fag-hag. All he had wanted was some time with Kissy.

It was the most frustrating situation Burke had ever been in with a woman. To have had her and then to be refused, as if it had only taken her one go to determine never again—it was not exactly flattering. But she had made it clear the price of seeing her was the pretense that he had never fucked her. They could only be friends—she didn't say it aloud but it was in her body language, the very fact that she invited him into her home, into her family life, so casually, as if he were no threat to it. A Friend Of The Family. Maybe she felt sorry for him.

He did not have time for her but he found himself making it, working up ways to stay in touch. Quickie phone calls, howyadoin', and once in a while, time to have coffee? Grab a bite of lunch with me? If he had a chance at a ticket to something, fund-raisers, games, shows going through, he called her first. She let him take her and Dynah to the Ice Capades and he came up with the extra ticket for Bernie Clootie's kid. Bernie had an exam, worse luck. The little boy stuck to Burke like a big-eyed burr—poor little daddy-starved bastard. Apparently he made a hit with Dynah too, because all of a sudden he was invited to a tea party. Fortunately, he couldn't make it. But he sent Dynah a rosebud, which impressed the hell out of her, Kissy informed him.

The rest of his invitations went begging. Trying to evoke a little jealousy, he had gone out with some other women and made sure Kissy knew about it. And it helped, taking off the clothes of another woman, any woman, jamming her—then he only wanted what he had, not what would not have him.

Then the season ended—the only one that counted in the Clootie household—and Junior was back in town. Burke got serious about his golf. He had another go-round with Narcissa. Stretching leather, he thought. He noticed a lifeguard at the country club, cute little eighteen-year-old. He flirted with her a little, and in late August, after a wedding reception she had worked as a waitress, fucked her in the locker room.

When the summer ended, he had decided not to call Kissy. But inevitably he ran into her—in Denny's. She had the kid with her, a little outing for Dynah. The kid grew all the time, it hit him. "Like a weed" was no joke. It bothered him. Time was getting away from him. He had expected to be married by now, to have started a family. It was not much consolation to tell himself that if he had married, he would probably be divorced, like most of the cops and lawyers he knew. Eighteen-year-olds were going to be scarce on the ground in the future, and he did not look forward to more Narcissas. And the voters were suspicious of never-married bachelors over forty but he had less and less time to find a wife.

He stopped reading the sports page and watching the sporting news on the tube so he would never have to encounter the name or face of Junior fucking Clootie. Who was successful and wealthy and had a beautiful little girl who was growing up fast and an ex-wife named Kissy at his beck and call. Some nights, Burke stared at the moon hanging in his skylight and fantasized about getting Clootie's phone number, calling him, hissing at him, "I fucked her, I fucked your wife and she loved it!" Except she hadn't loved it enough to let him do her again. It wasn't enough, just once. He didn't like it being her decision that once was enough. It gnawed at him.

∞ 28 ∞

"**M**arry me," Burke blurted.

They were at a show at the School of Fine Arts, not one with any of her pictures—a fund-raiser for the hospital, black-tie, hundreds of potential campaign donors. She did not attend such events very often, but it was the School of Fine Arts and she was connected there the way he was in the courthouse. She had not come as his date—they were both dateless—but he had spent the evening keeping track of her and finally cornered her, only by then he had had a few.

She laughed. Not rudely. Ruefully.

They both pretended for a while he had never made the proposal. They went on as before: *Howyadoin'? Take a break? Time for a burger?*

About six weeks after the fund-raiser at the School of Fine Arts, she brought a print of a picture of the courthouse she had done that he wanted to give to Butch as a birthday gift to his office. She undid the bubble wrap around it and showed it to him.

"It would look nice in a museum frame," she said.

He nodded agreeably and then it was out of his mouth again. "Marry me."

She started and he made a pass at her, grabbing her clumsily, forcing his mouth on hers. He had the advantage of surprise, unnerving her, and maybe she was inhibited by where they were, but she only struggled a moment and then she let him kiss her. And responded.

And Butch opened the door. "Oh," he said, "excuse me," and closed it quietly.

Kissy backed away. Her skin was flushed from her hairline to the cleavage the undone buttons of her blouse revealed.

"I'm serious, Kissy," Burke said. "I want to marry you."

She looked at him as if he had proposed knocking over a 7-Eleven. She walked out.

He slumped into his desk chair and kicked the bottom drawer. "Shit."

His secretary peeked in at the door. She looked abashed. "Sorry, I was in the ladies'. The Man wants to see you."

At Burke's rap on his door, Butch looked up from the paperwork on his desk and pointed his chin at the chair he habitually assigned to people just before he tore off their heads and handed it to them. "Keep your private life out of this office. The taxpayers get shirty these days about public servants getting stiff on their time."

"Yessir." Humble as shit in the face of an outrageous hypocrisy. Butch had written the book on getting laid on the taxpayers' time.

His boss sat back and eyed him speculatively. "So you're messing with Clootie's wife—"

"Ex-wife."

"Keep your skirts clean, Mike," Butch said, passing him a file. "Clean this up too."

"Yessir." Tug the forelock. God, he was good. Butch didn't have a clue. Tell me, Butch old buddy, your bag-of-bones cunt of a wife like it up the ass as much from you as she does from me?

Crouching in his samurai drag, the goalie waited. The net was a cave at his back. He fanned gently. He waited, waited on the game, the puck, the black period that punctuates every hockey sentence. For some time he existed in this state, on the frozen white plain, alone, while the game, the puck and the skaters, shuttled beyond his reach. Until at last the loom of players suddenly reversed, the lines racing toward him. The goalie jittered and jived, waiting, waiting, waiting to implode or explode, to fall down or stand on his head—whatever impossible reaction the puck demanded. A right winger broke out, made a pass, and erupted past the defensemen. Without looking, he collected the puck from his left wing and picked up more speed as he rushed the net. A defenseman was suddenly there, angled to intercept the offense. The goalie dropped low. For an instant, a blank instant, the puck was on the goalie's stick, stopped as the winger tried to stuff it, and then the winger crashed into him. A fraction of a second late, the defenseman impacted the winger from behind, his knee underneath him, and in the tangle of the three players, the winger fell backward, his left skate kicking up.

As the defenseman and the winger scrambled to their feet, the goalie paused. He had felt a slight tug at his neck, as if the back of his collar had been given a jerk. Yet there was a new distance to the ice, to the long white field, and new unnameable sensations. Dropping his stick, he sank slowly to his knees as if to pray. Indeed, his hands rose, he shed his glove, but did not clasp his hands after all. They found his mask and lifted it as he keeled forward, still slowly, still carefully, into the dark flow from his throat.

Seven minutes, he knew, ridiculously, he had seven minutes before irreversible brain damage, and he would like to lift his head to look at the clock, to see the numbers counting down the seven minutes of this new period, this new game he had suddenly begun.

Something had happened, something had gone wrong. A disaster. It was as if Kissy were watching, again, the dragon breath forking contrails as the *Challenger* fell from the sky in pieces and the voice of Mission Control announced with terrifying calmness, "There has been a major malfunction." Ah yes, fuck yes. There had been a major malfunction. Junior lifted his mask and the dark arterial blood from his severed, majorly malfunctioning jugular, opened by the winger's skate blade, gouted upon the ice, an act she knew at once she would see in replay over and over and forever. She waited for the voice, for Mission Control to confirm what she saw—Junior, malfunctioning, folding slowly into his own blood. She was in shock, her heart clenched hard enough to hurt. Fallen to her knees from her seat at the edge of the couch, she clutched her own throat unaware.

Dynah had watched the first period of this game before being put to bed with the usual promise she could finish it tomorrow on tape. It was only chance Dynah was not watching, was not here next to her, to watch Junior malfunctioning. It would happen. Sometime in the years to come she would be able to see it, on tape, or inadvertently, see Daddy bleed to death.

It was quick, minutes only, and unconsciousness even quicker. Junior was malfunctioning and she could not stop it. In minutes he would be finished with it. It was all too perfectly Junior, too improbable, too bizarre, and as usual he was leaving her.

On her knees, like a pilgrim on the steps of the cathedral of Sainte Anne de Beaupré, she crawled across the room and fell against the console and hit the power button. The screen winked out. Blink and it was gone, Junior was gone. She had silenced Mission Control.

Mike Burke might have his law degree from Sowerwine and his membership in the bar, he might work in an office right next to the DA's, up the hill in the courthouse, but it always seemed to him, when his work took him to the station house, that he had never really left the cop shop. He was in and out of the place nearly as often as when he was a uniform. If there was anything to miss, it was the bond with his fellow officers. Once you left the street, you might retain the respect they accorded to veterans, but you lost something too, you weren't on the line anymore, not the way they were. You weren't building the bond anymore, the way they were.

He was where he wanted to be and headed where he wanted to go, but especially around his old partner, Pearce, he found himself proselytizing Pearce to raise his own sights, get his ass off the street before it got too comfortable behind the wheel of a street unit. Pearce never failed to listen closely, nodding in agreement about the wonderful things the two of them could do together in the courthouse, leap over tall buildings, stop speeding bullets for truth, justice, and the American way. If he hadn't seen Pearce listen with the exact same intensity to every piss-stained old wino he had ever hauled out of Dunkin' Donuts and off to the shelter where they stored the drunks, he might even think he was having some effect on him.

In the middle of one of these futile shoveling sessions in the bullpen, Pearce sprawled in his chair, Burke straddling a chair pinched from another desk, the desk sergeant shouted *Oh Jesus!* Burke and Pearce reached reflexively for the weapon in the belt that Pearce had dropped on his desk, going to red alert though they had no idea yet what the problem was. There was no debate; Burke let Pearce have the weapon and snatched the pepper spray holstered on the same belt. All to naught—it was the television under the counter that had so shocked the desk sergeant. The cops in the bullpen gathered around, and in silence, sweating from their own adrenaline, they watched the goalie bleeding out.

"Unreal," Burke muttered. Clootie, the lucky one, the man who had everything, spurting from the neck like a sacrificial goat. Burke grasped Pearce's elbow. "Hey, man," he said quietly. "I'm going over to Kissy's. She'll need help."

Pearce tore his gaze from the screen and something else came into his eyes, and he knew Burke saw it and made no attempt to hide it. Pearce knew him too well, had heard him on the subject of Kissy when they were pulling shifts together.

All right, thought Burke, I'm no angel, I've had a hard-on for her, why should I not do the right thing now, be there for her?

Some of the ground floor of Junior and Kissy's house showed lights. Dunny Clootie's wagon was parked haphazardly in the drive. It was still running, the driver's door standing open. Parking brake on, but the wagon was still in gear. Burke put it into park and turned it off and closed the doors, leaving the keys in the ignition.

The side door Dunny had used was still open, heat and light spilling out of it into the chill of a winter night. The place was quiet. Not even the sound of a television, Burke noted. But there were small noises, of secretive grief. He closed the door behind him and went through the kitchen and down the hall into the living room.

Kissy knelt on the floor, rocking back and forth, choking on snot and tears.

Dunny knelt next to her, embracing her, crying and snuffling himself. His hair stood straight up. His shirt was zipped into his fly.

"Jesus, Jesus, Jesus," he moaned, or prayed—there was no way of telling.

Burke put his arms around Kissy from behind. "Come

on, baby, come on, now," he urged her, drawing her to her feet.

Dunny followed, more or less automatically, unwilling to let go of Kissy. "D'ya see it?" he sobbed. "D'ya see it?"

Kissy was white and shaking. She looked up at Burke, turning toward him, away from Dunny. Burke had seen devastation more times than he could count. He remembered Kissy herself after the accident that had killed the Greenan girl. He remembered her shock in the aftermath of the fight between her old boyfriend and Clootie. But this time, it was different. Her distress had more resonance just because they knew each other now as people, and their fleeting intimacy added to that sense of knowledge. This time, she was shattered, in more disarray than he had ever seen her, so much she was allowing him to see it. She looked up at him with a vulnerability that placed her totally in his power.

"Is there anything to drink?" he asked Dunny. Just to give Dunny something to do.

Dunny nodded and fell into step, doing what needed doing, doing the something he needed to do. He came wandering back, having unearthed a bottle of Courvoisier, never opened, wrapped in foil and with a red ribbon and Christmas tag still on it, apparently a holiday remembrance from someone.

Burke poured some of it into Kissy, into Dunny, and into himself. He wrapped Kissy up in blankets and sat her down on the couch with Dunny holding on to her. Then he called the station house and goosed the watch for some coverage for the neighborhood; the media would be descending on this house. He made himself the man in charge. There were calls to take and make: Bernie; Mark; Dunny's girlfriend, Ida.

Junior's agent called; shaken, too, into tears and incoherence. And shortly thereafter, the manager of Junior's team got through, and the first hard information came in: Junior was, at last report, still alive. Burke began to make arrangements.

He booked a jet from a charter service at the airport. A car and someone from the team to meet them. Dunny's girlfriend arrived, and Burke sent her upstairs with Kissy to pack some bags and wake Dynah up enough to dress her for the trip. He set up a police escort to the airport. He met

the first media at the door and told them what he knew—
alive at last report—and promised he would give them
everything he could as soon as he got it. Then he had them
pushed off the street and bundled Kissy and Dynah and
Dunny into the back of a unit and ignited the show—
bubble lights and sirens, something for the media to run on
the eleven o'clock news—and delivered them right onto
the tarmac next to the jet. The owner of the charter service
had rushed out to oversee the fueling of the jet himself;
he told Kissy this one was on him, and began to weep
himself. Burke thought of going with them, but he could
see Dunny had recovered himself considerably and it was
the best thing, give Dunny the responsibility. Gently he
brushed his lips over Kissy's cold ones and she looked up
at him with eyes swollen and shadowed with exhaustion
and tears, and she was still looking at him as the pilot
lifted the door of the Lear into place. As if it would all
come out all right, if only she never took her eyes off him.
If she just did everything he said.

She was still terrified and still furious as she waited
with Dunny and Dynah at Junior's bedside in the hospital
for him to wake. The cut, she had been told, was ten inches
long, but she hadn't seen it; it was hidden under the bandage on his neck. Sitting there, looking at him in the slackness of unconsciousness, she could not help thinking of
Ruth. There was no visible evidence of it, but his heart had
stopped; he had actually flat-lined at one point, died. He'd
been where Ruth was, passed her, possibly actually
reached the gates of hell, and the doctors had whistled him
back. He was rather pale and thinner, as if the blood lost
had had significant weight and volume that the transfused
product had not. The doctors were confident there had
been no brain damage, at least none anyone would notice
in Junior. No doubt they had checked with Mission Control. She clasped her hands tightly against the shaking that
seized her. Fury had taken up residence in her throat,
stopped there only by the need to appear sane and calm
and in charge. For Dynah. Dynah couldn't afford to have
Daddy with his throat cut and Mommy screaming.

Burke was there when she brought Junior home by air
ambulance and she squeezed his hand and kissed his

cheek, though she was distracted. Dynah was fractious and demanding, Junior dazed with drugs and perhaps disbelief that he was still in the land of the living, and the media blowflies were fluttering around, in everybody's face and way.

It was a couple of days before he dropped by, almost too late, ten-thirty at night, and only a few lights still burning in the house. But the kitchen window still showed light, and that was where Kissy was, having put her household to bed. There was a little woodstove in one corner, and she had been reading, curled up in a rocking chair. The white irises he had sent her were on the kitchen table, a little cluster of glowing white-and-green life. She let him in, they embraced as old friends—he noticed she was quite a lot thinner—and she offered him coffee.

"Got a beer?" he asked.

She nodded and brought him one, and a glass that he waved off.

"How's it going?"

She shrugged. "Okay. Dynah's thrilled to have Daddy home. He's making progress."

The weight she had lost added to the look of strain. She shifted restlessly around the kitchen, twitching, picking up things and putting them down again.

"I never thought he could get killed," she said. "He's been doing it so long, I forgot it was dangerous. I can't watch it anymore. I hate it. And he can't wait to get back to it."

Burke, perched on a stool, watched her thoughtfully. "Risk is part of life, baby," he said neutrally.

She crossed her arms, holding herself together. "I hate his life, I never wanted it! He hasn't got any right to make me afraid all the time, so he can play a stupid fucking dangerous game! What if Dynah had seen it happen? What if she had had to live with that memory for the rest of her life?"

"I've worked a dangerous job in my life," Burke told her.

"It's a necessary job—"

"Yes, but—"

"There's no comparison."

Implicitly conceding she was right, Burke did not argue the point.

"The shock is very fresh," he said.

She flung herself into the rocking chair and stared at him.

Burke leaned toward her. "Where do you want to be in ten, twenty years?" he asked. "It's your life too, Kissy. If it's not going to get better for you—"

"I've got a kid," she blurted. "I can't just blow out of here, the way my old man did. Goddamn it, I'm raising her. We're going to have a settled life. I'm not dragging her from pillar to post, I'm not leaving her with some baby-sitter to raise—"

"Of course not," he said. "Look, whatever you do, I'm here for you."

Her eyes welled. She nodded.

Burke managed to stay in his dear-friend mode. But inside, he was elated. Now she was leaning on him, it would not require much leverage to tip her off her feet again.

Rarely home this time of year, Junior watched the shift of weather outside the window as if it were doing it just for him. He had never been at greater peace with himself. Dying didn't just concentrate the mind wonderfully, it cast everything in a new precious light. In those moments of watching his own blood pool before the world went gray and then disappeared, he had known he was dying and, most unexpectedly, had never been happier. He had been grateful for his life and full of love for Kissy and Dynah and his dad, for Bernie and Casey and Mark—he had been so very lucky, thank you. There had been no tunnel of light, no floating above his own body, no pale ethereal Diane telling him it wasn't time yet. Consciousness had returned as Kissy's voice, murmuring in his ear that she was there, Dynah was there, everyone was there with him, and his throat had felt tied at the bottom, like the Scarecrow's head was in the *Wizard of Oz*, and it was sore, like somebody had clotheslined him.

It was very pleasant, lying abed reading cards from well-wishers in a roomful of hothouse flowers that might have been displayed around his coffin otherwise. He was hungry all the time, and Kissy cooked for him and Dynah treated him as if he were her baby doll, feeding him with one of the tiny spoons from her tea set, from the tiny china with the blue forget-me-nots. She cuddled up to him on the bed and they watched whatever the satellite caught for games, or game tapes from various sources, and made bets with each other about who would win Pig-in-the-Middle the next time they played it with Dunny.

He had nightmares, not surprisingly; a lot of times he woke up in a puddle of sweat, and once it was bad enough for him to piss himself. It was the throat-cutting, every time. The doctor called it posttraumatic stress syndrome—the brain took a savage hit of adrenaline and the effects lingered, he said, keeping you in the same hyper, scared-shitless state, even though the crisis was over, and of course you couldn't sleep, which messed you up. So now he was taking an antidepressant that left his mouth a little dry and made him fart but got him sleeping like the dead. And the farts were just noise that amused the hell out of Dynah.

The days went by, lengthening as he grew stronger.

Kissy was putting in long hours at night in her dark-room and sleeping in another room so as not to disturb him. One evening he stayed awake, past Dynah's bedtime, the bedroom door open so he could hear the rustle and pad and clink of her locking up downstairs. At last he heard her on the stairs. He rose on one elbow. "Baby," he said as she peeked in at him. "Come in and talk to me."

"I'll be right back, I'm going to check Dynah."

He relaxed against the pillows. She looked tired. Maybe it wasn't the right time. But he had a hard-on already and it felt great—not just the hard-on, it felt great to have one. She came back and he patted the bed. She sat down on the edge of it. He touched her mouth with his fingertips. But when he cocked his head to place his lips on hers, she turned her head away.

"What?" he asked. He didn't understand. He'd showered earlier, shaved carefully, brushed his teeth. "Is my breath bad or something?"

She stood up and pulled a chair away from the little secretary on the other side of the room and set it down next to the bed. She sat down on it and put her hands in her lap and struggled to look at him. "This is hard to do," she said.

His stomach flip-flopped, and he felt his blood draining away. His flesh rose in goose bumps.

"There's someone else in my life," she said, carefully, as if the words had sharp edges and might cut him. Or her. "I've decided to marry him."

It felt like someone had kicked him in the chest, and he laughed, shock triggering the inappropriate reaction. "Yeah," he said, "it must be wicked hard, fucking me over right now."

That brought a satisfying tremor to her mouth. He still didn't believe it. It was so incredibly cruel, it couldn't be a joke, but the words had come out of her mouth, Kissy's mouth, and the woman sat there, avoiding his eyes, his wife, his Kissy, whom he loved so much he had thought of her when he had been dying.

He rasped the word that was like a stone in his mouth. "Who?"

"Mike Burke."

He dropped back against the pillows. "Jesus Christ."

"I've already started transferring your assets back into your name—"

He sat up again, making himself dizzy. "Fuck my assets! Why don't you just cut my fucking throat for me and do it right this time!"

She shrank from him, her hand covering her mouth, tears in her eyes.

"I don't give shit one about my fucking assets," he said. His voice had gone hoarse on him but he wasn't going to cry, he wasn't going to fucking bawl.

"I'm going right away," she whispered, "in the next few days—"

"You're not taking Dynah."

Her hands wrung each other in her lap. "Yes, I am, yes, but you'll see her all you want—"

"I want to live in the same house with her, that's what I want."

She pulled herself together. "That's not possible."

"Why are you fucking doing this? Are you in love with that asshole?"

"Yes, I am."

Lying. Lying through her teeth. To herself. She couldn't love that asshole. "I don't believe you, not him, fucking Officer Friendly—you are fucking him, right?" She didn't answer. She just stared at him with her overflowing eyes, like Dynah when she had pulled some shit and got caught. What had he struggled through so many sessions with Sarah to learn? She was a separate person he could not control. No shit. He took a deep breath. "I left you alone too much and he's the kind of shithead can spot a vulnerable woman ten miles away. All right, I understand it, I can forgive you, Kissy. I think you owe us a chance to try to fix it, you owe Dynah—" He was weeping despite his best effort to control it, and his anger exploded. "She's my kid, you can't take her away from me and make that prick her stepfather—"

She had come to her feet. "Junior," she said in a voice so soft he had to strain to hear it, "I'll never have to watch Mike get his throat cut." She bolted from the room.

Bolting from their life. He sat in silence after those words, still hearing them, word by word. He fingered the bandage on his throat. "I didn't do it on purpose," he told the silence. "It was an accident. It just happened to me. It's not going to happen again."

What she had said was crazy. She was crazy. What had happened to him had driven her nuts. Which made what Burke was doing worse, taking advantage of a woman temporarily out of her mind. The thoughts insisted on being thought—that cocksucker dicking her and her wanting it from him. The woman who was so much his, it was like she was part of him. He pushed the sheets away and unsteadily sought to stand. His chest hurt and he struggled to breathe. He could hear his heart knocking along in there like a weaving drunk. All he was wearing was pajama bottoms. He felt cold and sick and his chest hurt so bad he wondered if he was having a heart attack. He found a robe and went looking for her.

She was sitting on the floor of the bedroom she had been using, her back to a wall, with her head in her hands. He sat down on the edge of the bed and looked down at her bent head and heaving shoulders.

"Things happen to people," he told her. "I didn't die, Kissy—"

"Yes, you did!" she accused him.

"That was just my heart stopping, I came back. Kissy, I'm not dead and I'm not going to die for a long time. Don't you understand there's no guarantees? Burke could die tomorrow—fuck, I hope he does, I may kill him myself." He slid to his knees and tried to take her in his arms. She fought a little and then she let him. "Baby," he murmured, "baby." The robe had come apart in his sliding off the bed and her face was against the hair on his chest and it was all wet with her tears and his. Her face was wet and salty as he kissed it blindly.

"Does this change anything?" he ventured, one bare leg resting comfortably between hers. The way she looked up at him, he saw it didn't. He rolled onto his back and stared at the ceiling. "You gonna tell him you let me fuck you?"

She came to her knees next to him. She looked half mad, her eyes glazed and unfocused. She didn't answer. He watched her pull her T-shirt over her head. She didn't bother to put her underwear or her jeans back on. He wanted to fuck her all over again.

"I've arranged for an auditor to go over the books so you'll know I was straight with you."

Back to the taped announcement.

"I told you I don't give a fuck about that—"

"I'm putting the house in your name—"

"I gave you this house, I gave you the fucking money, your jewelry, they were fucking gifts, you don't give back gifts, Kissy, it's an insult—"

"If you keep this house, it'll make it easier on Dynah, if she comes here to you—"

"That's real thoughtful, I'm so glad you're so fucking concerned with Dynah, you're crazy, Kissy, you've lost your fucking mind, you need a shrink, I've been telling you for years you need to deal with some shit—"

"I don't want her messed up by us fighting over her—"

"You don't think it's gonna mess her up, you splitting us up? Just don't forget she's my kid, not his—"

"He understands that—"

"I don't give a fuck whether he understands fuck-all—"

"I'm not your enemy and neither is he—"

"Wrong, wrong, you're fucking wrong about that one, he is my fucking enemy and you're fucking him—"

"It's got nothing to do with you, Mike and I—"

"Nothing to do with me? I can't fucking believe my ears!"

"Lower your voice, please, you'll wake Dynah."

Angrily he snatched up his pajama pants and legged into them. "I'd like to know how you think you're going to explain this to her." He tried out a mocking falsetto. "Mommy likes Officer Friendly now so she's gonna live with him and of course Dynah has to come along—fuck that, Kissy." The more he thought about it, the madder he got. "I want full custody, I'm gonna sue you for it, you and Officer Fuckhead can just fuck off together and I'll raise Dynah."

"How? Leaving her with a housekeeper all the time or dragging her on the road with you, hotel to hotel?"

Junior sat down on the edge of the bed and put his head in his hands. "I hate you." It sounded like something Dynah would say when she was crossed and he knew it and understood for the first time what an expression of power-lessness it was.

She left the room. After a moment, he followed her and found her in the bathroom, on the toilet, pissing.

He stood in the door and watched her. "Be funny if I knocked you up. I hope I did."

She stood, yanked the flush lever, and then stalked to the shower and turned it on.

"I don't hate you," he said. "I love you. You know it."

She stepped into the rush of water without looking at him.

With all his heart, he cheered on his sperm, the fast strong ones that were racing up her tubes in search of an egg. She wouldn't leave him if she caught, he was certain of it. Now he thought about it—it must be against the odds, her not catching all the times they'd had sex without contraception. At least he hadn't used anything—he sup-posed she could have been sneaking the Pill, though why she would want to keep it a secret from him, he couldn't imagine. Unless she had been fucking around on him all along. He still couldn't believe it. He couldn't believe she had let anyone else fuck her, especially not Officer Fuck-head.

He went back to bed, piling on extra blankets and quilts because he had the shakes. You spent days flat on your ass, it sapped your strength something wicked. Couldn't even fuck without it exhausting you. Closing his eyes, he tucked his body fetally against the cold. He was too wiped out to fight any more tonight. But he wasn't giving up. Sarah had tried to get him to accept the end of the marriage before, but he had owned his feelings, the way Sarah had said he should, and his feelings were he would not give it up. Sarah had visited him briefly in the hospital and he had called her once to tell her he was okay and taking anti-depressants. He should call her, but she would only start throwing the usual bread crumbs that were meant to lead him out of the forest, to the conclusion he should quit. He would fight for Kissy all the way to the justice of the peace, and if she actually married that shithead, he still wouldn't give up. She was just temporarily wacko. He ought to have pushed harder to get her into therapy, to change the script she had learned from her parents. It wasn't him getting his throat cut that had flipped her out; it was her denial that love carried the risk of loss.

He imagined grabbing Officer Fuckhead by the throat and telling him, "It was great last night, we balled on a twenty-thousand-dollar silk Oriental rug and I made her come four times. Maybe you ought to rethink this idea of marrying Kissy."

He would do it—only Kissy would be so furious with him she would move out anyway. She didn't need a ticket from Officer Fuckhead to leave him if he pissed her off enough, even when she was sane. Attacking Officer Fuckhead would not work. He had to restrain his own instincts to go beat the living shit out of the prick and throw his body off the Mid-Dance. Being with him had to be her choice. Love and acting like a grown-up had washed out the divorce—until that shithead came along. He had to believe it would wash Officer Fuckhead away too.

∞ 29 ∞

It was easier to promise himself he was going to be sweet and rational and unruffled than to do it. She started packing up her darkroom and files and he thought he was going to explode, all he could think was what a waste of energy it was when she was just going to have to move it all back when she came back to him. He followed her around, picking at how she was going at it. "What are you doing, lifting that heavy shit? Hire somebody to do it, for Christ's sake."

She glared at him and wiped her hands on her Levi's. "Fuck off, Junior."

He sulked off to the kitchen and made tea and toast that tasted like cardboard and chewed up and swallowed about the same way. Then he threw it up. He couldn't keep anything down since she told him. If he kept on puking, he wouldn't be able to keep his antidepressant down and then what would happen to him? All he remembered about the fine print sheet that came with the prescription was that suddenly stopping the med could have dire consequences. He might sink into a catatonic trance or wind up at the mall with an automatic weapon. He still couldn't bring himself to call Sarah. He would wind up bawling over the phone, admitting she had been right all along.

He had to talk to the old man. Kissy had set up an appointment at the house for the next day with a CPA to go over their financial affairs. He was going to need someone he trusted to tend the day-to-day details. If it wasn't going to be her, there was only one choice. It was humiliating to have to call Dunny and tell him Kissy had decided to leave him for someone else.

"What?" Dunny was stunned. "Who?"

"Mike Burke," Junior said, spitting out the name like it was a mouthful of sour milk.

"The assistant DA?"

"He's a fucking asshole, what difference does it make how he fakes earning a living?"

"All right, all right, calm down, I'll be right over—"

And then in the early evening, Officer Fuckhead himself came to his house, from which the aforementioned son of a bitch was stealing the householder's wife. And Butch Mc-Donough's bumboy brought with him a U-Haul truck in which to remove the stolen wife's most precious belongings to the Lair of the White Fucking Worm. It was halfway into the Valley but scenic and secluded and safe as houses, Kissy informed him, in the open garage door while Officer Fuckhead was backing up the U-Haul.

"Officer Fuckhead lives in a house?" Junior asked. "I thought he lived up Butch McDonough's asshole."

Kissy's mouth twitched but she didn't allow herself to laugh. On the strength of that little tremor in her mouth, though, he patted her on the ass. She jumped about a yard to get away from him.

"Don't call him that, please," she begged. "It's so childish."

"Okay, I'll call him Asshole."

He had already told her he wasn't going to shake the fucker's hand, and she must have told Fuckhead because the asshole didn't offer it when he got out of the truck and slimed his way to the garage.

"Howyadoin'?" Officer Fuckhead asked casually, which struck Junior as the most astoundingly banal, stupid, insulting greeting he had ever heard.

"I'm just back from the dead and ready to party," Junior said, "and my wife's leaving me for some fuckhead—"

"Stop it," Kissy said. She stalked away.

Fuckhead watched her go and then he turned to Junior. "You got a pile of money, Clootie, and probably you can hire some hotshit shyster, but you don't want to forget you live in my town. You ever get dirty again, there won't be any plea bargains—"

"Fuck you very much," Junior said. "Hold your breath till you turn blue. Nobody signs a contract with a million-dollar price tag on it without insurance, and the insurance people got a thing about losing money. They got a provi-

sion they can drop a drug screen on me in the middle
of Midnight Mass with the Pope giving me Communion,
they feel like it. I'm a fucking altar boy and you can't
touch me."

Fuckhead just looked at him and then turned on his heel
and followed Kissy into his house. His house. How often
had Fuckhead been in his house when he wasn't home?
Had Kissy let Fuckhead fuck her in their bed, in the hot
tub, or on one of those rugs they had chosen together?

Dynah was with Bernie and Casey at Mark's, out of the
way. He went there, had some beers in the backyard with
Mark, who had only gotten home a day or two earlier when
his minor league season ended. Mark knew all about Kissy
leaving him and muttered he was sorry, which did not do
shit one to make Junior feel better. Bernie could hardly
speak for her fury at Kissy.

"Play a few rounds tomorrow?" Mark asked him. "You
can use a cart."

He touched his throat, the scar still covered because it
upset Dynah. Use a cart. Like an invalid, like one of those
old men with the monstrous chest scars from bypasses of
their clogged-up hearts. His heart was clogged, his heart
hurt. He got up abruptly and went into the house and threw
up the two beers he had put away.

When it was time for Dynah to hit the hay, he took her
home and read to her and put her to bed. And then he
turned on the tube and spun the dish to pull in some playoff games to watch. He didn't bother with lights but sat in
the dark, in case Dynah came downstairs and saw he was
weeping. The lights crawled over the wall from the truck
returning, dropping off Kissy.

She came in and he looked up from the couch in the
dark and asked, "How long has it been going on?"

She started and peered at him, her hand at her breast. "It
doesn't really matter, does it?"

"Sure it does."

But she didn't let him get close enough to smell her. She
was gone, swiftly, up the stairs, into the bathroom. To take
a shower. To wash away the sweat of moving those boxes,
the sweat of lovemaking, the smell of her lover on her. He
would never touch her again, he thought, not with that bastard's fingerprints on her. He wanted to break things, to
kill somebody, to kill himself.

He found himself going to Dynah's room, needing to know she was still there. She didn't have any idea what was happening. Kissy was going to tell her tomorrow. She was so deeply asleep, she never even reacted to the shift of the mattress under his weight. She cut her hair herself, with nail scissors, to look like Kissy's. Her hair was very curly and it took a lot of gel to spike it like Kissy's. It was a lovely dark riot. He was moved by his daughter's sleeping beauty and surprised again by bone-deep gratitude. Kissy had given him this child; she could never take her away. He put his hand over the back of hers, spread on the mattress, and she smiled in her sleep, her hand turning to his, palm to palm, fingers weaving with his.

Butch's handshake was firmer, his clap on the back heartier, his congratulations as unreserved as anyone else's in the office, but Burke perceived an irony in it.

"All right, all right," Butch said, at the end of an over-time session a few nights later, tossing a file onto his desk at the same instant he closed the file on his computer screen. He cocked his head at the antique cupboard he used to house a discreet high-priced selection of hard stuff and the proper crystal for its consumption. He touched the hollow of his throat and coughed politely.

"Double double?" Burke asked with a grin.

Butch popped his eyebrows and Burke got up and poured them both a double shot of double malt.

"Ah, you're a luvely man," Butch said in his mock-wardheeler's brogue, and raised his glass in Burke's direction.

Burke accepted the salute in kind and settled back to savor the taste of the boss's booze.

"You're sure about this, are you?" Butch continued, expecting Burke to follow the change of subject.

"Right time," Burke told him, "right woman."

Butch grinned mirthlessly and nodded, his big thick bricklayer's fingers dwarfing the squat knobby crystal. "Hand it to you, laddie, you've been discreet. I never heard a word of it, and even after I tripped on the two of you that day, you never let on it was serious."

"We weren't either one of us looking for anything serious." Burke studied his glass as if it held a secret.

Butch blinked. "Tell me you haven't knocked her up, now—"

Burke laughed.

"Oh, all right, then." Butch dug around in the back of a drawer, found a pack of cigarettes and held it up. When Burke shook his head no, Butch shook one out and lit it up and sprawled back in his chair. "She straightens you out, does she?" Butch laughed. "Oh, the women are the divil. Baggage, me dad used to call 'm. This baggage has a little baggage, laddie. Shotgun marriage, funny sort of half-assed divorce, bit of the artist—*kooky* was the word when I was young."

Burke let it hang a minute, while Butch blew smoke rings. "She'll never be an issue, Butch. She's not political herself, she just wants to do her own work. I'm not worried about the divorce thing. There's a lot of divorced voters out there. You and I know nobody's for divorce, everybody thinks there's too much of it, but everybody is convinced their own divorce was entirely justifiable. There's a lot of voters out there married to someone who's been married before, a lot of voters raising somebody else's kid. There's no big scandal here—"

"No, no"—Butch flapped a hand dismissively—"times have changed, I wouldn't worry about it at all. You're not running for anything for a while yet anyway—"

"Years off," Burke agreed, "maybe never." He looked Butch in the eye. This was the big one, the one that counted. "I've waited a long time for the right woman, Butch, and she's it. I love the woman. I'd marry her if it meant I was dead-ended right here."

Eyes moist, Butch reached across the desk to grab his hand and shake it. "Fabulous," he said. He sank back into his chair and picked up his glass. "Piece of advice, laddie. Contrary to conventional wisdom, marriage is not a two-way street. It's not a fifty-fifty deal. It takes a hundred percent from both parties—" Butch practicing his wedding breakfast speech. He laughed and heaved himself from his chair in the direction of the booze.

Burke shook his head no to the waggle of the bottle in his direction. Butch always liked that, his seignorial rights to the bottle ceded.

* * *

By arrangement, Junior was to leave Dynah with Bernie to be picked up. But it was Junior who came out of his father's house with Dynah on his shoulders, bouncing her heels off his torso, giggling while she tried to cover his eyes to make him blind.

"What's he doing here?" Mike demanded.

Kissy was irritated herself to see Junior there. She stopped herself from snapping how the hell would she know at Mike. She got out and held out her arms to Dynah, who dove into them. Handing Dynah's things to Mike as if he were the chauffeur, Junior never looked at him but concentrated all his attention on Dynah, hugging and kissing her good-bye. He held the door for Kissy to slip back into the BMW Kissy had given Mike as a wedding gift. The smile he wore for Dynah disappeared. Kissy braced herself for some nasty remark, but instead he went as solemn as a pallbearer.

"There's some bad news," he said, glancing past Kissy toward Dynah, who was checking her tote bag for something. "I guess it's bad news."

"Spit it out," said Kissy.

"Ruth Prashker died a couple of hours ago."

Knowing Kissy was away, Mrs. Cronin had called Bernie, who in turn informed Junior. They conferred as to which of them would take the duty of telling Kissy. Junior insisted.

The event so long awaited felt unreal now it had occurred. She didn't know how to feel. Distractedly, she heard Junior express his condolences. She thanked him. He reached for her hand.

At the same instant Mike, behind the wheel, reached for the same hand, only to encounter Junior's. Both men flinched in reaction, and for an instant were close to snarling at each other. Junior stepped back slowly from the BMW and stood at the curb, watching them drive away.

Just before noon, Mrs. Cronin told her, while the cleaning lady polished the furniture of her room, Ruth had taken a breath, a long reaching sigh, and a moment later the cleaning lady realized she had not taken another. There had been only the rub of her polishing rag on the wood surfaces and the squeak of her rubber-soled shoes, only her own breathing behind the sterile mask she wore in Ruth's room. She had approached Ruth's bed and studied her still and silent body and then called Mrs. Cronin from her kitchen, where Sylvia had been preparing a lunch for herself.

Kissy had paused only long enough to switch her gear to the Blazer. She had even brought Dynah with her, too distracted to consider how appropriate a place it was for a child. The Prashkers and Mrs. Cronin were making calls and arrangements and receiving a few close friends and relatives, who were taken into Ruth's room for a final visitation in that setting. Mrs. Cronin seemed glad to see Dynah. She took her into her lap and they drew pictures together while Kissy set up.

Ruth's appearance was not very changed from the last time Kissy had seen her, ten days earlier. Ruth's joints had been flexed, limbs withered and stiffened, despite regular physical therapy, her face fixed too, expression frozen in permanent stony blankness, for some time. It was the continued rise and fall of her chest that had been extraordinary, as if a statue had suddenly taken a breath. In this last photographic session the Prashkers were permitting, Kissy tried to summon up some feeling, even of relief, but there was nothing there beyond curiosity at her own void of emotion. It would show in the last photographs, she thought. That was not wrong. She had not been engaged in revealing appropriate sentiments, only what was.

There was grief among the survivors, but after so long a time of waiting, it was diffused and there was undisguised relief. And gratitude for the tasks at hand, the business of notification, arrangement, ritual. While everyone was preoccupied, Dynah made her own curious survey of the goings-on and of the room where the body lay. On tiptoe she crept to the bed and stared at Ruth's dead face a moment until Kissy looked up from changing film and saw her there. When she drew her quietly away, Dynah went willingly enough but her eyes were troubled.

On the ride home, she told Dynah the story she had told her several times over the years, when Dynah was curious about her relationship with Ruth. She had always edited it as seemed appropriate for Dynah's age. Dynah had it straight now, that Ruth was not Esther, but the tale of sudden death and coma, of a long struggle for release, was unavoidably disturbing to her. It evoked her confused memories of her grandmother's sudden death and was complicated with the knowledge that Daddy had had a bad accident and people said—Casey was very insistent about it—that Daddy had died. Dynah was struggling with the concept of death, of cessation, and how it could come to one person with great and sudden finality and to another as a long sleep from which there was no wakening and yet another person could die and be brought back to life.

"Ruth was like the princess in the story," Kissy told her, "the one who pricked her finger and slept for a hundred years."

"Only she didn't wake up," Dynah concluded.

"That's right. She didn't wake up."

"Will she come back someday?"

Kissy shook her head. "I don't know. Lots of people in the world believe we do come back, to live other lives."

"I'm going to," Dynah said. "And you'll come back and be my mom and Daddy will come back and be Daddy."

Kissy did not have the heart to disabuse her.

Mike had gone to the office. Once Dynah had been read to sleep—she was clingy, understandably, in a new environment after a week's separation from her mother—Kissy dug out the Ruth material and pin-mounted it on the wall of her new darkroom. It included the snapshot Mrs. Cronin had given her of Ruth as an infant, and later family pictures she had copied from the family albums—Ruth as a child, Ruth's school pictures, Ruth in her high school prom gown. Latest were work prints of her last visits. She reversed the chronology, going backward in time to the first weeks of Ruth's coma and then before the accident. At the end, the infant Ruth looked at her from wide, startled eyes. Kissy touched the infant lips with her fingertips and was, at last, clenched with grief.

COMA VICTIM DIES bannered the leader on the lower fold of the *News*. And at the bottom of the front-page column under Ruth's high school graduation portrait, bold letters announced ADDITIONAL CHARGE AGAINST CONVICTED DRUNK DRIVER. Ruth Prashker's death meant a new charge of manslaughter would be filed against James Houston, Jr. If convicted of the death of Ruth Prashker, Houston could receive an equal or greater sentence.

By the time Kissy saw the paper, Mike had already left

the house for an early visit to the Y. First day back, it was going to be a tough day. And indeed, she did not see him again until nearly eleven. He let himself in the front door and went straight into the living room, where he unlocked the liquor cabinet.

"Are you really going to indict Jimmy Houston again?" Kissy asked from the doorway.

Mike looked up from pouring his drink. "I'm not going to do it—the grand jury is." He stirred the red-amber fluid in the glass with his forefinger and then sucked at the finger. "I am, however, going to prosecute it."

"Isn't that a conflict? You were a witness."

"As a cop. An officer of the court. I'm still acting as an officer of the court. I haven't changed sides. Butch is okay with it."

"What's going to happen? Another trial?"

Mike downed half his drink. He closed his eyes and rolled his shoulders, as if trying to shed some invisible burden. "I'd be surprised if there were." He looked at her. "You shouldn't have to testify again."

"I wasn't thinking about that. What's going to happen to him?"

With an irritable clink of bottle against rim, Mike topped his glass. "He's going to get another ten years and in all probability he'll still be alive at the end of it, which is more than you can say for Ruth." She didn't say anything but he grew angrier for some reason and glared at her. "I don't need this, Kissy. I need to be able to come home and talk about my work to you and especially about how I feel about it, because I can't do this job with my feelings in the way. I have to deal with them on my own time. I need you to be the safe person I can spill them to. What I don't need is you dumping your feelings on me about any case of mine. Don't ask me to feel sorry for this asshole—or any other asshole whose file winds up on my desk. It's just going to bitch us up. Do you understand?"

He knew he was being heavy-handed. She could see it in his twitching hand, the sweat on his upper lip. She gave him a tight nod and went upstairs. Dynah was asleep in their bed. She had to move her.

A little while later he followed her into the bedroom to apologize. He was tired. The pricks at the office had diverted all the shit to his desk while he was gone. When he began to kiss and fondle her, she was unresponsive but he kept on going, though he had a difficult time of it. Any attempt to help from her only made him angry. And being angry, he could do it.

He attended Ruth's memorial service with her. Junior was there too, and came up and took her hand and kissed her lips lightly and said he was sorry again. And Mike clutched her other arm tensely the whole time as if she were going to run away from him. She resented not only his insecurity and possessiveness but the draining of her energy into resentment, the negative emotional state that made her feel ill. In fact, she wondered if she was ill—bitten by some virus, some bug, there was always one going around.

Mike called her from work a few days later to tell her that as he had expected there would be no trial—Houston was going to plead and ask for immediate sentencing. And in due course she watched a nightly TV news broadcast in which Jimmy Houston, in an ill-fitting suit and with his hair shorn tight to his skull, went into the courthouse between two state troopers to enter his plea and be sentenced. He looked older, as she expected, but it still made her feel a little light-headed. She hadn't seen him since the day he went to prison. It was like looking at an old sepia print of some long-dead ancestor and recognizing her daughter's face.

The judge handed down another ten years but made it concurrent—meaning, the newscaster on the courthouse steps explained, the time already served counted against it.

"Was it a deal?" she asked Mike when he got home and was making himself a drink.

"Nope. He pled guilty, period, and threw himself on the mercy of the court. The judge liked his prison record—" Mike laughed.

Kissy gave him a quizzical look.

"He was premed, remember?" Mike's eyes glittered with amusement. "Did some nursing courses before he went in too—he's not stupid, you know. They put him to work as a practical nurse in the prison hospital. Last three years he's been nursing prisoners with AIDS." Mike shook his head in wonderment. "Volunteered for it—anyway, Judge Durand thought that was above and beyond evidence of remorse. With all the good time he's accumulated, he'll be out in another six, nine months." Kissy didn't say anything. Mike grabbed her and pulled her into his lap and kissed her. "Much ado about nothing."

Mike's house was severely lacking as far as Dynah was concerned. It did not have a big-screen TV with a satellite feed. Or a swimming pool or a gym or an indoor ice rink, like Daddy's. Her dollhouse was at Daddy's because her new bedroom under the eaves was too small and low-ceilinged to accommodate it. She had to ride a different bus to a new school. The neighborhood was strange, not a real neighborhood at all, but a house here and a house there and all of them isolated in their patch of creepy woods. The unpaved driveway was all bumpy under the wheels of her skateboard, the nearest kids her age a pair of brothers who didn't like girls—they must be fags, she told them, and then Kissy.

"That's an ugly word," Kissy said. "Where did you pick that up?"

"Daddy says Latham is a fag, and I asked what a fag was and he said a boy who doesn't like girls."

"A lot of boys go through a phase of not liking girls," Kissy explained. "Latham's my friend. It's rude to talk about whom people sleep with. Okay?"

"Yeah." Dynah's mouth was down, her eyes unhappy.

"You're not going to call anyone a fag anymore?"

Dynah shrugged. "Okay. I guess Darren and Shane are just flaming assholes—"

"Dynah!" Kissy made a mental note to speak to Junior about his language around Dynah.

Not that language was the only problem. There was bedtime. Dynah whined and cried and threw tantrums on a scale unequaled since she was two. She screamed that she hated Mike's house and her new bedroom and she wanted Daddy. And then, in the night, she would come weeping to Kissy and Mike's bed. And get in between them.

Mike wanted to lock the bedroom door. Kissy rejected the idea vehemently. He backed down quickly, suggesting they could lock Dynah's door.

"Don't be an idiot," Kissy said, hearing the shrillness in her own voice with dismay. In honesty to herself she had to admit it was a relief to have Dynah there, a comfort. It made her uneasy to know she was using her child to desexualize her marriage bed, but lovemaking had become a trial and a sore point. She had made every excuse—the pressure of her leaving Junior, excessive honeymoon expectations, the adjustment of living together—but more often than not, Mike could not sustain an erection. She had had her expectations, built on her memory of their first encounter. He drank much more than she had realized and undoubtedly that was a factor. There was something amiss with her too—guilt, she guessed. She did not sleep any better than he did, with Dynah in their bed, and her head ached all the time from the unsatisfactory rest.

He threw up his hands. "You deal with it."

Junior had Dynah on weekends and also picked her up after school three days out of five for swimming. He fed her supper on those days and then brought her home close to bedtime. At Dynah's insistence, he had to stay and put her to bed—and then she went angelically. Kissy bent over backward to make Dynah accessible to him, for Dynah's sake. It seemed natural to have him around at bedtime, putting Dynah to bed. Too natural. It troubled her that it was Mike who felt like an interloper, an extra wheel, even to her.

Though not at home until after Dynah's bedtime most nights, Mike was aware Junior was in the house, and he seemed always to call during that time period, supposedly to let her know he was going to be late. He fumed about it, letting his jealousy show. Maybe it also was something to be expected, but he had known she had a child and could not dispute it was in Dynah's best interest to maintain her relationship with Junior. The time would come when Junior would go away, Kissy reasoned; things would be different. Making adjustments was just part of the process for all of them.

One night while Junior was tucking in Dynah, Mike called to say he would be late.

"Mike says good-night," Kissy told Dynah, coming in to kiss her. He hadn't, really, but he was always working so hard to finish and get home.

Dynah made a face. Junior laughed.

He followed Kissy downstairs. "Fuckhead working late? I feel safer already—"

"Don't call him that, please—"

"I could use a beer, you got one—"

She went into the kitchen and took one out of the refrigerator and handed it to him. Junior right behind her.

"Thanks." He spun off the cap. "I could use some sugar too."

"Go home. The sugar bowl's empty." And it was. The last time she had felt anything resembling sexual desire was with Junior the night she told him she was leaving, and there had been more of desperation in it than anything else. She had been through a phase like this—an absence and a numbness and a kind of disgust—before, in the months following the abortion she had had at fifteen, and again in the first six months of her pregnancy with Dynah.

He grinned and leaned against the counter, picking contemplatively at the label on the bottle. "She swam like a dolphin today. We should think about a private school with a top-notch swim program. These public schools suck. She's bored out of her mind."

"So you're giving her extracurricular lessons in gay-bashing and locker room language—"

He laughed.

"I don't want her calling people fags and assholes—"

"Fuck me raw, baby, she hears those words in the school yard—"

"But not from me and not from you—"

Junior shrugged. "All right. I won't call people fags in front of her. I reserve my right to call anybody an asshole who is one—"

"Asshole," Kissy said.

He grinned, refusing to be insulted. "I love it when you talk that way. I almost called you the other night—had a few beers in me and I was horny as a rat, I wanted you to talk dirty to me over the phone but I didn't know if Fuck—excuse me, Mr. Wonderful was out making the world safe for scum or at home in the bosom of my wife—"

"Go home," she said.

"Come with me." He slipped an arm around her waist. "Or come with me right here. We don't need to be home."

She walked out of his arm to the door and flung it open. "Good night, Junior."

He handed her the beer bottle and kissed her neck. "Call me if you need anything."

∾ 30 ∾

Dynah rose on the last day of school from a sound night's sleep between Kissy and Mike. She sang loudly in the bathroom and dressed herself in exuberant clashing colors. She hopped and jumped down the stairs and skateboarded into the kitchen.

Mike confiscated the board and put it on top of the refrigerator, telling her, "Skateboards belong outdoors, honey."

Throwing herself into a chair, Dynah shot him a poisonous glare.

Mike looked at Kissy, who merely cocked an eyebrow. Rattling the paper, he took a long irritation inhalation before dropping his gaze to the headlines. The coffeemaker huffed and hissed, signaling the pot was ready.

Dynah jumped up. "I'll get your coffee, Mike," she announced.

She sashayed to the coffeemaker, filled Mike's mug, closed two hands around it, and minced gingerly to the table. At Mike's elbow, she suddenly tripped and, with a theatrical little cry, spilled the hot coffee into his lap.

Mike reacted predictably.

Dynah spun about to shriek at Kissy. "Mike said fuck! He said fuck!"

"All right, Dynah, I'm not deaf," Kissy told her, and ducked Mike's shirt as he flung it at her.

While Mike was changing his suit, Dynah dumped his briefcase on the floor and stomped the papers like grapes.

"Kissy!" Mike roared.

She came running from the laundry room where she had been rinsing coffee from the shirt. Mike was crawling around the kitchen floor, muttering swear words and gath-

ering up scattered files. Outside there was a crash of glass
breaking. They rushed to the doorway. Dynah was racing
for the school bus pulling up at the corner. The windshield
of the BMW hung in a web of shards and there was a good-
size rock caught like a fly in it. Dynah stared at them im-
passively from the back window of the bus as it wheezed
into motion again. She held up a rigid middle finger.

And not for the first time, Kissy wondered if Dynah
really was Junior's kid, if somehow Junior's germ plasm
had gotten homogenized with Jimmy's.

"Jesus Christ," Mike said, despairingly near tears.

"You're late." Kissy thrust the keys of the Blazer on him
and watched him rush away.

Junior thought it was the funniest thing he had ever
heard. "Just for the amusement value, I'll pay for the
windshield."

"Be serious a minute. Tell me you're not filling her up
with a lot of Mike-is-the-devil."

"I never mention Fuckhead's name, baby," Junior said.
"If she's pissed at him, maybe it's got something to do
with him breaking up her family—"

"Blame me if you have to blame somebody. What matters here is Dynah—"

"What I've been telling you since you went nuts on me—"

"This is our life now, Junior, she has to come to terms
with it—"

"Give her to me," he said. "I'm going to be here until
camp starts. I can take care of her—"

"We'll just be starting at go in August—"

"Baby, you can always come home, you come with her
and I promise you, she'll settle right down."

Kissy hung up and leaned against the wall, both fists
clenched. He wasn't going to help her, the bastard wasn't
going to help her one bit. She wiped her eyes and blew her
nose. Fuck you, Junior, she decided. She was overreacting.
Just like Dynah. This was going to take some patience,
maybe a lot of patience. Patience and consistency. Dynah
would have to make an apology to Mike. The skateboard
was off the road for a month minimum.

"Can't you for Christ's sake get her out of our bed?"
Mike said on hearing this plan. "I would sincerely like to

get laid again sometime without being terrified she's going to walk in on us."

"All right. We can lock the door, just for that," agreed Kissy, "but the rest of the time the door has to stay unlocked. The worst thing I could do now is literally lock her out."

Mike rolled his eyes. "She used to like me. What happened?"

"You know what happened. You took Daddy's place."

He nodded wearily. The last time he had found Dynah asleep with Kissy, he hadn't even bothered to move her. He had slept in the guest room.

Next day he came home with a fishbowl and a plastic bag of bright orange goldfish. Dynah sniffed. At bedtime, when Kissy came to tuck her in, she was sitting in front of the bowl, watching the fish closely. They hung in the water for long moments, and then, like little orange semaphores, darted and flickered.

"They're stupid," Dynah said. "All they do is swim around. They're fucking stupid."

"You're being rude." Kissy took out Dynah's pajamas and handed them to her. "Mike gave you a gift. Even if you don't want a gift or you think it's stupid, it's only polite to say thank you."

"It's a lie. I'm not thankful. I'm not supposed to tell lies. I don't want those stupid fucking fish and I'm not going to tell Mike thank you." She kicked a sneaker across the room. "Fuck him raw."

"Stop talking like that—"

"I want Daddy!" Dynah's voice shook. Her face reddened. She fell to her knees and grabbed Kissy around the legs. Taking great gulping sucks of air between the words, she wailed, "I-want-my-Daddy!"

Junior had sweated away most of June, as he had the weeks since his return, in skating and conditioning. He was as strong as he had ever been. At least working himself into exhaustion every night channeled his restlessness. His mind was clear; he knew if he was going to come back, he had to live in a state of permanent training. He was still taking the antidepressant, which he was sure was the only reason he was sleeping. To what degree the drug affected his emotions he couldn't be sure, but he did notice that when a big black hole opened up underneath him—a fairly regular event—and he fell in, he also climbed out rapidly, and with the sense that a short crying binge was a reasonable reaction to the shocks of the past few months. He wasn't supposed to drink while using the antidepressant and mostly he didn't—boozing wasn't compatible with serious training either. The drug lowered his tolerance, he noticed, made him a cheap drunk. Couple beers and he was on his ass. Every time he had to bring Dynah back to Kissy, he thought about suing for full custody, and gritted his teeth with the unspoken vow that he would be a monk if that was what it took to persuade a judge he was competent.

It drove him half crazy to go into the house Kissy shared with Fuckhead. She was everywhere in it and that was bad enough, because she was forbidden territory now. Or he was persona non grata, in exile from her. It was also wrong, and not just because of Fuckhead's spoor. It was fundamentally wrong because he was on the outside of it, and subtly wrong for the change it represented in Kissy. She was a stranger in it, a stranger to him, a stranger to Dynah. She had placed a stranger in the middle of their lives.

He insisted she and Dynah take the cottage for the last two weeks of June and all of July. He would have it and Dynah the first three weeks of August. Kissy was inclined to go along because it was what Dynah was used to doing. What Junior liked best about it was that the place was too far away to allow Mike Burke to commute, nor could he get more than two weeks off to be with them, what with having taken a week of vacation time to honeymoon. Among Burke's tribe, Junior thought, a summer cottage was a signal of status and so was being too overworked to actually use it with the wife and kids. So the family fucked off to the lake most of the summer and the workaholic yuppie pricks stayed in town and reverted to their college days, playing pickup basketball in the evenings before they hit the bars for a few drinks and to hustle some extramarital snatch. Junior also guessed the thought of six weeks without Dynah had its own appeal to Mike Burke. Of course, Fuckhead would do some tossing and turning, wondering if Junior Clootie was at home in Peltry or had snuck away to the cottage.

McDonough threw a big Fourth of July barbecue Kissy had to stay in town to attend, and then she was going to take Dynah to the cottage.

"I miss you too," Dynah said. She covered the receiver and raised her face, alight with excitement, to Kissy. "Daddy wants to come up and spend the day—"

Kissy took the phone.

"I thought I'd come up Saturday and you could have a day off—go shooting by yourself or into town if you wanted—and Dynah and I could just hang together—"

Dynah clung to her, "Please, please—"

"All right," Kissy conceded. "Just the day."

The gravel of the drive rattled and rolled under the wheels of the Benz at six. No motor—Junior had coasted down the hill so as not to wake them. But they had the jump on him. They were already getting into their bathing suits, to begin the day with a swim.

"Daddy!" Dynah squealed, and bolted downstairs to throw herself into his arms.

Kissy took her time, pulling a T-shirt over her tank. Downstairs, Dynah was riding Junior's shoulders and whooping while he turned in circles on the lawn. Kissy let him brush a kiss onto her lips and then went back inside to start coffee.

Junior stuck his head in at the kitchen door. "Hitting the water, babe?"

"Uh-huh."

"May I join you?"

"Of course."

With the shucking of his T-shirt, he was ready, in the baggy shorts he'd worn up from town. The scar on his throat was obvious but not horrible.

"You look good," Kissy said, regretting the fact as much as she immediately regretted saying it aloud.

"Takes a long time to come back." He flexed strongly. He swept Dynah off her feet again to shrieks of delight. "Now I am strooong."

With Junior sporting a few yards away with Dynah, Kissy savored a few moments in the water to herself, undistracted with watching her child. Sheerly and insistently sensual, the cool caress of the medium, bearing her up, holding her—it always made her grateful to have a body, to be able to feel consciously. Dynah dove from Junior's shoulders and shot off through the water. And Junior rolled, arm rising and driving forward, head lowered, in one smooth motion into a powerful stroke. He disappeared beneath the surface. Kissy turned on her back to let the early light warm her face. And she felt Junior like a current beneath her and then beside her, as he broke the surface. He rolled over, hand falling on her opposite hipbone, and drew her down below the surface. They sank quietly, looking at each other with open eyes, hair raised by the water in soft feathery spurts. He caught his legs in hers and she kicked free and went topside in one quick thrust. And he was still down there, his hands closing on her hips, his face suddenly between her legs, a feathery sensation that might have been the current or his tongue flickering in the hollow of one thigh. Gasping, she twisted away. He came up grinning. She rolled away and toward Dynah. He never gave up. Let him within tongue distance and he would give it a try. And grin whatever the result.

Once out of the water, he volunteered to cook breakfast. Toad in the Hole, Dynah demanded, meaning an egg fried in a hole in a piece of bread. One of the highlights of the dish was the privilege of cutting out the hole with a glass.

When Kissy came back downstairs, barefoot in dry T-shirt and shorts, he wanted to know what she was going to do with the day.

"Thought I'd take some pictures of you and Dynah," she said.

"I miss that." He had taken up using a point-and-shoot to take pictures of Dynah occasionally. Dynah used it to take pictures of him too, but sometimes there wasn't anybody else to take pictures of the two of them. "Oh, I've got a check for you."

He paid child support directly into a bank account. After their divorce, their finances had gone through the same reconciliation as they had and once again had had to be separated. It was an exercise Junior resented. He found money counting boring to start, and then the whole business reinforced the reality that Kissy had left him, for Mike, taking Dynah with her. Having prided himself on his openhandedness to her, he resented the lawyers and accountants formulating what he ought and had to do, which seemed to imply he could not be trusted to do it. Since

Kissy would not take the house or cottage, Junior had settled half their value on her, half of all the rest of their assets, which, in fact, existed largely as a result of his
earnings. Though she had done some investing for him—
good job too. She didn't want any of it; he had to threaten
to give her shit over the custody arrangement to make her
take it. She glanced at the check—her half of the dividends
from a mutual fund—and slipped it into her checkbook.
Their financial affairs were going to be entangled for the
foreseeable future. Which was what Junior wanted.

Having cut the holes in the bread, Dynah was outside
again, dumping the box of cans and bowls and buckets and
other household utensils that were castle-building tools,
on the sand.

"How's she doing?" he asked as he broke an egg into
one of the frames of bread. "You know, she acted up with
me too. Sometimes I couldn't do anything right. She had
me but she didn't have you and she was still frustrated. I
thought I understood what it was like for you to be a single
parent when I was away but—"

Dynah burst in and jumped on him. He caught her by
the waist and boosted her one-handed up onto the kitchen
counter.

"That's not true," he said, "what I just said. I knew all
along."

Having thrown off the confession like a pebble skipped
across the water, he turned his attention to Dynah and
breakfast. They had made plans over the phone—sand
castling and lots of water time, a game of hearts, a dress-
up dinner at a local inn. For Dynah that meant spiking her
hair like Kissy's, belting an oversized purple T-shirt over
yellow leggings, and wearing several multicolored plastic
bracelets. She wanted to pierce her ears but he and Kissy
were still holding the line.

"You're invited," he told Kissy.

"Sounds like fun."

"I'd like to stay over, take you both to Sunday brunch
too. I've got a room at the inn for tonight."

Dynah was too happy and excited to turn it down. Kissy
figured she had better save her no for his next come-on.
She was playing with fire, and didn't kid herself that she
didn't feel a little warmth from the flame. Bemused, she

resorted to busywork, checking batteries in a flash. Junior looked good all right. Like staring into the sun.

She kept him at the end of the camera lens all morning, while he and Dynah sported on the beach and in the water. After they had a picnic lunch on the beach, she flopped down in the shade. The heat and the food in her tummy had the usual soporific effect. She was half asleep when he bent over her and kissed her. It was so light at the start she thought she must be dreaming and then it got serious. She opened her eyes and turned her head hastily and his tongue tickled her ear.

"Stop," she murmured.

Dynah hadn't noticed. She was intent on the elaborate castle under construction.

"Couldn't help it." Junior grinned. He squatted next to her, plucking at the sand with his fingers. The grin faded. "I've been really angry at you sometimes. But I know it was my fault."

"No," she said, struggling against the brilliance of the light, the weight of the heated air, the sleepiness dragging her down. "No."

Dynah sprawled loose-limbed in the backseat on the drive back from dinner, in the soundly exhausted sleep that rewarded a day in the sun. Her skin was dusted with gold like pollen on apple petals.

"Thanks," Kissy told Junior. "It's been a lovely day." She meant it. A lovely reproach of a day. She didn't suppose it was possible to compose a life of such days, but she was grateful to have the one.

The phone was ringing as he carried Dynah into the cottage. Kissy picked it up. A few moments later, when he came downstairs, she was loading iced tea glasses from a late-afternoon snack into the dishwasher.

"Mr. Wonderful?"

She didn't like the term but it beat Fuckhead. She closed the dishwasher and punched it on. "Uh-huh."

They moved toward each other simultaneously. She closed her eyes and let it happen. Let him take her upstairs. His fingers groped for Mike's rings on her hand and gently took them off. She rested her brow against the scar on his throat and felt his heart beating through it, the quickening of his blood. The dishwasher churned the whole time,

sighing and whooshing and throbbing. She couldn't deny it
felt like coming home, like she had escaped some strange
house where nothing was where it was supposed to be,
nothing worked very well, some chilly, isolated, snowed-
in place. He wasn't Mike. She was glad of it and agonized
with guilt and sick at heart she had done this to herself, and
she hated Mike for leaving her in need of Junior. Knowing
she did not love Mike, she had not expected it would be so
difficult to *like* him, to understand him, to make a partner-
ship with him, without love. With Junior, she had been the
goose girl touching the goose, stuck to him like glue.

"You can't stay overnight," she told him, hunting her
rings among the sweaty tangled sheets. "It's too confusing
for Dynah."

"Me too," he said. "I've checked in at the inn and
there's a do-not-disturb on the phone and the room. Mr.
Wonderful was still in town as of forty minutes ago and
it's a three-hour run—" He nuzzled her ear. "I have to tell
you something—"

"What?"

"I'm in love with a married woman—"

She poked him in the armpit and he rolled onto his side,
shaking with laughter. When she came back from the bathroom, he was on his back.

"You've never told me anything about you and Mr.
Wonderful," he said. "You didn't pick his name out of the
phone book. You must have had some kind of thing with
him but I've wracked my brains and I never felt a false
moment—"

"Why do you want to know?"

"I don't know exactly. Maybe I need to know how big a
chump I was."

She turned on her back and stared at the ceiling. "You
weren't a chump." There was a constriction in her throat
that kept her from adding *"I was."*

He sat up and she turned her head to look at him. "I was
an asshole," he said. "It was my fault. I did something or I
didn't do something I should have. Don't tell me it was
getting my throat cut. That made you crazy, but there had
to be something before it that pointed you at Fuckhead. I
know I left you alone too much—"

"It just happened. What's done is done. I can't change it

now. I have to make it work. I made a promise. It has to be this way."

Then she turned onto her side. She heard him sigh and waited for him to say she had made the same promise to him, first, but he didn't. He tucked himself up against her. He told her how much he loved her and that he always would, and would always be there. As her thoughts floated toward sleep, it came to her he had always had what he wanted and maybe this too—not just her going to bed with him but her marriage to another man—would make it easier for him to pursue his career. The thing he loved more than anything else, even when it rose up and tore his throat out.

"Did you sleep with him?" It was Mike, at five-thirty the next morning. She had picked up on the first ring. She dropped the receiver into the cradle, glanced at the clock, and pulled the pillow over her head. The linen was fresh; she had changed it as soon as Junior left. She had stayed up to wash and dry it and get it back into the linen closet. Late-night laundry, the wages of sin, she thought ruefully.

He rang back five minutes later. "I'm sorry. I can't help it. You were with him a long time. Don't tell me he doesn't hit on you."

She didn't say anything.

"I think I can get Friday off, come up Thursday night," he said. "Or should I just fuck off?"

"I'm thinking about it."

Something came up Thursday but he got away at Friday noon and was at the cottage by four. Tense and tired, dark shadows under his eyes. "I didn't sleep real well this week. Must have missed Dynah climbing in with us." He took a couple of beers out onto the beach, and Kissy put Dynah to work setting the table for supper and followed him out. She sat down on the chaise next to him. He looked at her tiredly. "I only have a little work with me. We'll have a nice weekend."

His eyes flickered away from her, toward the lake. He fell silent. The smell of the beer hung in the air like bad breath. He was miserable and it was her fault.

She guessed Junior had been right; for a little while, she had been crazy. As Dynah couldn't cope with the idea of death and turned instinctively to reincarnation as a compensation, she herself did not have the courage to love anyone other than Dynah anymore, and about her child she had no choice. She thought she understood for the first time, watching Junior dying on the ice, what the real meaning was of the stained-glass images in the window of the Sowerwine chapel—the rearing horse, the skeleton being thrown. The white horse was not Life, the skeleton not Man falling into Death. The name of the white horse was Death, and it was the bones of Love, which went ironically, pointedly, naked of flesh, that it threw down. The fact remained she had made a mess of it. She had disrupted Dynah's life and changed Mike's and she couldn't go back on it. And why should she? It wasn't as if Junior was going to be there, waiting for her, at home.

It wouldn't happen again, she promised herself. Junior would be off to camp and she would have the winter to work at making a marriage and a baby with Mike. She owed him that. Maybe Junior would meet somebody. Or already had and would pick it up again and find out how quickly a girlfriend could convert an affair into an engagement and then a marriage.

She went up to bed before Mike. He stumbled on the stairs. If she hadn't been able to smell the whiskey he had started drinking after supper, she could have read the state he was in by the jerky clumsy effort of his disrobing. He dropped heavily onto his back on the bed next to her and caught his breath and then he rolled onto her with the same heaviness. The shadows in the room barred his face and his eyes were in darkness but she could see his mouth, loose with drink and desperation, as it descended to hers.

"What did you expect? All I can think about is him being here—"

"He came to see Dynah—"

"And try to fuck you."

She got out of bed and went into the bathroom. She was spitting mouthwash into the basin when he came to the doorway.

"It's been driving me bugshit all week," he said. "I'm sorry—"

"I'm married to you," she said, glancing into the mirror. "I left him for you."

Mike nodded but he didn't look as if her words were

much consolation. He was a lawyer; he knew she had not denied sleeping with her ex-husband.

She would not say anything more to him. She wanted to pack up Dynah and leave. Only guilt kept her there. She reached for her toothbrush. Her hand was shaking. He watched her a moment and then went back to bed. She brushed her teeth and washed her face and moisturized it. She had lost weight, bone had come forward, making her look older—nose thinner, eyes set deeper, flesh less taut. Not like Ruth, really, but making her think of Ruth. The way she had faded. She had to take care of herself, she thought. Junior was always telling her that.

∽ 31 ∽

On the first of August Junior moved into the cottage with Dynah and Kissy went back to Peltry. Dynah cried over the phone, wanting her to come back. She returned to the cottage for the second Saturday and did not get back to Peltry until two in the morning. Mike was still awake, waiting for her. Silent, staring, hurt, more than a little drunk—but waiting. He put his arms around her and held her and with his eyes closed, inhaled deeply. Smelling her. Was she too scrubbed, too fresh from the shower that like a profane baptism washed away the evidence? He went to his knees, face to her stomach, as if to beg, and wept.

She should leave him. But she quailed more than a little. She knew Mike quite a lot better now, and most of what she had learned suggested he would be as much of a bastard to leave as he was to live with. At other moments, she could not bring herself to care about the mess she was in. It was her work that mattered, and Dynah; it was probably ridiculous and spoiled to expect more than what she had. And then, she was a grown-up, she had done this to herself and must somehow make it come out right.

As in a half-forgotten memory, she saw herself framed in the windows of a glassed-in porch. She could hear her own muffled shouts of anger, the ones caught inside her now. She stood flat and brittle and translucent, tensed against the blow, the breakage, the disintegration. Moonlight the color of a white horse filled everything in a blur to the tops of the black-leafed trees and flooded her like an X ray, a flash of spectral light, casting her bones like a shadow, an augury, upon the floor.

* * *

Nothing was ever what you built it up to be, Mike Burke told himself. He had had to stop himself from busting her face for her. She admitted it was thoughtless, if not outright provocative, to come in so late. She slung bullshit about not leaving until eleven because they were playing Hearts and Dynah hadn't wanted to quit and the three-hour drive. She promised she would never do that again. Given he wanted to believe her, he cautioned himself against gullibility, but there was no real evidence. He was in a bind—if she was doing it, she was making him look like a fool, and if she wasn't, then he would look like a jealous asshole.

When he told her he wanted to have a dinner party, have Butch and Narcissa and some people from the office in, she cocked an eyebrow like a dog cocking its leg.

"What's the menu, cannibal stew?"

He snorted laughter. "Very funny. It's as necessary to receive guests, and receive them well, as to be one—"

"Not for me it isn't—"

"All I'm asking is for you to hire a goddamn caterer if you can't be bothered cooking, and wear something appropriate and not be a bitch—"

"Hire a goddamn caterer yourself, Mike, and wear a yellow ribbon on your dick—"

One of those times he could swear she *wanted* a black eye. The least he should have for his heroic restraint in not giving her one was the goddamn dinner party, and he said so. Eventually she did one for him, and it was exceptional, all her own cooking served by a willowy young thing from the Art School, ring in the wrong ear—Mike had had a moment of alarm when he first saw him, wondering if she was going to pull some stunt, have them waited on by a faggot in a mask and a cock ring. But no, it was very sedate, pleasant, and Kissy managed to keep a lock on her lip all evening. She looked fabulous too—maybe a little too much tit on view. Butch could hardly look anywhere else, and Narcissa was enraged.

"Next time, wear something a little more discreet, okay?" he told Kissy.

"Next time take them all out to a fucking restaurant," she said, and flung the dress into the trash can.

With enormous forbearance, he retrieved it and hung it up. Somebody had to be a grown-up.

* * *

Marriage was an even greater adjustment than Mike Burke had expected. They were very different people to start. Her taste was flamboyant, exotic, eclectic, and cluttered; he liked everything in its place. With years of living by himself, he had his habits deeply ingrained. And Kissy had hers. And had been spoiled, undeniably spoiled, by money and an indulgent, absentee husband. She liked to work late at night, so even when he worked late, she was not in bed when he got home, and quite often was still working when he rose. She turned down the corners of pages in books to mark her place and left them spread open on their bellies so their spines broke. She had no discretion about personal hygiene, leaving her box of tampons right out on the top of the toilet tank. She bleached and colored her own hair, and the chemical stench made his eyes water and stuffed up his sinuses and made the house smell like somebody was running a ticky-tacky little home beauty salon with a cutesey-poo name.

He needed his space and he got everything arranged that way—his space, her space, the kid's space—and she and Dynah just ignored it, like they couldn't see it, couldn't see the boundaries. If they did not have a woman coming in to clean, part-time, the place would be a minefield of photographic equipment and Dynah's kid-junk—tripods and skateboards and Dynah's kid-junk—tripods and skateboards and Dynah-size hockey sticks and rollerblades and hockey skates—all vaguely hostile, edges and points and loose strapping like traps. Kissy and his mother had disliked each other at first sight. Now that she was his wife, Kissy reacted to reasonable suggestions and hints from his mother about housekeeping and child-rearing with dead silence or amused laughter, and once, a cheerful "Oh, fuck off, Margarite."

She was entirely too free and easy with her language around Butch or his other associates. Fuck this and fuck that might be the lingua franca at the Art School, but it was just potty-mouth from the lips of the wife of an assistant DA. It made her sound slutty or as if she had had too much to drink. She blew off social engagements without apology—once she showed up late at a barbecue at Butch's in raggedy Levi's and a short-sleeved chemical-stained T-shirt that showed she didn't shave her armpits.

Which he had gotten used to but made her look eccentric. Dykey.

Just lately she had gotten fascinated with nose rings—there was a whole series of work prints in her darkroom of teenagers with nose rings. With seven holes in one ear and three in the other, she was already far enough out, he told her. If he ever came home to discover she had had her nose pierced, he thought, he would break it for her. If she wanted to pierce something else, she had places where a ring or two would be kinky enough to do him some good.

And there was Dynah, from whom they had no privacy. The kid begrudged every bit of attention Kissy ever gave him, which was not goddamn much to start. He had never realized how hyperactive Dynah was when he saw her only occasionally. His mother thought the kid needed medication.

Burke had assumed that once Kissy was his wife, her ex-husband would be out of the picture, or at worst, a voice on the phone arranging kid swaps. Instead Clootie was a hellish presence, like greasy dog shit on his shoe, endlessly underfoot all summer—dropping the kid off or picking her up, having a beer or a cup of coffee waiting for her. The bastard bald-faced sat there in the kitchen of Mike Burke's home and flirted with Kissy in front of him.

Clootie had paid for a room the night he was at the cottage with Kissy and Dynah, but of course that didn't mean anything. Burke took to driving by Clootie's place to see if Kissy's Blazer was in the driveway, by his own house late at night when he was supposed to be working late, to see if Clootie's Harley or Benz was parked behind the Blazer. He checked the parking lot outside the Sowerwine Athletic Complex to see if the Blazer was there at the same time as one of Clootie's vehicles. He went through the clothes hamper, looking for changes of bedsheets, panties, sniffing all of it for semen, for sexual musk. He searched the darkroom and Kissy's files for recent negatives or prints of her ex-husband.

He thought about bugging the phones but it was too risky. Bugging someone without a court order was not only illegal, it was a firing offense and a career spoiler. He told himself she had to stay on some kind of terms with her ex-husband, who could make her life difficult over custody or child support and other financial issues.

Some of the other guys in the office checked out the summertime action but he refrained with a calculated restraint—who wants hamburger, he told them, when there was steak at home. Because if it wasn't steak he had at home, then he was one of them, another schmuck with his dick hostage to the little woman, the kiddies, and a mortgage. He had not waited as long as he had just to marry a paper-doll-chain woman. One of Kissy's appeals had been her indifference to convention—she was a challenging woman, an artist, more than any of them could satisfy or sort out. She would take some breaking and he would do it, one way or another. A baby would take up her time and energy, along with her body. Clootie would lose interest in her once she swelled up. Be good for Dynah too, to have a sib. He figured in a year or so, particularly with a baby in the house, he could persuade Kissy to let the kid go to Clootie, who could well afford to stick her in a boarding school or hire a nanny.

During his two weeks at the cottage, he banged Kissy—or he tried to—until she wore loose gauze cover-ups all day to hide the bruises on her thighs. She wanted it too—he couldn't help suspecting she was trying to prove something to him. It was the same when he got her home in August. No Dynah. He came home for lunch and they spent it in bed. He came home late and she was waiting for him.

"You want me and Grampa to pick you up and take you to the airport with me tonight?" Junior asked Dynah.

"All right," Dynah said with elaborate indifference. She slammed down her board and pushed off through the kitchen.

"She's not in a good mood," he told Kissy, who stayed by the door, waiting to close it on him.

"I noticed," she said curtly.

"And neither are you—"

"Go away, Junior," Kissy said, "you do it so well."

He reached out for her and she turned away from him.

"I don't want to leave like this—what's wrong?"

"Go away," she repeated, and walked away from him, following Dynah into the recesses of the house.

Junior packed automatically, brooding over the change in Kissy. She had come to the cottage again and they had

had a wonderful time and, after Dynah was asleep, made love again. And now she was furious with him, apparently because he was going away. *She* had left him, was living with and married to that fuckhead Burke, and *she* was pissed at him for going away. As he had for years. It was his job. What was he supposed to do? Retire at twenty-seven and spend the rest of his life trailing around after her like some Old Fart after The Wife?

As the plane caught the rise of the air and banked out of Peltry, Junior relaxed against the seat back. The plane was a door in a time machine between worlds. Step on in one world, step out in another. He shed Peltry easily, thinking of mythology he had read, some story of a bear casually stripping off his pelt and going bloody and naked, suddenly human, into the world of men. As he had savored everything since his near death and virtual resurrection, he lived these moments of transition with a new intensity. The emotions were all real—he really did hate leaving Dynah and Kissy, hated it especially this time, with Kissy angry at him—but this was his life and he had nearly lost it. It would be gross ingratitude to demand more than he had.

Camp too was part of his continuing return to life. The smell of the ice, water crystallized not into the delicate geometry of snowflakes but into another world that composed a radical topography, a moon-colored glacial plane as hard as bone and as cold as the moon looked, excited more than just the hairs inside his nose—it thrilled him. He breathed it in and made it his own. The click and clack of the stick and the puck, the scrape and swoosh of steel edge cutting ice, sang to him. He put on his gear that smelled like his own worn hide with the glee of a flayed bear finding his old skin. He could not help grinning and laughing.

The media were thick as maggots on a dead cat. He was the most revered cliché in the world of sport—the athlete on the comeback trail. He got to see a lot of his own face in print, on ESPN, with the livid scar on his throat and the plastic flap designed to deflect another skate blade at the bottom of his mask, a device he had always before declined to wear, trusting foolishly to a throat pad that had slipped at the only moment that mattered. It shook him a little; the scar looked longer and uglier and more dramatic than he remembered. He had not seen the replay of the accident before, and now it was an inevitable, unavoidable prelude to the TV coverage of his comeback. It fascinated him—was that really him?

He remembered something he had forgotten. At the instant it happened, he had lost the puck. *Where is it? Where's the puck?* He remembered the thought. He remembered a fraction of an instant's relief, as he saw darkness in the periphery of his vision, down low. It was underneath him. And then the realization that the darkness was growing, it had no edge, it was fluid, as if the puck had somehow melted. In the replay tape, he saw the puck, the only other darkness, a solitary little punctuation, in the frame as the camera closed on him, sinking to the ice. And then the replay entered his dreams. He began to cry out, on dream ice, in what in his dream was a dream replay— *Where is it? Where is it?* And see his blood flow over it, see it disappearing, become part of the darkness. But that was at night, in dreams, nightmares, and even in the dreams, he knew he was only dreaming.

He played with a hard-edged brilliance, as if dying had clarified everything he had ever learned about the game, and with more aggression, out fast to clear the puck, bravismo meeting breakaways. He called out to his teammates, hearing his own voice, his game voice, with wonder that it could still be heard at all. The Voice of the Turtle, he had phrased it to himself, the net the shell on his back, the padding and gear that thickened his body turning him, as Dynah had pointed out, into something like a Ninja Turtle. Ninja Goalie, she called him. *Thy rod and thy staff,* he amended in what was at first a private joke to *thy stick and thy puck,* but he found himself, as he tapped the posts to center himself, repeating it as a refrain, a mantra. *Thy stick and thy puck they comfort me.*

The Drovers had a new coach, Gunnie Ringgren, who had spent fourteen years polishing turds in the minors. All his focus was on The Game. He had never believed it was his job to baby-sit grown men. If a player had trouble at home, or got into trouble, it was his, the player's, lookout. Coach Ringgren had always told his players that a professional left his personal problems outside the arena. But in this, his rookie season as an NHL manager, he was dealing with franchise players for the first time, guys who were paid more than he was and knew it. Management had put together what should have been a good club, as far as the talent went, but it wasn't where they wanted it to be. In the playoffs, in other words. The loss of their million-dollar goalie the previous season had been disastrous in terms of the playoffs, though they were making up some of it in ticket sales this season, people coming to see the guy, back from the dead and all—add a little ghoulish resonance to the next time they watched their tape of the throat-cutting. Management wanted Clootie performing too. The goaltender had a super camp, which certainly augured well, but he gave Ringgren the spooks.

Gunnie had had a dream in which he had been on the ice again, himself, trying to shoot past Clootie—only the puck had passed directly through the goaltender and Gunnie could see it happening. It had been as if Clootie were transparent, a ghost, and then Gunnie had realized the ice was heavy, and looking down, saw he was skating on a plane of glistening red blood.

Gunnie had worked with his share of Russians and other Eastern Bloc players, and once you got it through their heads they had to work for the money, had to sweat, hit, and compete, this wasn't a Socialist league where you only played a game or two a week—in the NHL your Socialist Hero medal and seventy-five cents bought you a cup of bad arena coffee—then the ex-commies usually buckled down. But this one was a public relations nightmare.

At the start of any job, there was usually one nasty thing, some kind of purge or enema, you got handed. Management had made it clear Ringgren was going to take the starch out of the Russian's shorts or trade him. As a man for whom sex had always held a place of interest many leagues distant behind hockey, fly-fishing, baseball, bridge, and the novels of Louis L'Amour, except for one week when he was seventeen, Gunnie was mystified how to begin.

"What am I s'pposed to do, put a padlock on the guy's zipper?" Gunnie complained to his wife.

"Buttonflies," his wife said, "all the young people wear buttonflies now. Idle hands do the devil's work, Gunnie. The boy needs a hobby."

Gunnie called in the Russian.

"Look," he said, "this is an embarrassment, all these women suing you all the time. I know two thirds of 'm you never even met and they're just looking for the bucks—all the same, management's trying to sell this game as family entertainment. You prove you're a man with your stick and your fists, not your dick. This isn't the NBA with a bunch a cheerleaders in hot pants shaking their tatas and their moneymakers during halftime. This is a sport with some tradition. You're from away and all, you were young— seventeen was it?—when you defected, and I can see where a young guy could get his head turned a little. Now you need to concentrate on your game, put your energy into your game, not getting laid. You gotta have it that bad, why the hell don't you just get married, for pete's sake?"

"Hoot tried to be married," Deker pointed out, "even when she divorced him. Then his wife married some fuck-head. Many of the guys are divorced—"

"It's just screwing!" Ringgren shouted. "It ain't the be-all and end-all. Get some perspective on it, for pete's sake!" He shoved a beginner's fly-tying kit across his desk at Deker. "My wife says you need a hobby."

Deker examined the box. He thanked the coach politely. Feeling bad about his outburst, Coach added a fishing magazine with an article about places to fish.

Junior came upon Deker on a bench in the locker room, studying a fly-tying kit, a fishing magazine splayed open on the floor.

"Coach gave me this," Deker said. "What is be-all and end-all meaning, Hoot?"

"What really counts. Winning the Cup. Getting laid." It was out of Junior's mouth before he could reflect on the wisdom of putting it that way to Deker. He tried not to even think about either one, himself.

Deker sighed. "These are for fishing, yes?" he said, holding up several as yet undecorated fishhooks.

Junior confirmed they were.

Handling them gingerly, the Russian promptly pricked himself. "These are some sharp hooks. I have not fished myself."

"You better not," Junior said, "not with hooks like that. I guess the idea is you stand in a cold mountain stream up to your nuts and you're too numb to feel it when you hook yourself. Also you wear canvas pants. You going fishing with Gunnie?" Now that he thought about it, Deker freezing his nuts off up some trout stream might be one small step for mankind.

"I am getting a hobby," Deker said. "Coach's wife is telling him."

"Good." Junior patted him on the shoulder. "A man needs a hobby. How 'bout hitting the greens Saturday morning?"

Eighteen holes of golf could be multiplied into thirty-six, to fill up some of the afternoon, and there was always somebody up for Sunday too. It was a great old time-waster, he never cried like he used to in therapy, and he was getting good enough to compete in pro-am tournaments. He might even have a second career in golf after he retired from hockey. Sooner or later, though, he had to go home to the crooked little house he was still renting, that still smelled faintly of dead Fucking Cat. Or if on the road, to some hotel room.

For the first hour at home or wherever, it felt good just to be himself. Then he made his calls home. His real home. Peltry. And it didn't feel so great after that. He spent a lot of time looking in bathroom mirrors at the scar on his throat. Dynah had taped pictures of herself and Kissy over the bed in the crooked little house for him to close his eyes on every night. He had thought of bringing women there and knew he never could. Not when he opened his eyes on his daughter's gap-toothed grinning face.

It was in his contract that he could have a room by himself but on the road he had found himself a roomie, a Mormon named Waltrip. The Walrus didn't drink, smoke, or screw around on his wife, and was always willing to look for a putting green or a golf course. Wally was as good as a sleeping pill when he started droning on about the Church and the Book and Junior enjoyed an occasional theological tussle with him on the bus. Wally always promised solemnly to think over Junior's points. With a matching solemnity, Junior had worked his way through most of the Book of Mormon. Wally was all right. On the other hand, Wally had a very serious conscience and beat himself up a lot over every little pass or shot missed. On checking into a hotel, Wally also invariably found a channel with infomercials to watch. He had the mildly irritating habit of telling you the cuttingly witty and irrefutable remark he *should* have made at some critical juncture of his life, like when his useless brother-in-law brought back the lawn mower with the blades all chewed up, as if you gave a shit. But he wasn't a pig or anal, just a normal guy who maybe stank up the bathroom once in a while but was otherwise okay—not one of those guys who lived for fag jokes or short-sheeting your bed like it was fucking summer camp. And most important, he would be acutely embarrassed by any libertine lapses by Junior.

It was his life, Junior told himself, the life given back to him. Loneliness was part of it. Loneliness was winter to summer, the shadow to the light; it made him appreciate it when he wasn't lonely. When he started feeling sorry for himself because he was lonely, he knew it was time to go to the nearest pediatric cancer ward and visit some sick kids. He had to improvise. He guessed he had flunked out of therapy; Sarah had told him they had gone as far as he seemed to be willing to go. He wasn't being faithful to Kissy, she had said, he was being obsessive. He was tired of trying to figure out his own motivation. All he knew was he hadn't met another woman who made him feel the way Kissy did and he didn't even feel like looking.

His dad brought Dynah out for Thanksgiving. Not surprisingly, she fussed and sulked some about her mother not being there. Once he was alone again, he had to think about the change. Because he had gone away and come back so many times, it had been easy to pretend it hadn't happened. But this time, Kissy hadn't brought Dynah to be with him. When he went home at Christmas, Kissy would not be waiting at the airport for him.

It had been strange, to be an adulterer with his own wife. Not talking about what they were doing, not talking about her being married to someone else, just doing it. Not like they were a long-married couple, running a routine, but like strangers, jumping off a cliff together. And then she had turned angry.

He did not believe she had really left him *for* Mike Burke, or that she loved Burke one scintilla. But she had left him. Maybe she had just been crazy but what if she weren't? What if she had been looking for a reason to leave him? It only took considering just whom she had bailed on him for to make that idea look plausible. Obviously he had deluded himself, to some degree, about how well their arrangement had been working. He had assured himself, before his accident, that she had what she wanted, a permanent home in Peltry, which he agreed with her was probably better for Dynah, and also there was family for her, his family. But she must have found his absence, the sexual deprivation, more difficult than he had realized. Even as jealousy welled at the thought of her seeking satisfaction with Fuckhead, he had the small but meaningful comfort of being sure she hadn't achieved it, not enough anyway to keep her away from him. It still troubled him to think maybe Fuckhead wasn't the first—well, he knew that was true, she had admitted there had been someone else his rookie season. But maybe there had been others, maybe a new one every season.

While he practiced heroic celibacy and set new records in self-satisfaction. He thought of Deker, frowning, sweating, fingertips swollen and bleeding, hunched over the fly-tying kit. A man needs a hobby. His hand closed around his cock. He could see the golf course in his mind's eye, its reaches a winter moonscape ghostly and insubstantial with snowcover, flawless as a naked woman's skin. Call it the fairway. He could see himself planting his naked feet, thinking through the stroke, the trajectory, following it mentally even as he took the shot. Whoosh. A silent shivery furrow, throwing weightless white into the air.

Christmas Eve at home, a pool party with his dad, who brought along Ida; and Mark and his new girlfriend, Sandy; and Bernie and *her* new guy, Yuri, another Russian, one Mark had introduced her to; and Casey, and Dynah, and Kissy—it was almost perfect. Fuckhead had stayed away. It was possible to pretend he didn't exist. But Kissy was as friendly as frostbite.

"Are you okay?" he asked her under cover of the noise the kids were making.

She glanced at him. "Uh-huh." And then drew her hand back at his hopeful touch.

Dynah stayed overnight and Kissy had to come back to pick her up, to have her Christmas with her and Mike— just a couple of hours—and then she brought Dynah back to spend the rest of his time home with him. His jokes, his longing looks, his tentative approaches, went unanswered.

Only when they were going over schedules did he have her attention.

"I'm going crazy," he blurted. "I want you so much—"

She closed her datebook and capped her pen.

"Kissy—"

"Don't start," she said. "Just don't even start—"

It had been a long time since he really wanted to get drunk and stupid, since he really wanted to do some damage. But all at once he was thirsty, all at once he longed for the spacey numbness of smoke, all at once he wanted a dog to kill and a bridge to throw it off. But he had a little girl to take care of, a little girl who had been waiting for him for weeks.

He had to bring Dynah back to her the day he left. Fuckhead was in the doorway. Fuckhead put his arm around Kissy. She stood stiffly, as if the arm were a chain weighing down on her hips. Fuckhead wore a smug little smile. *I've got her. I'm going to fuck her tonight too, just because I can.*

The Ruth photographs consumed her. She began work on them as soon as Dynah was in bed, before Mike got home from his evening stint—he went back to the office nearly every night. And she kept on working through his return and his going to bed. She rarely finished before it was time to get Dynah up for school. Sometimes she got good stuff out of it, sometimes it stank, when she let herself think about anything but the work. After Mike went to work, she slept on Dynah's bed, in her clothes. She got up just before it was time for Dynah to get home, took her to Junior's, where she could swim and Dynah could do whatever she wanted, swim with her or skate with Dunny. Junior's father now lived in the apartment over the garage, to caretake the place for Junior. Sometimes Dynah did both and Dunny brought her home after Kissy went home to throw some kind of meal together.

Mike made no complaint; she thought he was relieved not to have to deal with either her or Dynah most of the time. Until the course closed for the winter, he golfed weekends. He was on Butch McDonough's City Rec League hoops team in the cold months. She could count on his being half in the bag by the time he turned up at home. Sometimes he kept on drinking. If she was lucky, he passed out before he got horny. Or she could try to put him off with a blowjob before he was drunk enough to blame her and demand something more. It was tricky. She discovered she had an amazing capacity to divorce herself from his touch on her body. As she shot and developed and printed photographs, it crossed her mind occasionally how little actually showed on the outside of anything, anybody. Nobody just looking at her, at Mike, at the two of them together, could ever tell their secrets.

Sometimes Junior slipped into her dreams, under the guard of her exhaustion, and she was with him again, in their old bedroom, with the wall of family photographs above, just as it really was. She could see all of their history together. They looked different—younger and unscarred. There was the strange quality of people in aging photographs, that they had been somehow left behind, in another country on another continent. Among the family photographs was one of Ruth, the first one she had ever seen, the one the paper had cropped and used after the accident, which ought to have told her it was a dream because that picture had never hung anywhere in that house, let alone on that wall. She could not look at it. She looked down at Junior, at his throat where the white line was like a thin rope and his pulse throbbed beneath it. His eyes were clenched, his face asheen with sweat, and he was pale too, and his throat swelled and worked and he rolled his head and cried out to her. She thought she could feel him inside her but it was only dream cock. He was not really there. He was somewhere else.

He called her, in reality, from wherever he was. What plane of existence, whatever parallel universe. His voice coming over the phone line like a message from the dead. "Are you okay? You takin' care of yourself?"

"Don't ask," she answered.

≈ 32 ≈

"**W**e have to talk," Mike said.

They were in the kitchen just after Dynah had bolted out the door to catch the school bus. "We're not talking—" She glanced up from the paper. He leaned over and took it out of her hands. He glanced past her at the clock on the wall, steeling himself against the little scream he must be hearing in his head, the little white rabbit, shrieking, *I'm late, I'm late.*

"Excuse me?" she said.

"I need your attention—" He dragged his chair closer and took both her hands. He spoke in what she thought of now as the Voice of Reason. "I work too much and you work too much. We both have to make some concessions—"

All at once she was on the verge of tears. She took her hands out of his to wipe at what she could not blink back.

"I love you," he said. "I want this marriage to work—"

She wanted to laugh. "It is working, all work, just like you said. Mike, I don't even think I like you, let alone love you—"

He was stunned. His mouth opened and shut and his face went all white and strained. "For Christ's sake—what have I done wrong?"

"You treat me like a whore, to start—do you think I like being abused by a drunk every weekend?"

After a long strained moment of silence, he asked, "Is that how it seems to you?"

She turned her back on him. How's that for talking, Bozo? The coffee had an ammoniac smell. She emptied the carafe and rinsed it out. Her mouth tasted of the coffee she had drunk, the same pissy taste. Beans old and rancid, the coffeemaker needed cleaning—whatever it was, she needed to do something. She held on to the carafe tightly to stop herself from slamming it down into the sink, reducing it to a spray of glass splinters.

"I'm sorry," he said, his voice breaking. "Jesus, baby, I'm sorry, I thought we were just playing games—it was the booze, I didn't mean to hurt you—"

"You drink too much—"

"Yes," he agreed quickly, "I've been hitting it a little bit hard, there's so much pressure, you don't know—I'll cut back . . ."

He came up behind her and massaged her shoulders and kissed the nape of her neck.

"And what?"

"You want to see a counselor? I'll find the time, it's all right, lots of people do that now—"

"Can't you do something without checking to see if everyone else is doing it?"

"Yes, of course I can—Kissy, help me with this, I need you, I need you to help me, we both have to work at it—"

They were both so good at working, she thought.

"I want us to make a baby. My biological clock is ticking," he joked.

She did laugh. It didn't happen so often, him joking, that she could afford to ignore it. She had never believed a child was a magic cure for an unhappy marriage or that a child should be brought into the world for any other reason than to give it the gift of life. On the other hand, she had wanted another one for several years, and she knew what a transforming thing a child was to some men. Dynah had changed Junior.

Mike wanted to make it work. He was contrite, he said he would change, and he did—immediately. He stopped drinking. And laughed about how good he felt. He hung a calendar—the *Sports Illustrated* swimsuit calendar Butch had given him for Christmas—on the wall of the bedroom, where he charted her fertile cycle, as determined by thermometer readings, and marked her likely fertile period in red. He had his semen tested—in fact, had had it done before bringing up the subject to her—and been assured of a normal sperm count. He wore boxer shorts because jockey shorts were alleged to diminish sperm production. They had intercourse no more than twice a week and never two days consecutively. If it didn't work, he told her, he had heard of a procedure where sperm could be concentrated and then used to artificially inseminate the prospective mother. Kissy already felt as if she were being serviced. She began to think the first thing she would do after a positive pregnancy test would be to tear down that calendar.

Dynah was with Junior while he was home during the All-Star break. Trying to distract herself from the knowledge that he was near at hand, Kissy locked herself into her darkroom. Somehow it got to be six a.m., and her stomach was all butterflies and her shorts and T-shirt were as wet as if she had been running through a downpour or swimming in them. Trembling with dehydration, she went straight to the fridge and drank orange juice from the carton. She had missed the early lap swim at Sowerwine. Though she was tired, she would not be able to sleep without a workout. She could go to Junior's, let herself in and use the pool there and have breakfast with Dynah—and Junior. It would be safe; Dunny would be there too.

She didn't see any sign anybody was up yet. The pool room was quiet, the water still and beckoning. Easeful passing over her skin. After forty minutes of laps her muscles felt oiled and strong but she was still wired. She showered and changed back into her Levi's and T-shirt and went barefoot, boots in hand, to the kitchen to make herself toast and coffee. There was coffee in the coffeemaker, the faint rumor of breakfast in the air that she confirmed was already a past event by checking the dishwasher—cereal bowls, orange juice glasses, crumby buttery knives in it, and then she remembered it was a school day. Dunny must have gotten up to put Dynah on the bus. Or taken Dynah to school and maybe gone on to the supermarket or some other errand—they would have missed the Blazer because she had parked it on the far side of the pool wing, where it wasn't visible from the street. She went upstairs, checking into Dynah's room automatically. The room was empty, the bed made as she had taught Dynah—pull everything up straight, coverlet thrown over everything, nothing had to be tucked in.

Junior was awake, lying on his back with one arm under his head. There was an empty juice glass on a tray at his bedside.

"Hi," she said.

"You have a good swim?"

"Uh-huh."

He lifted his head, shifted to his side, lifted the sheet.
"Come get warm."

The room wasn't cold but she was shivery. She slipped
under the sheet next to him. He was bed-warm.

"Skinny-dipping?"

"Yes. I forgot it was a school day. I was going to have
breakfast with Dynah—"

"She brought me some o.j., told me to sleep in—" He
cupped her head, drew her down against his chest. She listened to his heartbeat. It was very calming. He was naked
and seemed extraordinarily whole to her, dense of substance, fuzzy as a teddy bear, alive.

"You're all wired up," he said. "I can feel you shaking.
You on something?"

"Up all night working." She sat up and started talking
about it. Junior listened closely, asked a couple of questions, and made her laugh. Talking about it didn't calm her
at all—it made her more excited. She was talking too fast
and laughing too much over nothing, and Junior reached
up and touched her cheek and she realized the wet was
running down her face, her neck, toward her cleavage, and
she laughed again. His hand spread over the side of her
face, he pressed gently and she closed her eyes and let him
draw her down again. His hand was on her thigh and she
trembled and his mouth brushed hers. She struggled away
from him.

He sighed. Sitting up, he threw off the sheet. "Take a
bath with me?"

She wiped at her face with her fingertips and then at her
nose with the back of her hand. "All right."

His cock subsided as he moved around the bathroom.
He started the Jacuzzi filling and laid out towels and a bottle of bath oil. She undressed again with a touch of awkwardness, more of defiance. He offered his hand and she
took it and let him steady her as she climbed into the tub.
At the sight of her, naked and in the tub, the water splash-
ing around her ankles, he was aroused again. He stepped
into it and pulled her up against him, his cock poking naturally to her bush. She looked up at him and he took her
hand and put his cock in it, and she laughed, this time
without hysteria.

The water rose around them. They held each other comfortably, with an occasional calm kiss, a little squeeze. Her skin grew pink. He feathered her pubic hair with his fingers to see the strands dew with bubbles. His dick floated in the water and she slid down and gently sucked it between her lips. The sudden warm wet sealing of her mouth, the pressure, the tug, made him close his eyes. A little while later she thrashed under him like she was drowning and he was forcing her under. Taking them both down. There was no Kissy there in her eyes, no one at all, only the black core of her pupils as wide as shotgun bores. Her mouth twisting, throat stretched out and pulsing with guttural noises. He let her orgasm draw out his own. It felt like something tearing. They were like two halves of a door ashudder on its hinges for a moment. She was making a noise through her teeth, a clenched wailing.

She slept so deeply, he hated to wake her, but half-past one rolled around and Dynah would be out of school soon.

In the kitchen, Dunny was having lunch. He seemed unsurprised to see Kissy, her skin rosily aglow, hand in hand with Junior. "There's tomato soup on the stove, cheese for sandwiches."

"Thanks but I have to go." Kissy gave them both affectionate kisses and went off toward the pool.

Junior watched her go. Then he reached for the bread and started to make himself a sandwich.

"You might try to be more discreet—" Dunny pushed his chair back and left the table to twitch aside a curtain and watch the Blazer leaving.

"Why? I want her back. I just have to wait for her to work it out on her own—"

"You think she's ever going to leave him?"

"Something's gotta give," Junior said. "She's all tied up in knots."

"Maybe she's one of those people has to be unhappy," Dunny ventured. At Junior's look of incredulity, Dunny made a hasty amendment. "What do I know?"

"I told Wally," Junior said. "He brought it up. He said I was obviously happier and asked me was I getting laid? Surprised the shit out of me. He was red in the face, he was so embarrassed, but he was also really proud of himself for being kind of crude and manly. Letting me know it made him happier to get laid—letting me know he knew that kind of happiness when he saw it. So I told him yeah, I'm having an affair with my ex-wife. He was shocked but he handled it very well. He hemmed and hawed and said, no shit, he said, golly you must have a lot of unsettled issues. He must have caught one of those talk shows, Couples That Have Affairs with Their Exes. I told him no, not really, I never wanted a divorce and I still love her. So he says what about her? So—what about you?"

They were in bed, in a hotel penthouse suite in Detroit. It was Dynah's school vacation and Dynah was asleep in one of the suite's two bedrooms. Kissy was checked into a room across the hall. Mike had been furious about the trip to see Junior, but she had curled her lip at him and braced herself for a black eye or a split lip and an ultimatum. To her surprise he had blinked. He had managed a strangled laugh and visibly pulled himself together.

"I guess I'm being an asshole," he had said. "I expect Dynah's as good at short-circuiting romance between you and Clootie as she is at shutting us down."

Kissy made no reply. She had made her argument already. Dynah wanted to spend the time with her daddy. Dunny could take her to him and take care of her when he was working. But she wanted a vacation with Dynah too, and if Detroit was not exactly where she wanted to spend it, it was a compromise that served everyone. He could take it or leave it.

She meant, of course, to sleep with Junior. Right or wrong, moral or immoral. If Mike thought he could control her, he was as mistaken as Ryne had been and Junior too. To have him buckle like a plastic bumper only confirmed that his assertion of rights over her was hollow. Junior at least not only would give her a decent fucking but make love in the bargain. She had thrust out her chin and inhaled deeply, filling her lungs with what she recognized as the brisk invigorating air of headstrong self-justification. It was fuel for her heart and desire.

"Has it occurred to you, you're married to the wrong guy?"

She rolled over and punched the pillow. "I tried being married to you and what it came down to was Dynah and sex when you could spare the time, sort of what we have now—"

"With the added complication of Mr. Wonderful—why don't you just elope with me? Don't go back. We can let the lawyers sort it out."

Kissy laughed. She had left her photographs in Peltry, hostage to Mike. She had no doubt he would destroy them if she failed to return. That was obviously a mistake. She would do something about it as soon as she was back—move copies to a safe place—Latham's would do. Distractedly she wondered if she was overlooking something else. Was there any other way Mike could still get to her?

Junior was cautious about it but it wasn't the first time he had asked her to bail out. Still, for every time he talked about how she should leave Mike, he never did anything—for a while she had been tense with fear he might pick up the phone and call Mike to say "Hey, asshole, I'm fucking Kissy again." But he didn't. In fact, he admitted he was piqued by the whole idea of the affair. Most likely he was only waiting—for her to quit Mike on her own, for Mike to drive her out, for Mike to catch her and be the one to leave. She didn't know if he ever thought about where it might all end. Junior didn't understand that just because she had her times with him, she could live with her mistakes.

Kissy was late, very late. If she blew this one off, he was going to kick her ass. The more Mike Burke thought about it, the more he thought he really would. She promised. She had fucking well promised.

The party was in a private room at the best restaurant in town and had been under way for over an hour. Even with the exits all propped open for the sake of air circulation, it was stifling—summer heat in early June sitting on the whole town like a thunderhead. The cigarette smoke and body funk and used air just sat there. Mike was drinking Scotch—he had been able to stick to beer most of the time, he had to have a beer or two or people would think he had a drinking problem. Like the old man before him. He would find himself taken aside by some fat old reformed-drunk copper who would invite him to go to AA with him. And his future would suddenly be narrowed down to a bottleneck, oh yes, a bottleneck, he would have to cram himself into it and crawl through until he was inside the bottle, the man-in-the-bottle, like a ship-in-a-bottle. That was how AA worked, you bottled yourself up in your alcoholism and your sobriety, and everyone saw you through the green glass of it and you saw everything through it, bobbing along, safe in the sea of booze.

But this was a special occasion.

Butch was getting red in the face. The buffet was down to crusts and flakes of fish and they were calling for the cake.

"Hey, Mike," Butch bawled, "where's the little wifie? She coming out of the cake?" And he waggled his shoulders, shaking imaginary tits.

The room rocked with laughter, then applause and whistles.

"Sure," Mike called, raising his glass to Butch.

Then there was another swell of glee near the door as Kissy shouldered her way through the mob. Which parted for her, amid more applause and wolf whistles, Butch leading the chorus with two fingers in his mouth.

She was three inches taller than usual, in fuck-me spikes. The dress she had refused to let Mike see before the party was a shimmer of deep red silk that skimmed her body like a pour of Bordeaux and split over her left hip, revealing long flashes of leg as she moved toward Butch. Her hair was the same wild rumple as always, but a line of garnet studs edged one ear and a cranberry-size one winked redly from a band of gold cuffing the other ear. She bought her own jewelry, she said, but he wondered.

Butch bit her bare lobe under the garnet cuff as he hugged her and then kissed her full on the lips. Narcissa smiled faintly. Butch's right hand spread over Kissy's haunch. Mike grinned and laughed. By the time he reached them, Kissy had extricated herself. Mike put his hand on her waist and they kissed theatrically, to another outburst.

The cake came blazing in, diverting everyone's attention.

"You might as well be stark naked," he told Kissy under cover of crowd noise. "Did he give you any tongue?"

She jerked her hand out of his and he grabbed her again by the wrist and held on to her. "Every guy here wants to fuck you," he said, surveying the room with an amused look but with his voice angry under the irony. He smiled at her as if they were having a pleasant conversation. "Where the hell were you?"

"The brakes let go on the Blazer, I had to drop it off and then wait for a cab—"

"You shouldn't be driving that piece of shit—but it's handy, isn't it? Having all kinds of car trouble to cover being late everywhere, every goddamn time, to every thing—"

"Fuck you, Mike," she said, as if she were saying excuse me.

She didn't leave. He watched her work the room, make nice to all the wives, giving the guys a look at what she had, and she even went over to Butch again and shook her tits for him, jokingly. Narcissa was not amused. Mike hooted and whistled louder than the other guys. He wasn't worried about Narcissa. Eventually she would come around to hinting that her party for Butch had been something scandalous. The Wild Bunch. She loved those big fat best-sellers about horny lawyers.

"So did you have a good time?" he asked Kissy when they were home. He was drunk and it was payback time. Dynah was at Clootie's. He didn't have to keep his voice down. "What about it, did you like shaking your tits for Butch?"

Ignoring him, she placed her evening bag on the table under the mirror in the front hall and hung her coat— flamboyantly embroidered purple silk that made the little flag of a dress look like an undergarment.

"It was your idea, Mike," she said, giving the coat a little tug to straighten it on the hanger. "You were the one who wanted me to look hot. You bayed as loud as the rest of them. You and your buddies, you're a bunch of suburban suits who get off on the thought of wife-swapping."

She stopped at the bottom of the stairs and started to take off her heels, pointing her left foot backward to grab the shoe by the back of the spike—he had always found it one of the sexier steps in a woman taking off her clothes. She had the shoe in her hand when he caught her by the wrist and she staggered against him, off the one heel she still had on. As she pushed reflexively off his chest, he cracked her across the mouth and her leg on the spike went out from under her. Crying out, she fell sideways against the banister. The spike she had taken off was still in her hand, in a convulsive clutch. He grabbed her arm and yanked her to her feet. One foot bare, the other wobbling on the spike, she couldn't get her balance. He shook her like a rag doll. She raked his face with the spike in her hand and he threw her backward onto the stair, knocking the wind out of her.

He was crying. Tears streaked down his face, stinging in the welt the heel had raised in one cheek. "You bitch," he said. "You castrating bitch."

She groped for the heel still on her foot and slipped it off and then rolled over and up onto her knees and dragged herself to her feet. Her back hurt, her backside hurt. She went upstairs into the bathroom and locked the door. Leaning against the basin, trembling, she wiped off her makeup with cotton balls and flung them into the trash basket. She splashed cold water over her face.

"Kissy." His voice on the other side of the door made her jump. "Are you all right?" He sounded choked. "I'm sorry. Please, open the door."

Slowly she unlocked the door.

He opened the door and stood there, uncertain where to put his hands. "I'm sorry."

Her head hurt. Behind her left eye, it felt like a drill was violating her brain. She turned away from him and fumbled in the medicine cabinet for aspirin that she dry-swallowed. Then she scooped water with her hand to wet her throat.

He stepped aside to let her pass back into the bedroom.

She unhooked a hook and eye and the silk dress fell to her hips and slid past them, and she stepped out of it, plucked it from the floor, and hung it up. She undid her bra, stepped out of her underpants. She put on a pair of pajamas. He was watching her but she didn't look at him at all.

She got into bed and pulled the blankets up to her chin and clenched her eyes shut. She tried to breathe evenly but it came out in a long shiver.

Mike knelt on the floor next to the bed as if he were going to say his prayers. "I feel like the odd man out," he mumbled. "I can't give you any of what he gave you—money—not even a baby—"

She turned her face away from him.

He went downstairs again. She could hear him locking the doors, turning off the lights. The drawer of the desk in his office, opening, stealthily, the drawer where he kept the bottle of Scotch she wasn't supposed to know about. Pouring himself another drink.

He came back up the stairs with weary steps and she listened to him undressing. He was careful with his expensive clothes. The wooden hangers clunked as he hung his suit in the closet. His weight bore down the edge of the mattress. She could feel his body heat and smell his aftershave and the booze on his breath and the nervous sweat on him. His fingers touched her hip tentatively and smoothed the fabric of the pajamas against her skin. She wanted to scream but she didn't move.

"I was drunk," Mike said. Two days later, he could face her. "We both went too far."

Too far. *She* had gone too far in her dress, in her behavior. *She* had provoked *him,* however unintentionally.

Nothing ever happened in a vacuum, he pointed out in the Voice of Reason. They were both of them tense over their continued infertility and under other pressures too— meaning the shadow of Junior Clootie over their marriage. He found motivation for her: she had been unconsciously testing his commitment. He insisted he did not really believe she was sleeping with Junior again.

"For Christ's sake, Kissy, say something," he demanded tearfully.

She didn't. She wouldn't even look at him. It was as if he had ceased to exist for her. He was a piece of furniture to step around.

He stopped pestering her with apologies and explanations and excuses. Every morning he went to the Y first thing, and he was always brightly, cheerfully un–hung over. He worked late, falling asleep most nights on the couch in his study.

She had a new lock on her darkroom and another on the adjacent room that served as her office. She had her life all arranged so he did not see her more than four or five times a week in passing, unless he made a special effort to get home for supper.

They had no social life anymore. She simply ignored all invitations and he went out by himself. It was being noticed—nobody asked him anymore how Kissy was. They asked him how he was in that careful way people did when they had heard you had something terminal. He had never imagined that it might turn out like this—that Clootie could take her back so casually. It was eating holes in him—the whole town whispering his wife was putting horns on him. She had not slept in their bed since the night of Butch's party, an occasion that still made him a little sick to his stomach.

He could not divorce her. He wasn't some twenty-year-old who could write off a marriage of such short duration as a youthful error. There was another thing. He needed her money. It had changed his life and he couldn't go back to being poor. The back of his neck got hot every time he allowed himself to think of his own venality. Sometimes before he went to bed, he went to her desk and took out her bankbooks she didn't even lock up, so he could check her net worth. The money from his house had helped to buy the one they had now, but she paid the mortgage on the rest. She met most of the household expenses, either from her own money or the child support. She had put the BMW under his ass. He could never have afforded to dress or drink or eat as well on his salary alone, especially not with a wife. They lived well. But she managed well too. Something happened to Clootie, there would be a whole lot more. She was a trustee for Dynah as well, and he would be willing to bet she was Clootie's major beneficiary too.

Clootie was revoltingly healthy.

He had wild thoughts. Setting Clootie up. It would be tough to make anything stick to a guy as rich as Clootie—a pro jock too. Fucking pro athletes hardly ever did any time, even if they got caught with a boxcar full of shit or videotapes of themselves fucking ten-year-olds. The best thing that could happen, that would fix everything, would be if Clootie got real stupid and did something to himself. Or it looked that way. OD'd, ate a tree on his fucking bike—and made Kissy richer. It wouldn't matter then if he called it quits—she would have to cough up a fat settlement.

Thinking about it gave him something to do. Maybe it kept him from actually doing something that would really fuck up his life—realistically, practically, a bad marriage was as common as sin and nothing to a murder charge. And then he would wake up and her side of the bed would

still be smooth and cold and empty. Two in the morning,
three—she was still in her darkroom.

It came to him one night this had gone on long enough.
He got up and slipped into some sweats and went downstairs to his office. It was weird, sitting behind his desk at
three-seventeen in the a.m., his bare feet on the carpet, the
house as dark around him as an empty cave. Her darkroom
was on the other side of the house and he wouldn't hear
her leaving it, but he would know as soon as she went into
the kitchen. He turned on the desk lamp and in the small
yellow pool of its light, opened a file from his briefcase.
When he heard the water spurt on and rattle into the glass
carafe of the coffeemaker, he started. It was nearly five
and he was still on the same page and didn't remember a
thing of what he had read.

She was measuring coffee into the basket. She looked
up at him and through him, making him feel invisible, and
then her gaze dropped to the measuring spoon dipping into
the brown-black well of coffee grains in the grinder.

"I hate the way we're living," he said. "I never see you,
I never see Dynah. I didn't get married to live with a couple of strangers and sleep alone."

For a moment, she made no reply. She mounted the
basket in the machine and flipped the switch.

"That's too bad," she said in a warily neutral tone.

He pulled out a chair and sat down heavily. Conversations in the kitchen, he thought. He did not really have any
idea what to say or do next. It made him bitter. He was
drowning and she wouldn't throw him a goddamn rope.
"Just tell me what it is I have to do to make it work."

He raised his eyes and she was glancing at him sidelong from across the room. The armpits of her sleeveless
T-shirt, the waist of her sweatshorts, were dark with per-
spiration. The darkroom must have been a sweatbox all
night. Her face was damp, her eyes dark with fatigue. Her
hands twitched. She wouldn't look right at him.

He got up and she flinched, body turning, one hand
coming up fearfully and then falling, defeated. She straightened up and faced him, her face dead-white, the tiredness
around her eyes like bruises. His throat was too tight to
speak. He lurched toward her and threw his arms around
her. She stiffened and he fell on his knees in front of her

and sobbed against her belly. After a time, her hands touched his hair tentatively.

It was strange, Burke reflected, how she kept breaking and remaking him. He was like one of her prints. There was an essential Mike Burke, the negative of him, and the paper Mike Burke, the potential one, and she kept forcing light through it and baptizing it in chemical baths and his face would come up, like a swimmer breaking the surface of the water, and take on depth and dimension, and he would see he was not the person he had thought.

It was real. Other people saw it too.

Butch stopped him after a meeting in the office and asked how he was doing and the malignant diagnosis hush was gone. It was the way it used to be, rich with is the boy still kicking ass and taking down names, are we still in bidness?

Mike laughed.

Butch cleared his throat. "Everything okay at home?"

"Trying to make a baby—"

"Good move," Butch agreed. "Need any pointers?"

He was supposed to laugh, so he did.

"Haven't seen you and Kissy for ages," Butch continued. "I'm going to char some chicken Sunday afternoon, if you can take a break from the fucking—"

"Damn, I'm sorry," and Mike was, too, "I'm taking Kissy and Dynah to the cottage this weekend—"

"Oh, well—come back early yourself, then—"

And Butch put the word out at his cookout that Kissy wasn't there because she had gone to the cottage and left Mike to fend for himself. It was an opening for Butch to tell Mike sending Kissy away for the summer was no way to make a baby. So everybody knew they were trying and the marriage must be okay. Mike raised a toast to Butch with real feeling behind it.

33

"**S**o are you pregnant?" Junior asked her.

She shifted onto her back to look at him. "Possible, I guess—but I don't feel like it—why do you ask?"

He punched up his pillow and flopped back down again. "My dad told me he heard it from somebody getting a haircut—courthouse security guy or some such. He wanted to know if I'd been careless again—"

"What did you tell him?"

"Told him I'd been trying to knock you up for years and it hadn't happened—maybe I should get a test."

She laughed. Rising, she went down the hall to check Dynah.

"Dead to the world," she reported. "She's a little warm—went straight-out all day. Got the shivers a couple of times—"

"I noticed. I'll keep her down for a couple of days—we're due for a Hearts tournament—"

Kissy slipped into bed again.

"You're sleeping with him again, aren't you?" Junior asked.

Eyes closed, she hid her face against his chest.

He sighed, tightening his arm around her. "I'm not angry about it, baby. I'm going to camp—"

"Yes," she said.

He didn't know whether she was answering his question or confirming his departure.

"Come with me, you and Dynah."

"Where?"

He had no answer. He had become expensive; trading him would finance buying some cheaper, younger talent.

Baseball was on the verge of a strike, and everything he had heard pointed the NHL in the same direction. Strike or lockout, over much the same issues. His future was very unsettled. He closed his eyes to visions of coming home and finding Kissy swollen up with that fuckhead's kid. Maybe he would get lucky and she would swell up with his baby again. But he had doubts—all the times they had done it without protection and no baby but Dynah to show for it. He really wondered if there could be something wrong with one of them. He did not want to know, though, not for sure.

They had a working deal—he went, she stayed where she had family and work and Dynah was settled, and when he came back, she was available to him. The downside was she had somebody else. Was that unreasonable? For her to have another life without him, as he had one without her? It was unconventional but not very different from what they might have had, still married to each other. Except he didn't have another woman. And he didn't know how much Burke knew—he must know or suspect, though he was such an asshole, maybe not. Maybe this was the best deal he could work out—for now. Maybe instead of hating Mike Burke, he should be grateful the guy was such a limpdick he tolerated his wife fucking someone else. But that could describe him too—he was tolerating her fucking Burke. She just lies there, he told himself, she just takes it and Burke's got a little tiny prick like a baby's finger that hardly even touches her and he comes in ten seconds, his semen a wet little drop of spit with no force behind it, it just dribbles back over his teeny tiny nub of a prick. It's like a raindrop on the windshield of the Benz—splat. Nothing. It's nothing to her, nothing more than a tickle. Masturbation is light-years better. If wishes were cocks, he thought, giving the pillow a savage punch, Fuckhead could choke on mine.

"Your friend Houston's out soon," Mike told Kissy, passing her the paper. "One of that batch they're booting out under court order, to make room. He was close anyway, what with good time."

Kissy barely glanced at the brief article in the paper before putting it aside. Her friend Houston. Not even close. She was glad for him that the long ordeal of prison would soon be over. The pictures of Ruth were showing at the

School of Fine Arts. There were publishers looking at them, her agent presenting a book proposal. Jimmy Houston getting out was another kind of closure, as the buzzword had it.

She called to Dynah to hurry up or she would miss the bus.

After he had talked to Dynah, that evening, she told Junior.

"Weird," was his response. "Give you the spooks?"

"No. I'm fine about it."

Officially, he called every night to say good-night to Dynah, but most nights he called again, later, on the line she had had installed into her darkroom and nowhere else in the house. She had a headset that left her hands free for work or whatever. Sometimes they didn't say anything for long periods of time but they could hear each other breathing. Sometimes he wanted phone sex. Or she did.

They did not have to talk about how things were going for him. The good news was he had been traded to the Caps. It brought him into the same organization as Mark; they might someday play together. It also meant, of course, he could see Dynah—and her—a little oftener. The bad news was that the owners had turned down the last offer from the Players' Association. Short of a miracle, he expected to be home again soon—good news in one way, but frustrating from a professional point of view.

The lockout started October 15; anticipating it, Junior had come home on the eleventh. No one knew how long it might last, but the baseball strike had killed the second half of the season and the World Series and there was not only no progress in the negotiations, there was talk there would be no baseball the next season either. It could happen to the NHL. A lot of the guys believed this commissioner meant to break the Players' Association and was taking all his cues from the baseball owners' efforts to do the same in their league. The minor leagues were playing, so Mark was working. Since he was so close to home, Junior paid Mark a visit and worked out with Mark's club in Portland and hashed the issues with him.

Everybody agreed the smart thing to do was stay in shape, stay game-ready, in case the lockout ended suddenly and the season could be salvaged. He could work out at home, or at Sowerwine, where the Spectres were happy to have him spicing up their drills and scrimmages. It was a lot like being in college again, though he definitely felt older, the kids were so young: *God was he ever this young, was he really this old, where had the fucking time gone?*

He had time to spend with Bernie and Casey—Bernie still going with Yuri but not at all sure she wanted to marry a hockey player, and wanting her degree too—and with his father, caretaking his house for him. And time with Dynah, of course. The rough part was being in the same town with Kissy, seeing her when he picked up Dynah or dropped her off. If he could not be playing, he decided, he would put the time to good use and break her up with Burke, once and for all. But she had a show at the School of Fine Arts, her Ruth pictures, and she had a lot of excuses for avoiding him. Which he began to resent. He was there, which is what she had always said she wanted, and she didn't have time for him.

He had Dynah at Thanksgiving. She helped him and Dunny and Bernie prepare the big meal. She was in a wild mood, and he encouraged her, horsing around with her, whipping her up. Too late he realized she was overstimulated— she started giggling and couldn't stop. When he put his arms around her to try to calm her, she grabbed a turkey leg and bashed him with it. He let her go and she scooped up fistfuls of mashed potato and threw them like snowballs at him. It turned into a screaming tantrum. She wanted Mummy.

Once she was just bawling, he got her into the Jacuzzi and the hot water and exhaustion made her stuporous. No way was he dragging her back to Kissy. It was raw and cold and she was practically sick. Maybe she really was coming down with something and that was why she was so excitable, so easily upset.

When Kissy called to say good-night to Dynah, he didn't mention the tantrum, only told her that she had already dozed off. He could tell Burke was in the room with Kissy and he stuck to making arrangements for the next day.

Dynah was better in the morning but he decided to keep her out of the pool and take it easy. They walked to the campus. Kissy's pictures of Ruth were coming down shortly and he wanted to see them one more time. He sent Dynah into

the side gallery, where there was a special show for kids. He
had the place to himself. They were really something, he
thought, as he moved slowly from one place to the next.
After a while he forgot about Kissy's being the photographer and thought only of Ruth, dying by inches before
his eyes.

Dynah came skipping back and they set off across campus. It was cold and windy and they took the shortcut
through the copse. Despite the weather, someone occupied
the bench in front of the memorial. Junior slowed out of
curiosity. Whoever it was sat hunched forward intently as
if he were trying to see through the stone. Dynah danced
ahead of him and in front of the man on the bench.

"Dynah," Junior called, "wait a minute. Come back."

He stopped beside the bench and she came running back
and looked up at him questioningly.

"Sit down," he said. "I want to sit a minute."

She plopped onto the bench quite willingly. The man at
the other end glanced at them and then resumed staring at
the stone.

Dynah wriggled restlessly. "Why, Daddy? You aren't
tired."

"No. I just haven't sat here in a while. This is a favorite
place of your mother's—"

"I know. It's a memorial. We come here all the time."

The man at the end of the bench looked at them again.
He was wearing glasses, rimless round glasses, and a scrubby
little beard that made him look like a refugee from 1967.
Junior looked at him a moment.

"Houston," he said suddenly. "You're James Houston."

The man blinked and then nodded as if in rueful accep-
tance of the fact.

"Have you been to the gallery?" Junior blurted, his face
growing warm.

"Yes." Houston rocked forward on the bench. "I've seen
the pictures."

"My wife took them." Junior felt exceedingly foolish, as
if he were babbling. "Kissy Mellors. She kept her maiden
name. She never used mine. She was a witness—"

"I know." Houston nearly whispered the two words.

Junior thrust out his hand. "I'm Junior Clootie."

Houston hesitated, then shook hands. His grasp was
bony and dry. He was thin but not wasted. He looked wiry.

Tough. There was a coldness about him. He made Junior think of a long-dead actor, David Janssen. Not because he really looked anything like Janssen but because of his body language. Janssen had played the hero of a series called *The Fugitive*. There was something very fugitive about Houston. Tension. Isolation.

Junior put his arm around Dynah's shoulder and drew her closer to him. "Mr. Houston, this is my daughter, Dynah. Dynah, this is Mr. Houston."

Houston gazed at Dynah a little distractedly, nodded to her with the unease of the adult uncomfortable around children.

"Kissy's and mine," Junior said. "Dynah's with me over the holiday."

Houston's gaze returned to Dynah and settled there.

Junior stared at Houston. Staring at Dynah. His hand closed convulsively around Dynah's and he came to his feet, dragging her after him. "We should go now. It's getting cold."

"Pleased to meet you, Mr. Houston," Dynah said.

Houston nodded gravely. "Pleased to meet you, Dynah."

Junior paused and turned back to Houston. "You come back here for any particular reason?" It wasn't very polite, but delicacy gave way in the face of urgency.

A little smile played over Houston's lips. "They accepted me for medical school here years ago. My grandfather left them some money. They decided to be kind and reaccept me."

Junior nodded and nudged Dynah along.

Though Dunny was supposed to bring Dynah home, it was Junior who came up the walk with her. He handed Dynah's overnight bag and a shopping bag full of kid vids to Mike Burke, who took them, with a little jerk of impatience, and deposited them immediately and firmly on the floor.

"Mummy, can I watch a vid?" Dynah begged.

"One." Kissy smiled at her.

Dynah grabbed the shopping bag and made for the nearest TV-VCR.

"I need to talk to you about something," Junior said.

"Talk away," invited Burke.

"No." Junior shook his head. "I need to talk to Kissy alone. This is her business and mine."

Incredulity and anger stiffened Burke's features.

Junior held Kissy's gaze. "She can discuss it with you later if she wants, but I want to talk to her about it first—"

"Schools again?" Kissy sighed.

Junior fell on it—she was handing him a subject. "Yeah." He thrust a chin at Burke. "Twenty minutes at Denny's, have some cops watch us if you want—"

Burke was furious but there was nothing he could do.

Junior said his good-byes to Dynah while Kissy got a jacket.

In the Benz, she stared silently out a window. He didn't drive to Denny's. He drove down into the Valley and tucked the big car into a patch of pinewood that in summer was a picnic area. Overlooking the stream, it was well screened from the road and in steady use at night as a pickup, make-out, dealing spot.

"I ran into an old friend of yours today," Junior told her, watching her closely. "On campus, at the memorial."

She turned her gaze to him with only faint curiosity in her eyes.

"James Houston," he continued.

Her eyes focused sharply on him and she smiled slightly, but she didn't say anything. There was an eerie calm in the way she looked at him.

"He's out of jail," Junior continued. "He's come back to go to med school. I guess they let him in on account of his grandfather left them some money."

She nodded.

"He's Dynah's father," Junior said.

Kissy nodded again, slowly. "Her biological father. You're her father in the only way that matters."

He laughed shakily. "Thanks. Really, I mean it. That's the nicest thing you've ever said to me."

She smiled as if it didn't matter—it was just too obvious.

"Were you in love with him?"

"No."

"Does he know? About Dynah?" She shook her head no. "I got the feeling he didn't. The way he was looking at her, I think he knows now."

She cleared her throat. "It doesn't matter. I can't imagine he'll claim her."

"He'll be around. What if Burke finds out?"

"Why would it matter to him whether she's yours or someone else's—"

"I don't know. I'm asking you. He probably wouldn't be too thrilled to know his wife's kid was a bastard by a convicted felon—"

She looked away from him. It was clear she was indifferent to whatever Mike Burke's reactions might be. And then she shifted in her seat, moving toward him, taking his face in her hands, kissing him.

He was surprised by its urgency and then grateful. The cops patrolled the area randomly and anyone might come through—it was incredibly indiscreet, but he didn't care. And he guessed she didn't either. They luxuriated in just making out and he thought about asking her to go back to the house. Then he didn't want to do that at all, the place they were was part of it. All they did was open their clothes a little, unbutton shirts, undo his pants—of course, she had to take more off—and then she straddled him. It lasted a long sweet time, much of it with eyes locked in silence, and she did nearly all of it, inside. And even after coming, they stayed together, her head tucked to his shoulder.

"Come back to me," he said.

She pressed her fingers on his mouth, sealing his lips. "I'm thinking maybe what I should really do is be single. Maybe I'm just no good at being married. I'll tell Mike we had a fight over sending Dynah to a private school. I won."

He watched her go into the house. He felt stupid about Houston, and about her too. She had kept a secret from him for all of Dynah's life. Houston had been her lover—for a night, a few nights, a week, it couldn't have been any more. And she had conceived Dynah and married him and borne Dynah and lived with him, off and on, for years, and never breathed a word to him. He felt as if he had never known her, really. She was as alien to him as Ruth Prashker, in the prints in the gallery—that woman in the photographs receding by minute increments into a very great distance.

The gallery always seemed shabbier as the pictures came down—the litter of packing materials, the half-undressed look of the room. People wandered through on their way to somewhere else and sometimes they loitered, looking at the ones still up, but she didn't pay any mind as she went about dismantling the show. Latham and his teaching assistant were helping her. She was on her knees, taping a packing box, when another man entered the gallery. Even in new unfaded Levi's and hardly worn high-tops, she recognized the walk, the legs and feet. She glanced up as he stood over her. Older, older than his years, he was twitching with nerves.

"Hi, Jimmy," she said, turning her attention back to her packing.

He scooched down next to her. "Hi. I thought I might see you here." He looked around. "Am I in the way?"

"No."

He sank back, setting his back to the wall, crossing his ankles, and resting his forearms on his knees. He studied her wordlessly awhile as she worked.

Latham drifted by, had a look at him, widened his eyes at Kissy, and floated away to gossip with the teaching assistant.

"I've been in to see the pictures several times," Jimmy said. "You did a hell of a job."

"They're going to be a book. The manuscript's complete except for an introductory essay."

"You've done well out of that night," he observed, "the pictures, a book, a husband, a kid—"

She slashed a box knife through strapping tape. "You always had a cruel streak, Jimmy."

He was silent for a moment. She pushed the box away and sat back on her knees.

"Yes," he agreed. "I did and I do."

"You don't have any interest in her, then?" Just a question, cool and inquisitive.

Anger sparked in his eyes, tensed his voice. "Fuck yes. I can't help it. Don't expect me to thank you, Kissy. You want to talk about being cruel. Dynah's another thing I lost. Did you ever think about it that way?"

She sat very still and then she shook her head.

"I read a lot," he said. "Stuff I'd never have looked at before. Popular fiction. I read a bunch of stories about this guy, this boat bum. He thought he was some kind of white knight. He went around helping victims who couldn't get justice from the law. Stole their money back and shit like that. And he was always fixing up shattered women." He stared off at the opposite wall and gave her a glimpse, for an instant, of a man who had lived a long time in his own head. "Anyway, at the end of the series, this kid of his turns up. It turns out one of those women had his kid and never told him—"

"You refused my letter—"

"I know, I don't blame you—anyway, this thing keeps coming up in other stories. A kid turns up some guy never even knew existed. And the kid is always smarter than hell, a fucking world-class athlete, gorgeous—in other words, the spit of Daddy. Never an ugly, fucked-up, stupid brat. And the kid always knows who Daddy is because all Mom's done, besides feed and clothe and raise the kid for eighteen years, is sing Daddy's praises. She didn't want to live with him or maybe she didn't want to trouble him, him being a free spirit and all, but she was honored to whelp his get and make him a legend to his kid." Jimmy grinned. "Men are incredibly egotistical, aren't they? When I was reading those stories, I was muttering, what was this guy doing? Trusting the women to take care of the contraception or didn't he give a shit or what? And the whole time, I trusted you—it never crossed my mind I'd knocked you up or that, if I had, you'd actually gone ahead and had the kid."

"I'm sorry I hurt you, Jimmy," she said.

He shrugged. "I killed two people. I got a nerve bitching about anything, let alone a kid. She might turn out to be the only thing I ever had anything to do with that was any good."

"You're going to school?"

"Got the rest of my life, don't I? If some drunken asshole doesn't run me down crossing the street."

"Do you want to see her?"

He shook his head. "No. Not yet anyway. Maybe someday."

"Good luck, Jimmy," Kissy said.

He took her hand and kissed her cheek lightly. "Thanks. You too."

Latham hustled over as soon as the door swung shut on Jimmy. "New boyfriend?"

"Old one," she said, "sort of."

"He looked familiar. Do I know him?"

"James Houston."

Latham's nostrils flared. "No—"

"He's going to med school here."

"Fascinating—is he still madly in love with you or was I seeing things?"

"Seeing things." She laughed. "We were never in love."

"Oh." Latham pursed his lips. "Liar. I just realized why he's so familiar-looking. You're a wicked, evil woman. Does Junior know?"

"Yes, and shut your mouth, Latham. Lots of other people don't."

"Oh, all right," he agreed.

Butch touched his elbow chummily, gesturing toward a table in the corner. Burke took his double from the bar and followed Butch.

"Howyadoin'?" he asked.

"Great, great," Butch said, surveying the room for people he knew, nodding, throwing a grin, a wave, here and there. He stopped a waitress and asked for a beer.

"Thanks for inviting me along," Mike said.

Butch winked at him. They had come up to the state capital to lobby the legislature for tougher sentencing. It went down well with the voters and got the both of them in the paper. The bill in question had drawn prosecutors from all over the state, providing a great opportunity to make personal connections. There was another meeting tomorrow that would allow everybody to put Saturday night on the arm too.

Butch's gaze fell to Burke's glass. "How many of those have you had?"

Burke held up two fingers.

"Why don't you quit right there?"

"Sure," he agreed. "No problem."

The waitress dipped between them, leaving Butch's draft.

"Want another, Mike?" she asked.

He grinned at her. "No, thanks, honey."

She smiled back and twitched away.

"Nice ass," Butch said. "You want my job?"

Burke started. "Sure. Someday."

"I've made a decision, Mike. It's time for me to take a shot at the First District."

Laughing, they shook hands. Burke raised his glass and Butch raised his in a toast to the new endeavor.

Then the two men focused intently on each other and Butch laid out the plan. "You'll run the office for the next two years, while I'm campaigning. You have to make me look good and keep my skirts clean. Can you do it?"

"Absolutely."

"I get elected, I resign, and you move up and run the next time as a sitting DA. And if I lose, I'm going to step out of the way and give you my endorsement. I figure if I'm not in Congress by then, I better go private and turn some serious bucks until the next good chance at Blaine House comes up."

Burke thought it was just as likely that if Butch lost, he would stay right where he was and make him wait another two years. But he nodded. "Sounds solid."

Butch tapped the edge of his glass with his fingertip. "I gotta ask. You clean, Mike? No little awkwardnesses that might come up?"

For a moment, Burke met Butch's eyes evenly. Then he said, "You know me as well as my own mother does, Butch. You worried about something?"

Butch checked with his own beer and then at him. "I was you, I'd switch to beer. At least in public. The voters have gotten puritanical, 'specially about drinking. People see you very often with hard liquor in your hand, they don't need much else to start whispering you got a problem. Whole town knows your dad did."

Burke laughed. "Sure. Hell, I've gone months at a time without so much as a beer—"

Butch nodded agreeably. "I know. I'm not worried. I'm talking about public perception. And one other thing—you and Kissy—"

"We're solid," Burke said. "Rock solid."

"You don't go anywhere together—"

"She feels like an outsider." He gave Butch an earnest look. "She's not political. She's an artist, a little flamboyant, she feels like she doesn't fit in—"

"That dress at my birthday party." Butch laughed. "I loved it—but I knew she was joking, she's so sophisticated—"

"She's insecure, maybe she overdoes it," Burke said. "I'll try to get her out more."

"Okay. I'm sure Narcissa would be really pleased to

help her get comfortable—you know, have a lunch for her, give her a little support and guidance—"

"Would she? That'd be fantastic—" He went on mouthing the right things. He could push Kissy a little bit. It wouldn't kill her. She did fuck all. He could imagine her at lunch with Narcissa, though. Jesus.

❧ 34 ❧

Nobody ever buzzed his door except the kid with the pizza, and he hadn't ordered any. Jimmy Houston squinted through the spyhole. It was Kissy. He had trouble unlocking the door.

"Hey," he said, "what a surprise. How'd you find me?"

"Registrar," she answered. She had a plant, the pot wrapped in brilliant foil, in her hands.

"Come in, come in." Receiving his first guest sent his spirits soaring with an excitement akin to that he had felt at six, peeking out the window at the first birthday party guest coming up the walk.

The place was just an attic walk-up in a shitty neighborhood, but it was cheap. The ceiling under a mansard roof was high and the windows piercing the mansard gave him a view over the rooves and trees. And it came furnished, more or less—thrift store junk, but the mattress was brand-new and nothing was actively uncomfortable. The important thing was that it wasn't a jail cell.

She handed him the plant—a sansevieria, mother-in-law's tongue, a plant you couldn't kill with neglect or abuse and that lived decades. An ironic plant. He grinned over it and thanked her effusively. Then, for a moment, he was at a loss. "Coffee," he said, not asking, just remembering, speaking out loud to himself—that was one of the things you could offer a guest.

Unzipping her jacket, she nodded agreeably. He fumbled to help her. It was a bike jacket, black leather with fringes, but otherwise plain. Cut for her though, he could see. She was wearing cowboy boots and faded Levi's and a long-sleeved Henley shirt that hugged her body. He couldn't help remembering. As he had on seeing her in the gallery.

She looked the same, she looked seven years older, she looked better, she looked too good to be true.

While he made the coffee, hands shaking, scattering black grounds over the counter, she looked out the windows. The street lamps lighted the bare trees from underneath. He was anxious to see the branches green out, the light through them.

The coffeemaker was new, as were all his appliances—a modest TV, a no-frills VCR, a stack of stereo components. He had purchased them with unexpected pleasure. Best of all was the Mac computer set up on the battered Salvation Army thrift store desk. He could have bought a used car for the money but he told himself he wasn't likely to kill anybody with a computer. He didn't know if he would even try to get a license. He had a bicycle and he loved riding it. Loved walking. Loved running in a world without walls.

"Déjà vu," he said, and laughed.

She smiled quizzically.

"You coming to see me," he explained. His mouth went suddenly dry. "Did you come to get laid?"

This time it was her turn to laugh. "Déjà vu, all right."

He realized he was strangling the coffee mug he had taken from the cupboard. He put it down carefully, extracted another one, and lined them up neatly. "I was a shit to you," he said. "I'm afraid you want me to be a decent human being. I resent being asked. If you could cut me some slack"—he wet his lips—"I've been on pause for eight years."

"It's all right, Jimmy." She didn't seem to be angry. Ironic. She was ironic, like the ugly, heroic plant she'd brought him.

"Were you there? When Ruth died?"

"No. I just missed her."

He came around the counter and sat down on the couch and stared at the floor. "You did the right thing. You tried to make something out of it. I tried to make something out of seven years in prison. I thought of it as composting. Turning the shit to fertilizer."

Kissy perched on the arm of a frayed old stuffed chair. "It's over."

He nodded. "As much as anything ever is."

She rose again and moved restlessly around the efficiency.

"Tell me about Kissy," he said. "How did you happen to wind up with that cop?"

She shrugged. "Bad karma."

Oops. The coffeemaker burbled. He jumped up and rushed back to it, taking refuge in the safe, neutral question: what did she take in her coffee?

"Nothing."

With the counter between them, she took her coffee, thanked him, sipped it, put it down. He watched her mouth, her hands. She wasn't wearing a wedding band but the ring finger bore the marks. She'd taken it off for the night.

He met her eyes, cool and aware of where he had been looking, what he had been checking, and he burst out laughing at his own daze of fear and desire.

"The last woman I was with was you," he said. "I'm scared shitless."

She came around the counter and paused there a moment, an arm's length from him, examining him as if he were a subject and she were checking the lighting on his face. He breathed in the smell of her, let his eyes feast on the texture of her skin, the juxtaposition of her features. Little signs of aging, the corners of her eyes, a faint vertical crease between her eyebrows—it was all beautiful and overwhelming to him. She touched his mouth with her fingertips. He caught her wrist and turned her palm to his mouth and licked it. Tasted the salt with a little moan, his tongue on skin again.

A woman in his arms. A female body against his. A woman's mouth, breasts, curve of ass, the yield between the legs. He was fifteen again. Hard in an instant and ready to come at the touch of bare flesh. Grinding against her.

"Easy"—she laughed breathlessly—"slow down."

Abashed, he stood there awkwardly while she moved calmly to the bed and leaned against it to remove her boots.

"I don't have a rubber," he said suddenly, in a stew of panic and relief that he wouldn't have to risk failure.

"It's all right." She smiled at him.

"That's what you said the last time. I should think you'd be worried about AIDS, if not a baby."

"I'm not worried about AIDS, Jimmy."

"What about a baby?" He laughed with incredulity. "Is

that what you want? You got one from me already—I should be good for another one?"

She laughed too. "It's all right, Jimmy. I won't have another one without asking you, if that's what you're worried about."

So what if she did? She hadn't asked anything of him with the first one. He'd had a lot worse things than an unwanted child forced on him. He kicked off his sneakers, fumbled at his buttons. "Let me," she said. Her fingers worked the top button of his shirt, the second, then her fingertips were inside, on his chest, rolling over his nipples. Her left hand gently cupped his crotch, stroking up to squeeze his cock. He grabbed her hand to hold it there. Pushed her back onto the bed and fell onto her, tongue into her mouth, fingers frantic at the waistband of her Levi's. And losing his hard-on. He couldn't believe it. He was going to shoot off any second but his dick was deflating like a blown tire. It was like an amputated limb, the sensation there, but no substance; he had a phantom erection.

Off her, on his back, he tested his cock in horrified disgust and found it limp as boiled spaghetti. "I can't," he said. "I want it so bad."

On her elbow, looking at him, her mouth ripened with kissing, she was unperturbed, itself exciting to him. "You're all tied up in knots. Lie down and let me get you relaxed. Have you got some lotion? I'll massage you awhile."

Once her hands were on him, he realized how right she was—his body was tight with tension.

"Junior does this for me," she said, working his shoulder muscles. "I learned it from him."

"Does?"

For a long moment she was silent, long enough to worry him that he had pissed her off.

"I made a mistake," she said. She laughed with a distinct ruefulness. Her hands worked down his back, kneading gently, warming the muscle.

"Sounds like you made more than one," he ventured.

"Oh, yes. You know about mistakes. You do your time, you know?"

"No." He twisted to glance at her. "If it's that kind of mistake, you file for divorce. At least that's the way I've heard it works."

Her knuckles dug into his buttocks and he decided he was totally grateful for her mistakes, especially that she had made a lousy marriage to the cop and was, consequently, massaging his ass. Raising his hard-on from the dead. Her lotion-slick fingers eased down the crack of his ass, tickling his anus, and his balls tightened like knots. He rolled over and she wrapped her fingers around his dick and stroked it with a wifely expertise.

" 'Show me,' " he whispered, quoting himself.

She hesitated. "I'm seven years older. I've had a baby—"

"I haven't seen a woman in the flesh in all that time, Kissy—"

"You do it."

As he unbuttoned her shirt, his fingers steadied. Bare skin, bra, the fullness of her breasts, the peaks lifting the fabric. Exposing her shoulders, the heavy delts of the swimmer, her muscled arms. The sound of the cloth as he took down her Levi's made his throat tighten. Seven years and a baby and her body took his breath away.

Her fingers circled the base of his cock and guided him into the heat, the glove of her flesh. And stopped him there, squeezing him. He was harder than he had ever been as a younger man. Her hips rolled up to meet him. It's not worth dying for, the posters screamed on the walls of the prison infirmary. The men there were dying of it. But. The bodies here, the bodies here, his and hers, they were living.

"I have to go." She had told him her husband was out of town for the weekend.

"Spend the night."

"No." No explanations. She owed him nothing, not even excuses.

He watched her dressing. "Come back tomorrow night. I want to wake up with you still here."

She glanced up at him from buttoning her shirt. "I'll try."

The silence thickened after her departure. He was more alone. He pulled the sheets up under his chin and replayed it all in his mind. Glad he had not gone to a prostitute, as he had fantasized he would in the first hour of his freedom. It had been worth every second's wait—hesitation, reluctance, fear, to be truthful—to be with Kissy, with whom he had a history. Meager as it was, it was still important. She had been his succor once, had borne his child, and come to him again. Her motivation was a mystery to him but he was grateful for her. Gratitude was part of the hard lessons he had learned.

What was he doing, balling the wife of the assistant DA? Talk about risk factors. Fuck it. Life was fucking wonderful in its weirdness. And horrible, too, but not when he had just had a woman for the first time in seven years. He loved her, he thought. Maybe he was a mug to love a woman for letting him fuck her, but he did. How could he not?

End of January: Junior had been back at work for a week. He had watched Peltry fall away beneath him with an almost palpable relief. It wasn't just the joy of going back to work, of being able to salvage the season. It was an instant of recognizing this was his real life, his work. He could feel Peltry clinging to him, weighing him, trying to draw him back down to earth, to *its* earth, and into it. Leaving meant leaving everything he couldn't fix. Straight out the back, Jack.

They were on the road, leaving everywhere, going somewhere, anywhere. Hotels and planes. Crowds that were fucking delirious to see them. One day he went into a bookstore and there was a woman working there who came up and asked if she could help him. They fell into conversation and he asked her out. Her name was Miranda and she was a few years older than he was, divorced and childless and a recovering alcoholic. He felt immediately comfortable with her. She met him after the game for dinner and he slept with her that night. First, though, he told her he wasn't exactly single and she laughed and listened quietly to his explanation and said all right, she wasn't expecting anything. But he had her phone number and he had not thrown it away. He kept thinking about her, wondering if he should see her again and see if it went anywhere. He had a compulsion to tell Kissy, but she never seemed to be able to come to the phone when he called Dynah, or else there was no answer but her phone recorder, or Officer Friendly.

Flying out one night to the next venue, he retrieved his phone messages through a seat-back phone on the jet. There was a message waiting all right. Her voice, strained through his phone recorder and the satellite hookup to the plane. She said his name. She laughed and then she broke into a sob. And he knew she was pregnant. What else would make her laugh and cry at the same time? He had finally done it. He had made her pregnant. She hung up and the machine rolled on to the next message, her again, calmer.

"Baby," she whispered. "Tell me what to do . . ."

"Yes," he said to the taped message, "absolutely. I'll come back for you as soon as I can. I promise. I will. I do. Yes—"

"Forgive me," she said, her voice quavering again. "I'm all alone and sometimes I don't know what to do—"

Junior dialed her number, fuck the time and Fuckhead if he happened to answer, but the phone was busy. And it stayed that way, as if it were off the hook. Disconnected.

They were going to be late. The shit always blew up when you were halfway out the door. Burke threw down his briefcase on the hall table and took the stairs two at a time. At least Dynah was out of the house, spending the night with Dunny and Ida. A night without a skateboard or some other piece of kid-crap to trip on, without having to take the little bitch's tantrums, was worth celebrating.

Kissy was in the bedroom, still in her slip, the TV on in the corner.

"For Christ's sake, aren't you dressed yet?" he said, ripping off his tie.

"I just saw my brother Kevin," she said. "On CNN. In Groszny. He's a cameraman, his camera said CNN on the side—"

"Great, great. Get me a drink, will you?" That was about what she was good for. He'd never even met her fucking brother. She hadn't heard from the jack-off for—what? ten years?

He didn't wait for an answer but headed straight for the shower. The hot needles of water made him gasp. Her hand appeared through the steam with a glass in it. He grabbed it, keeping it out of the water as he backed up against the shower wall into a safe place and got a swallow of it. Silky liquid heat in his gut. Worth every penny.

Kissy turned off the TV. It *had* been Kevin, she was sure of it—older, of course, looking like her father around

about the time he blew them all off. She would call her
mother later and let her know he was still alive. She would
call CNN and find a way to get in touch with him. It was
such a relief to know Kevin was okay, if you could call
working in a war zone okay. The point was he had made
himself a life, he wasn't dead of drugs or AIDS or living
on the street somewhere. He had gotten out and survived.

She shimmied into her dress. Gold. Shivery gold, short,
low-cut. Opaque stockings the same color so her legs
looked gilded. Turning sideways, she drew the fabric taut
over her abdomen. Her hand spread over her belly. She
smiled. She put an earring through her ear. It was a huge
chandelier earring that filled her whole hand.

"Goddamn it," Mike said from the bathroom door,
"can't you find anything that doesn't make you look like a
high-class hooker? I thought we had an understanding.
What happened to going to the hairdresser and getting
your hair colored to something resembling real hair, decently cut?"

"That was your understanding with yourself. I like my
hair the way it is." Kissy feathered her hair in the mirror,
making it stand up more. "I like this dress. I like these earrings. I don't look like a hooker. I just don't look like a Junior Leaguer. I'm not."

He hunted cuff links out of a drawer. "You're my wife.
You're supposed to look like a grown-up."

Kissy cocked one knee, slipping a high heel on. Then
she did the other one. "Mike," she said. "about me being
your wife—"

Dress shirt tucked in, he zipped his fly. "Where's my
tie?"

She pointed at the bed, where his tie and cummerbund
were disposed. "I quit."

"What?"

"I quit."

He turned to the mirror, adjusting the cummerbund. "I
heard you. You quit what?"

"You."

He stared at her and then he laughed bitterly and picked
up his jacket. "We're going to be late."

"You're not listening. I'm leaving you—"

"Not now. We have a very important dinner to go to."

She sat down on the bed and looked at him. Her fingers worked at an earring, taking it off.

"Your timing sucks, Kissy," he said wearily. "If you want a scene, we can have one tomorrow. I'll give you all the scene you want."

She heard the threat in his voice. He could see it in the way she paled. Her throat worked. It made him furious. She started this shit and then turned into a fucking bunny rabbit in his headlights. He grabbed her by the arm and yanked her to her feet. "You didn't get dressed up just to give me shit. Though I'm sure it adds to your enjoyment. Don't make me late, Kissy."

He got her by the elbow and goose-marched her down the stairs, her reattaching her goddamn earring. She shook off his elbow and straightened herself out, giving him a look that was supposed to freeze him dead, he guessed. She took her coat out of the closet. And putting it on, she had a smile on her face. A snotty one. Dynah came by it naturally.

"We'd better take the Blazer," she said. "The roads are greasy and it might turn to snow."

"The Blazer looks like shit. I don't know why you didn't let him buy you a new one—"

"If somebody slides into us, better the Blazer gets dented than the BMW."

You couldn't dent her hard head with a snowplow. She knew what kind of shape he was in and she was shooting her mouth off, arguing with him. But—she was right. Visions of his BMW with a crumpled hood made him feel a little sick. They were late anyway, and he could park the Blazer far from the main entrance and joke about having to bring it because of the shitty weather. Another thing he did not need. He did not need this shit. What he did need was another drink. And fuck Butch if he didn't like seeing him with a glass in his fist. Butch had ducked out early to go home and change and had stuck him with all the late-breaking crap. Butch didn't have a high-riding cheating bitch like Kissy mouthing off at home. Well, he did, but Narcissa was different. At least Narcissa wanted what Butch wanted. He got himself a drink and took the glass with him to the Blazer.

At the party, he watched Kissy smiling and chitchatting. Men looking at her, grinning, turning to each other to remark on her tits or her ass in that gold dress. Devil at home, his mother used to say, angel outside. Kissy was an angel on the outside, the devil inside. His eyes stung and he emptied his glass and went looking for a refill.

The weather sucked and Junior sat on the runway waiting for clearance on a plane full of people trying to get somewhere else. They were all impatient but he could hardly sit still. He unbuckled his seat belt and roamed the aisle, distracting himself with riffling the magazine stash and getting in the way of the attendants. He touched his neck, the hard rope of scar there. He had forty-eight hours' personal leave before his next start. He could feel them draining away while he sat on the fucking plane.

The message she had left was clear to him. He wasn't going to wait until the end of the season. He was going to get off the plane and go straight to her and take her out of there, her and Dynah. He craned to peer out the window—the rain was letting up. Thank fuck for small favors. He made his way back to his seat.

"Let Kissy drive," Butch said in Burke's ear, clutching his elbow as they shook hands good-night. "Give her the keys. You're toasted—"

"You bet." Burke laughed, happy-drunk on the outside, red-eyed-murderous inside. If only he had a glass in his hand still, he would be rearranging Butch's face with it.

He pressed the keys into Kissy's palm and closed his hand around hers tightly, so the edges of the keys bit her flesh, as they went out in the sleet. It was nasty stuff, in around the collar and splashed up the legs, and somehow they were soaking by the time they reached the Blazer, on the far side of the lot.

She tried to hold on to the keys, telling him, "Mike, you're drunk."

He dug the keys out of her palm, digging his nails in. He took her by the elbow around to the passenger side. "Get in." She started to open her mouth. "Get in the fucking car, Kissy." She closed her mouth tightly and got in. He climbed in the other side and stuck the keys in the ignition. "Put your seat belt on."

She buckled up, with him watching her. He faced the windshield, turned the key in the ignition, and the motor turned over. And then something exploded into her face, hammering her nose, driving her head into the seat back. Her body jerked with the impact and she could not see, could not breathe, and when she did, she sucked in air and it was wet, she choked, she was trying to breathe blood. She buried her face in her hands. He had hit her, backhanded her, she knew dimly, broken her nose, she knew what it felt like, what it sounded like from the inside—her hands were full of her own blood, it was running through her fingers. The Blazer was moving, speeding up, and it turned steeply, the momentum shoveling her against the door. She was choking and sobbing. She could feel her eyes swelling up as she tried to focus them. The blood in her hands was black and then it was red in the lights from the street and the traffic and then it was black again.

"Are you happy now?" he asked her. "Are you proud of yourself? You're a fucking mess."

She fumbled for the door and he slammed the button on the door locks. Then there was a crash and glass flying— she cried out, hiding her face from it. He had smashed the glass he had brought out of the house against the dash, and as she lifted her head and peered past her fingers, she saw he grasped a great bloody shard of crystal in his left hand, pointed at her. She shrank from him.

She would not sit still for him to hit her again, she decided. Her gun was in the glove compartment. She had not looked at it in an age, let alone cleaned it, but it was loaded. The only problem was the compartment was locked, to keep the gun safe from Dynah, and Mike had the key, dangling from the fob in the ignition. They were in the driveway now, approaching the house, and she surreptitiously slipped off her heels, groping for the door handle with one hand, fumbling at her seat belt with the other as he brought the vehicle to a stop. She heard the click of the door lock mechanism—he was letting her out. The door swung open and she fell out, onto the gravel. It bit into her hands and knees and then into her feet, bare of anything but the film of stocking as she staggered into a run. He wasn't expecting her to run away from the Blazer, away from the house, and he shouted angrily.

The shadows of the woods were so near, she dove into them. He shouted again, furious at her disappearance. She could not stop, he would find her, but she was clumsy and panting and her eyes were swelling, making it harder for her to see, and he could track her by the noise she made. Somehow she stayed ahead of him, gaining a little, finding a path, the beaten dirt, mud in the rain, easier on her feet than the twigs and stones and slimy leaf mulch in the woods. Behind her, he stumbled and thrashed and roared like some maddened beast. She shrugged off her coat and dropped it, hoping he would slip and fall on it. The path went downward into the Valley, and her lungs ached with the cold wet air and the effort and her face ran with the rain. She was grateful for the rain; it eased the swelling of her eyes. She knew where she was, she told herself, she knew where she was, and he didn't, he didn't know the Valley the way she did, he didn't know where she was, not exactly. He was drunk. She fell and scrambled to her feet and the trees conspired against her, slapping at her, thrusting out their roots to trip her, but she stayed ahead of him, and then she no longer heard him. She paused, briefly, terrified, listening with her whole being, and could no longer hear him. She ran again and paused again and heard only the blowing rain and the 'Pipe. The 'Pipe was at her feet, water rushing through the void, and everything in it was hidden from her, but she knew where she was. Moving more slowly, cautiously, she crept through the fringe of woods on the banks of the stream. Perhaps she would find some lovers parking, someone who would help her. But the night was so wretched there was no one, apparently, no one horny or passionate enough, or strung out enough, to brave the elements.

Her clothing was as wet as her skin and she thought she must be blue with the cold. She stopped to strip off her ruined stockings. The road that wound through the Valley was empty of traffic; she could walk out on it, run if she had to, and make her way to the first house she came upon that looked safe. Hesitantly, she stepped onto the pavement. She hugged herself against a fit of shivering and began to trot, just to try to move her blood, generate a little warmth.

Lights swept around the next curve and she ducked sideways but too late; she recognized the shape of it in the dark and the configuration of its lights. In her panic, she had gone to the wrong side; the Blazer was nearly between her and the woods. She bolted for the bank of the stream, hearing the squeal of the Blazer's brakes behind her.

"Bitch!" he screamed out of the darkness and the downpour.

She thought of how icy the water would be. But she could swim for it; he would never follow her into the water. She yanked her dress up to her waist as she ran, to free her kick.

And then she tripped and fell heavily on the embankment. She scrambled to her feet, her palms muddy, and Mike was behind her, grabbing one shoulder with what felt like claws. Crying out, she wrenched herself free, but he had grabbed a handful of her dress and now he got the other hand into her hair and yanked it painfully. Frantically, she tried to remember what to do, what moves she was supposed to make, but the self-defense course had been so long ago. She turned on him and screamed into his face so hard it hurt her throat, and for an instant, he flinched.

"Leave me alone!" she cried out, "leave me alone! I took pictures of the bruises the time you kicked me, you bastard, and they're where you can't get them. If you hurt me, they'll come back and haunt you—"

Disbelief, horror, and fury twisted his features; it was like watching a demon taking possession of him. Suddenly his hands were around her throat, and her mind went blank. Her body, though, remembered a long-ago lesson, and her knee jerked upward, making solid contact. He gasped; his hands loosened, he staggered away.

And slipped in the mud, lurched, and staggered, fighting the pitch of the embankment, and slipped again, to his knees. He looked up at her and she kicked him, her bare foot driving into his chest. His breath went out of him in an audible oomph, and he tipped backward, surprise flickering briefly in his eyes, or perhaps it was only the rain that caught the light in random ways. He was in the water, and he splashed and gasped and floundered. She stepped backward, carefully, keeping her eye on his struggle, but finding the gloom of the nearest tree, so he could no longer see her. She cast about with quick glances for a stick or a rock to protect herself with, but before she could find one, she saw him standing in the water, the current rushing around him. He must have put a foot down wrong; suddenly he slipped again, falling back into the water with a sobbing little cry, and then he was fighting the current. She did nothing; she was letting him drown, she thought, though she could save him. She was a strong-enough swimmer; she knew it. He was screaming now, screaming to her. *Help, help me, Kissy*—pleading, sobbing.

She turned her back and moved quietly toward the road, toward the Blazer, that he had left running there, door open, waiting for her. Behind her, he began to curse, curse her very specifically, and she felt a great weariness but she did not turn back. She reached into the Blazer, turned it off, and removed the keys from the ignition. Unlocking the tailgate door, she shoved aside the accumulation of gear she carried with her and opened the compartment where the jack was stored. With the jack in hand, she closed the tailgate and removed the cover of the spare tire. One end of the jack fit the bolts that held the spare in place. The wet and dark did not help, but she managed to get the spare off its mount at the price of a few dings in her own hands. And then she rolled it across the pavement and banged and shoved it through the brush to the embankment.

He was still there, his struggle weaker and more desperate, but he was all out of breath to waste on cursing. He must be so wet and cold.

"Mike!" she shouted hoarsely, and the wind whipped his name away, and she shouted it again. He seemed to see her then, and she stepped into the water's edge and threw the tire at him. She felt a sudden elation; he would be saved, and she would have done the right thing.

He reached for it, she could see him straining, and then the current caught it, and shoved it at him, and it hit him in the chest. Surprise stiffened his features and then he disappeared, in the blink of an eye.

For a moment, she stood there in disbelief and then cried out his name again, but there was nothing there anymore except the tire, riding the current.

"You were supposed to catch it!" she shrieked. "It would have kept you afloat—" It came to her then that if Junior had tried to save Mike with the spare tire, he would have managed to do what she had: kill him.

The water rushed onward, over the rocks and against other rocks, against tree roots it had exposed, finding its way to the larger river. It had carried drunken men, and drowning men, and dead men—and women and children too—to the black cold embrace of the Dance. It would carry others.

It was hopeless, she thought, but the very futility of it drove her, stumbling and staggering, back to the Blazer, and to the keys she had left in the tailgate. To the car phone. She closed the door and turned on the engine and hit the heat and made her call. And then there was nothing to do but wait. She wondered if Sergeant Pearce would be among the rescuers she had summoned and hoped he would be; she trusted him, and thought if anyone would believe her, he would.

She was shaking; she hugged herself. She doubted she would ever be warm again. Peering through the windshield, she looked up at the sky. No moon. The clouds hid its ironic grimace. Still, it was there; she felt its stony coldness in the chill, the rain, and the rushing water, in the miserly light that was no more than reflected, heatless, and drowning. Perhaps she should feel some relief, but instead grief upwelled in her, filling her throat with an ache, as if she had swallowed a stone. Grief for Mike, because he had lost whatever chance he might have had to recover, to have some happiness. And with that grief came a renewal of what she had felt for Ruth, and for Diane too. Lives lost, and places empty.

A snowflake as big as a moth splatted its pale fragile crystals against the windshield, and then another and another, and she watched the hypnotic random spatter. It made cat paw marks, only there were so many it was like a dozen ghostly cats danced and climbed on the glass.

"Where's Junior?" she asked herself aloud. She needed him; she might be able to get warm again if he would hold her. She leaned back and closed her eyes, and on the wind there rose a distant plaintive siren.